THE CURE

THE CURE

JOHN STEWART

THE CURE

iUniverse books may be ordered through booksellers or by contacting:

iUniverse
1663 Liberty Drive
Bloomington, IN 47403
www.iuniverse.com
844-349-9409

ISBN: 978-1-4502-9551-2 (sc)
ISBN: 978-1-4502-9553-6 (hc)
ISBN: 978-1-4502-9552-9 (e)

Print information available on the last page.

iUniverse rev. date: 10/27/2021

Dedicated to my wife.
"You inspire me!"

Tim

Chapter 1

The alarm buzzed at 5:35 a.m. Tracy reached over for the second time and hit snooze. The bedroom fell silent again as Tim rolled over. The room was cold. Denver had its fair share of cold weather, but this winter was shaping up to be a doozy!

"Damn, Tracy" . . . . Tim said as he pulled the covers up to his neck. "Did you forget to turn the heat on again last night?"

Tracy pulling the covers back over her body from where Tim had pulled them away. "No! . . . I don't know. Why is it always my fault?"

"Because you were the last one to come to bed," Tim grunted as he rolled away from her.

"Well, don't roll away from me. Come keep me warm!"

"I have to go. My flight leaves in just over two hours. I should have been in the shower twenty minutes ago."

"I hate it when you leave."

"You know the deal. We talked about this plenty of times."

"God, Tim, why do you have to be so cold? I just miss you when you're not here." Tracy threw the covers back over her head and began to cry.

1

"Look, Atlanta is my home. You know that. I'm here for one week a month and then it's back home. We have talked about this a dozen times."

"Yeah, we talked about your divorce a few times before, too! What about that?"

Tim got up and walked across the bedroom into the bathroom. The apartment was Tim's Denver home during his one week a month travels. For what he used to pay in hotel bills each month, he easily paid for a furnished apartment. It made his lifestyle away from his Atlanta home much easier for him and his girlfriends.

The water came on in the bathroom and Tim shut the door, sending the bedroom back into pitch black. Tracy fell back onto the pillows, wiping tears away as the alarm went off again, scaring her half to death. She pounded the top of the clock radio and silence fell over the room. Sitting up, she buried her face in her hands.

Tracy began to mumble into her hands. "What am I doing here?"

Five minutes later, she was dressed and walking out the door with her overnight bag. As she began to close the door, she looked at her keys, and at the key Tim had given her just months before. As the tears kept falling, she took the new key off and threw it onto the counter next to Tim's key chain and wallet.

Turning and walking out without even bothering to shut the door, Tracy yelled, "Screw you, Tim Billings! Find someone else in this town to have sex with."

After shaving and getting dressed, Tim came out of the bathroom expecting to see Tracy still asleep. He stared at the door to the apartment, which was standing open, with Tracy nowhere to be found. The long carpeted hallway outside Tim's apartment only had one person standing in it. The neighbor stood half asleep in the hallway, staring into Tim's apartment.

"Mr. Billings, is everything alright? I heard a woman yelling out here."

Tim scratched his head. "I guess so, Mr. Stevens. I think my . . . . " Tim looked up, not knowing what to say as Mr. Stevens shook his head and began to go back inside.

"Crap!" Tim said as he shut the door.

Then he noticed Tracy's key lying next to his on the counter. He walked over and picked it up, smiling as he dropped it in the drawer.

"Good! She was getting too attached, anyway. That's the last thing I need is a girlfriend getting too attached and screwing up my marriage before I have things all in order."

Tim got his bags together and began to head for the door. "Whoops! Almost forgot." Tim walked over to the bedside table, pulled out his wedding ring, and slipped it back on his finger.

The apartment was furnished nicely and Tim had bought a few things to make it more personal. A huge picture of the Eiffel tower in Paris, his favorite city in the world, hung over the couch. A Persian rug he and Tracy picked up one afternoon shopping when they first met, and a 50" flat-plasma screen for watching the games during football season. All in all, it was very different from the family oriented house in Atlanta that his wife had decorated.

The cab had pulled up at the curb out front and the cold air bit at Tim's face as he walked out onto the Denver street just after 6 am. The ride to the airport was not bad this early in the morning and Tim always tried to book his flight out early. With the time difference back to Atlanta, getting out early meant missing the rush hour on 285. Tim never went into the office on travel days, although the office downtown was only twenty minutes from the airport.

As Tim got out of the cab, the all too familiar headache began again at the base of his skull. Tim massaged his neck and head as the cab driver handed him his bag. He paid the cabbie and turned to walk into the concourse once again. The cabbie looked at the money in his hand and shot Tim a bird for the two-dollar tip. "Thanks, asshole!" he said.

Tim never looked back as the glass doors to the airport closed behind him. The check-in counters were packed, as usual on a Friday. His elite status granted him a no wait line of his own at the Delta counter. As usual, he was greeted with a smile and a friendly hello but Tim did not return the greeting. His headache and the morning's fight with Tracy had set him in foul mood by now. He wanted a drink and some peace and quiet.

Four hours later Tim stepped off the plane in Atlanta. Tim was glad to be home in the much warmer 60 degree weather. He looked at his watch: 3:10. "Good, I still have time to go by Scully's and get a nice scotch before I have to deal with going home."

He began the long walk through Atlanta's sprawled out concourses and huge escalators. Traveling through the busiest airport in the world had its ups and downs. He hated parking in the economy lots because of the forever walk, so he always sprung for the more expensive garage parking on these trips. Hell, what did he care? He was billing the client anyway.

As Tim got to his car, he turned his cell back on and two messages immediately beeped to get his attention. Reluctantly, Tim hit the voicemail button, assuming at least one of the messages, if not both, would be from Tracy, telling him what a jerk he was. As he expected, the first message was from Tracy, very angrily telling him that she never wanted to see him again. Tim deleted the message without even hearing it to the end. "Stupid girl," rolled off Tim's tongue as he played the next message.

In a much softer voice, a very monotone Sue Billings, Tim's wife, voice came on the line. "Tim, the doctor's office called the house to confirm an appointment for Monday. 9:00 o'clock. Just thought I would pass it along," the call ended.

Tim hit the delete button and stared at the phone before finally dropping it into the console. Tim reached back, cupping his neck, massaging the headache that was still pounding the back of his head. For the last several months, Tim had been getting headaches in the same place almost daily. He had forgotten he had his secretary make the appointment to see the family doctor.

Tim drove out of the airport smiling at the all-too-familiar, "Welcome to Georgia" sign right at the entrance to the expressway. It was good to be home again. Rush hour traffic had not started yet, but in another 30 minutes or so, it would. Rush hour in Atlanta started at 4 and ended at 7. The longest hour he knew where there was absolutely no rushing involved!

Tim pulled into Scully's parking lot just before 5 and was glad to be there. Usually there was a regular crowd there and Tim knew that a few scotches later his headache would be gone; he might even chance a poker game if there were a few suckers hanging around.

Tim pulled his BMW in beside the red Cadillac he knew belonged to George Cotton, and as he got out, he saw the tail lights of Peter's 911 across the parking lot. It looked like his two-card suckers were already inside and ahead of him on the drinking. It would indeed be a good night.

Scully's was an older place in Roswell, maybe an old steakhouse at one time. Heavy wood trim everywhere and a big wooden bar just as you came in the door. The lighting was low and the carpet in the place may have been the original when the steakhouse was built. Scully sure didn't spend a lot on changing the place when he bought it years ago. Nonetheless, it was warm and full of friends. Tim loved this place almost as much as he loved himself! Well, maybe not that much.

Tim walked through the door and was greeted by several friends as he approached the bar. Tim laughed and felt like he just walked into an old episode of *Cheers*! Tim slapped Peter on the back as he walked by and took his seat at the end of the row. "How's it hangin' fellas?"

Both men held up their glasses and smiled. Peter and George were older than Tim by at least twenty years and had made their money early in life. Scully's was a very frequent hangout for these guys and a card game was always welcome. Tim sat down and the bartender sat the 12 year old scotch on the rocks down just like clockwork.

"How are you doing, Mr. B? Did you sue anybody today?" The bartender was a kid in his mid-twenties, someone Scully had obviously recruited straight from the Bronx to give the place that New York feel. Never mind that Scully himself was a skinny redneck from south Georgia who made good selling his farm off before the recession and decided to open a bar in north Atlanta with most of the money.

Tim smiled at the kid. "No, not today, Billy! It was a travel day for me."

Billy smiled. "Oh! That's too bad. You let me know when you boys need another drink, okay?" Billy turned and walked away to give service to the pretty blonde down at the other end of the bar.

Tim never looked back at Billy as he faced his friends. "Well, gentleman, we playing cards tonight?" The partial grin crept onto Tim's face as he waited for an answer.

Both guys turned to look at Tim. George spoke first. "Did you bring enough money for both of us to leave here a few hundred richer than we came?"

Tim slapped the bar and laughed. "I think you took my money last time, you old codger. It's my turn to leave with the money and I bet both of you the winnings that I get that blonde's number down there before I leave, too!"

"You're on!" Peter spoke up. "You ain't that smooth, boy."

Tim nodded. "We'll see! Shall we?" Standing to go back to the usual table in the back to play, he caught the eye of the blonde at the bar and smiled. She smiled back. The battle was half won.

As the guys played cards Tim kept his eyes on the blonde and now the two friends that had joined her. As Billy took drink orders from the men, Tim bought round after round for the ladies. Each time they all turned and smiled as they raised their glasses. Tim raised his back and smiled.

"See fellas, win or lose here I will get that phone number."

George looked at Tim a little sideways. "Tim, aren't you married?"

Tim turned from the girls and looked at George. "Yeah! We are about to get divorced though. She is a do-good lawyer and thinks I am an asshole. We haven't had sex in forever. I need a woman that turns me on. You know what I mean?"

Both men sat there quietly and didn't answer Tim. "What? Don't tell me you guys have always been faithful to your wives."

Peter spoke up first. "Yeah, Tim, I have. When you find a good thing, you take care of it."

Tim laughed. "Whatever! You guys don't know what I have been through. My career has been hell at times. My wife doesn't understand me at all. I have given her everything she ever wanted. She doesn't give a crap about me. Nothing I do is ever good enough for her and my kids are just as bad."

George laid his cards down on the table. "Tim, let me tell you something. Twenty years ago, my wife and I were not doing so well. I made a mistake with a girl at work and had an affair. It was a defining moment in my life."

Tim smiled again. "That's what I am talking about. Was it good?"

Shaking his head, "No, I had thrown away everything that was important to me in my life for sex that meant nothing. I had broken the trust of a woman who had loved me for twenty-three years for nothing, for absolutely nothing."

"George! Relax, man, let's enjoy the game. Man, you guys are heavy tonight. I won't pick up the girl. Let's just play."

George stood. "Your moral compass is way off, Tim. You need to go home and make your flower bloom."

Tim looked at George with a confused stare. "What? What flower?"

George picked up his scotch and finished the last swallow from the glass. "Peter, it's been real. I will see you next time."

Peter sat back in his chair. "See ya later, George."

Tim watched George leave and turned back to Peter trying to understand. "What the hell is wrong with George?"

"Nothing's wrong with George, Tim. You need to listen to the man." Peter leaned into the table, laying his cards down as well.

"What, you about to lecture me too, now?"

"Nope. You have your own life to live my friend. I think I will go home and tell my wife how much I love her. Take it easy." Peter stood and waved at Billy as he walked past the bar. "Good night, Billy. See you next time."

Tim sat there for a few minutes staring at the pot of money on the green-felt covered table both men had walked away from. Tim slid the pile over and plucked the bills from the stack one by one. Tim stood pulling a long drag from his glass and began to walk towards the women.

Tim and Sue's house was a large red brick two-story that sat on a corner lot. Lights lit the front of the house and it was easily nice enough to be on the cover of any *Better Homes and Gardens* any day. The lawn was manicured and the bushes were all color coordinated in the spring with blooms.

Most of the time, Sue felt like she lived alone raising the two kids, Annette twelve and Jonathan eight. Tim was never there, when he was he was most often withdrawn or watching TV.

Sue was working on a case in the kitchen table, at the round mahogany table with carved detail down each leg. Annette finished a history report beside her. Jonathan was watching TV in the living room, too loud as usual, with his feet resting on the coffee table.

Sue looked up and barked, "Jonathan, feet off the table."

"When is Dad supposed to be home?" Jonathan shouted back over MTV's *Big Brother: Episode Number Who Cares!* Slowly removing his feet from the table in defiance.

"I don't know, sometime tonight."

Annette looked up from her book at Sue's face. "Mom, are you okay?"

Sue turned to Annette, "Yeah, why?"

"You looked so sad when Jonathan brought up Dad. Are you guys getting a divorce?"

"Annette, why are you worried about that kind of stuff? Your dad and I are . . . ."

Her sentence fell away as she realized she didn't know what she and Tim were any more. It had been so long since she really cared for Tim that she realized it must have been obvious on her face. Sue began to cry. Annette sat there staring at her mom for a second before slamming her book closed. "I hate him!"

Annette walked away from the table towards the stairs, leaving Sue sitting there, not knowing what to do with the situation. Sue agreed with Annette. She hated Tim, too, and had for years. Tim's job had become a monster. The fact that she knew he was having at least one affair with a woman in Colorado didn't even faze her. She was numb to all of it. She was in a marriage she couldn't stand and her kids knew it. At least Annette did. Jonathan wasn't too aware of feelings yet. His world was consumed with Play Station and TV.

Sue sighed and stood up from the table. "Jonathan, turn the TV off and go get your room clean. Dinner will be ready in a few minutes and I want you down here with hands washed, helping me set the table." Jonathan stood up, turned the TV off and fell to the floor, playing dead.

Sue smiled. "Don't make me come in there and beat you, kid!"

"Whatever, Mom!" Jonathan laughed as he rolled over.

"Get going. Dinner will be ready soon."

Sue went to Annette's room. The sticker-covered door was closed, but Sue pushed it open with a half knock. Annette turned and looked at her as a text message ding rang out.

"Mom, I really don't want to talk about this."

"Annette, you just said you hate your own dad. We are going to talk about this."

"Mom, he is never here and when he is he acts like he hates us. He has never been to one of my school functions. He doesn't even know that I have a part in this year's play at school." Tears began to run down Annette's face as she turned back to her computer.

Sue stepped over the clothes strewn all over the floor and shoes piled up. The room looked as if a tornado had touched down dead center and threw everything in all the drawers all over the place. Each wall had posters of boy band singers and movie stars that Annette was sure to marry one day.

Sue sat on the bed for a minute and let out a sigh. "I am sorry, baby. I know it hurts. Your dad does love you, I promise. He just has a hard time showing it. That's all."

Annette spun in her chair. "Why are you defending him? He treats you worse than anybody. I don't care if he ever comes home!"

"Annette, don't say that. I don't know why he is the way he is, but life isn't perfect. Sometimes people just get lost and forget who they are. It doesn't make it right or easy but it doesn't mean you stop loving them. Sometimes they need more love to get through it."

"I don't love him. I don't even know him. If I never saw him again it wouldn't matter."

"Don't talk like that. I am sorry things are this way. You will always have me! I love you very much."

"Do you love him?"

Sue stood. "What I do is not for you to worry about. That's my stuff to deal with, not yours."

Annette stood and hugged her mom. "I am so sorry you have the life you do, Mom. I know you're not happy. When Dad is here, you barely even talk. I love you too, Mom. You will always have me, too."

Sue turned to leave the room. "Dinner will be ready soon. You okay?"

"I will be fine. Thanks for being my Mom."

"No problem." Sue stopped at the door turning back to look at the room. "The carpet in here is somewhere under all this stuff. I want to see it the next time I come in here. Do you understand me?"

Annette turned back to the computer. "Yes ma'am."

Back at Scully's, Tim was walking towards the bar. He had picked up an easy hundred dollars from the poker game and was ready for his next conquest. The lady's at the bar. As usual, Tim had already dismissed what George and Peter had said about being faithful. They were old school and Tim always did whatever he wanted anyway.

Tim looked at the ladies at the bar. One was dressed in blue jeans, tight, with a nice figure and a sweater that was loose but not so loose that it hid the nice upper body she had. The girl to her right was in a blue dress. She had probably come from work. The dress was cut just below her knees but fit very well. Low cut in the front, revealing nice cleavage, but not too much. The third girl had her back to Tim and was in a suit, very sharply dressed, with her hair pulled back into a very nice ponytail. A career girl. Tim laughed. Maybe even an attorney. The mystery of these three was too much for Tim to pass up.

Tim walked up to the ladies and raised his glass. "Ladies, who have I had the pleasure of buying drinks for tonight? My name is Tim."

The girls all turned to look at Tim and then, smiling, looked at each other. The blonde broke the silence first. "I'm Jenny. This is my friend Sarah, and this is Fay. What happened to your friends?"

"Oh, you know. Old guys have to get in bed early. What brings you lovely ladies into Scully's tonight? I don't think I've ever seen any of you here before. It's nice to see such beautiful women in here."

Sarah laughed. "Easy, tiger, don't hurt yourself."

Tim smiled. "Oh, I won't. If I can stand in front of a jury and convince them that my client is innocent when he clearly is not, this won't hurt me at all."

"So you're an attorney?" Jenny asked.

"Yes, I am, and a good one at that."

"No confidence problem, I see." Fay giggled and stared down at her drink as she said it.

"No, they teach you in law school to get over being shy or scared of a crowd. If I have to take all three of you out for dinner tonight, I will."

Sarah reached over and picked up Tim's left hand. "What about that, Counselor?"

Tim looked at his wedding ring and started to laugh, "Just waiting on the divorce papers to be signed. I just keep up the appearance for the kids. It's not their fault, you know."

"Really? Whose fault is it?" Sarah stared at Tim.

Tim looked at Sarah in her fitted suit, wondering what she did for a living. All three just stood there looking at Tim, smiling while they looked at each other, all waiting for someone to take the lead.

Tim broke the silence, "So what about that dinner, ladies? I am starving. There is a fantastic steak place right next door."

Jenny and Fay continued to smile. Sarah picked up her purse and shook her head no. "I'll see you girls later."

Tim grabbed Sarah's arm. "Wait. Come on and go with us. We'll have fun, I promise."

"Sorry, Tim. No married men for me! Thanks for the drinks, though."

"Oh, don't be like that, it's just dinner. No harm at all."

"Good night, guys." Sarah walked out.

Tim turned back to the other girls and smiled. "Shall we go?" Tim called out to Billy to settle the check. Billy did so, and the three of them were off to dinner. Tim was pleased with his winnings for the night as the girls got into his car. If he was really good, he would end up with both of the girl's numbers and maybe even both of the girls. They spent the next two hours eating and laughing as the night went on. By the end of dinner, Tim had gotten both phone numbers and had already begun to plan dates with each.

Tim started for home around 10:30 and knew he would have to invent a story to tell Sue before he got home. She hardly asked anymore when he got in late, but Tim was always prepared. Any good attorney knew what the answers were going to be before the questions were ever asked.

Sue was tucking Jonathan in when she looked at the clock to see what time it was. 9:45. Another Friday night, she thought to herself, and Tim is not home. Wonder who he is with tonight?

Jonathan looked up at his mom. "What's wrong, Mom?"

"Nothing, baby; why?"

"I don't know; you made your mad face just now. Did I do something wrong?"

Sue smiled at Jonathan. "No, baby. You didn't do anything wrong. I am not mad. I was just wishing your dad was home so he could say goodnight. That's all."

"Are you mad at him?"

"No baby, just sad that he has to travel so much. I am sure he misses you guys."

"What about you, Mommy, doesn't he miss you?"

Sue began to cry. "I'm sure he does, baby. He misses us all. Now close those eyes and I will tell daddy to come give you a hug when he gets home."

Jonathan closed his eyes and Sue lay down beside him, holding his little hand in hers while he fell asleep. Sue laid there listening to Jonathan's breathing for a while, thinking about divorcing Tim. How much would it affect her kids? How ugly would Tim be over money and the kids? She had no worries about Tim trying to take custody because the kids would interfere with his playboy life too much.

Sue stood up from Jonathan's bed as she heard the garage door begin to rise. Anger began to build inside her. He was home, and Sue was going to tell him tonight that it was over. If she was going to do this all by herself, then she might as well be by herself. That would give Tim the freedom he so desperately wanted anyway. Sue was determined to make him pay, though. She was a lawyer, too, after all. She was taught by the same professors as Tim. Hell, they had shared classes all through law school, did homework together and studied well into the night, countless times. Sue knew how to work a judge just like Tim did.

She stood in the kitchen with no lights on, waiting for Tim to come in. The anger inside her was as hard as the granite counter top she leaned against while she waited. The lights from outside lit the room like a scene from any horror film. Sue waited like the killer to pounce on Tim as soon as he came in. Her tears were pushed back now, her arms crossed and anger ready. She waited.

Tim stopped as he came through the door. "Jesus, Sue, you scared the shit out of me! What's your problem? I see you're not even going to let me get in the door this trip before you start bitching at me about something."

"Why so late Tim, what pressing business has kept you late this time? Or should I just say, what's her name?"

"What's wrong with you? I got in this afternoon and stopped by Scully's to have a drink. You don't usually wait on me to come in the door when I am coming back in town. What's different about today?"

Sue had her back to him completely now, looking out the window into the darkness.

"Well, your son wanted to know what was wrong with me tonight. I told him that I was sad that daddy wasn't home to tuck him in. I couldn't tell him the truth."

Tim stopped looking at Sue. "What's the truth, Sue?"

Sue turned back pointing her finger at Tim in rage. "The truth is that I am sick of you acting like you're not married! I know about the girl in Colorado, Tim! Who knows how many others there are?"

Tim dropped his overnight bag onto the hardwood floors and threw his hands up in the air.

"Bullshit, Sue! What girl in Colorado? There is nobody in Colorado but a client that I work very hard for so that you can live in this nice house, drive your nice BMW and not worry about anything."

"I heard you on the phone before you left, telling her what flight you would be on and when you would be at the apartment. You think I'm stupid, but I'm not. I'm a lawyer, too, in case you have forgotten. A lawyer who scored higher on the bar exam than you did, by the way. Asshole."

Tim laughed. "Yeah, that's why you do pro bono work instead of working for one of the major firms like me. You're not aggressive, Sue. The big boy attorneys would eat you alive. What's this all about, anyway? Why are you grandstanding me, lawyer? What do you want from me?"

"I want a divorce. And I do pro bono work because I want to help people, not get rich off of setting criminals free like you."

Tim laughed out loud. "What you need to do is be quiet and enjoy the life I have given to you. Keep doing your free work for the poor and raise our kids. That's what you need to do!"

Sue turned and began to walk out of the kitchen. She heard the kitchen door open and slam shut. Tim was gone. She heard the screech of tires on the driveway as he drove away. It had begun. Sue and Tim had been dodging this subject for the last year, and now the words had been spoken. Sue never thought she would be the one to start it. She always expected that Tim would just stop coming home from Colorado eventually and the divorce would be done via mail or express courier. She was not expecting a face-to-face confrontation. Sue stepped into the half bath and began to throw up. Her nerves were shot and her stomach was bearing the brunt of it. One hand gripping the white porcelain bowl and the other grabbing at her wrenching gut, Sue threw up her dinner and everything else in her stomach. The tears flowed down her face. Her life was a mess and she knew it.

Everything Tim had said was a lie, except the part about the big-time lawyers tearing her apart. They would. Sue had always done better than Tim in school, but during debates, Tim would dominate. His personality and confidence set his destiny early on in law school. He had what it took to sway a jury, stand toe-to-toe with any other attorney, and tell him he was wrong about his client. Sue knew that she would never be that strong. She knew that a divorce with Tim would be a nightmare. The sweet romantic guy that she fell in love with so many years ago was gone forever. He had become hard, cold and calculating. Tonight he had stood in that kitchen and denied the relationship in Colorado, a bold faced lie. His face never even quivered when she had dropped the bomb of knowing the truth. He remained calm and cool as he deflected what she had said. He had become someone that Sue didn't even know anymore.

Sue sat on the bathroom floor, holding her head over the toilet, waiting for her stomach to calm down, when she heard the water stop upstairs. She looked up at the ceiling as more tears rolled down her face. Annette was out of the shower and Sue did not want her to see her this way. Annette was struggling enough; she didn't need to deal with this yet.

Sue stood gripping the white pedestal sink. Taking the monogrammed hand towel, she wiped her face clean and threw the towel in the trash. Sue looked at the angry hurt woman in the mirror for a long minute. She closed her eyes and began to slowly speak the words, "Pull it together, Sue!"

Sue came out of the bathroom as Annette bounced down the steps. Startled by Annette, Sue jumped at the sound of her voice.

"Hey Mom, whatcha doing?"

Sue grabbed her chest. "Gosh, Annette, you scared me."

"Why? I just asked what you were doing. Why would that scare you?"

I was just going to bathroom and heard the water shut off. I just didn't expect you down here. That's all."

"When I was getting in the shower I thought I heard the garage door. Did Dad get home?"

Sue stood paralyzed. How would she answer her daughter; with the truth, or a lie? "Yes, he was here. We had a fight and he left."

Annette stood there looking at Sue. "A fight about what?"

"Just stuff, don't worry about it."

"Is he coming back?"

Sue felt the tears again. "I don't know."

Annette's face tightened. "I hope he doesn't!"

"Annette, don't say that. It's never good when a marriage is in trouble. You have to be willing to fight for each other. Your dad and I have got some problems, but . . . . "

Sue's sentence fell short as she realized she really didn't want to fight for Tim. He had become a monster, and all Sue could think about was how she wanted her and the kids to get away from him before permanent damage was done.

Annette stood there, waiting for Sue's answer. "Mom, I hope he never comes back. He doesn't love you or us. I hate him!"

Annette ran out of the kitchen and back upstairs. Sue yelled out for her to stop, but Annette was gone and she heard her bedroom door slam. Sue walked back into the dark kitchen, bent down on the island, and began to cry. Her life was falling apart and she couldn't do anything to stop it, nor did she want to. It was time to move on without Tim Billings. She deserved better than this. She deserved to be loved. Tim didn't care about her and she knew it. Tonight had proven that.

The Doctor

Chapter 2

The Marriott hotel room was furnished nicely. Tim stood at the mirror on the back of the bathroom door getting ready. The marble floor and counter top were covered with towels from Tim's shower and the night before. The view from the tenth floor was of Lenox Mall, one of the more expensive places to shop in Atlanta. Tim had always liked Buckhead and thought he might move here when the divorce was done.

He was still wearing the clothes he had worn on Friday. His neck and head were killing him this morning. He thought about not going home over the weekend and was a little surprised that Sue had not tried to call him at all. Tim smiled, thinking how convenient it was, though, since Jenny had called, and decided to come to the hotel that next night for dinner and never left. As he was about to leave the hotel room, Tim turned back, looking at the bed and at Jenny lying there naked, half covered with the sheets. Maybe when the divorce was underway and he moved out, Jenny might make a good girlfriend; she sure was good in bed. Of course, he still had Fay to test out, too. She might even be better! When Tim got to the lobby, he stopped at the desk to check out and pay for the room.

"Are you checking out for good today, sir?" The desk clerk asked.

"I am, but I need a favor. I have a friend still asleep in the room. Can you call up in about an hour and tell her check out is at 11. She can stay in there until then if she wants."

"I certainly will, Mr. Billings. Is there anything else today?"

"No, that's it." Tim signed the credit card receipt and tipped the desk clerk ten dollars.

"Thank you, sir. We will take good care of your guest. Please come back anytime."

Tim got to his car and put his luggage in the back. Grabbing the back of his neck, he thought that this was probably the worst headache he had ever had. He thought for sure he would probably end up at a chiropractor's office before the day was finished. He must have hurt his neck playing tennis or something. The pain was unbearable! He was glad to be going to the doctor. As Tim slid into the leather seat of his red BMW, he quickly reached for the bottle of Advil he kept in the glove box. Chasing three down with a sip of Starbucks bold coffee, he started the engine.

Tim pulled out onto Lenox Road and headed for the doctor. As he looked back at the hotel, he thought about Sue and what he should do next. Their marriage had not been good for years. His love for Sue had begun to fade fast when he started to travel to Colorado. Meeting Tracy there had changed everything. Tim thought about his kids and the damage he would cause to them when the truth came out. Eventually he knew his kids would know that he had cheated on their mother. How would he deal with that? How would he teach his son to be a good man when he himself had not been one?

Tim shook the thoughts out of his head as he pulled into the parking lot at the doctor's office. His head was pounding, and thinking about the things he had done wrong was not helping. Tim decided as he went into the doctor's office that he would go home tonight and talk to Sue about things. After all, fourteen years together and two kids said a lot. Tim didn't know what it said, but it was a lot and he needed to take things slow. Divorcing Sue would be messy and he really just wanted things to stay the way they were. He did realize that it may be too late for that now. Sue not calling at all was a bad sign.

The waiting room was the usual mix of people seeing a general physician, a mom with a sick kid; an old couple hard of hearing and annoyed about being there, talking loudly about the ordeal; a man holding his head up by propping his arm on the arm of the chair.

"Great!" Tim thought as he came into the room. Coming here with a headache and leaving with the bubonic plague!

Tim had always hated going to the doctor for anything. He had been healthy most of his life. Rarely did he ever catch the normal colds that the kids had each year. His immune system was pretty strong. Actually, aside from this neck injury or whatever it was, Tim had not been to the doctor in ten years.

Tim got to the window and knocked. A nurse slid the glass back and just looked at Tim. "Can I help you?"

"Tim Billings, I have a 9 o'clock appointment."

The nurse grabbed a clipboard and began to stack papers on it. "Please fill these out and I will need a copy of your insurance card and driver's license. Don't leave anything blank! The doctor is running late, so have a seat."

Tim cursed under his breath and pulled out his cell phone as he walked away from the window.

"Shelly!" Tim barked as his assistant answered the phone at his office.

"Hi Tim, did you remember the doctor's appointment this morning? I sent you a reminder email on Friday." Shelly was the most efficient woman on the planet! She remembered everything.

Shelly had worked for Tim for the last few years. She knew things about Tim that no one else did. She knew about Tracy in Colorado and several other ladies in Atlanta that got their calls put through to him when he specifically had said, "hold my calls!" Shelly just looked the other way and did the job. In the break room, however, Shelly would tear into Tim with the other assistants often. "Cock Hound" was the most common term the girls used about the attorneys that liked playing the field while their wives stayed home, oblivious to whom they were really married too.

Tim replied abruptly. "Yeah, I got it. I am here now and they have already told me the doctor is running behind. I'm thinking about just leaving."

"Wow, that sucks, do you want me to try and reschedule?"

Tim paused, feeling his head pound with pain. "No, my neck is killing me and I have a headache the size of Montana. I need to stay and be seen. Push my 11 o'clock back until tomorrow, and hopefully I will be at the office by lunch. Order in for us today. We need to go over those proceedings for Colorado and the Smelt case for next week."

"Sure will, boss. You want your usual, Chinese?"

"No, not today, I don't feel that good, how about a salad from Johnny's?"

"Okay, anything else?"

"No, I will be in as soon as I can." Tim hung up the phone and looked around the room, trying to pick the best place to sit so he wouldn't catch something new. Everyone had spread out so much that there was no way for him to get a safe distance from anyone. Tim stared at the old couple and decided they were his safest bet. She had a cane so they were probably there about arthritis or something like that. Hopefully not something that was contagious. Maybe they were there for Viagra! That would be a funny conversation.

As Tim sat a chair away from the old woman, she turned and smiled with a very small, "Hello."

Tim smiled and returned the greeting. She turned back to her husband and asked, "Is that our son?"

The husband looked up apologetically. "No, Martha, our son lives in Dallas. We are still in Atlanta. He is coming next month to see us."

She smiled. "Well, good. He sure looks like Steve, doesn't he?"

Tim turned away from the conversation and thought about his own life. He didn't ever want to get that old. He never wanted to lose his memory to the point he didn't even know his own kids. Tim hesitated. Did he really know his kids now? He had hardly been in there life at all for the last few years.

As Tim answered question after question on the doctor's forms, he watched patients go in and out of the offices, husbands and wives, women and children. He looked at their faces and thought about how each of these people seemed to have people with them that cared. Tim realized that Sue probably didn't care anymore at all. In fact, Tim realized that no one cared about him anymore. Sue's face on Friday night when they had fought was cold and void of the love he once knew. Tim thought about what he had done over the last several years. He thought about the fact that Sue had heard his conversation with Tracy in the driveway before the last trip. He was talking to her about when he would get in and that they could go to dinner at her favorite restaurant that night. What an idiot he had been for talking to her at the house. He knew better and it had gotten him caught.

Tim let his mind turn to Tracy. What was she to him, really? Did he have feelings for her at all, or was it just sex? He had met Tracy almost two years ago. She was a paralegal for the co-counsel on a government case. They had spent some late nights preparing testimony and going over the case. Tim had never cheated on Sue at that point. Tracy listened to every word that came from his mouth; she adored him. At first, it had reminded him of when he met Sue. They had these passionate conversations about law and the future, politics and everything going on in the world. Sue hung on every word then, just the way Tracy was now. Tim allowed himself to fall in the trap and ended up with her that second night, after the other attorney had to leave. Tim and Tracy had sex on the couch in his office and Tracy had gone back to the apartment with him that night. It had begun an affair that had lasted for the last few years.

Tim found that, like with most bad things, once you cross that line it was hard to turn back. First it was just Tracy, and only when he was in Colorado. Soon it was Wendy in the Atlanta office, and then another from the coffee shop, and so on, up to last night's indiscretion with Jenny. He had to stop this behavior, if there was ever going to be a chance with Sue to fix their disastrous marriage. Tim knew he had to change.

"Mr. Billings" rang out and jarred Tim from his thoughts. He looked up at the nurse standing at the door, seemingly annoyed that Tim had not jumped to his feet already. Tim stood up, grabbing the back of his neck, as the sudden movement reminded him of the pounding headache he had.

The nurse stepped forward. "Are you okay, sir? Do you need some help?"

"No. I just have a terrible headache this morning. Sitting out here for the last hour has not helped it."

The nurse turned at that point, taking the clip board from Tim's hand and leading him to the nurses' station to begin the process. She recorded Tim's height, weight and blood pressure and told him to follow her down the hall to the next waiting area. Tim walked into the small exam room and sat down. He started to ask for water, when the door shut and he found himself alone. As he stared around the room, he felt creeped out by the diagram of the human body on the back of the door, with layers of skin gone, showing muscle and bone throughout the body. Worse yet, the exposed eye in the picture never seemed to stop looking at him the whole time. Tim sat in the chair next to the table as he kept looking back at the door and the muscular/skeleton figure.

"Christ!" Tim cried out as he got up and lay down on the exam table. The faint sound of a busy office outside the door kept Tim's attention for just a moment as he closed his eyes to keep the bright overhead light from shining into his eyes. He slowly began to drift off to sleep as he lay there waiting.

Tim began to dream he was being chased by a man with a gun. He was in a strange dark alley in a big city. It was night, and the man was screaming as he chased Tim. Tim was running wildly down the alley as bullets flew past his head. Tim ran out into the busy street at the end of the alley, avoiding the mad gunman, only to be hit by a passing car, which knocked him to the ground. Tim woke with a jolt as the doctor shut the door to the exam room.

"Well, Mr. Billings, were we having a bad dream?"

Tim sat up holding the back of his head. "Wow, I was dreaming that I was being chased by a guy with a gun. It was terrible, Doc!"

"That's a pretty bad dream; you feeling guilty about something?"

Tim's eyes squinted as he stared at the doctor who seemed to have heard all of Tim's thoughts while in the waiting room. "No, not really. Do you think that's what the dream means? I'm running from some evil in my life?"

The doctor laughed. "Mr. Billings, I am no psychiatrist, but I can recommend a good one if you want to follow up with that dream. I'm just here to help you with these headaches you are having. By the looks of how tightly you are gripping at your neck and head, I would say they must be pretty bad. My nurse said you looked kind of dizzy in the waiting room when you stood up. Is that true?"

"Not really. I just stood up quickly and lost my balance a little. The headache is bad though, Doc, seriously."

"Okay. Let's take a look at a few things. Turn around here and face me." The doctor began looking into Tim's eyes with a light.

Tim flinched at the bright light.

"Does the light hurt when I shine it at your eye?"

"It hurts how bright it is; want me to shine it in yours?"

The doctor smiled again. "Have you ever suffered from migraines before? Has anyone in your family had them?"

"Not that I know of, my mom and dad were pretty healthy when they were alive."

The doctor stepped back from examining Tim for a second. "When they were alive? What happened, if you don't mind me asking? Anything medically related?"

"I don't mind. My mom died of cancer last year. My father was killed ten years ago in a car accident."

"Hmmm," The doctor exclaimed. "Is there a history of cancer in your family?" looking at Tim's paperwork.

"Not really. I think maybe one of my grandparents and my mom. That's about it. I don't have any brothers or sisters."

Looking back at the chart, "I see. About your headaches, it says here your neck hurts up into the base of your head. Have you injured your neck recently? Any blows to the head or neck that might have caused a problem?"

"I don't think so, but I run and play tennis so I might have twisted it wrong or something."

"And how often do you get these headaches?

"Every day now, it's been like that for the last few months."

The doctor stepped away from Tim again. "For the last few months? Why would you wait for months to come see a doctor about a problem that affects you every day?"

Tim turned red with embarrassment. "I don't know. I don't like going to doctors. No offense, but I'm an attorney and I see hundreds of malpractice suits come through my office every year."

"Hmmm, maybe you're not such a smart attorney, are you?"

"What!"

"If this thing causing these headaches, Mr. Billings, is something bad, like a tumor or cyst that we could have removed two months ago, with very little problems, has now grown into a larger problem, that would not be good. Agreed? Early detection is always the best thing for these types of problems."

Tim looked at the floor like a kid in trouble. "Yeah, I see your point. Two months ago, it was just a headache that with a few aspirin would go away. I called it stress and moved on. It just wouldn't get better, so I had my assistant schedule the appointment. Sorry."

The doctor smiled and patted Tim on the shoulder. "Hey, no worries, I'm sure it's nothing, anyway. You probably just need a vacation or maybe some glasses."

"Glasses, I see just fine."

"How old are you Mr. Billings?"

"I will be thirty-eight this year. Why does that matter?"

"Maybe just some forty-itis kicking in early. Does it hurt you or strain your eyes to read smaller print? I would imagine you do a good bit of that in your line of work."

"No. I can read just fine. No problems."

The doctor walked around behind Tim and began to feel along Tim's neck and upper back. "Any pain in the areas I'm touching?"

"No, not to the touch, this headache radiates in that whole area though. It starts at the back of my head and radiates down my neck."

"Hmmm."

"Doc, why do you keep saying that?"

27

"Saying what?"

"Hmmm!"

"Well, Mr. Billings, because the things you keep saying change my direction of thought as to what I think the problem might be."

"Great! That's just great. So what are you thinking is the problem?"

"I think I want to run some blood work on you and get you down the hall for an x-ray of your neck area. Let's just see what we have going on in there. Make sure we don't have a disk problem or bone spur or anything like that. I will probably send you over to get a CAT scan once we get your blood work back if nothing shows up. See if we have anything growing in there that shouldn't be. No worries, Mr. Billings. We will get you fixed up. I will get you some really good Tylenol for days like today. That should help." The doc stood back and began to write some notes down in the chart.

"Okay. That sounds like a good plan. Can I take one or two of those Tylenols now? My head is pounding."

"Yeah, the nurse will take care of that in just a few minutes and take some blood, then get you down to x-ray. I will tell her to go ahead and give you a sample now. That will last you until tonight when you get your prescription filled. Okay? Does that sound good?"

"Sure, Doc. Whatever you think, I just want to get rid of these headaches. I am tired of having one every day, know what I mean?"

"I do, Mr. Billings; just sit back and the nurse will fix you up. I will get the results of the blood work back in a week or less. If they are normal, I will give you a call."

"And if they're not?"

"Then I will see you back in here right away. Don't worry. It's probably a pinched nerve or something like that. We can get you to a good orthopedic doctor and get it straightened right out. I am sure you will be good as new in no time. Just do me a favor, don't wait so long before you come see me when you have a problem."

"I hear you, Doc. I won't, I promise."

Tim got done with everything and left for the office. The headache was beginning to subside a little and he liked the Tylenol 3 the doc had given him. He really didn't want to deal with these headaches anymore.

Tim got to the office to find his in-box full of paperwork. His phone messages were ridiculous and Shelly was waiting to pounce on him as soon as he got settled. Tim had always found Shelly to be very attractive, but she was ridiculously happy in love and he knew there was no chance. They would get into some personal chit-chat every once in a while, but she would bring it back to business quickly. Too bad, Tim thought. She would be a lot of fun.

"Shelly, what's happening?" Tim exclaimed, as he put his brief case down beside his desk.

"Your 11 o'clock wouldn't wait until tomorrow. She is furious over this lawsuit and is waiting in the front waiting room for you now. She said she would wait all day! You have 50 messages from last week, including one from Tracy, marked urgent!"

Tim looked up at Shelly from the papers on the stack at his desk. "Urgent?"

Shelly nodded. "I don't want to know. The partners want to have a dinner meeting downtown, Wednesday night, 8:00 pm; no exceptions and you have court tomorrow at ten. Besides that, life is normal. What did the doctor say?"

"He said I'm dying!"

"Good, then dinner with the partners won't matter and I will tell the lady in the lobby to go screw herself. She wasn't very nice to me anyway! I guess that means you'll be working a two-week notice then, huh!"

"Ha, ha. You'd like that, wouldn't you?"

"No. I would probably end up working for Bob since his assistant quit. The only thing worse than working for you, would be working for nasal Bob."

"Well, the doctor said it was probably nothing. They took some blood and did some x-rays of my neck so I will see later this week. I'm too mean to be dying of anything. If I was I would be suing someone over it."

"Huh, Sue is probably hitting you in the back of your head at night when you're sleeping, trying to make your death look like an accident." Shelly smiled, turning on her heels and walking back into her office.

Tim watched her leave, scanning her from head to toe. "Hmm, very nice today, Shelly!" Tim whispered as she left the room.

Shelly smiled as she walked away. "Stop looking at my ass, Tim!

Tim looked away, trying not to get caught.

The Results

Chapter 3

During the next week, Tim and Sue talked several times about their marriage. Tim moved across the hall into the guest bedroom to give Sue some space. He confessed to the affair in Colorado, but swore to Sue it was over. Sue didn't speak to him for two days after that. Tim wasn't sure if he should move out of the house, or stay, hoping for things to get better. He really didn't know and Sue wasn't talking much.

On Friday, Dr. Simmons' office called Tim's cell phone. Tim answered quickly when he saw the caller ID. The nurse told Tim the doctor wanted to see him back in his office right away. Tim's heart hit the floor.

"What's going on?" he asked the nurse.

"Mr. Billings, it's not my position to even comment. The doctor wanted to get you in here right away to talk about the results. When can you come in? I have two appointments open for Monday and several for Tuesday."

"The hell with that," Tim barked. What do you have open for today? I can come down there right now."

"I'm sorry, sir, we don't have anything for today. The doctor is booked all day."

"Lady, you get me ten minutes with him today. I'm on my way. The doctor said if there was nothing wrong he would call. If there was something, he would get me back down there right away. Obviously, there is something wrong if you are trying to get me worked into the next appointment. Now, what does the chart in front of you say?"

"I'm sorry, Mr. Billings, I can't . . .

Tim hung up the phone and yelled for Shelly. "Shelly, cancel the rest of my day. I am going down to the doctor's office right now."

Just as Tim was walking to the doorway, Shelly came walking through it. "What's wrong? Did they tell you something was wrong?"

"They won't tell me anything. I'm going down there myself get to the bottom of this. Just transfer my calls to my cell. I will deal with what I can on the ride there."

Shelly stood in the doorway as Tim left the office, almost running towards the front lobby. Bob was coming out of his office as Tim went down the hall. "Get out of the way, Nasal!"

Bob backed up into his office as Shelly began to laugh, stepping back into her own office to keep Bob from seeing her laughing.

Tim walked into the doctor's office fifteen minutes later and charged the front window. "I need to see Dr. Simmons right now."

"Mr. Billings, I told the doctor that you were on the way and he understood. Come on back and let's get you in his office, he will work you in between patients, okay?"

Tim let his shoulders relax a little. "Okay, I appreciate that."

Tim followed the nurse back down the corridor to a small, but clean office in the back. He sat down and began to look around the room. There were several diplomas on the wall as well as awards for various achievements throughout his career. Pictures of what looked like family lined the desk. The doctor and a younger, attractive woman were displayed in an 8x10 frame. Tim picked it up and was trying to guess her age as Dr. Simmons came through the door. Tim jumped and went to put the picture back on the desk.

The doctor smiled. "My oldest daughter, if you were wondering. She graduated from medical school that day. I am very proud of her. How are you, Tim?"

"Scared to death at the moment. Tell me what's going on."

The doctor sat in the chair next to Tim, instead of across the desk. "Tim, your x-ray didn't really show me much of anything. Your blood work, on the other hand, did. I want to get you in for a CAT scan as soon as possible."

"What did it tell you?"

"Tim, your white blood cell count is really high."

Tim shook his head. "Okay, what does that mean?"

"High white blood cells mean your body is fighting an infection."

"What kind of infection?"

I don't know. A few other levels in your blood were not good, so we want to do some specific testing. I am going to refer you to a specialist for that."

"What kind of specialist?"

"I am going to send you to an oncologist."

Tim's face went white as he focused on the doctor. "Oncologist. Do I have cancer?"

"You have some indicators that might be cancer-like. That's why I want to run these other tests right away. I am not saying it's cancer for sure, but it runs in your family and your x-ray does show a dark area at the base of your skull." The doctor reached over and touched the back of Tim's head. "Right about there."

Tim dropped his head into his hands and began to shake his head.

The doctor put his hand on Tim's shoulder. "Listen, Tim, we need to do more tests. I can't say for sure either way with the basic blood work we did on you. We need to get you to a specialist and let them do their thing. Cancer is not the death sentence it used to be. There are a lot of good treatments out there that are really breaking some new ground. You're young and healthy, Tim."

"Is it a brain tumor? Is that why I am having these headaches?"

The doctor was quiet.

"Dear God, it is, isn't it? That's what you think, don't you?"

Doctor Simmons held up his hands defensively. "Tim, I just don't know. We need to do a CAT scan and an MRI with contrast to see both the bone and the soft tissue inside your head. We need to do more extensive blood work to be sure."

"Oh my God, I can't believe this is happening to me. Doc, I can't have cancer. I'm 38 years old. I am way too young to have cancer. I don't smoke. I run, play tennis! I don't understand." Tim was standing now, pacing back and forth.

"Tim, sit down. This is a disease that can affect anyone, young or old. It's not just for the old. The good news is that you are young, healthy and strong. That will make a big difference. You live in Atlanta. Emory is one of the best research hospitals in the country when it comes to cancer. Remember, we are not even sure that's what it is. Your white blood cell count is very high and that is just one indicator. This is not the end of the fight for you. If it's cancer, it's only the beginning. How severe, or to what extent you have this, is not even determined yet."

"Doc, cancer is bad no matter what. I have a career where I travel once a month. I am a partner in one of the largest law firms in Atlanta. I have two kids and a wife that depend on my income to live. I can't have this disease. I want the test done now. Who do I need to go see?"

"Tim, calm down for me, okay? Getting worked up over this and having a heart attack is not going to make things better. Cancer is bad, but it's treatable. If, and I say that loudly, *if* you have a brain tumor it could be benign. Your white blood cell count could be high because it is fighting an infection. You could have other things going on that have elevated your white blood cell count. We just need to get all the tests done that we can and get all the answers. Then we can fix you. Okay?"

"No, it's not okay, Doc. You just sat here and told me, I might have cancer. Nothing is okay anymore. I may be looking at the biggest life changing event in my life. Everything I know may be about to change. This is a terrible day! This day will mark all the rest of my life. This is the day that I begin the countdown to my own death from this disease. Cancer has no cure. People beat it for years, but it comes back. It always comes back!"

Doctor Simmons swallowed hard. "Tim, I know this is a lot, the stress you are under right now is probably the greatest you have ever felt, but you are wrong. There are people that survive cancer all over the world. Cancer is a mysterious disease, but not always deadly. Some people get treatments done and the cancer goes into remission. We just don't know until we get things going. I am not even sure you have it. Let's not get ahead of ourselves, okay?"

"Doc, it's brain cancer! How many patients survive cancer that starts out with a brain tumor?"

The doc shook his head. "I don't know, Tim. I am not an oncologist. Cancer is not my specialty. There are a lot of great doctors in this town that are really excellent at this stuff."

"I want the best. I want to know who the top doctor is. I don't care where he is; I want to go to him. How do I find that out? Do you guys have ratings or something? I want the best. I have money, I can afford the best."

"Well, as I said earlier, you are in luck. Emory, right here in Atlanta, is one of the very best. Their research is rated among the top in the country and the top doctors are there."

"What do I have to do to get in there to see one of them right away?"

"I want to set you up with an oncologist first. He will run specific tests and review your MRI and CAT scan. I will get you the information on Emory so you can make the appointment. I went to school with a guy over there named Wells. He is one of the best in their oncology department. He will guide you on how it works. Listen to me; go see Dr. Roberts first. He is the oncologist associated with my office. He's really good and will know exactly what's going on with you."

"Doc, you know what the deal is or you wouldn't be sending me to a specialist. I have a brain tumor, don't I? Just tell me the truth."

Dr. Simmons sat back in his chair, dropping his hands down to his legs for support. "It looks like you do to me, Tim! I'm sorry. Normally I would never tell a patient without further testing, but from the x-rays and the blood work, combined with the headaches you have daily, that's what I think. Again, Tim, you may not have cancer at all. If the tumor is benign, they can get in there and get it out. The technology these days is outstanding."

Tim fell back into the chair beside the doctor. "I'm scared, Doc!"

"I know you are, but right now you need to be strong and persistent. Go see these doctors. The faster you get things done, the faster you will be on your way to recovery."

"I will call the guy at Emory as soon as you get me the information."

"You have to go see Dr. Roberts first. Emory will not talk to you until they know for sure what you have—if you even have cancer, Tim. Go through the process. Let's see what you are dealing with and then go after

it. This all could be minor surgery with minimal time away from work."
Dr. Simmons patted Tim on the back.

"Why me, Doc? I don't smoke. I drink some, but I'm really a healthy guy.
Why does this have to happen to me? Are you sure about this? Maybe I
need a second opinion."

Dr. Simmons stood. "Tim, you do whatever you think you need to do. I
want to set you up to see Dr. Roberts as soon as possible. In the meantime,
let's get you down to the CAT scan people and get that done. Dr. Roberts
will need that when you go see him. If you want a second opinion, that's
fine, too."

Tim remained sitting. "I don't want this, Doc. I have so much going on in
my career. This will ruin everything."

The Doctor sighed. "Son, you have to face the bad things in life head on.
Running from this won't make it go away. You can get all the second and
third opinions you want. Go home. Talk to your wife about this."

Tim shook his head. "Forget that. She and I are not on good terms; hell,
she hates me."

"I'm sorry to hear that, Tim. Having a good support network is crucial.
Maybe you need to go home and work on that."

"Give me the information for the doctor. I will call in the morning and
make an appointment. I also want the number for the guy at Emory. If
this is cancer, I want the best."

"That sounds better. Talk to your wife. If this turns out to be cancer, you
will need your family. Call me and tell me what is going on. Feel free to
call me with any questions. Okay. I am really behind. I have to go. Please
keep in touch."

"Thanks, Doc. I guess. I will call you with any news."

The two shook hands and the doc pointed towards the door. Tim stood and walked to the door. The doctor informed him that the front nurse would give him all the numbers he had asked for. Tim appeared to be in a trance as the doctor handed him off to the nurse standing in the hall.

As Tim walked away, the doctor said, "Tim, take care, okay? Keep in touch."

Tim never turned back or spoke as he moved down the hall with the nurse tugging at his arm.

The next few days were a blur for Tim. He had Shelly make all the appointments he needed. The CAT scan was done and the appointment with the oncologist was next. Tim pressed through the day as always, but the only thing on his mind was the ever-pressing news to come after every appointment. Shelly was constantly reminding him of meetings and appointments related to work. Tim was just waiting for the next step to find out the rest of his life. Work was really not important. What someone wanted to do over some wrongdoing really didn't matter anymore to Tim.

Shelly stood leaning against the red mahogany door leading into Tim's office. "Are you okay?"

Tim looked up. "Hey, Shelly, I just wish I knew. I hate this waiting crap!"

Shelly smiled. "Well, that's because you're a control freak and this is kicking your ass."

"Gee, thanks, Shelly. Did you come in here to cheer me up? Because if you did, maybe you should work on a better technique."

Shelly smiled. "No, I came in to tell you the partners had me divide up your work load for the next week. Go home. Get this testing and stuff done. Everybody knows how stressed you are over this. It's understandable. How did Sue take the news?"

Tim just stared at the desk.

"Well?"

Tim wouldn't look up at Shelly. He knew there would be a disapproving look, and he just couldn't take it.

"Jesus, Tim! You haven't even told her, have you?"

Tim swiveled the high backed leather chair away from Shelly and stared at the bookcase behind his desk. "We're not doing so well. I think we are getting a divorce."

Shelly sighed. "Oh man, what a mess. You have to tell her. Maybe it will help."

"Nothing will help. I just don't love her like I used to. We are not the same people we used to be. I don't even know her anymore. It's too late."

"Bullshit!" Shelly said with conviction. "That's bullshit, Tim."

Tim spun around in his chair to see Shelly now standing at his desk, with her hands on her hips. "What do mean, bullshit?"

"I mean, the problem is Tracy in Colorado, or the other girls here in Atlanta. Stop thinking with your dick. Sue is the mother of your children, for Christ's sake."

Tim interrupted Shelly, standing quickly. "Who do you think you are?"

Shelly stepped back. "I am the person that takes your calls, cleans up behind you when you're not looking. I am a friend as much as an assistant, and if you don't want to hear the truth, then leave, or fire me. You're a jerk! Sue has been good to you and you have left her behind. It's too late because you decided it was. Go home and fix the problem. Don't be like the rest of the jerks in this world that leave good women behind. Fix it!"

As the tears began to form, Shelly turned and walked out of Tim's office. Tim started his rebuttal, as a good lawyer would, but the words froze at his lips. He slowly sat back down, starring at the now empty doorway where

Shelly once stood. Shame began to fill his soul. Shelly had stepped over the line, but she was right. Tim wanted to go in and fire her on the spot, but he knew she was right.

Shelly had been a great assistant to Tim over the years. Whenever she and Tim had gotten into it over something, she was usually right. Tim sighed and sat back knowing that she was right again. How could he fix the years of damage? He would have to tell her everything and that was just too much.

Tim searched the top of his desk and put a few of his files into his brief case. "Shelly, can you come in here?"

There was no reply. "Shelly," Tim said again, as he walked to the doorway joining his office to hers. She was gone. Her computer was off and her chair was pushed in. As Tim turned back into his own office, he felt more alone than he ever had. He had no one he could go to. Tim's parents had both passed away, and there was no one in his life to hang onto.

The walk from his office to the car was silent. Several people had spoken to Tim as he walked the wood lined hallway, but they all got blank stares and nods. All Tim could think about was the possibility of cancer and going through it alone. When Tim reached his car, he stood beside it for a long minute before unlocking the door. He put his briefcase in the back seat and turned to look out across the parking deck into the park across the street. Tim shut the door to the car and locked it, now walking towards the stairs that led to the street level. Down one flight and across the street put Tim walking on the soft grass of the small, but well-kept downtown Five-Points Park.

The Fight

As Tim headed for the fountain in the center, he went back over his life and all he had done. His career was on fire. He was strong and young. His marriage was a mess, but it was just his first, anyway. Everyone in the firm had been married two or three times at least. Why should he be any different? The air outside was cool, but not bad for this time of year. Atlanta never really had bad winters. As Tim looked around, he noticed the park was almost empty. A couple of homeless guys huddled near a small statue trying to keep warm but that was about it. On the far side, there was a couple walking along the sidewalk, oblivious to anything around them. Past that were the busy city streets of Peachtree Street and Marietta Blvd. As the wind blew, he felt the chill of being alone.

Tim walked around the fountain and finally settled on one of the many park benches facing the fountain. His thoughts were bouncing between the possibility of cancer, divorce, death and the rest of his life. The gentle cascading of the water in the fountain was almost hypnotic. The sound of the city faded away as Tim's mind reflected on all of the problems in his life. The wind blowing through the dead leaves of the trees around the park faded to silent.

He had not spoken to Sue in several days and didn't know what he would say even if he did. Tim wondered if she had already drawn up divorce papers and was just waiting for him to show back up so she could serve him. Tracy had called three times, leaving him long messages about overreacting and wanting to talk. Jenny called once, just to say hi.

His life was a mess. His next appointment was with Dr. Roberts tomorrow and he just didn't want to go. For the first time in his life, Tim was afraid, really afraid. This doctor would most likely tell him he had a cancerous brain tumor that would ultimately lead to his death. He was way too young for this kind of news. It wasn't fair.

Tim thought about his kids, how he really had been so busy that he didn't even know them. Then the thoughts of his mom came flooding in. She had died of lung cancer. She had smoked when she was younger, but only for a few years. It was enough to do the damage in her. Tim was also not really around for her, either, when she went through all that. He wished he had been now. The fact was, Sue had been the hero for her. When she got sick, she moved to Atlanta to be closer, and Tim bought a condo for her. But he never really spent any time with her before it was too late. Her cancer was very aggressive and the chemo never helped. The time between her diagnosis and her death was just over a year. Would it be that fast for him? he wondered. What would Emory do for him, if he was willing to try any of the latest drugs? Tim had money that even Sue knew nothing about. He could offer a pretty hefty donation to Emory if they would give him the most aggressive treatment. Tim didn't want this, and the more he sat on the bench the madder he got at what life had just given him.

Tim's brain was going 90 miles an hour when it all came to a halt as someone sat down on the bench beside him. Tim jumped because he had been in such deep thought that he didn't even hear the man approach.

Tim turned quickly to see the young black man looking very intently at him. "Whatcha doin' out here, man?"

Tim stared at the guy, confused, trying to understand why this guy would be talking to him, when he felt the tip of the gun touch his neck from behind. All the city noises rushed back into Tim's brain. The sound of horns from the streets, the wind in the trees and the fountain. Tim spun around to see the second young man holding a chrome revolver, which was now pointed at his head.

"Come on man, gimme yo' money! The watch, too!

Tim froze. He looked between the two men, boys really, not believing this was happening to him.

"Now, fool!" The gun hit Tim's arm.

Tim felt his coat being snatched open by the guy who was sitting on the bench and a hand reaching inside his suit pockets.

Tim snatched the coat back and grabbed the guy by the shirt. "No!" Tim yelled at the one man while turning to look at the guy with the gun.

As Tim turned, he could see the young man's eyes begin to widen, whether with fear or anger, Tim wasn't sure. In reflex, he started pulling away as the young man raised the gun up to fire. While he was still holding the first guy by the shirt, the gun went off. The ringing in Tim's ears was so deafening that he closed his eyes and waited for the pain of the bullet.

Tim began to lose his balance as he felt the weight of the first guy in his grip. Realizing he still had the man by the shirt, he felt the guy pulling away to run. Tim let go, his eyes still closed as he dove to the ground to take cover. The whole world was moving in slow motion, the screams that were around him, all seemed to be far away and very faint.

Tim's face hit the cold ground; he rolled away from the gunman. His ears still ringing from the shot but oddly he felt no pain at all. Had the guy missed him at point blank range, or was he just in shock? From the ground, Tim opened his eyes for the first time to see where the men were. Looking in the direction of where he thought the gunman was, he realized he was nowhere to be found. The guy was gone.

What seemed like forever was, in reality, only a couple of seconds. As Tim turned to look towards the first guy, what he saw was surprising. T-Bone Fisher was lying on the ground, just past the end of the bench, with a single gunshot to the middle of his forehead. What was to be a robbery and mugging had turned in a split second into murder, and Tim was dead center.

Now there were several people looking towards the park from the surrounding streets, and Tim was still on the ground in front of the bench. Tim's ears were still ringing and the first guy wasn't moving. Tim began to stand up, the weight of what happened started to crash in on him. He felt his legs begin to shake as the air outside seemed to drop ten degrees. Tim held firmly to the back of the green park bench not taking his eyes of the still open eyes of his attacker. He slowly began to hear the distant sirens over the ringing in his ears. Tim eased down on the bench and sat down, still staring at the man and the small pool of blood that had formed around his head.

"He's dead!" Tim said out loud, as he looked up, realizing he was still alone.

Tim pulled his cell phone out of his pocket and dialed 911. The recording came on telling him they understood it was an emergency and the next available operator would be right there to help.

The phone picked up. "911 emergency, what is your emergency?"

The words fumbled out of Tim's mouth. "My name is Tim Billings. I'm in the park, Five Points, at the corner of Peachtree and Marietta. There's been a shooting . . . a murder."

"Sir, stay calm for me. Okay? Tell me what happened. Are you injured or in danger?"

Tim for the first time looked around at the crowd beginning to gather. "No, I'm fine. I was in the park and two guys tried to rob me, near the fountain. I fought back and the guy with the gun shot at me. I don't know how he missed, I ducked and the bullet hit his accomplice in the forehead."

"Sir, the police are already in route. Is the man dead?"

Tim looked back at the man, and saw blood filling the cracks of the cobblestone sidewalk around his head. "I think so; yes, he's dead! He was shot in the head!"

"Okay. Sir, just stay calm for me. Where are you now so I can tell the officers?"

"I'm sitting on a bench at the fountain, staring down at this guy. I hear the sirens. I didn't shoot him."

"Okay. Sir, just stay there and stay calm. I am telling the officer everything right now. Hold on the line for me. Don't hang up."

Tim looked up as two police cars came sliding up to the curb fifty feet away. Two cops came out of the cars with guns drawn. Tim could hear the 911 operator calling his name as he raised his hands at the approaching officers. One officer made his way towards the guy on the ground and the other never took his eyes off of Tim.

Tim was now shaking in fear of what had just happened. "I'm unarmed!"

The officer closest to Tim began to speak. "Keep your hands where I can see them."

"I didn't shoot this man, officer."

"I don't care what you did. Keep your hands where I can see them."

"I am. I was getting mugged here. Not the other way around."

The officer reached Tim and pulled him to his feet, quickly searching him and looking over the situation. He looked at the other officer who was now crouched down at the mugger's head, checking for a pulse. Tim and the officer watched as he shook his head no.

Tim heard, "Come with me, sir."

Tim turned to look at the officer now holstering his weapon. "Tell me what happened."

Tim walked with the man away from the bench looking up now at the crowd. "I walked from the parking deck at my office." Tim pointed across the grass at the parking deck.

"Okay. What time was that?"

"Maybe thirty minutes ago. I came over and sat on the bench there just staring at the fountain. I was really lost in my own thoughts when the guy on the ground sat down beside me."

"Was he armed?"

"I don't know. Not that I know of. It scared me when he sat down. I wasn't paying any attention at all."

"You said there was a second man to the operator. Where was he?"

"He came up behind me shortly after the first guy sat down. He stuck a gun to the back of my neck and told me to give them my money."

"And then?"

"I felt the first guy start to open my coat. I fought back. I turned to see where the guy with the gun was when he raised it to shoot. I turned my head and ducked just as he shot."

"When did your ear get cut?"

Tim looked at the officer like he was speaking a foreign language. "What?" Tim reached up and for the first time felt the blood and the cut in his ear.

"Oh my God," Tim exclaimed. "I didn't even feel that. My ears are still ringing from the shot. I knew he was close to my ear but not that close."

Tim started to wobble a little. The officer grabbed Tim's arm. "Alright, let's sit down on the edge of the fountain. Okay?"

Tim looked up to see three more police cars and an ambulance pulling up on the grass near the dead guy. "Jesus! I can't win. I have the worst luck ever."

"Why is that, Mr. Billings?"

"Because I basically just found out I have a brain tumor this week and now this. I was out here just thinking about all that has happened. On top of all that, my wife wants a divorce. I have the worst luck ever!"

"I am sorry to hear all that you are going through, but I think today it wasn't about luck. You have to pay attention to where you are in this city. It's not always good to be out here all by yourself. Can you tell me what happened next."

"Well, next the guy with the gun pulled the trigger. I ducked, just barely, obviously, and he shot his friend in the face. I still had the guy's shirt in my hands and thought he was just pulling away to run. I didn't know he was hit until I was on the ground."

"Did the guy with the gun run then, or what?"

"Yeah, he was gone! I had closed my eyes and dove for the ground behind the bench so I really don't know what happened right then. When I hit the ground, I looked for the guy but he was gone. He must have seen his friend get hit and he took off then."

"Was there anyone else around at the time?"

'Officer, I really don't know. I didn't even see the two guys approach me. I sure wasn't looking during the struggle. After it was over I did look for the guy with the gun in all directions, but the park was empty."

"Well, Mr. Billings, it sounds like you got very lucky today. Most muggers don't use deadly force. They may punch you in the face or knock you to the ground but that's it. These two guys must have thought you were a good target. Did they take anything?"

Tim reached to his back pocket and he still had his wallet. His watch was still there and his money clip was still in his front pocket. "No, I'm good I think."

Another officer approached. "Sergeant, can I speak with you?"

"Mr. Billings, if you will give the detective your information and numbers where you can be reached, we should be done here shortly."

Tim nodded and the detective began to take down all his information. The sergeant went over to a lady standing in a group of officers. She had seen the whole thing from about two hundred feet away. She told the men the story just as Tim had and pointed the direction that the gunman had fled.

The officers had identified the dead man as William "T-Bone" Fisher, who had lived in East Point most of his life. He was a small-time criminal with two counts of possession and one stint in juvie for the armed robbery of a convenience store.

He and his accomplice were nothing but a couple of thugs, just hanging out, looking for trouble. Tim was an easy target. It sure went wrong today, though. The officer looked over at the body covered in a sheet now, with the crowd trying to get closer to take a look. What a waste, he thought. For less than a $100, another young man is dead on the streets of Atlanta.

The sergeant came back over to Tim. "Your story checks out. There is a witness who was standing about two hundred feet away. She saw the struggle start and the shot fired. The other guy ran down Peachtree headed south and turned in behind that building. That's all she saw. Not much of a description—black guy, my height, wearing jeans and a black jacket, hat on his head. That's all she could give us. What about you? You were face-to-face with the man. Can you describe him in detail?"

"Not that much. It was only a few seconds and then it was over. He did have on a white shirt under his jacket. Some kind of writing all over it; I couldn't read it. The hat was a stocking cap deal. You know like all the kids wear these days."

"What color?"

"Black! He did have some facial hair. Just a rough beard like, that's about all I got. It happened so fast. I just don't remember anything else."

"That's okay, Mr. Billings. Listen we are going to take you to the hospital now so they can treat your ear. You may need a stitch or two. I need you to come down to the station after that and give me a full statement. We will have an artist try and draw the guy with your help. That's probably as far as this thing will go. Two junkies trying to score some money but it went south. You're wrong about yourself, Mr. Billings. You're a very lucky man. That could be you lying over there under that sheet. Be thankful you're alive. If you want to call your wife, it's okay, I'm sure she will want to know you are okay. Looks like you will make the news tonight."

Tim turned to see several camera crews already setting up and the reporters giving their commentary. "Great!" Tim said. "Just what I need on top of everything else going on." Can I just go to the hospital now? I don't want to talk to any reporters. The last thing I need is to be on the 6 o'clock News. I will have everybody and their brother calling me tonight."

"Sure. Mr. Billings, let's get you to the ambulance."

"Christ, can't I drive my own car? It's right there in the parking deck."

"No sir, I'm sorry. You are technically in our custody until the doctor releases you. We'll get you back to your car after we get your official statement. Sorry, sir. We don't want to be sued by anyone."

Tim laughed. "Did I tell you I was an attorney?"

"No sir, just a lucky guess. You kind of look like an attorney. Let me ask you this, why did you fight with these guys when they had a gun pointed at you? Are you carrying a lot of cash on you or something?"

Tim thought for a minute. "No. Not really, maybe a hundred bucks."

"Then why risk your life?"

Tim shook his head. "I don't know. I just had had enough. This whole week has been full of doctors and people telling me that my life may be over and I was not going to let some punk-ass kid do it, too."

"Why are they telling you your life is over?"

"They think I have cancer, a brain tumor. A brain tumor located where the gunman held his gun to my head. How ironic would that have been, if I had been shot in the brain tumor and died, instead of the tumor killing me?"

The sergeant looked at Tim for a minute. "Sir, do you think you did what you did because you don't care if you live or die?"

"No, sergeant, I did what I did because I do want to live. I did it because at that moment I decided I would fight for my life. You see, I came over here to this fountain today because I was at the end of my rope and hopeless with this cancer stuff. I was depressed and didn't know what to do. When that guy stuck that gun to my head, I knew right then I wanted to live. I am successful and have a lot of life to live ahead of me. I decided right then to fight for it. I yelled out 'No' and grabbed the guy's shirt with both hands. I turned back to see where the gun was just in time to duck. Nobody is going to take my life away."

"Well, Mr. Billings, that's pretty amazing, let me tell you. That guy today would have shot you in the head, stole everything you had and never thought about it again. You got lucky today. I hope you are just as lucky with the cancer. You fight like you did today and I'm sure you will beat it, too."

Tim smiled and climbed into the back of the ambulance. An officer climbed in with him and they headed for the hospital. When all was said and done, Tim got two stitches in his ear. He had heard at least a hundred times by the end of the night how lucky he was. After all this, Tim still didn't feel very lucky. He still had a brain tumor. In the end, he still would die, but instead of one quick bullet to the head, it would be a long, drawn-out battle with an enemy he would never see. His worst fear was not the demon that had a gun in the park earlier; it was the demon that lived inside his body. That demon grew every day, killing him a little at a time.

At about 8:30, a uniformed officer delivered him back to his car in the parking deck. As he unlocked the door, he looked out of the parking deck into the park where his life had almost ended earlier that day. There were still some news vans on the curb and a few spectators trying to get their face on the news. Tim stood there, staring out at the park for several minutes, thinking about the fight that had taken place and the fight that would begin tomorrow with the oncologist. Would he tell Tim it was cancer for sure, or would he get lucky again? Tim didn't think tomorrow would turn out so lucky for him.

The officer got out of the car after several minutes. "Is everything okay, Mr. Billings?"

"Everything is fine. I was just looking at the park and thinking about today. You can go, I will be fine."

"No sir, my sergeant said to follow you out. Take your time. I will be here when you're ready." She got back into the car and backed up into a parking space.

Tim looked one more time out at the park. "You didn't get me today, and you won't get me tomorrow, either." He threw his coat into the passenger seat and climbed in. Tim waved at the officer as he backed out of the space and jammed the accelerator.

As Tim drove, the fight in him began to rage. People beat cancer all the time, so could he, he thought. Tomorrow he would see Dr. Roberts and move on quickly to the researchers at Emory. He would get to the cutting edge stuff right away. To hell with all the "normal stuff." He would buy his way to a cure. Tim knew how to work the system. He was a master at it and had been doing it for years. After all, money can buy anything.

As Tim approached his neighborhood, he thought about Sue. Would he even bother telling her about today? Maybe she saw it on the news. He gritted his teeth as he thought about how things were at home. This cancer thing would be hell to go through alone. Maybe he needed to tell Sue. What if it got her to put the divorce on hold for a short while? Tim really wasn't sure what to do anymore about Sue. At a quarter to ten, he pulled in the garage. Tim just sat there for awhile thinking through the conversations he needed to have. How it would play out. Tim did this all the time before court, but this time it was his life on the line. It was his own needs he had to have help with this time.

"Hi, honey. Interesting day today, I found out I may have cancer and oh yeah, I got part of my ear shot off today in the park! How was your day?"

What a mess things had become. As Tim sat there, the garage light came on and the door opened. Sue stuck her head out and looked at Tim. The look of confusion on Sue's face slowly went back to the cold stare Tim was getting used to. Sue shut the door and the light went back off. Tim got out of the car and headed inside.

As Tim walked in through the garage door, he saw Sue starting up the steps. "Sue, wait, please!"

Sue stopped on the steps and turned back to face the kitchen. "What, Tim?"

"We need to talk."

Sue stood her ground on the steps. "No, we don't, Tim. You don't have anything to say that I want to hear. I want a divorce. I will have someone in my office do the paperwork."

Sue turned and started walking up the steps. The lights went off and Tim heard her door shut.

"Wow, this will be harder than I thought." Tim said to himself as he sat in the dark in the kitchen.

By the time Tim got upstairs, the hall was dark and a small glow of light was the only thing coming from under Sue's door. Sue's lamp by the bed was most likely on. Tim stood outside her door for a long moment, wondering if he should just go in and tell her everything, or wait for a better time. He truly didn't know which way to go. Tim Billings as an attorney had knocked down hundreds of imaginary doors with juries to get through and free his clients. He was never afraid; but with his wife, Tim was terrified. He was terrified because the crimes that had been committed were by him against her. He was a repeat offender, and way past the three strikes that judges often gave common criminals in the system.

Twice, Tim raised his hand to knock on the door, but turned away and went into his room and closed the door.

Sue came to the door when she thought she heard Tim walk up. She wondered what Tim could want to talk about. Sue wondered if it was confession time for him, or if he just wanted to go over the divorce. The last week had been miserable around the house. Before she told Tim she wanted a divorce, at least things were livable. They got along, as long as Sue just acted like nothing happened. She knew Tim was going to the doctor for his headaches, but he had not said a word; maybe he wanted to tell her about that. She had assumed it was sinus related or a pinched nerve and he was probably taking something by now.

She wondered how long this would go on, before Tim came home with divorce papers drawn up. Sue had said she would do it, but Tim would try and control how the divorce went, and Sue knew it. It certainly wouldn't cost him anything or be any trouble. One of the paralegals would do the work and one of his buddies would sign the papers. She had thought about it at work, but had not done anything. She hated to throw away so many years of marriage, but being happy was not something she had known in forever. She didn't want to go through life married to a man she knew was cheating on her, either. Sue got back in bed, saddened by what life had become. She decided she would talk to Tim tomorrow and come to a decision. She couldn't deal with it tonight. In Tim's absence over the years, Sue had dealt with the kids and the house and everything that went into making life happen. She had been up early with Annette getting her to school with a class project. Life was hard with no husband to help.

Tim got in bed after taking a quick shower and thought about how crazy the day had been. His partners had basically sent him home with not as much as a hope that the doctors will say it's not cancer. He had been mugged and shot, witnessed a murder and had been questioned by the police all afternoon. Life was insane all around him. He lay there wondering why. What in the universe had changed that directed all this bad attention to him. Tim started to wonder if God was punishing him for his bad behavior. He had not talked to God in so long, he doubted if God would even remember who he was, much less want to help him. Besides, isn't that what everybody does? Don't talk to God for ages, and then something bad happens, and you yell his name.

Tim closed his eyes and lay there for awhile, trying to sleep, but it wouldn't come. The drugs the doctors gave him at the hospital had worn off, and his ear was killing him. Tim kicked off the covers, rolled over and stared at the ceiling. Light cascaded across the ceiling from outside street lights, illuminating the room. It was 12:45 a.m. and sleep was nowhere in sight. His life was a mess, but hopefully tomorrow it would begin to get back on track. Hopefully the x-rays would show nothing major and a day in surgery would do it. Tim was ready to get on with his life.

At 2:00 a.m. sleep finally came.

The Specialist

Chapter 5

Tim woke the next morning tired and stiff from the day before. It was about 8:00, and Tim's appointment that morning was at 10:30. He showered, got dressed and went downstairs. Sue was standing in the kitchen, drinking coffee and reading the paper. As Tim walked in the room, she looked up, surprised.

"What are you doing home?"

Tim walked to the coffee pot. "I have another doctor's appointment today."

Again, Sue looked surprised. "Another appointment; what's wrong?"

Tim made a cup of coffee and searched the fridge for something to eat. "Don't worry about it. I'm sure it's nothing."

Sue sat her coffee down on the granite counter top. "What do you mean nothing, Tim? What is the appointment for and what did they say at the first appointment?"

Tim turned and faced Sue, "It's an oncologist!"

Sue stared at Tim noticing the bandage on his ear. "What, an oncologist? Do they think you have cancer and what happened to your ear?"

"I've had a rough few days. Don't worry about it."

"What are you talking about Tim? What do you mean, a rough few days? Let's start with the ear . . . What happened?"

Still leaning into the refrigerator, he replied, "I got mugged yesterday. I was in the park near the fountain and this guy sat down beside me while his partner stuck a gun to my head. Don't you watch the news? It was all over the TV last night."

"What!"

Tim stopped and turned to face Sue, closing the refrigerator door. "I couldn't believe it was happening at first. It all seems like slow motion to me now, but it happened really fast."

Sue felt her heart jump as Tim spoke. "So what happened to your ear?"

Tim cleared his throat, "I got shot!"

Sue walked over close to Tim. "Tim, what the hell, you got shot? Why didn't you tell me last night when you came in?"

"I tried, but you walked upstairs."

Sue sighed. "I'm sorry; I thought you were trying to . . . It doesn't matter; I just didn't want to hear it anymore so I went upstairs. I heard on the news that there was a shooting downtown in the park by your office, but I really wasn't paying attention. That was you?"

"Well, sort of. The guys who were mugging me got violent and one of the guys—the guy with the gun—tried to shoot me. I ducked and the bullet grazed me, but hit the other guy in the head."

"Jesus, Tim, is he dead?"

"Oh yeah, the bullet hit the guy right in the forehead. I dove to the ground and by the time I looked back up the gunman was gone. The other guy was on the ground, dead."

"Oh my God, you are lucky you weren't killed. Now I understand why you took today off. You must have been scared to death."

"I really didn't have time to be scared until it was over. I sat there staring at the guy on the ground, in shock at what had just happened. It was crazy. Then the cops questioned me for a few hours about what happened. I ended up with a few stitches, but other than that, I am okay. That's not why I took the day off, though."

"Why, then, the doctor, what's up with that? You said you were going to an oncologist. Tell me why you are going to an oncologist?"

"Sue, it's no big deal. My blood work was not right and there is a dark area where I get my headaches. The doctor referred me to an oncologist for more tests. It looks like I might have a tumor, but I don't know if it's cancerous yet. Don't worry about it. You have made it clear that we are finished. You won't have to deal with it either way."

"God, Tim, you can be such a jerk! We wouldn't be here if it wasn't for you. I have been a good wife to you. You shut me out of your life, Tim, just like you are now. Why is it you don't think I am good enough for you?"

Sue turned, throwing the paper in her hands on the counter. As she walked off, she swore under her breath. Tim started to say something, but again Sue's words hurt and he let her walk away. He looked at his watch and decided to go ahead and leave. He could stop at the corner coffee shop and get a Danish and frappuccino. Tim looked one more time towards the stairs, but Sue was gone. Tim had made a mess of his home life and it was too late to repair the damage. He grabbed his keys off the hook and headed for the garage.

Sue was crying as she went into her room. Tim could hurt her faster than anybody else on the planet. She hated that she still let him get to her so easily. He didn't care about her at all. It had been all about him for years. Sue was just there to take care of the kids and keep the house nice. He had not even said anything on their last anniversary. Sue ended up taking the gift she had bought him back after several days and bought herself a necklace instead of the $400 pen set she had bought Tim.

After Tim got breakfast, he headed for the doctor. He didn't know how to act, not going to work. His days usually started early and he worked until at least six. This morning he had slept in, got dressed in casual clothes and was going to make the doctor's appointment in plenty of time. Everything was different this morning, except the headache that was now creeping up the back of his head. God, he was tired of the headaches. Stress like this morning, arguing with Sue, just made it worse. Whatever the outcome today, he would be glad to get rid of the headaches.

Tim thought to himself, that he could get used to this life of leisure if a few things were different. Maybe after this tumor and the divorce he might just make that happen. He had been putting money away for a long time from some of his less than scrupulous business deals. Some of Tim's clients were not such nice people and quite often had thanked Tim for the not guilty verdict by giving him large sums of cash. He was very good at hiding money in untraceable offshore accounts. He thought that with the right investing he could live pretty well.

Tim smiled as he pulled into the doctor's parking lot. First, he needed to deal with this tumor, or whatever it is and get it behind him. He did the normal check in at the front desk, but this office was much smaller and the waiting room was surprisingly empty. The receptionist told him it would only be a few minutes, and to have a seat. Tim felt very alone in the room all by himself; unlike the last waiting room that was full of people, he had no one to look at or make fun of. He was alone to deal with this thing both here and at home, he thought.

The door opened and the nurse called his name. He walked back into a small exam room. This differed from Dr. Simmons' office. There were pictures of cells and information about cancer treatments on the wall instead of diplomas, medical achievements and family photos.

Dr. Roberts came through the door just minutes later. "Mr. Billings, how are you this morning?"

"I've been better, Doc, how are you?"

"I'm good. I got the x-rays and the blood work." Turning to the x-ray viewing board and snapping several CAT scans into the lighted board.

"Well, tell me some good news, Doc."

Dr. Roberts came over and sat in the chair next to Tim. "Mr. Billings, can I call you Tim?"

Tim laughed. "Doc, nothing good ever follows a doctor asking you if he can call you by your first name. How about I say no, and you give me good news!"

"Tim, I am going to be honest with you about things from the beginning. If you want me to call you Mr. Billings, that's fine. The news will be the same either way."

"'Tim' is fine, Doc; let's hear it."

"Tim, you have a tumor in the lower part of the back of your head. Right now, it's about the size of a golf ball. The test that Dr. Simmons did does indicate cancer, but we will do more and determine that for sure."

Tim sat back in his chair and began to rub his face. He could feel the tears welling up in his eyes. He had tried to mentally prepare himself for this moment but it had not worked. Hearing the doctor say he had cancer hit hard. It was spoken now and real, the brain tumor was real. His life had just changed forever. Whether he survived or not, it was changed forever. The doc sat quietly while Tim continued to rub his face, trying to shield the tears that were now coming.

Dr. Roberts leaned towards Tim, touching his knee. "You okay, Tim? Hearing that affects everyone differently. The emotions you are feeling right now are okay to have. Most people feel like they were just handed a death sentence. That's not the case. Okay? There are a lot of really good treatments out there now and a brain tumor is not near as scary as it used to be. Yours is in a very good position for removal."

"Really? Not scary for who, Doc? I got to tell you, it scares the shit out of me!"

Dr. Roberts smiled at Tim's expletive. "I understand. Let me rephrase that, it's not near as scary for us doctors. We can do a laparoscopic procedure to remove the tumor. It's practically day surgery in some cases, whereas 10 years ago a brain tumor was major surgery."

Tim looked at the doctor, "I want the best, Doc!"

"You want the best of what, Tim?"

"I want the best and latest treatment for cancer there is. Dr. Simmons gave me the name of a doctor in the oncology department at Emory. I want to go see him and get the latest, most-advanced treatment there is."

"I understand that. You're a fighter. That's good and you need to be. You're going to go through some rough times, Tim. Fighting will help you make it through. Emory has some great things going on. But what makes you think I'm not the best, Tim?"

Tim flushed with redness looking up at the doctor. "I didn't mean you weren't good, Doc, I just . . ."

Dr. Roberts laughed. "It is okay, Tim. I understand what you're saying. I am good at what I do, though, but the guys at Emory are on the cutting edge. You actually fit a good profile for being in their test program. You're young and in good shape. Who did Dr. Simmons recommend?"

Tim fumbled with his pockets looking for the business card the nurse had given him. "His name is Dr. Wells. Do you know him?"

"Yep, Jim Wells. He's good, but I think there is a better guy over there for you. I want you to call a Dr. Hampton. He is head of research in the brain cancer section of Emory, a really smart guy. I wouldn't tell him you want the best. He might not think that's funny."

"Is he the best?

"Yes! He is the best of the best. I will send him your file and what I think is going on with you. I also will send along my recommendation that he put you in the experimental group. You call him and leave your information with his office. He will evaluate the case and call you if he accepts you in the program."

"You get me in touch with him and I will make him accept me!"

"Tim, I read your file and I know you are a powerful lawyer in Atlanta, but I am telling you, don't try and bully your way into this guy. You're an excellent candidate for the program and I will send your information over to him. He and I are friends and we serve on the same board at Emory. Be patient. In the meantime I want to run a few more test so we can pinpoint exactly what you have."

"Okay, Doc, that sounds good. I want to beat this thing. I'm way too young to die of cancer."

"Maybe God wants you to do some good with your life still."

Tim looked at the doctor quickly, "I don't know, Doc. I think maybe I have done some bad things and God is just getting ready to really start punishing me!"

The doctor laughed, "God doesn't punish, Tim, and He forgives. Maybe He wants you to ask for forgiveness so He can bless you."

Tim hung his head, "I'm not so sure, Doc. Life was pretty good for me a few weeks ago; however, it seems lately with every turn I run into more bad news."

"Tim, let me tell you about the road you're about to go down. It's a hard one. Cancer is a very destructive force on the human body. Chemo is a hard drug. You're going to feel much, much worse before you start feeling better. Hang in there. God is with you no matter what. Now might be a good time to get back in touch with Him and make it right."

"I thought doctors weren't supposed to talk about God with their patients. Isn't that against some kind of rule?"

Dr. Roberts laughed. "No, Tim, that's teachers. Doctors can talk to you about whatever we want to and God is someone you need to work things out with!"

Tim smiled faintly. "Maybe, Doc. Maybe . . ."

"We will run some more tests to determine the type of cancer you have. I'm sending you to one of the best neurosurgeons there is to go ahead and get ready to get this brain tumor out. We will test it to see if it is cancerous or not. Once that is done we will start treating you for the cancer."

"Okay, I'm ready."

"That's good. The nurse will be in here in just a few minutes to take some more blood. I will have her call the neurosurgeon's office now to see how soon we can get you in there. You call Dr. Hampton this afternoon and leave a message. By the time he gets it, I will have sent him an email with your file attached. By this time tomorrow you will be on your way."

"Thanks, Doc!"

"Remember, Tim, this is going to be a hard fight. Don't lose sight of the end. You're young and in good shape. You can beat cancer."

"I know, Doc. I'm as ready as I can be. I'll work on that God thing, too, maybe."

"No 'maybe,' Tim, you better work on that now. There will be days when He is the only one who will be with you."

Tim endured the taking of blood again and all that the doctor explained about x-rays and the huge amount of information that his new life would involve. As Tim left the office, he thought about God and what the doctor had said. What an unusual place for someone to care about his relationship with God. Tim thought about Sue again. Another relationship he had let go over the years that needed to be fixed. Unlike God, Sue might not be so forgiving. He had treated her like she didn't matter for years.

That afternoon back at home, Tim called Dr. Hampton. Surprisingly, he answered the phone. "Hampton, how can I help you?"

Tim stuttered, not expecting to get the real guy. "Uh, this is Tim Billings. Is this Dr. Hampton?"

"Why, yes it is, Tim. I was expecting your call. I got Dr. Robert's email about an hour ago and I would like to talk to you right away. I think I have some things that may interest you."

Tim was shocked. "Really, I can come right now? I could be there in 30 minutes."

"Sorry, Tim, today is no good, but I have time tomorrow around eleven. Can you be here then?"

Tim was silent. "Can you be here at eleven, Tim?"

"Yes, I'm sorry. I didn't expect to actually talk to you today and really didn't expect to see you so quickly. Yes, I can be there, no problem. Where is your office?"

The doctor provided the address and directions, including where to come once he arrived on campus. Tim could not believe his luck. Maybe God was not completely against him, after all. Tim thanked the doctor and with one final sentence, he was gone:

"See you guys at eleven!"

Tim sat back in his chair, confused about what he meant by "you guys." Tim had not mentioned bringing anybody. Maybe Dr. Hampton assumed Sue would be along. Tim thought that in any normal relationship the wife of a cancer patient would be along. Tim and Sue were not what he would call normal. Sue at this point probably was glad Tim had cancer. If he died from it, no need for a divorce. Tim cringed at the words floating in his head. Sue didn't hate him; she was just tired. He knew in his heart she didn't want him dead, either.

"Dead," Tim said out loud for the first time. He had not really thought about death before. He had always been so alive, so strong. In the courtroom, in the heat of battle, he could feel the blood rushing through his body. Court always made him feel alive. He had always been adventurous, he always liked to do things that made his adrenalin pump. Now he was feeling the rush of his blood because death was so close, closer than it had ever been before. It was a real possibility now. It was an outcome that he would be faced with if the surgeries and the drugs didn't work . . . Before, he could always count on his skill and agility to avoid death. Jumping from airplanes or riding a motorcycle through the mountains was dangerous, but his skill was a factor. For the first time, skill had nothing to do with it; God did!

Tim sat back in his chair smiling for the first time in days. He got up and decided to go down to Scully's and have a drink with the boys. His last encounter was not so good but maybe a card game would be. He started walking out of his office as Annette was coming down the hall. He had not seen her in a week, it seemed. They stood face to face in the hall. Both froze, not really knowing what to say.

Tim spoke first. "Hey, sweetie, how are you?"

Annette stared at her dad, saying nothing.

"You're just getting home from school?" Annette still said nothing.

Tim had no idea what to say to Annette. His own daughter stood in front of him and he was again at a loss for words. A man who was paid very well for words was completely at a loss.

Annette stared at Tim and quietly spoke. "Are you going to die?"
The words hit Tim like a Mack truck. Tears began to roll down his cheeks. Her gaze never left his eyes. She was cold and without feeling.

Tim gathered himself like many times in a courtroom when something unexpected was said, almost wanting to say, Objection! He cleared his throat and wiped his face.

"No, sweetheart. I . . ." The words just hung there as Tim looked at his daughter, who really didn't care. He didn't know her. And because of that, he didn't even know how to talk to her.

Annette changed her gaze from Tim to the floor. "Mom said you have cancer. Do you?"

Tim kept trying to stop the tears coming from his eyes. "Yes, I do Annette, they think so, anyway. That doesn't mean that I am going to die, though. Did Mom say I was going to die?"

Annette never looked up and began to move past him toward the stairs. "No, she just said you have cancer. Everybody dies that has cancer. My friend's dad had cancer. He died."

As she walked by Tim, he turned to face her. "Annette, wait, I want to talk to you."

With that, she was gone. Tim walked back into his office and fell into his leather chair. The two-minute conversation had exhausted him. He pulled the bottle of scotch from his desk and poured a large shot into his empty coffee cup. As he began to drink, the mess he had made at home saddened him. He had a wife that had stopped loving him and wanted a divorce, a daughter that hated him and was apparently glad he might die and a son he had not played ball with in years.

With those thoughts, he finished the scotch and headed for Scully's. He had had enough for one day at home. Besides, he was celebrating the call from Emory. He was ready to fight this thing with everything he had. He was used to fighting in the courtroom every day. He could do this, too.

As he pulled into Scully's, he recognized a few regular cars sitting in the parking lot. He was glad George and Peter were not there, as far as he could tell. The last conversation was a little judgmental and he really didn't want to deal with it tonight. As he walked in, Billy from behind the bar let out a warm, "Mr. B, how are ya!"

Tim smiled. "I'm good, Billy. I'll have my usual."

Billy nodded. "Coming right up; some of your boys are in the back. Already got a game going. Get in there and get you some money, sir. I'll bring your drink to ya."

"Thanks, Billy."

Tim headed back and the guys all smiled as Tim came in the room. Things like, "Tim, my boy" and "There's a sucker right there" were called out. Tim laughed and took the only empty seat.

As he got seated, he greeted the guys with, "I'm taking all of yawl's money tonight!"

The guys laughed and dealt Tim in the game. Billy arrived with the first round of scotch and Tim felt like he was back to normal. As the night went on, he lost most of the hands he played, but he didn't care because the room was full of laughter and joking as he told the story of getting shot in the park. The guys could not believe what had happened. The rest of the night, they called him "hero" and bought his drinks. He was really glad to be around the guys; for the first time in a while, he didn't feel alone. He didn't even want to bring up the tumor. Why bring the mood down? He thought.

The night ended with Tim and a couple of the guys eating a steak and having a few beers. Charlie asked Tim about Sue, and Tim shook his head.

"I'm getting a divorce, Charlie. Sue hates me. We haven't been good for years; I'm a jerk, anyway. She's better off alone."

Charlie laughed. "I could have told you that. You suck at poker, too. We took all your money tonight. You need me to buy your dinner?"

"No, Charlie, I'm good. I still have some of your money from the last time."

"Not my money, maybe Ted's," Charlie replied, pointing at Ted, who clearly needed a cab at this point; he had been drinking scotch all night, plus three beers with dinner. He was wasted.

The cab got there and they poured Ted in the back seat. Tim offered to come get him the next day and bring him back to get his car if he needed. Ted raised a hand at Tim, and Tim shut the door. He and Charlie stood there watching the cab drive away.

Charlie laughed and hit Tim on the arm. "Want to go back in and have one more for the road? I'm buying!"

Tim smiled at Charlie. "No, I better get going. It's been a long day. I'm ready to get to bed."

Charlie laughed again. "With who, dog? I heard you left here the other day with two women. Did you sleep with both of them or what?"

Tim shook his head looking at the ground. "Man, who told you that?"

"Billy told me. You're going to see one of them now, aren't you? You never go home before midnight. Come on man, tell me the deal."

"No, Charlie, I'm done with that stuff. I need to make some changes in my life."

Charlie stepped back, "What! What did you do with my friend Tim? Cause you are clearly an impostor."

"Man, leave me alone. I just need to treat Sue better. She's a good woman, Charlie, and I think I might have really screwed up with her."

"Wow! I can't believe what I am hearing right now."

Tim reached for his keys. "Man, I got to go."

"No, Tim, hold on a minute. This is not the Tim I have known the last few years. What's going on? Talk to me."

"It's just been a tough week, dude. Getting mugged and shot, plus a bunch of other stuff. I just need to get some stuff right in my life. I have really screwed up at home, Charlie. My daughter can't stand me. She all but told me today that she wants me to die."

"Oh, shit! Why? What brought that on?"

"Nothing. I really need to go. I appreciate you caring, Charlie, but this is stuff I need to work out on my own. I'll see you later. Okay?"

Tim walked into the dark parking lot, leaving Charlie standing at the front door. As he got to the car, he looked back and Charlie was still standing there. He felt bad for not telling him about the cancer and everything else, but he didn't want everyone knowing about it. Ultimately, there was still a remote chance they could remove the tumor and get all of it at the same time. He could end up cancer free and then there would be nothing to tell. As Tim drove out of the lot, he could see Charlie going back into Scully's for that last drink. Tim laughed at the thought of having to represent him in a DUI case. Charlie was headed right for one, with as much as he drank in a night and then always driving himself home.

Tim's ride was a short one and he was home in ten minutes. He had driven it so many times he could do it drunk or sober if he had to. Tonight was not so bad; he had gone easy on the drinking on purpose. He had a big day tomorrow, and he certainly didn't want the doctor rejecting him because he reeked of alcohol.

It was about 11 when he came in, and the house was quiet. The kitchen was clean and all put away as usual. Sue was a good mom and wife. The kids were always fed and the house was always clean. He noticed a chocolate cake on the counter and cut a piece for himself. As he leaned back against the counter in amazement, he shook his head at how good it was. It had been a long time since he had tasted one of Sue's homemade chocolate cakes.

As he went over to the refrigerator to get a glass of milk to go along with his cake, he noticed one of Jonathan's school papers hanging on the fridge with a big A+ at the top of it. Tim pulled it off the door to look at it after he poured his milk. As he read the book report on Thomas the Train, he could see his son standing in front of the class reading it. It hit Tim like a ton of bricks: he had been so busy with his life that he had not even seen his son ever get on the school bus, nor had he ever been to an open house or school function. Jonathan was in the 2nd grade already and Tim had missed it all.

Once again, tears begin to fill up his eyes. "Jesus, Tim, how many times can you cry in one day?"

As he took a sip of the milk, he hung the report back on the fridge, realizing he had missed a lot of his home life while chasing his career. Being "the man," he had to make things right.

Tim finished the cake and made his way upstairs. At his door, he paused and looked at Sue's door again. Should he just go in, crawl in bed with her, and say I'm sorry for everything, tell her he loved her and make it right? There was a glow of light under the door; she was awake in there.

As he took a step towards the door, the light went off. Tim froze again, standing there for a minute before turning back towards his room. At the dresser, looking at his reflection in the mirror, he asked himself, "What is wrong with you, Tim Billings?"

Shaking his head, he got ready for bed. That night, as Tim lay there, he began to pray, for the first time in a long time. He thought about what the doctor had said that day and he wanted to get some things right in his life.

Tim fell asleep praying into the night.

Sue lay in bed wide awake for an hour, wondering about herself and Tim. She wondered what she would do if they found cancer in him. Would she help him, or walk away? She wasn't sure she could do either one. Tim had been everything she wanted in college. Strong, good looking and intelligent. They were everything to each other for years.

Sue tossed and turned until finally getting out of bed. She put on her robe and walked into the hallway. Dim light cascaded from the bathroom shining towards Jonathan's room, and Sue smiled, thinking of her little man. As she turned, she could see the door to Tim's room open about a foot. Sue walked over quietly and looked in.

Tim was asleep, snoring as usual. Sue pushed the door open a little further and leaned against the door jamb. Looking at him now, in the dim light, she was not sure if she even knew the man anymore. They had been inseparable at one time. Now there was nothing but separation. How could it have gotten this bad? How could he have turned his back on his wife and kids?

Tears began to spill onto Sue's face and she backed out of the room, closing the door behind her.

As the door shut, it woke Tim with a jolt and he sat up in bed. Tim shook off the sleep, looking around the room. Finally, he got to his senses and realized the door to his room was shut. He remembered it being open when he went to sleep. Tim got up and put on shorts, making his way to the door.

Tim opened the door and looked into the hallway. It was quiet and the only light was from the bathroom. Tim opened the door wider and stepped into the hall. As he did, the hardwood squeaked with his weight. Tim stepped back, balancing his weight to his other foot. Stepping carefully again, he made his way down to the bathroom.

Sue stood inside her bedroom, with her hand hard over her mouth, covering the sounds of sadness trying to escape her. She was so tired of crying over Tim. Sue couldn't move as she heard the toilet flushing and Tim coming back down the hallway. His steps slowed at her door, and Sue feared he would open her door to look in, just as she had him.

Tim stood at her door, listening for any sound. He heard nothing, and turned back to his room to go back to bed, this time shutting the door as he went.

Sue eased back to bed and covered herself with the thick comforter on the bed. The cold she felt was all the way to her bones, it seemed like.

Emory

Chapter 6

The next morning, Tim was up early. He got dressed and came downstairs to find everyone in the kitchen. Jonathan's face lit up as he walked in the room.

"Morning, Daddy. What are you doing here?"

With a big smile on his face, Tim picked Jonathan up as he ran to hug him. "I came down to eat breakfast with you, buddy, is that okay?"

"Sure it is! Mom makes the best eggs ever! Do you want some eggs, like me?"

"I do, if Mommy would be nice enough to make them for me." Tim looked over at Sue reading the paper. "Please!"

Sue looked puzzled at this new behavior. "Sure, I will. How many eggs would you like?"

"Two is good. Thank you."

Sue looked back at Jonathan who was still in Tim's arms. "Sweetie, get down and finish your breakfast. The bus will be here soon."

"Aw, man! I wanted to eat with Dad."

As he put Jonathan down, Tim said, "I can take the kids to school. I have time."

Sue turned back to look at Tim again, when a loud "Yes!" came from Jonathan. Sue just looked at Tim and shrugged her shoulders. "I guess."

"All right, Dad, sit by me."

Tim walked over and sat next to Jonathan. "Hey, good job on the book report, son. A+! That's great work. Keep that up and you can be a lawyer like Daddy."

Sue dropped the pan hard into the sink as she heard the words come from Tim. Without looking at him, she shook her head no, as she continued to make his breakfast.

Jonathan was all smiles. "Yeah, I know. The teacher said I did a good job. Could I work in your office with you one day, Dad?"

Tim rubbed Jonathan's head and smiled. "You bet, in the office next to me if you want."

Sue sat the plate down hard in front of Tim. "How about you become a doctor, Jonathan? We have enough lawyers in this family already," sending half a smile in Tim's direction.

"Maybe Mom's right, big guy. We need a doctor in this family."

"No, I want to be just like Daddy and stand in front of the jury!

Sue turned away. "God, that's just what I need."

Tim smiled again at Jonathan. "You can be anything you want, son. Anything! Now eat up so I can get you to school."

Tim turned towards Annette, who had been quiet this whole time. She slowly ate her eggs and didn't look up at Tim.

"What about you, Annette? Want me to take you to school, too? It will be fun."

Annette picked up her plate. "No, thanks! I'll take the bus."

With that, she took her plate to the sink, grabbed her book bag and headed out the door. Tim watched his daughter go in silence, knowing he had to get through to her. She hated him and he didn't even know why, really. Maybe she had noticed how he had treated her mom and was mad for her mom's sake. He wasn't sure, but it was complicated, and might take years of therapy to fix!

"Cool!" came Jonathan's voice from behind Tim. "It's just the dudes!"

Tim laughed. "Yeah, just us dudes."

As they sat there, Tim realized he had no idea what time school started. He was pretty sure where it was, but that was about it. Sue had left the room and so had Annette. That left Tim and Jonathan. Would he know what time? Do second graders know that kind of stuff, or do they just show up when their mommies tell them to? He had no idea.

"So, little man, what time are you supposed to be at school?"

"Dad . . . it's 8:30; you don't know that?"

"Yeah, I was just seeing if you did. Okay, hurry up; we need to get going. We don't want to get you in trouble. You might need a lawyer if you do!"

"Dad, you're so crazy. You should take me to school all the time. You're funny."

They finished breakfast and got ready to leave.

Sue came back in the room. "He needs to be there by 8:15. Parent drop-off is on the right side of the school. You will see the line of cars. You need to hurry or he'll be late."

Tim smiled. "Thanks. Listen, Sue, can we talk later tonight? I have a lot I want to tell you and I would like to talk about Annette, too."

Sue looked at Tim, trying to figure out his angle. "I guess. I suggest you don't go out then tonight. I go to sleep about 11."

"No, I won't be out anymore. I do want to talk tonight."

"Come on Dad, let's go!"

"Okay, little dude! Go get in the car. I'm on the way; you drive."

Jonathan smiled. "Dad, I'm only eight. I can't drive."

On the way to school, they drove with the windows down, and Tim let Jonathan turn up the radio. Tim was enjoying every minute of the ride with Jonathan, trying to remember when he had been as carefree as Jonathan was. Tim did not want to die or miss the chance to see his son grow up. He had missed too much already. This morning, as short as it had been, was the best time he had had in a long time. Tim kept noticing Jonathan looking over at him, and he'd smile while singing along with the songs as best he could. Every verse that Tim sang wrong would make Jonathan laugh out loud. Tim loved every minute of it!

They got to school and pulled into the drop-off lane. He was surprised to see the line of cars. Tim turned down the music and smiled at Jonathan.

"I don't want to get you trouble with the principal!"

Jonathan laughed. "Oh you would, too. She's mean, Dad."

"She is? You better behave, then. Getting in trouble is not good. Your mom would be mad at you."

Jonathan looked at Tim with sadness in his eyes. "Dad, are you home from work today because you're sick?"

Tim turned the radio off. "Why do you ask, son? Who said I was sick?"

"Annette did. She said you were dying. I don't want you to die, Daddy. Are you?"

Tim was furious with Annette, but melted as he looked at little Jonathan's watery eyes. "No, son, I'm not going to die. Annette was just being mean and I will talk to her today about that. I am sick, though, and may need to go into the hospital soon to have surgery."

"What kind of surgery?"

"Brain surgery. I don't have one and I'm going to get them to put one in for me."

Tim laughed and poked Jonathan. That brought a smile back to his face. They pulled up and the drop-off girl opened the door with a smile. Jonathan grabbed his book bag and hugged his dad.

"Bye, Dad! Thanks for the ride. It was cool!" With that, he was gone.

Tim mumbled the words, "I love you son," as the door shut. He was almost afraid of the words. Annette was a different problem. She must really hate me, he thought. He would have to work things out with her. One thing was for sure, he didn't want her telling everyone he was dying. He would talk to Sue tonight, and maybe after that he could sit with Annette and try to work some things out.

Tim started heading downtown. He had enough time to go by the office for a minute and then on to Emory. It had been days since he had been in the office and, strangely, he hardly missed it. He had worked for the firm since college and had worked hard, 10-to 12-hour days, almost every day. This time off was more than paid for, he thought. Fifteen years of long, hard days, plus being one of the top billers in the office, had granted him some pretty good benefits over the years.

Tim pulled into his regular spot and got out of the car. As he did he could see the park and the bench where he had been wounded and where T-Bone had lost his life. Reaching up, he felt the small bandage that still covered the wound. That was a close one, he thought.

It felt a bit strange as he walked into the office. He was dressed casual, which was a first, and it was nice to see everyone. Just about everybody he walked past asked how he was doing. He answered with quick 'I don't knows' and 'okay for now' before finally making his way into Shelly's office. As usual, Shelly's desk was occupied with piles of paperwork.

Shelly looked up with surprise. "Tim, oh my gosh; how are you? I sent you several emails asking how you were but didn't hear back from you. Is your Blackberry working?"

Tim laughed. "It is. I just really don't know that much yet. I'm going to Emory today to talk to a specialist. How are things here?"

"God, don't ask! The other attorneys are trying to pick up your slack along with their regular case loads and it's a mess. I'm signing your signature about ten times a day. Don't tell anyone. Some of the stuff I just don't have time to explain so I just sign your name and put it in the proper out box."

"Aren't you the daredevil. You get caught doing that and you may need a lawyer yourself, you know."

"Maybe I shouldn't have told you."

"Ah, don't worry about it. I won't tell, and I will swear I signed it if anybody asks me. Besides, if you need an attorney, I'm not doing too much, anyway."

"How are things going? I'm sorry about the last time you were here. What you tell Sue is none of my business. I'm sorry."

"Shelly, forget it! Besides, you were absolutely right. I have some work to do at home and I am trying."

"So, what are the doctors saying? Everyone keeps asking me what's going on and when you're coming back."

"Well, apparently I have a brain tumor the size of a golf ball that will be coming out soon. Preliminary tests indicate cancer, but, of course, I won't know for sure until they take the tumor out. After that, I hope to be on some of the leading edge treatments at Emory. That's what I am doing today. Meeting with them to talk about treatments for cancer and what they can do. I want the best there is, and Emory is it."

Shelly was beginning to cry. "Tim, I am so sorry. Have you told the partners what's going on at all?"

"No, not yet. I am meeting the neurosurgeon this week; after I do that I'll set up a meeting to talk about the whole thing and how it will affect me work-wise. I'm going to beat this thing, Shelly, don't you worry. You're not getting rid of me that easy."

"You're too mean to die, Tim! I'm sure you will beat this, I know you will."

Tim smiled and walked into his office.

"Hey, want to sign some papers for me? I have several motions here and a couple of draft orders I need to get out today."

Tim smiled again feeling right at home. "I have a few minutes. Come on, let's have them."

"Thanks, Tim. I don't want to go to jail for impersonating an attorney."

"You won't. I told you I would swear I signed whatever, as long as it's not my will or something."

Shelly laughed and Tim signed the stack. Looking at his watch, he signed the last form. It was almost ten.

"Oh, wow, Shelly, I have to go. I am meeting this doctor at 11. Listen, set up a meeting with the partners for late next week. I will know what the plan is by then as far as surgery, schedules and all. In the meantime, I'll come by every few days to help with signatures and things you need from me. Hopefully this will just be a temporary problem and soon we'll be back to normal around here."

"Well, I'm not admitting to missing you. I just don't want to end up down the hall! So go get well, okay?"

Tim blew Shelly a kiss as he went out the door. "I'll email you when I know something."

On the way to Emory, he thought about the office and how good it made him feel to be there. He realized being in the office for only those few minutes made him feel alive. Tim really loved being an attorney. The fight for someone's freedom in the courtroom was like nothing else. Literally, lives were sometimes at stake. He loved the fight and he was good at it, but this time he would be fighting for his own life.

As Tim walked up to the doors of Emory, he could feel his nerves. He was nervous about Dr. Hampton. Tim was afraid that something would prevent him from being a candidate for whatever program the doc had mentioned on the phone. He began to prepare himself, just as he did for court, to argue his own case. He had kids and a thriving career, and a wife he needed to do a lot of work with to make things right. The doc didn't need to know that, though. He was young and in shape. He was the best candidate, no matter what!

Tim opened the door and went in, his mind reverted to begging as the best plan. He would beg Dr. Hampton to take him, and even bribe him, if needed. After all, he wanted the best and he felt strongly that this guy was probably it.

The receptionist informed him that Dr. Hampton was finishing a meeting with the dean and would be out shortly. Looking at the small coffee table, he noticed it was filled with medical journals and cancer magazines. Tim didn't even know that such magazines existed. What could they possibly talk about in there? Cures? Tim reached for one of the magazines as Dr. Hampton came out.

"Mr. Billings?" Dr. Reid Hampton crossed the room with his hand out.

Clearing his throat, he replied, "Please, call me Tim."

"No problem, Tim. Everyone around here calls me 'Reid,' but you call me whatever you want; doesn't matter to me. Did you find the place okay? Where is your wife?"

Tim looked down at the floor. "She couldn't come today. Work. Is that a problem?"

"No, not for today. Tell her I am sorry she couldn't make it. This is exciting stuff we are embarking on. Are you ready?"

Tim stared at the doctor for a minute, and Reid stopped, feeling that there was a problem. "Tim, are you okay?"

"I just thought you would be older. How old are you?"

Reid began to laugh. "I'm 28, Tim! Is that a problem for you?"

"You're out of med school, right? You're not a student at Emory now, are you? You look like you're about 20."

"I know, I get that a lot. I am out of school. I graduated from Emory med school when I was 23. I skipped a few years of high school and one year of college. You're in good hands, I promise. I did my residency at Johns Hopkins."

Tim nodded affirmatively.

"After residency, I applied here at Emory to be on the research team. My dad died of cancer eight years ago, and, well, I vowed to cure it, so here I am."

"Wow, so how is that working for you?"

"What's that, Tim?"

"Finding a cure; I sure could use one."

"I'm real close Tim, real close."

Reid continued to talk about some of the research and various testing procedures. Tim was lost with all the turns and various rooms they had gone through. Reid would casually introduce Tim to people as they walked through, although most of the people there never lifted their heads up from the microscopes they were staring into. A hand would go up, or a low "Hi" would slip out.

Reid turned to look at Tim as they turned onto another corridor, "Almost there, Tim. I am very excited about considering you for this program. You fit the profile well."

Tim smiled. "What program? Dr. Roberts said you were head of the brain research over here. I feel like I am going to some dark lab in the back of the building where I may never be seen or heard from again."

Reid laughed. "That's funny. You're a funny guy. Sorry, I usually park behind the building and come in the back. My lab and office are back here. I like it quiet. We are pretty serious in the brain tank!"

"I hope so."

The two men walked into a small room and Reid handed Tim a white suit with booties and gloves. "This is a sterile environment. Sorry, but no one goes in without suiting up. Our test subjects are in here and I thought you might like to see what we are doing."

Tim nodded and got dressed. As they walked into the room, Tim saw the place was full of cages. They ranged from small ones to larger ones on the ground. Reid began to explain some of the causes of cancer and what they have been able to figure out about the growth of cancer and how it spreads in the body. He showed Tim cage after cage of mice being treated with the latest and greatest chemotherapy and other treatments. As Reid got to each cage, he kept saying, "This subject has cancer and is being treated with . . ."

Tim listened and walked. "Doc, I don't hear you telling me about any cured subjects. I thought you said you were getting close."

Reid smiled at that question and pointed across the room. "Over here, Tim, let me introduce you to some cancer-free subjects."

Tim smiled. "Now that's what I wanted to hear."

Reid began with small mice. Each had been given cancer, then treatment, and now was cancer-free. Tim was impressed, but he was no mouse. Reid got to the end of the room where the big cages were, and in a row were four chimpanzees.

Reid stopped. "Okay, Tim, this is what you wanted. These four little guys are some of the first officially cured from cancer patients ever. Not in remission, cured."

Tim stared at the chimps playing and looking at him. "Doc, these are monkeys. How does this have anything to do with me?"

Reid smiled and put his hand on Tim's shoulder. "Well, Tim, a month ago all four of these guys had active, live brain cancer that was spreading to other parts of their bodies and today they are cured."

"So, what are you saying, Doc?"

"I'm saying if we can cure it monkeys, we can cure it in humans. They each had brain tumors just like you. Tim, the FDA has approved us to test this on humans. A very limited number of humans, but humans nonetheless. That's incredible news, don't you think?"

"No, I don't think. They're monkeys, for Christ's sake, Reid. How do you know what you have done to them will work on me? My life is at stake here. I only have one shot at beating this thing and you want me to be the first human to try something out that worked on a monkey. That scares the crap out of me."

"Well, you don't have to be. There are other candidates that I can get. You can go back to Dr. Roberts and start chemo."

Tim grabbed Reid's arm. "I didn't say that I didn't want to be here; I just don't know how you can be sure that what works for a monkey will work for me? Humans?"

Reid smiled and put up his hands. "Come on, Tim, let's go into my office and let me explain the process and how we test. I think it will help."

"Fine; lead the way."

Tim and Reid came out of the clean room and disrobed from the sterile gear. They crossed the corridor and went into a small, but well-kept, office. Reid took his place behind the desk and offered to get Tim something to drink. Tim ordered scotch on the rocks and Reid laughed out loud.

"Sorry, Tim, I don't have any of that here. Do you want a water or soda?"

Tim smiled. "I'm good. Doc, I don't know about this whole deal. I want the best but I am really not sure about being the next monkey."

"Even if it meant I could cure the cancer that is spreading through your body?"

"See, Doc, there you go. What do you mean cure me? Are you telling me that you have really found the cure for cancer? That would be huge and all over the news."

"It will be in time, and, yes, I'm telling you it appears we have found the cure. I need good candidates to try it on and the government approved it for human testing just two days ago. Your timing couldn't be better."

"The cure!"

"Yes Tim, we are cautiously optimistic we have found the cure for cancer. Would you like to be cured?"

Tim laid his head back on the chair staring up at the ceiling. "Yes."

"I'm sorry I didn't quite hear that, Tim; did you say yes?"

"Yes! How risky is it?"

"There are some risks that go along with this procedure. So far, we have had a 100% success rate in our subjects. That's key. We have tested it every way that you or I can imagine and we still are at a 100% positive response."

"Okay, what's the catch?"

"Well, like I said on the phone, you meet the criteria we are looking for: young, in good physical condition with no other health issues, brain-related cancer, and married."

"Why is my marital status one of the qualifications?"

"Your wife will be a big part of the recovery. I am a little surprised she didn't take off work to be here today with you. She must be very important, what does she do?"

Tim's stomach turned inside. "She's an attorney like me. It's hard for us to leave sometimes with court and things. Maybe I can get her here for the next visit."

Tim thought about the words he had just said. He wondered if Sue would ever come. His situation at home may be the very reason he would be turned down for this.

"Well, you need to get her down here so we can go over the deal and sign some paperwork. How soon can you get her in here?"

Tim hesitated. "Right away; I just have to get with her and see what her schedule is."

"Tim, I'm picking up some hesitation in your voice. Let me tell you a few things. Without your wife being involved, you are not a candidate. If we can't sign you up for this program, I will get someone else. There are only four slots open for human testing. We have one; Cal Tech, Berkley and Yale each have one as well. If I don't have a candidate on board within a week, I lose my slot. I was part of finding this cure; that's why I got a slot. I am not losing it! Can you be here tomorrow with your wife, or do I need to look somewhere else?"

"No, I will be here, no problem."

"Alright, man, let's celebrate. You are about to be one of the first humans to be cured of cancer completely. That's awesome."

"Yeah, Doc, that's awesome. What time tomorrow?"

"I am here at 6 a.m. Come as soon as you can. I have to go over the entire treatment program with both of you and then we sign the paperwork. The good news is Emory will be picking up the entire bill for you, too. Not only will we be removing the tumor and giving you the cure, but it will be paid for 100%!"

"Wow, really? That's amazing. Why?"

"The publicity for starters, we will be the first research department to cure a human from cancer. That's huge, Tim. Students will be signing up like crazy to get into Emory's cancer program. That's big money. I was meeting with the dean just before your appointment to tell him we had our man."

With that, Reid stood up and stuck out his hand. "Are you my man, Tim?"

Tim stood and shook Reid's hand firmly. "I'm your man, Doc. I will see you tomorrow."

Reid smiled. "Good, Tim! That's very good. Let me show you back out. I don't want you lost down here and end up in the psych ward locked up for the next three days."

"Really, you have that here?"

Reid laughed again. "No, I'm just kidding you, Tim. We don't study brain behavior down here; we cut them up and study the brain itself. Follow me."

Tim grimaced at the thought. "That's gross!"

Tim left Emory knowing now he needed to make it right with Sue for sure, no matter what. His life could depend on it. Sue had been so cold and hurt. How would he ever convince her to come and help him? Again, the only plan he could come up with was to beg and beg until she agreed. This disease had already reduced Tim from a strong, arrogant attorney who was not afraid of anything, to a begging-for-his-life-fool.

He had seen some of the care in her when he explained the shooting in the park. Maybe he could tap into what love there was left and convince her to help him, if only until the surgery was done. He could offer her more money in the divorce if she did. Sue had no idea what kind of money Tim really had, and he was way too good at hiding what he didn't want anyone to find.

Over the years, he had stashed away millions of dollars in offshore accounts. Donations he had received from some of his, shall we say, less than scrupulous clients. You help a drug lord get off from three counts of murder and they are grateful. He found out just how grateful when he found a suitcase in the back seat of his car the day after the trial with a note taped to it saying, Thanks for the not-guilty verdict, Rico. When he opened the case, he found bundled 100 dollar bills. Quickly he moved the money from here to accounts that were not traceable to anyone.

Tim would gladly make arrangements to pay Sue more than she would get in the divorce in return for her seeing him through this surgery and recovery time, but first he would just ask. As an attorney, he had learned never to give up too much too fast. Maybe there was enough love left in her to want to help him this one last time; if nothing else, for the sake of the kids.

Somehow, Tim would have to convince Sue to go through this with him, at least to the other side. He would be cured, and Sue could go on with her life. Tim knew inside he did still love her and he remembered what a great life they once had. If he had not forgotten that somewhere along the way, they may still have that life.

As he drove, he thought about what had happened that day. How he had hung out with his son, saw firsthand he was missed at the office, and had been told there was now a cure for cancer. All in all, this had been a great day.

As he pulled into the garage at home, he began mentally preparing for the conversations he had to have with Sue that night. He felt unprepared! As an attorney, you never went before a judge unprepared. She would be the toughest judge he had ever faced and there was more at stake with her verdict than any jail term for some stupid guilty client he had ever defended. His life was hanging in the balance, and she held the keys to his freedom.

Conversations

Chapter 7

Tim came in the house just after four, and Annette was sitting at the kitchen table doing homework. She looked up at Tim, startled, expecting her mom. Annette's warm smile turned cold as soon as they made eye contact. Tim's heart sank as he realized that his own daughter didn't love him at all.

Tim came into the kitchen and sat down at the table. Annette immediately got up, so Tim grabbed her hand. Annette glared at him, causing him to instantly let go.

"Annette, please sit down. I want to talk to you."

Annette kept getting her books together. "There's nothing to talk about, Dad. I need to do my homework."

Tim raised his voice just slightly. "I said, sit down!"

Annette flopped back into her seat. "What?"

"I don't know what I really did to you, but telling your brother, and I assume everyone else, I am dying is not nice. Why are you so mad at me? Christ, why is it that you hate me so much?"

Annette was shocked by Tim's directness. She stared at Tim, silent.

"Do you hate me?"

Annette looked away. "I don't even know you. You treat Mom like crap! You don't care about us. I wish you and Mom would just get divorced."

Tim felt the daggers sink deep into his chest and he struggled with what to say. How do you tell a twelve year old girl that you are a complete son of a bitch, and that she is right? That you have cared more about your career and your drinking buddies than you have for your children or your wife? Tim stared at the table trying to get the words out.

"See, you can't even say anything. Do you cheat on Mom?"

Tim looked up in surprise at the words coming from his twelve year old. "I . . . I really have screwed up."

Annette shook her head. "I hate you!"

"Annette, don't say that. You don't hate me. I'm your father."

Annette slammed her book shut on the table. "I wish you weren't."

Annette stood up and started walking to the steps. Tim was right behind her. As she made it to her room she began to slam the door, but Tim got his arm in the door before it closed. The door hit his arm with a thud and bounced back open. Tim pushed through and yelled, "Stop!"

Annette turned to face her dad, crossing her arms in a stance of defiance. "What? What do you want from me?"

"I do believe I am still your father and if I want to talk to you, I will, and you will listen."

Annette stood silent.

Tim was waiting for another response. "Okay, I know I have not been such a great dad, but you can't talk to me that way, and you can't tell your brother that I am dying."

"Well, you are! Everyone dies from cancer. That's what you have, right?"

89

"Maybe. But even if I do, I met a doctor today who says he has a cure, and they want me to be one of the first to receive the treatment. So, I am not dying."

"So, what about you and Mom, are you getting a divorce?"

Tim sat on Annette's bed and gazed down at the floor. "I hope not, but I have really screwed things up. I let my career and a lot of other things really get in the way of being who I should have been for your mom and you kids; maybe even too much to fix!"

"Why? How could you cheat on her?"

Tim looked back up at Annette. "I don't know. Somewhere along the way, I got lost. I became someone else and forgot everything that was important. I forgot you guys."

Annette began to cry, wanting to forgive Tim and love him, but the anger inside kept her from it. She stared down at her father, remembering all of the nights she watched her mom cry over him. All the school events only her mom attended. The birthday parties over the last several years that Tim had been on his cell phone for most of the night, not even watching her open her gifts. She didn't care about the money he made. She just wanted a dad who loved her and wanted to be around her.

"Mom says you will never change. She said people don't change."

Annette's door pushed open and they both turned to see Sue standing in the doorway.

"What's going on?"

Annette walked past her mom. "Nothing but lies."

Tim stood. "Annette! Thanks, Sue. Apparently you have been telling her what a son of a bitch I am and she believes every word of it!"

Sue smiled as she raised her eyebrows. "Truth hurts, doesn't it, Tim?"

She turned and walked down the hall to her bedroom. Tim went downstairs to fix a drink. He sat in his study for a moment, trying to regroup before he went to talk to Sue. He needed to win her over for the Emory deal. He needed her to go through this with him and then he would give her what she wanted. Tim paused at that thought. Was it what she wanted, or was it what he wanted? A few weeks ago, it was what he wanted, but now the lines were blurred. He had done some soul—searching these last few weeks and realized *he* needed to change some things, not Sue.

The words George had spoken at Scully's the other night kept ringing in his head. He had cheated and lied to Sue so much he doubted she would ever want to fix things. Tim sighed and finished his scotch. "Let's do this."

Tim got up and headed upstairs. He got to Sue's door to find it closed. He knocked, but got no answer. He stood in the hall waiting, like a kid in trouble, shifting back and forth one foot to the other. Finally, he said out loud, "This is ridiculous!"

He opened the door, but there was no Sue. He looked around the room and then even in the closet, she was not there. Then he heard the water running in the bathtub. She was taking a bath. He heard the water flowing and knew she was already in the tub. He wanted to talk now but didn't want to invade her privacy. He paced back and forth. The water shut off and Tim got quiet.

"Who's out there? Annette, is that you?"

"No, Sue, it's Tim." He paused.

"Can I come in?"

A quiet "I guess," came from the bathroom. Tim went in and Sue was up to her neck in suds, soaking in the tub.

"Can we talk for a little bit?"

"Tim, what's up with you; are you trying to make amends before you die?"

"What's with everyone thinking I'm dying? I'm not dying."

"So what is it, then? This morning you're taking Jonathan to school and tonight you're talking to Annette. Both are things you have not done in a very long time. This cancer thing must have you pretty scared. What do you want from me?"

"You sure aren't going to make this easy, are you?"

"Hell, no I'm not; what do you expect, Tim? You have treated me like dirt for years, me and the kids both. I expected any day for you to walk in and tell me you were moving to Colorado with whoever she is and leave us all behind."

He raised his eyes from the floor to Sue. "I didn't think you knew."

Sue laughed. "Tim, I'm not stupid. I do the laundry. If I think about it real hard, I could probably guess what kind of perfume she wears. Jesus, Tim, you're not even trying to hide it anymore. Not to mention the little phone call you had in the garage the last time you went out there. I heard you talking to her. So, besides talking about our divorce terms, what can I help you with?"

"Wow, this is going to be harder than I thought. Everybody hates me!"

"Oh, don't start the sympathy crap, Tim; you brought this on yourself. There was a time I would have done anything for you. I would have walked through fire if you needed me to. You threw all of that away for someone younger or prettier or whatever."

He sat speechless, staring at Sue as she spoke. He knew she was absolutely right, and he had made a huge mistake and lost a great woman.

"I'm sorry. I have made some really bad decisions."

"Yeah, Annette was right. There's nothing but lies here. Get out, Tim. I will draw up the papers next week. I want the house, my car, alimony and child support. You can afford it. I know there's money hidden, too. You're really not as smart as you think you are."

"Sue, wait. Calm down for a minute and let me talk to you about what's going on. I will agree to whatever you want in the divorce. I am totally in the wrong and I know it. You deserve all those things. I will pay it; I won't fight you, I promise."

Sue looked at Tim. "You must need something pretty bad, then. Spit it out, Tim!"

"The doctors have confirmed I have a brain tumor about the size of a golf ball at the base of my skull. The tests have already confirmed it's cancer."

Sue's anger in the moment left her with those words. "Tim, I'm so sorry to hear that. No matter what my feelings are for you at this point I certainly would never wish that on you. What are they going to do?"

"Well that's the good news. I went to Emory and met with a cancer research specialist today and he wants me to be part of some brand new procedure. He says, they have found a cure for brain cancer."

Sue squinted at Tim. "What? I haven't heard anything about that on the news. That's huge! It would be all over the place."

"No, not yet; this is brand new research. It's so new I will be one of the first of four humans to receive the treatment."

"Now that sounds scary. Are you sure you want to be part of that? It sounds kind of dangerous."

"They have cured mice and monkeys. I guess if the FDA has approved human testing, it must be safe. If it means I stay alive, what do I have to lose?"

"Okay, so what does this have to do with me? Are you afraid you might need someone to take care of you while you recover from the surgery? I might not be the best one for that right now. Why don't you get your

Colorado girl to come do it for you, or one of the others? I'm sure you can find someone to help you."

"Sue, there is no Colorado girl. There are no girls, period. I ended all of it. I promise."

"Whatever, Tim. Why should I believe a word you say? When did you end it, yesterday? I don't believe you and it doesn't matter. As soon as you're over this thing, you will be the same old Tim. It's who you are. People don't change."

"I have changed Sue, I swear, I understand where you're coming from. Here is what I'm asking. Emory will not let me be part of the research group if I don't have you come with me tomorrow. You have to be part of the deal or I can't be. This could be life or death for me, literally."

"What do you mean, be part of the deal? What part of the deal do I need to do?"

"If I don't have family support, I can't be considered as a candidate. Sue, I need you for this. If you will help me through this, I will give you whatever you want."

"Whatever I want? Are you offering me money, Tim?"

Tim was stumped. "I don't know what to do, Sue. I need you and I know you hate me. You have every right to, but I don't want to die, Sue."

Sue sat quiet for a minute. "Tim, I need to think about this. When do they want us there?"

"As soon as we can be. I know this is huge thing to ask right now, but once I am through this I will move out and agree to whatever you want. I won't fight you on anything. I'm begging you to help me."

"Get out, Tim; just let me think about this tonight. I'm starting to prune here. I need to get out of the bathtub. If I agree, and I'm not saying that I am, we are going to talk about that offshore account you have. Maybe we split that, too. Your kids should have the best! Now get out and let me have some peace and quiet."

Tim stood up and walked to the bathroom door. Turning to face Sue, "I really appreciate you thinking about it. It will mean everything to me, Sue. I am sorry for everything I have done to you and the kids. This morning with Jonathan was incredible. I don't want to miss them growing up. I know I need to change. I can do it, Sue, it's not just the cancer making me say that. I want to change."

Sue just stared at Tim. "Out!"

Tim left the room and went back downstairs. Jonathan was watching TV, and Tim came in and sat down beside him. Jonathan leaned against Tim, and he put his arm around his boy, squeezing him tight. Jonathan looked up and smiled at his dad. Tim's eyes began to swell with tears as he began to realize how much he had missed. He had a great family and he had thrown it away for nothing. If he got the chance, he would never make the same mistake again.

Sue came down after getting dressed and started dinner. Tim and Jonathan were still watching TV, and Annette stayed barricaded in her room. Sue watched the two boys in the living room, laughing at some sitcom and having a great time. Jonathan was so glad to have his dad back. He had not really felt the hurt like Annette. Besides Jonathan was so forgiving, he didn't care. Sue desperately wanted to be the family they once were. When Annette was little, Tim was a great dad. He was a junior partner at the firm then and although he often brought work home, he was home. As his career grew and the clients got bigger, so did his ego. The power and money consumed him and he was just gone.

Chicken and pasta tonight will have to do, she whispered to herself. As she put it on the plates, all she thought about was how desperate Tim was in the bathroom. He was willing to do anything! Sue wondered if she asked him to quit the firm and start over, would he? Be faithful and loving, would he? Be a good father and be in his kids' lives, would he? As much as she wanted the answer to be yes, she knew it would only be temporary at best. He had tasted life away from responsibility and marriage. He had money and power. There would be no coming back from that. There never is, but Sue was an optimist. She always would be. She knew she would help Tim. She loved him inside no matter what he had done. She took the vows she had made on their wedding day seriously and didn't want the divorce. She wanted to live happily ever after, but years of being a lawyer had shown time and again how happily ever after was only in the movies.

She called everyone to dinner. Tim and Jonathan came in smiling and talking about Will Smith as they took their seats. Annette didn't come down. Tim offered to go up, but Sue put up her hands, indicating no.

"I think she has had enough talking with you for one day. I will go see what's up."

Annette was doing homework with her iPod blaring in both ears. Sue walked in and pulled one ear bud from her ear. Annette turned it off and looked up at her Mom.

"What's up?"

"It's time for dinner."

"Is Dad down there eating?"

"Yes, he is. It will be fine. He won't say anything else. We talked."

"About what? Why is he trying to talk to me? He doesn't even know me. We have barely talked, like, this whole past year."

"Annette, your dad is sick and is facing life-changing times. He's scared and doesn't know how to handle it. He just wanted to be in your life today. He doesn't know how, but he's trying, and that's a step in the right direction."

"Oh my God, Mom, you're falling for his bull crap. He's never going to change. You said so yourself."

"Well, that may be true, but I don't want him to die; do you?"

Annette didn't speak.

"Annette Billings, you better get your head right. He is your father. I don't
care what kind of jerk he has been; he will always be your dad. He loves
you, Annette, and you love him. Yes, he has made some huge mistakes and
he knows it. They may even be mistakes I can't get over, but neither one of
us wants him to die. Come on Annette, think about what you are saying,
he's your dad. Do you really hate him so much that you want him to die?"

"I hate him! Okay, so I don't want him to die but I don't want to be
around him, either. I can't believe you, Mom. He cheated on you!"

She stopped talking and thought about the words she had just heard.
Annette is right. Tim is an ass. He had been with at least one other woman
for sure and Sue knew in her mind that there were more. How could she
ever love this man again?

Sue looked back at Annette. "Come on, it's dinner time. We are eating like
a family no matter how screwed up we really are."

Winking at Annette, she put her arms around her. "I will always be here
for you. We can be here for each other, okay. Come help me get through
dinner."

Annette smiled. "Okay. I will do anything for you, Mom, I love you."

"I love you, too, baby! Let's go be strong for your brother. He is just happy
to have his dad back, even if it is temporary. He doesn't understand what
you do. Be happy for him, okay?"

"Alright, I will. What's for dinner?"

"Chicken and pasta."

"In that white sauce stuff?"

Sue smiled. "That's what you like, right?"

"You know I do."

The two went down and sat at the table. Tim smiled at Annette and she offered a partial smile back. Tim looked at Sue with gratitude for the gesture. He knew it was Sue who had prompted that response. He still had a lot of work to do before Annette would feel anything again towards him.

They ate and cleaned their plates. Tim helped clean as much as he could. He had no idea what to do. He ate out so much, or in the past would eat and just leave his plate. Sue was kind of enjoying this new, humble Tim. Even if the marriage was over, she would milk this behavior as long as she could.

The kids had gone off to bed and Tim was desperate for Sue's answer. He kept looking at her while she was working at her laptop, waiting for her to break and give him the answer he was after. Sue loved the anticipation. Like waiting on a sequestered jury, he paced and made noise, trying to get Sue to break her concentration on the laptop. She laughed inside because she had finished with work thirty minutes prior and was just surfing the internet now. She checked Facebook and read posts, all the while watching Tim glancing back from the living room and getting up constantly to get ice or more soda. Sue was very amused.

Finally, after she felt she'd inflicted enough torture, she called Tim. "Let's talk."

Tim was in the kitchen in a second. "Okay, what do you think? Will you come with me tomorrow?"

"Let's talk about my conditions to this partnership."

Tim looked surprised. "Okay, what are the conditions?"

"You have to quit the firm!"

"What? Why do you want me to do that? I make a ton of money there. I can drop Colorado and take on a smaller caseload so that I am home more, but quit? Seriously?"

"I'm not finished. I want you involved in the kids' day-to-day life. I'm not the only parent here. I want you at school events, some parent teacher conferences and helping with homework on occasion, no matter where you live."

"Okay!"

"That's not all. I want half the money from the offshore account. You take care of it however you have to. I want that put away for my retirement."

"Is that all?"

"Wow, maybe I didn't aim high enough. Are you that desperate, Tim?"

"I am, Sue. I have made a mess of my life and I think God decided to get my attention."

Sue looked into Tim's eyes. "Tim, I don't think God even knows who you are anymore! But I do, and I won't be fooled again."

Tim smiled at Sue respectfully. "I won't fool you or make a fool of you, Sue. I promise."

"We'll see what the doctor says tomorrow. We may need to renegotiate."

Tim started smiling. "Does this mean you don't want the divorce?"

"Let's not get ahead of ourselves. I may agree to help you through the cancer, but that's all I can do for now. Tim, you have hurt me more than anyone on this planet. You cheated on me and left me behind like I didn't matter, like we didn't matter. I don't know if I can ever trust you again, or even if I would want to. Who knows what all you have done. I can't imagine the kind of person you really are; I have no idea."

Tim hung his head in shame. "I'm the same guy Sue, I just got lost. The job, the power and the money just consumed me. I've never done anything illegal. The money in the account was a gift from a client I got off of a murder conviction. You would be surprised at how some people say thank you."

"Yeah, I'm sure; with money and women, right? I really don't want to know."

"It wasn't like that. He set the account up and just sent me a note with directions on how to access it and a 'thanks' at the bottom of the page. The firm didn't know anything about it, either."

Tim looked puzzled at Sue. "How do you even know about that, exactly? I never had anything that even mentioned that account here."

"You're wrong. The kids were loud one day in the living room and I was trying to work, so I went into your office for some quiet. There, on your desk, was the account number and the website. I logged on and it only took me 3 tries to guess your password. You really should change that. It's been the same for ten years now."

"Wow, that was on my desk for one day and you just happened to go into my office on that day. What are the chances of that?"

"Tim, when you're living a life of lies, God doesn't look after you. He lets the bad things happen. God wanted me to know about the money for today. That's what happens when you lie and cheat. You get caught. Look at all it has cost you."

"I wouldn't have kept it from you forever. It was just out there for our future."

"Whatever, Tim, you're such a liar. Is that the only account you have like that, or are there others?"

"No, that's it, I swear. There's no more."

Sue looked at Tim with disgust. "You wouldn't tell me if there was; would you? I don't think you know how to tell the truth. You have been lying to clients and juries so long it's just who you are, a liar!"

"Sue, I know I have done some terrible things. I'm sorry. If you just give me a chance, I will change. I can be the man I used to be. Please give me a chance."

"I don't know if I can. You won't even come clean with me on everything you've done."

"I will. I have."

"How many women have there been?"

Tim stood in silence.

"Too many to count, or you just can't bear to tell me? Tim, which is it? You see what I mean; how can I ever trust you?"

"There have been four. They meant nothing to me, Sue, I swear."

Sue put her hands over her face. "Jesus, Tim. How long has this been going on?"

"Two years."

"At the office? In Colorado? Where at, Tim? Right here under my nose? Please tell me you never brought anybody here!"

"No, never; not at the office either. It was just stupid. I was stupid. I hated my life at home. I wanted to be rich and powerful and I never was that here. To these women, I was adored. They hung on my every word. You quit doing that years ago. I just quit wanting to come home."

Sue had begun to cry. "How could you do this to me? The mother of your children. I was a good wife to you."

She walked out of the kitchen and he felt his heart sink into his chest. He had hurt the only woman he really ever loved. Tim slid down the cabinet to the floor, burying his face into his hands, trying to get control of his emotions and the tears now rolling down his face. He knew he had really screwed up; he had lost the best thing that had ever happened to him, and over what? A woman that didn't even matter to him, someone he didn't care if he ever saw again. What an idiot he was.

He got to his feet and started upstairs. He couldn't let this conversation end like this. He needed to win her back. Sue was a good woman. She deserved better than he had given her. He needed her to know that. He needed her to know if she gave him a chance, he would show her how good he could be to her.

Once he got to Sue's door, he threw it open. She was standing at the dresser, holding a picture of the family taken a few years ago at Easter in the park. It had been one of her favorites and Tim had framed it for her as a present. Sue turned and stared at Tim long enough to take aim. The picture flew from Sue's hand straight at Tim. Tim swayed slightly and the picture struck the door behind him. Shattering glass and wood hit Tim in the back as the picture exploded on impact. Tim's hands were covering his head.

Slowly he dropped his arms and looked at Sue who was now standing in front of him. She slapped him across the face so hard he staggered back and hit the door just as the picture had. Tim quickly put his hands over his face again, but this time to keep from getting hit again. Sue stood over him, seething with anger.

"Get out of my room!" Her voice was strong and full of power and anger.

He rolled through the doorway and stumbled into the hallway. He was so dizzy from the slap he wondered if she slapped him or punched him. The door slammed so hard behind him that the pictures down the hall shook. He heard the lock being turned. Sue had had enough.

He made his way to his room, not believing what had just happened. His head was pounding. Now he was afraid Sue wouldn't go. Tim lay on the bed for hours, wondering if he had blown his chance at being cured. If she backed out, Dr. Hampton would find someone else. He thought about being honest with Sue, but in the moment, he couldn't do it. The truth might be too much and he didn't want to lose her completely at this point. The count on women was more like eight over the past three years, and the money was upwards of three million spread out over six accounts. He was glad she only knew about the one. That had been the first account and he was much sloppier about keeping secrets back then. He was so much better now. He sighed, thinking that was not something he wanted to be good at anymore.

Finally closing his eyes with the help of a handful of Tylenol, he fell asleep.

Sue fell to the bed crying after locking the door on Tim. How could she have let her life get to this point? She thought. How could she have been so blind? She hated Tim for who he had become and for cheating on her. What had she ever done to deserve it?

After an hour of crying and feeling sorry for herself, she got up and began to clean up the glass and wood. She picked the photo from the debris and looked again at the faces, now cut and ripped from being thrown against the door. She laughed at the comparison. The picture was broken, just like the family it showed. Everyone was smiling, looking like they were one happy family. Sue thought how at the surface things can appear to be just fine, but underneath there were secrets and there had been for a long time. She tore the picture in half and threw it in the trash along with the glass. That part of her life was over now. She would be single and never trust a man again like she had Tim.

She got into bed, still angry and swearing she would not help the man at all. Why should she? He had lied, cheated and kept money from her. There was no telling what all he had really done. How many times when he was supposedly in Colorado was he really somewhere else with some slut! The nerve, she thought. How could she have been so stupid?

She would make him pay the house off completely and still split the money in Zurich. She deserved at least that. Then maybe she would sell this place and move somewhere else. It's not like Tim really cared about seeing the kids. She was originally from North Carolina, and thought maybe she would go back to the Outer Banks and buy a place there. She would be restarting her life as well. She would have to do less pro bono work now, and take on a paying position at a firm somewhere.

She knew the interest in the kids was temporary. He was never really involved with the kids, ever. She felt like she had spent 15 years of her life for nothing. It had all been a lie.

She had always seen Tim as so strong and powerful. Even in school, he would dominate the room when they would practice arguing a case, but tonight he was so weak. He was like she had never seen him before. He cowered when she hit him. A reaction she never thought she would get from him. She thought how scared he must really be. How afraid for his own life he must be. Sue hated that she cared for him at all. He had treated her so badly she should just hate him and be done, but she couldn't. No matter what had happened or would happen, she would always love him. She always had from the moment they met. Something about him had grabbed her heart and would never let go.

Sue sighed, knowing she would go tomorrow and help the man. She hated him for what he had done, but didn't want him to die. She would go tomorrow and get through the surgery or treatment or whatever it was. She owed Tim that, for the good years. After he was well and back to his rotten self she would get the divorce and go on with life. She would discover herself for the first time and figure out what she liked to do for a change. She would have the money to do it the way she wanted, thanks to Tim's stupidity. But inside she felt an emptiness she had not felt before. All she really wanted was Tim back the way he was before. The Tim she had fallen in love with, and the man he was when the kids were young. She would forget it all if she could have that Tim back.

Finally, she fell asleep, exhausted from the day and the night's fight with Tim. Tomorrow would begin the rest of her life and Tim's too. She would agree to a financial arrangement with him and move on. There was no more love in the equation; it was business now. The deal was about her and the kids' future, not Tim's. Sue was standing up for herself this time.

Understanding the Cure

Chapter 8

S
ue woke up early to get the kids off to school. Tim was still upstairs. Maybe it was fear of what she would say, or just slow starting. She didn't really care. After last night, she had resolved to accept that divorce was her decision. She had lived in a dead marriage for the last several years; she could do it for six months more. At least now, she didn't have to pretend everything was okay.

As she finished up breakfast, Tim came downstairs. He looked a little confused. She noticed his out-of-sorts look. The anger she had last night was gone in an instant as worry flooded her mind. Suddenly, Sue felt bad that she had slapped him last night. What if she knocked something loose with the tumor? Tim came in and sat down at the table.

Sue reached out to touch Tim's hand, but stopped short. "Are you okay?"

Tim looked at Sue. "I don't feel so good this morning. My head is killing me!"

"Tim, I'm so sorry I hit you last night. I was so angry. I'm sorry."

He shook his head. "Sue, don't apologize. I am in the wrong here. I have been wrong for years. I'm sorry I have put you through it."

"I will help you through surgery and the treatment, but we are finished after that. I don't want you to think something has changed because I am willing to help you."

"I understand. I appreciate you being willing to help me. I really don't want to die. You may not believe me, but I want to be in my kids' lives. I want to be in your life, too, but I am afraid I blew that. I really am sorry."

"Let's just go, Tim, let's get to the doctor and get this thing going. You don't look so good this morning."

"I don't feel so good. I really think this thing is getting worse."

They left the house, with Sue driving. They arrived at Emory in about forty-five minutes. By then, Tim was better with the help of some drugs and Sue was beginning to not feel so bad.

Dr. Hampton greeted them in the waiting room and then guided them back through the maze of labs and halls. Once they arrived in his office, he made all the official introductions to his team for both Sue and Tim. Sue sat with arms crossed, throughout the introductions, still angry with Tim, but glad he was in the program.

Dr. Hampton kept prompting Sue because she was not engaging in the conversation. Sue would answer and then tune them back out, filling her mind with work and the kids to pass the time. Dr. Hampton really began to take note of her behavior. He stopped speaking and looked directly at Sue. "So, Sue, are you willing to help Tim through this?"

Sue looked at the doctor. "I'm here, aren't I? What kind of question is that?"

The doc smiled. "You are, but you're not. I'm curious as to why that is?"

Tim interrupted the question. "Doc, we have had a rough few days at home over all this tumor and cancer stuff. Give Sue a break, okay?"

The doc looked at Tim and smiled. "I need to know she is in this with you. Can I speak with Sue alone for a minute?"

Tim stood. "Why, Doc? Whatever needs to be said can be said here in front of both of us."

Dr. Hampton's team had already started clearing the office. Sue was looking very nervously at Tim.

Tim spoke again. "Doc, really I think . . . ."

Dr. Hampton turned and faced Tim. "I need to speak to Sue alone, Counselor. It will only take a little while. It will help me make my final decision about taking you into this program. Can you give us a minute? My colleagues will take good care of you. Sofia, can you give Mr. Billings a tour of the labs?"

Tim looked at Sue and then felt the tug of Sofia at his arm. He reluctantly began to move out of the room and Dr. Hampton closed the door behind him. Sue never looked up at Tim as he went out the door.

Dr. Hampton turned to Sue. "Sue, can I get you some coffee or soda, water?"

"No, Dr. Hampton, I'm fine."

He smiled and pulled a chair around the desk to sit across from Sue. "Sue, please call me 'Reid.' I don't want to be so formal. We are very casual in here with titles. We try and focus on the cure more than who's in charge."

"Okay, Reid, no problem. Why did you want to talk to me?"

"Well, Sue, most patients I deal with who bring in their spouse look more like a couple than you guys do. I have to be honest. Are you guys okay? Because you don't look it."

"We're fine, Reid, just a little fight last night, nothing to worry about."

Reid sat back in his chair putting his hands behind his head, "Really? I think there is more to it than that. You look like you could care less about Tim. Why don't you tell me the truth, because I will tell you the truth: if you guys are not okay, I can't take Tim as a candidate."

Sue looked scared. "Reid, we just had a fight and I am still a little bit mad at him. It's okay, I promise. I want Tim to have the best chance at beating this thing. He tells me you guys have found a cure; is that true?"

Reid smiled big. "Changing the subject won't work. I have never seen a wife sit as uninterested as you have today. Let me ask you a few questions. Tim seems like a pretty take-charge guy. What was the fight about?"

Sue sighed. "Really, Doctor, I don't see what this has to do with anything. I said we're fine."

Reid leaned towards Sue, "Sue, this cure we have found is a major cancer breakthrough. It will cure Tim's brain cancer for sure. We have had a 100% success rate in every animal we have tested; however, I cannot afford to take a chance. There are only four slots available from the FDA to test on humans. If you don't tell me the truth right now, Tim is out. I won't lose my slot over this."

Sue began to cry. "I said it was fine, Dr. Hampton, please don't take this away from Tim. I don't want him to die."

"Then tell me what you were fighting about."

"I don't want to, really. He and I worked it out and we're fine."

"Not good enough. I am sorry, Mrs. Billings, I cannot risk this knowing that you guys are not on good terms. It's way too important."

Reid stood up and began to walk to the door. "Wait," Sue cried out. "Wait, I will tell you."

Reid turned and sat back down. "Okay, let's talk then."

Sue told the Reid about the fight and all about Tim cheating on her and hiding money. She told him she had agreed to stick with him long enough to get through the procedure and well on the other side. Sue pleaded with him not to take the program away from Tim, and explained that though she felt they would end in divorce, she still loved him and wanted him to be okay. She wished she had the old Tim back.

Reid smiled at Sue as he crossed his arms over his chest. "You know, Sue; I haven't told Tim exactly how we cure the cancer yet. Do you know why that is?"

"I guessed you didn't want him telling anyone. I don't know why."

"As a scientist, I am always looking for experiments that give unusual results. We found the cure for cancer because we did experiments that produced unusual results. Sue, this little experiment will give you a unique set of results that just may change the rest of your life, not just Tim's."

"What are you talking about?"

"Well, you see we found with brain cancer, and maybe all different types of cancers, the cancer cells are produced in the neurons that store memory. We don't know why yet, but we found that they are the source. We did test after test and kept finding the cancer cells being generated in the memory cells. So to test for a cure, we eliminated the memory cell portion of the test subject's brain."

"Really! And it worked?"

"Yes, it did. It worked very well. Once we did that, not only did it stop the growth of new cells but the existing cells died like their mothership was eliminated."

"Wow, that's amazing. This will work on Tim?"

"You are not really following what I am saying, are you Sue? This procedure cures the cancer completely, but in all of our test subjects it wiped their memories clean."

"Will that happen to Tim?"

Reid smiled. "Yes, Sue, it will. When he goes to sleep prior to surgery, he may remember those women he cheated with, but when he wakes up, they will be gone forever."

Sue smiled, "Erased?"

"He will not remember anything about his life, *including you.* That is why you are important to him being a candidate. He has to have someone on the other side to teach him who he is again. It has to be someone he can trust, someone that loves him enough to do it and stick with him."

Sue sat staring at the floor for a minute thinking about what he had just said. "Wow, that changes everything."

Reid leaned in close. "That's why I am even more excited about you, Sue. See, I thought this would just be the first human truly cured of cancer, but Tim and you will be an experiment just the same."

"How is that?"

"Because, Sue, all you want is the old Tim back. I can give you a blank slate to work with. Tim will still have the same genetic makeup as he has now. He just won't have all the memories of what made him the man he is today. He won't know anything about his life at all—only what you tell him and teach him. You can make him into anybody you want."

Sue was beginning to get a grasp on the whole picture. "I can get rid of all the bad and bring back only the good!"

Reid smiled sitting back in his chair. "That's right. If you want him to be romantic, you show him how. If you want him to take out the trash, you tell him he always did it before. You have control over everything he will become. Didn't you tell me you wanted your old husband back, the guy you fell in love with before the world corrupted him? Before money became his only love?"

Sue sat back on the couch in the office and began to think of all the possibilities.

Reid leaned towards Sue. "There is a downside, Sue."

Sue's attention left the ceiling and returned to focusing back on Reid's face. "Great! What? Will he regain his memory at some point?"

Reid laughed. "No, he won't. However, he also won't remember anything about his career. You will have to support him for a very long time, more than just six months. That's why it's critical that the family unit be in place for the person to qualify as a candidate. Tim will have no career after this. He won't even remember law school. He won't remember you, his kids or anything. He will be like a newborn baby. Can you handle that, Sue? Because it will be exhausting at times."

Sue was quiet for a moment. "I can, if in the end I will have my husband back. I miss the old Tim, Doc. He was my best friend. He was someone I would do anything for."

"Well, Sue, you will have your chance. Now, he will be in rehab for about eight to ten weeks after surgery. We will teach him how to walk again and speak. So far, we have found most of the motor skills are still there. Obviously, with this being the first human test, we will want to watch him closely, documenting everything, tracking exactly what he does know and what he doesn't. This would give you time to erase his life at home. Make it so he can't get back to his old life at all. This includes any friends, work, anything that would bring back those bad habits."

"Can I do that? I would think people would think I killed him if he just disappeared."

"You can do it and I will tell Tim he will have to sever all relationships due to the extent of his memory loss. Once he goes into surgery, he won't remember anything, anyway. You could move to another state and he will not know the difference. Sue, it will be a year before he even wants to leave the house, much less without you."

Sue smiled as the light bulb went off in her head. "If I move us to a new town, throw away everything that was his aside from his clothes, he will be helpless to reattach to his old life. I could have my old Tim back."

"Yes, that's what I have been saying for the past ten minutes. Tim will only know what you teach and tell him. If you tell him he has a great relationship with his kids, he will assume that it's the truth and act that way. Believing it is half the battle. He will be in a position to believe whatever you tell him."

Sue was now excited and fully committed. "How long before we get started? I want to do this now. I don't want him to make any arrangements with his friends or girlfriends to find him."

Reid sat back with that. "Girlfriends? Is he that bad that you know about them, Sue?"

"Not really, but he admitted to four over the past few years. It may be more; but I am more worried about some of his clients. He knows some powerful people. The sooner the better, I think."

"Well, we can move quickly, but best case scenario is a week. We have to get him in to do biopsies and test him for transplants of brain matter. You see, we remove the memory area of the brain, but if we don't put new back, he won't regain memory for a long time. In fact, we can almost guarantee some deficiencies, no matter what."

"Like what? Are we talking retarded here or something less? Is he not going to have the ability to remember after this? Is that a possibility?"

Reid was laughing. "It is a possibility; however, it's not likely. We have had great success with transplants so far and we don't think there will be any problem. The body will grow back neurons on its own, over time. We just transplant a section called the hippocampus. It's the part of your brain that is responsible for long-term memory. He will be fine, it just takes time."

"Are you sure? It sounds kind of risky."

"You are surrounded with some of the world's best doctors, Sue. We are doing things inside these walls that will revolutionize medicine one of these days. We will fix him up just like brand new. The real fun will be watching you make him into the loveable guy he used to be. I want to see that, just as much as I want to cure him from cancer now."

"I want to get him in here and away from his life as fast as we can. He will arrange for someone to tell him everything if I don't act fast. Tell me what comes next."

"Well, next week we do the biopsies and then we will go in and take the brain tumor out. He will recover from that in few days and after that, we will go in and treat him for the cancer. Once the tumor is removed and the treatment has been completed, he will go to our live-in rehab center where they will make sure he heals well. They will immediately start working with him on bathroom skills, eating and talking—everything he needs to be ready to leave the hospital. I will have to give him at least a few days to prepare or he will think something is wrong."

"Okay. What if you tell him his condition is getting worse? He did wake up dizzy this morning."

"Dizzy?"

"Nothing major, I slapped him last night really hard and I think that got things agitated with the tumor. I'm sorry; I hope that hasn't messed things up."

"I need to examine him right away. If the tumor has moved, or is growing, that will affect how quickly we may need to deal with that part. It won't change him as a candidate. More severe is even better for this particular research. Let's get him back in here and tell him the good news. How do you think he will react?"

"I don't know, Reid. He loves his life and money a lot, but I think staying alive will help sway him. He's scared. I know him enough to tell you he is scared to death of this thing."

Reid opened the door and Tim and Sofia were standing in the outer office. Tim looked at Sue immediately and was taken aback by her unusual smile. Reid motioned them both into the office and closed the door.

The next hour was spent explaining to Tim all that was about to happen to him. Sue sat quietly and watched Tim's face as the Reid delivered the crucial information. His face went from excitement to utter fear in just the speaking of a few sentences. Tim stopped Reid several times having him go back over the total loss of memory parts again and again.

He understood fully the fact that he would lose everything in order to stay alive. Turning to Sue, he now had an understanding of her smile when they came back in. Sue would be in control.

"You like this little arrangement, don't you? Did you tell the doctor about me?"

Sue's smile faded. "Yes, I did, but only to save you as a candidate, Tim. He would have passed you over if I didn't. He knew we were not right."

Tim looked at Reid. "Is that true?"

Reid smiled at Tim. "Tim, it's true, and let me tell you something else that's true. You have a woman that loves you. She is willing to stand by you and help you learn life over. If she forgets to tell you some parts of your life, I think it will be better for the both of you."

Tim sat quiet for a long minute, embarrassed that Reid knew the truth. "So do I!" Tim said, finally. He leaned over, and without asking, kissed Sue for the first time in months. She was shocked by the gesture and found herself kissing him back. She missed his kisses more than she realized. Their passion was on fire years ago and she found herself hoping it would return, along with the old Tim.

Reid laughed at the kiss. "Well, that's a good sign!"

Tim turned and smiled. "I'm ready, Doc, as soon as we can get this going. I have a wife and kids to get to know. I have been away for far too long as it is. What's next?"

Reid nodded and looked at Sue. "I think this is going to work out just fine. We may just cure more than cancer here today folks. We may fix a few broken hearts as well!"

They went over a few of the immediate details and Tim was set to come back in two days to start the blood work. Sue was ready to change her life for the future and get her husband back, even if it would be a tough year ahead. Dr. Hampton had his candidate and would be the first to perform the surgery that would cure cancer. It was a good day for everyone, a day that would begin a new life for everyone in the room. Sue and Tim both signed the consent forms and they were officially underway.

On the ride home, it was quiet in the car. The talk was small and Tim was thinking about all he would lose with this surgery. In the same light, he thought about all he would gain. He was torn between the happiness and sadness of all that was in front of him. Sue was looking forward to the new start.

Tim looked at Sue. "I guess you're happy about this, aren't you?"

Sue grinned. "Well, I get rid of all the bad in you and replace it with good. I guess we will see how much of the bad in you is genetic."

"I told you I wanted to change."

"Well, good, but now it's not up to you. When you wake up, you won't remember anything about who you were. We just might have a chance at a life after that."

Tim laughed. "The partners at the firm are going to be pissed."

Sue smiled again. "Don't worry. They'll have some new hotshot in your place so fast they'll never miss a beat. They probably already do."

Tim laughed again because he knew she was right. It was a big firm and there were a lot of young, new, very promising lawyers just waiting for a chance. He could easily see one of them being promoted to start taking over his caseload. The firm was seventy-five years old, they knew how to survive and keep going.

Tim thought about the money he had put away. He would find a way to remember later where it was in case things with Sue did fall apart. He would need it to live on if that happened. If it did work out, then he would have it for them. It was good either way. The rest he didn't really care about. The firm had been good to him and he had made lots of money, but he wouldn't miss it. It was stressful being a lawyer. Maybe in his new life he would just work at Home Depot, stocking shelves and pointing out where the plumbing department was to shoppers.

Tim looked at Sue again. "Maybe this is God's way of keeping us together."

Sue was shocked. "When did you start caring about what God wants?"

"When He gave me a brain tumor to get my attention!"

Sue laughed out loud. "I told you, you were hardheaded. So how long has this relationship with God been going on?"

"Just a few days, it's not a big deal. I just started praying again. He answered me in a very strange way though."

"How so?"

"Well, I prayed for help and for this thing to be okay; for us to be okay. His answer was to erase my whole life. A do-over, I guess. I bet I am careful about what I pray for from now on."

"I guess you will be!"

"Sue, I know this will be hard for you. The end results may be great for us and I hope it will, but no matter what happens, I want you to know I really appreciate everything you are doing. It means the world to me. I really am sorry for all that I have done."

Sue thought before she answered. "Tim, I want the old you back more than anything, but this is still a financial arrangement between us. If it works out differently, that's great. I hope it does, but I'm not going through all of this to have you walk away as soon as you are better. In fact, the money in the Zurich account needs to be transferred into my bank account before the surgery. All of it!"

"All of it! Kind of tough, aren't you?"

Sue started to reply and Tim laughed. "I'm kidding! We will need it to live on over the next few years. It's no problem. I will go into the office tomorrow and make the arrangements. The money will be in your account by tomorrow afternoon."

Tim paused. "I hope this will be more than a financial arrangement by the time I am better. I want to be your husband, Sue. I want to be a father to my kids. I hope this will give me the chance to do that right."

Sue nodded. "Me, too; you sure made a mess of it the first time around! Not many men get a second chance, Tim. Don't blow it over some whore this time."

Tim cringed at the words. "I am so sorry that I hurt you Sue."

When they got home, they both began to make arrangements. Sue would need to work, so she began working on her resume and Tim began to list things he needed to wrap up in his life. He wrote a letter to Tracy in Colorado saying a final goodbye; he really had not brought closure to that. Next, his resignation from the firm. Everything that he was in life would end in a few days. Trying to prepare for that was almost impossible.

Getting Ready

Chapter 9

The next morning Tim called the apartment complex in Colorado where he was leasing a fully-furnished apartment. He terminated the lease and instructed them on what to do with the clothes and belongings he had left there. It was mostly small things, so he sent the superintendant a check and told him to give it to Goodwill or throw it all away. The man agreed and it was done.

Sue was off to her office early to begin preparing them for her leaving. She would start looking for a new job soon after Tim entered rehab. Tim felt bad that she would be supporting them for years while he learned a new life and career. She had turned out to be much tougher than he ever thought she was. She was standing tall while Tim was falling apart.

At about ten, he left for the office. He had called Shelly and told her to schedule an emergency meeting with the partners. She immediately started asking questions. Tim told her to just wait and let him come in; he would explain it all. Shelly hung up mad. She was not the kind of person that liked waiting. Tim smiled thinking how much he would miss working with her. She had been a lot of fun and was good at the job. Nasal Bob would like having her.

He began to really think about the part of his life that Sue, Shelly and the firm knew nothing about on the way in. Tim had almost three million dollars in other accounts out there and a lot of powerful friends. How he should handle that and he thought about Tracy and Jenny here in Atlanta. Should he speak to them at all or just disappear. He wanted to make sure things were final so no one would come looking for him later. There were a ton of loose ends for Tim to wrap up in a very short time period.

When he arrived at the office, everyone began greeting him as if he were dying. People came out, gave him hugs, and spoke as if they would never see him again. Tim had to laugh at how fast news traveled around the office. He finally got to his office and Shelly met him at the door.

"Okay, so what's up? Are you dying on me or what?"

"Damn, Shelly! It's good to see you, too."

"Cut the crap, Tim. What did the doctors say? Are you leaving for good? Is that what the meeting with the partners is about?"

Tim sat at his desk. "Ah, this feels good. When is the meeting with the partners?"

Shelly sat down in the chair across from his desk. "Are you going to tell me the deal or am I going to have to hurt you?"

Tim laughed. "Okay, okay! Gosh, you're pushy. First of all, I told Sue everything. We may be getting a divorce when all this is said and done, thanks to you."

"Not thanks to me, you're the one that wasn't acting right."

"You're right about that, but this cancer thing will cure all of that."

Shelly looked sad. "It's cancer for sure?"

Tim nodded. "Brain cancer no less; I don't do anything halfway. Let me tell you the good news."

"Okay, good news is good!"

"It's very good! The research department at Emory has found a cure for my type of cancer."

"You mean a treatment."

"No, I'm talking 100% cure."

"What? Tim, that's fantastic. Why haven't I heard anything about it? There hasn't been anything on the news at all."

"There won't be for awhile. I'm the first human to receive the treatment. How cool is that?"

Shelly looked a little shocked. "That seems a little bit scary; is it safe?"

"It's been approved by the FDA. I'll be fine. There is a catch though and it's a big one."

"What?"

"I won't remember anything after the surgery."

"For how long?"

Tim laughed. "Forever, my entire memory will be gone. Sue, the kids, here, my career, all of it, my memory will be blank."

Shelly looked confused. "I don't understand, Tim; how can that be?"

"They have found that cancer cells are generated in the part of your brain that stores memory. To cure it they will remove mine and transplant new in its place. It's a 100% effective cure, but the subject is left with no previous memory at all. Sue will teach me everything about who I am after that."

Shelly began to laugh. "You are screwed, my friend."

"What are you talking about?"

"Sue will make you into a completely different man. You know that, right? Good for her. You're a jerk, Tim; you need this. She will make you into a good guy. Good for you. I will miss working here, but I am glad for you."

"What do you mean you will miss working here? Where are you going?"

"I'm quitting! I have been looking for a new job for a month. I had enough months ago. When all this came up, I postponed it, waiting on you to come back or whatever. I'm done."

"Well, isn't that funny. Good for you. I hope you are happy wherever you go. I will be glad to write you a very strong recommendation letter. I would say I will give you a good reference, but I won't remember you in another week."

"That's okay. I won't remember you in another week, either!" Shelly laughed again.

"Whatever. You will miss me and you know it. We are the best team in this place. If this hadn't happened, I would have never let you leave."

"I wouldn't have given you a choice. Tim, I'm sorry you have cancer, though. I hope this all turns out okay. It sounds pretty radical. Tell Sue to keep me informed. I would like to know you're okay. I'm sure I will be here for another few weeks training the new person."

"Shelly, I think Sue will erase me from the face of the earth once I go under the knife. I don't think anyone but Uncle Sam will know where I am. I sure won't."

"That's a good thing Tim. Maybe there's hope for you yet."

Shelly got up and headed back to her office. "I have a huge stack of things for you to sign before you go talk to the partners. You need to brief me on any odd clients, too. I need to let the new attorney know what he is in for."

Tim looked up puzzled. "When am I meeting with the partners?"

"At two and don't be late."

Tim sat at his computer and went to his personal folder, typed in his password and the pages began to open. He had listed all of his accounts on one page. Women and contacts on another and information about business deals that he wanted kept secret. Some of Tim's clients had let him in on things to buy and that had made him a ton of money over the years.

After Tim printed all of the necessary information, he decided to write himself a letter telling all about who he was. He trusted Sue to make him into a good man on the other side; however, he may want to know some things about himself that Sue may not. If things didn't work with his marriage he wanted to make sure he was well taken care of, too. He worked until lunch time on the information and then told Shelly he was going to take care of a few things during lunch.

Shelly eyed the package tucked under Tim's arm as he left and skeptically said, "See you later" as he left. Tim crossed the street in front of the law firm's building and went into the bank. Inside, he paid cash for a safety deposit box for two years. He placed the package inside and sealed the envelope.

Tim stepped out onto the broken gray sidewalk in front of the bank. He looked up at the overcast sky and shivered from the cold as he began to walk. His head was hurting, as usual, and he tried to focus on other things rather than the pain. Stopping at the sandwich shop next to the bank, he grabbed a sub. He sat and ate at the window counter looking across at the park to the right of his building.

He wondered where the gunman was that had almost ended his life. Tim wondered whose fate was worse, his or that guy's. He would lose everything to gain his life, while that guy had nothing and had no life. As he ate, he pondered that it was better to have had a life and lost it than to never have lived. Tim thought of the old saying, "Better to have loved and lost then never to have loved at all." He thought about Sue and wondered if they would survive. He had loved Sue and still did, somewhere inside. She had been a good wife and didn't deserve what he had done to her.

He had enjoyed the life he had. He was wealthy and had powerful friends. He had known success and was good at the job. He had become one of the best lawyers in this town. Now he would become the best father he could. He would be the husband that he wasn't before. He would be faithful and true to Sue for sticking with him. He could do this, but the evil in Tim was still alive. The side of Tim that wins cases and gets ahead in life would plan for the future, no matter what happened.

He had the safety deposit box key in his pocket. His fingers rocked the key back and forth as he walked back to the office. Shelly was waiting for him again with paperwork to sign. Tim held up a finger for her to wait, while he took two more Tylenol for the pain, then he motioned for her to come in, and the signing began.

As they were working, Tim asked Shelly if she had the number of the private eye they had used here in Atlanta to track down people when they were hard to find. Shelly got the "what are you up to" look on her face.

She leaned back from Tim's desk. "What for, Tim?"

"Just because, Shelly; don't ask me questions you know I won't answer."

"Tim, you say you've changed, but you haven't. You're the same old Tim. I feel sorry for Sue."

"It's not like that, Shelly. How about feeling sorry for me! I am losing everything. I just want the guy to find me in a year or so and deliver a package I made, telling me all about myself. Just so I know. That's all, nothing bad."

"Really? Then call Sue now and tell her what you're doing. If it's nothing, it won't matter, will it? Better yet, just give Sue the package you left here with."

"I don't think so. Mind your business, Shelly, and be a good assistant, if only for one more day."

Two o'clock came, and Tim went into the partners meeting. He told them about the cancer and the treatment program he was getting ready to enter. The partners told him to make sure Sue knew their number in case things went bad. The firm would be glad to represent her in a wrongful death suit. Tim laughed and assured them he would. The partners gave him a nice bonus as a thank you for all his hard work, and wished him well. He assured the partners he had hoped one day he could come back, but he knew it would take him years to learn to be a lawyer again.

When Tim got downstairs to his office, Shelly was gone. On Tim's desk, he found a note and the private eye's phone number. Tim sat down and read the note.

"Dear Tim, I have enjoyed working for you over the years and I do hope all goes well. I wish you would reconsider the private eye. If you trust your wife, then give her the package for safekeeping. I'm sure if you tell her it's what you want, she will keep it. At some point in your life, you are going to have to believe in your marriage if you want to be happy. Sue is a good woman from what I know and you should hold onto her and let go of everything else. I'm sorry I couldn't stay to see you off, but I don't think I could see you, knowing you are the way you are. I didn't want our last words to be harsh ones.

I hope that God grants you wisdom and mercy. I pray he watches over you during this surgery and protects you from harm. I know there is a good man inside of you, Tim, get out of the way and let him surface."

Shelly gave her home number and told Tim to have Sue call her if she needed anything. The letter ended with a single word: Goodbye.

He sat the letter down on his desk and thought about the words Shelly had written. He knew she was right, and Tim was clinging to his wife. He did believe in her and trusted her, but he knew Sue would destroy any part of his history the minute he went under. He wanted to know the truth for himself in a year, no matter what was going on. He called the PI and arranged a meeting for later that afternoon.

As Tim began to pack up his office, other attorneys straggled in, saying their last goodbyes to Tim. All of the paralegals and assistants came in, and Tim felt loved by all. They all had good words to say and wished him well. Tim laughed at the thought of missing this if he remembered it! He began to joke with a few of his friends that he wouldn't miss them because he wouldn't remember them by this time next week.

Some of the senior partners came in as well and sat with Tim to say their last goodbyes and give him well wishes. Tim wrapped up the day at about five and got a few people to help him take his things to the car. As he pulled out of the building, he watched it fade away in his rearview mirror for the last time. He would miss being an attorney. The power he felt in a courtroom staring down a jury. Waiting for a verdict and opposing a defense attorney. It had made him a ton of money over the years and he knew he was good at it. He wondered what he would do with his life after the surgery. Would he have the same drive as he did now? Would he rise to the top of whatever profession he chose? Tim wondered, along with his memory, how much of his personality would be missing as well. He felt horrified at losing it all. He had worked so hard to get where he was. Was he making a mistake? Maybe he could be cured without losing his memory. People live every day post-cancer and do just fine. Was he being too hasty?

Tim pulled in the parking lot of the Starbucks and saw the PI standing by his car. Robert Stewart was an ex-military guy who had also been a cop for ten years before going private. He spent several years protecting some pretty high up executives in Atlanta, but got bored and started his own agency a few years back. Tim knew him from the protection days, but had used him to find a few people that needed to testify and were reluctant. Robert was good and he was trustworthy. Tim would pay him well, and in a year, Robert would find him and deliver.

Tim got out and greeted Robert. The two went in for a cup of coffee. They sat outside alone, and Tim told Robert what he needed him to do. In a year, he was to find Tim, wherever he was. Tim provided Robert with his social security number, a copy of his driver's license, and his birth date. With that much information he should be able to track him down. To help even further, Robert asked for Sue's information as well. Tim realized he had picked the right man. After writing it all down, he explained he may not remember Robert when he found him, but it would be okay. Just deliver the package and tell me I told you to do it. Tell me I need to read what's inside. Make sure you only deliver it to me. Don't leave this with anyone else. I prefer you watch the house and make sure I am the only one home when you do.

Robert knew better than to ask too many questions, but he did ask a few.

"Are you in some kind of trouble, Mr. Billings?"

"No, Robert, but I am having surgery and unfortunately one of the side effects will be permanent memory loss. I want to make sure I know who I am later."

"I see," he said. "Who will I be getting the package from?"

Tim handed Robert the safety deposit box key. "I have left the package in a safe deposit box at the Wachovia bank downtown, off Peachtree and Tenth, Box 1145. I also left instructions that one year from today a man would come and request to open the box. I will call and give them your name as soon as you have agreed to the terms."

Robert agreed and took the key. "Why don't you give me your address as well, if you think you might still be there?"

Tim smiled. "I doubt it. My wife will be supporting me at that time and I am sure she will move us away from the house we have now. She wants a fresh start, you see. I want to make sure I know my past."

Robert understood and agreed to the deal. Tim paid the man $2,000 and agreed to cover any more if required at the time. They shook hands and Robert was gone.

Tim sat, staring out into traffic as he finished his coffee, thinking about what he had set up and the information he had included in the package. Was he doing the right thing? Sue was really being strong by standing with him after all he had done. What if in a year he was happier than he ever imagined? Would the information change everything for them? Could he handle finding out the person he had been? Would it send Sue over the edge and cause her to leave him at that point?

He decided he would take the chance. He would want to know who he had been. He would make the decision then what to do with it. Tim drove home and unpacked the car. Sue got home shortly after and helped him carry in a few boxes.

Tim smiled at Sue as they got to the kitchen and she was looking through the things. "Listen; please don't throw away everything as soon as I go in the hospital, okay? I know you want to erase who I am completely, but there are some good things about me."

Sue looked at Tim. "I'm waiting."

Tim looked puzzled. "Waiting on what?"

"I am waiting for you to tell what those good things are."

Tim sighed. "Come on, Sue, you know I'm not all bad. We had some good years. We had a lot of good years. It wasn't until I made partner at the firm that I started getting stupid. Before that we had fun, didn't we?"

"Tim, I helped you do a lot of case study before that, remember? You would come home, eat and then go work in your office. I spent a lot of time watching TV alone. How about you don't be a lawyer next time around? Let me be the lawyer and you be a writer or plumber or something simple. Okay?"

"I don't know what I will be, except a burden. I'm scared of not knowing anything, Sue. Is this the right decision?"

"It's the rest of your life, you'll be fine. Thanks to your illegal gifts, we will have the money for you to go back to school and be whatever you want. Hopefully you won't turn into a jerk again. I would hate to have to kill you after you are cured from cancer."

"I heard that. If I die I will have that written down so you are the number one suspect."

"That's okay, write it down. As soon as you have surgery you won't remember what I said anyway."

"You are making me nervous, woman."

Sue laughed and walked out of the kitchen. "Put that stuff near the back door so I won't have far to take it when I throw it away!"

Tim laughed. "You better not. I have some very sentimental stuff in here I would like to have later in my life. Don't throw all this away."

Sue was laughing as she walked upstairs. She knew Tim was serious but Sue had already spoken to a realtor earlier that day. As soon as Tim went into surgery, she was selling the house and totally erasing his life. She knew if they were to have any chance at all, she would have to do just as Dr. Hampton had said. She wanted no part of Tim's current life. She had decided she would save some things from the early years of their marriage, but everything else had to go.

After Tim got the boxes put away in his study, he sat down at his computer. He pulled out the piece of paper he had made earlier, showing only the one account. He went on the website and clicked on accounts. Tim entered the password and his account came on the screen. This particular account had almost $800,000 now. At one time, it had a million, but Tim had taken $200,000 and invested in foreign stocks he also had hidden away.

The transfer was complete. The whole amount was now in Sue's account. He had made the arrangements earlier that day to cover the money from a legal aspect. Sue would owe some inheritance tax now, but it was not much, considering the amount of money. Tim had created an uncle in Germany that Sue magically knew nothing about. He wrote the letter to Sue explaining she was his only living relative from some law firm deep in Germany, no one would ever check. The money went through Zurich into her account in a matter of seconds. Later he would explain that if she would roll the money over into an IRA she could defer the taxes until she needed to take it out. This was the best he could do on short notice like this.

Tim closed down his computer and sat in his study alone for awhile. Sue called him for dinner finally and he joined the family. Jonathan was glad to be with his Dad, but Annette was still off in the distance. Tim figured with time she would come around. He would like that, and hoped that one day she would be proud he was her Dad.

After dinner, Sue and Tim sat at the table. Sue asked, "Are you ready?"

Tim couldn't answer. "How do you prepare for your own death?"

Sue understood and knew it was a big deal for him. He had worked hard since college at the firm and had done well. He was one of the youngest partners in the firm. He had made great money and big friends. This was death for him, but to Sue it was birth! It was the birth of hope that she would get the man back she had once loved. It was the birth of hope for her children to grow up with a loving father, one that wanted to be with them every day. It was the birth of hope that she, too, would get back her best friend and lover, who had walked out of her life several years ago.

Sue reached out and touched Tim's hand. Tim jumped at the gesture. "It's okay, Tim. I know this is a lot for you, and I know you're scared. We will be okay."

Tim smiled and reached up with his other hand to take Sue's in both his hands. Tears were beginning to form in his eyes. "Thank you so much for standing by me. I will never hurt you again."

"Let's hope not. I hope you become the man you were when we met. That's the Tim Billings I am helping to come back. The Tim Billings sitting here is a liar and a cheater."

Sue pulled her hand away and got up from the table. He raised his hands to his face to try and cover the tears now rolling down his face. She finished the dishes and he never moved from the table. As Sue started leaving the kitchen, he was still sitting at the table with his hands over his face.

Sue stopped at the kitchen door. "Tim, finish your business tonight. All of it! Say goodbye to whomever and close out all of the accounts. Tomorrow you get admitted for blood work and there is no coming back after that. Finish it!"

Sue turned off the lights, leaving Tim in the dark kitchen. She left the room and went upstairs. Tim thought about her words for awhile. He got up, grabbed his keys, and headed for the car. Sue stood at the window as Tim drove off saddened at the thought of him most likely going to some woman's place to say goodbye. She couldn't bear the thought and turned away. Sue turned on the TV in an attempt to lose herself in a movie. It didn't work. She was restless for hours while Tim was gone.

Tim pulled into Scully's parking lot and searched the cars, looking for George. As he turned down the last row of parking, he saw George's Caddy at the very end. Tim parked and went inside. Billy greeted Tim with the usual, and Tim just threw up a hand.

Billy responded: "The usual, Mr. B?"

Tim smiled at Billy. "No, Billy, I don't drink anymore! Have you seen George and the guys?"

"Yeah they're out on the patio tonight. Smoking cigars I think. You don't drink? Since when?"

Tim walked away and headed for the patio. He came through the doors and the whole gang was there, George, Charlie and Ray. Tim smiled as he walked over to the boys.

George spoke first. "Well, well, look who it is. Timmy Boy. Where you been?"

Tim reached over and took the cigar out of George's mouth and threw it over the rail. George looked at Tim like he was crazy. "Damn it, Tim, that was a $15 cigar you just threw away."

Tim pulled out his money clip and peeled off a twenty. "Here! Smoking causes cancer and you should stop it now."

"Whoa son, what's gotten into you?"

"Cancer, that's what."

All the guys turned to Tim. "What?"

Tim held up his hands. "Where is Peter? I was hoping all of you would be here."

Ray spoke up. "I think Peter is at his mountain house with his wife this week. They go all the time, you know. Call him, he'll answer."

"Oh well, guys, I am not staying, but there are a few things I want to say. First of all, George, you were right the last time we spoke. I have been screwing around on Sue and I was wrong. She is a great woman and I am working on saving my marriage. Tell Peter he was right as well okay."

George laughed. "Sounds like you had a come-to-Jesus meeting there, Tim."

"You could say that! It was more like a baptism by fire, I think, George."

Tim went on. "Charlie, I'm sorry about the other day. I didn't want anybody to know about the cancer yet, and I had just really found out myself. I appreciate you wanting to be a friend. That means a lot to me. You guys have been good friends, but I have to go back home to my wife."

Charlie grabbed Tim's arm. "What about the cancer, Tim?"

Tim laughed. "No big deal, just brain cancer, and this is the last time you guys will ever see me, so I guess this is 'so long.'"

"Are you dying? What do you mean, the last time we will see you?"

"No. I am going into surgery tomorrow, and when I come out of it, I will have no memory of my life at all. I won't remember anything about this place or you guys or anything. I am sure Sue will probably sell the house and move us somewhere else by the time I get out of rehab."

"Holy shit, Tim!"

"I know it's a bit much all at once, but it is probably the best thing that will ever happen to me. It's funny how sometimes you have to die to live."

George reached out and pulled Tim in for a bear hug. "You take care now, okay? You take care of Sue this next time around, huh."

"I will, George. I really will."

Charlie stepped in and hugged Tim, too. "If you need anything, you tell Sue to call me; I will be right there for you guys. Okay?"

"I will, Charlie. Thanks."

Tim started to turn and leave. Looking back at the guys, he said, "Play a hand for me every now and then, okay, fellas?"

They all smiled and said they would, and waved as Tim headed back inside. As Tim headed through the bar, Billy nodded at him again. Tim stopped and pulled out a fifty. He handed it to Billy told him thanks for being a good bartender. Billy looked shocked, holding up the cash in a dumbfounded way. "Thanks, Mr. B!"

Tim was almost running back to his car. He wanted to get back home and tell Sue where he had been so she wouldn't think the worst. For the first time in years, what Sue thought really mattered to Tim.

When Tim got home, the house was dark. He ran upstairs and could see the glow of the TV under Sue's door. He came to the door but was afraid to knock. Sue stood on the other side waiting to see what he would do. Tim knocked. "Sue!"

Sue opened the door. "Was she heartbroken?"

"I wasn't at some girl's house, Sue. I told you I was done with that. I went up to Scully's to say goodbye to the guys and, no, I didn't have a drink."

At that, Sue grinned. "It would have been okay, I think."

Tears pooled in Sue's eyes. Tim grabbed her around the waist and pulled her against him. "I love you, Sue. I will never forget that."

Sue squeezed Tim tight and buried her head against his chest. "I hope not."

"I won't. I won't forget, no matter what part of my brain they remove. I loved you the first day I saw you and I will again. That has nothing to do with memory."

Sue was crying now and so was Tim. Sue pulled him closer and shut the door. Tim picked Sue up and carried her to the bed. The two fell into the bed, embracing in passionate kisses as they used to when they first met. With every kiss, Sue's body ached with desire for her husband. They made love for the first time in almost a year. Tim had almost forgotten how beautiful his wife's body was. With each touch, Tim fell more in love with Sue. With every stroke, his passion for her came back tenfold, more than it had ever been. She gave in to her love for him. Forgiveness had always been her strongest attribute and she had wanted to forgive him. Now she had, and her love was pouring out of her.

As Tim finally lay down beside her, pulling her next to him and wrapping his arms tightly around her, Sue said, "I love you, Tim. I always have!"

Tim pulled her even closer. Their bodies almost becoming one, he kissed Sue again and again until the two of them fell asleep in each other's arms.

On the Way

Chapter 10

S ue woke first. Feeling Tim next to her was startling, since it had been so long. She slid out of bed and made her way to the bathroom. Tim never moved. She went downstairs to get the kids ready for school.

Annette came down the hall and noticed her dad's door open and the still-made bed. As she came in to the kitchen, she didn't see him there, either. Sue was smiling, making eggs and greeted Annette as she came in.

"Hi, baby! Want some eggs?"

"Sure. So did Dad not come home last night? I see he's not in his room."

Sue paused. "He is in my room."

Annette groaned. "Gross, Mom, why are you doing that? I can't believe you let him in your room."

"Annette, it's complicated; but the bottom line is, I love your Dad. I have been married to him for a long time. I don't like what he has done, and he hurt me and you guys, but he has changed, and after the surgery he will really change."

"No, he won't! He probably will while he needs you, but then it will be the same."

Sue explained to Annette that her dad would lose his memory completely. She explained how he would not know anything about his life or what he had done. Annette had a hard time believing what she was hearing. Sue went on to explain that she would have the chance to turn her dad back into the loving man he was. Annette had so made up her mind about her dad that she didn't want to hear anymore. She quickly finished eating and headed for the bus stop. Sue watched her walk to the bus stop, standing alone while she waited for the bus. Sue wondered what was going through her mind right now. Annette had decided to hate her dad for some obvious reasons, but there had to be more. Once Tim was in the hospital, she would talk more with Annette to try and help her forgive.

Jonathan was in the kitchen and ready to go. He ate pop tarts and drank a glass of milk before he headed out the door. Sue kissed him on the forehead as she helped him get his book bag. As Jonathan went out of the garage, she noticed Tim was still not downstairs. It was now almost 9:30 and they needed to be on their way by 10. Hopefully, he was getting ready and not still sleeping.

Sue went back upstairs to her room and Tim was lying in the bed. Sue laughed and grabbed his toe as she walked past the bed. "Get up, sleepyhead!" Sue kept going and went into the closet to get dressed. She threw on jeans and a blouse and started putting on her makeup. Tim still had not moved from the bed. Sue leaned into the bedroom. "Tim! Get up. We need to go."

When Tim didn't respond again, Sue began to worry. She started walking towards Tim and called out again. "Tim!" As she reached Tim, his eyes were open and blinking but he was not moving. Panic overwhelmed her.

She grabbed Tim's face and turned it toward her. "Tim, what's wrong? Why aren't you moving?"

He was trying to speak, but nothing was coming out. He couldn't move. She began to cry as she pulled back the covers and started moving Tim's arms. Now in a full panic, she grabbed the phone from the nightstand and called 911. As she waited, Tim was still trying to speak and move. He barely began to turn his head. Sue was now on the line with emergency asking for an ambulance. She was telling the operator her husband was scheduled for surgery this week at Emory but he seemed to be paralyzed. The operator told her not to try and move him, and the paramedics were on the way. Sue hung up and sat next to Tim.

As she told him the ambulance was on the way, he began to speak. "I can't feel anything."

She began to touch him down his body, asking if he could feel any pressure. Quietly, he said, "No."

Sue got some shorts from the closet and put those on him. She was afraid to try a shirt, not sure what might happen if she moved him. Within a few minutes, she could hear the ambulance siren, and then they were pulling in the driveway. Fortunately, there was a fire station just up the street from their house. She ran downstairs to let the paramedics in and show them the way. Two paramedics came in with medic bags and a stretcher.

The paramedics entered the bedroom and began to take vital signs. One paramedic worked with Tim while the other paramedic touched Sue's shoulder. "Ma'am, can I ask you a few questions?"

Sue wiped tears away but couldn't take her eyes off Tim. "Yes."

"Did anything happen that might have caused an injury to his neck or back?"

Sue briefly looked at the man. "No, he has a brain tumor. We are going to Emory today to admit him for surgery."

"Okay. Right now, we are going to get him stabilized and transport him to Northside. Has he had any symptoms like this before?"

"No, none."

"Has his doctor said anything about side effects relating to this brain tumor?"

"No! Why is this happening?"

Tim was now talking a little to the other paramedic and moving his head some. The paramedic was touching his neck and shining a pen light into his eyes. He was still not moving his body. As Sue and the other paramedic looked on, the paramedic motioned for help to move him to the stretcher. Sue stepped to the side to let the men work. They carefully moved Tim from the bed to the stretcher. Tim looked scared to death as his eyes met Sue's. Sue stood with both hands over her mouth, scared to death as she watched his motionless body being moved. She worried that this may prevent him from being eligible for the procedure at Emory.

With Tim safely on the stretcher and strapped down, the paramedic turned back to Sue. "I am sure this is a temporary side effect from the tumor. Do you have the number of his doctor?"

Tim spoke quietly. "It's in my wallet. Dr. Hampton's card."

The paramedic again touched Sue on the shoulder. Sue was frozen. "Call his doctor. Let him know where we are taking him. He will need to call the emergency room and speak to the doctor in charge. I'm not sure what they will do first, so try and get them talking quickly. You can ride with us or follow behind. I'm sure Emory will transport him there, but we can't, we have to take him to Northside. Are you okay?"

Sue was still looking at Tim. "I guess. Can I talk to him before you take him?"

"Sure, but it needs to be quick."

The paramedics stepped aside and Sue walked over to Tim. "I'm scared, Tim."

Tim smiled. "It will be okay. Just call Dr. Hampton. Tell him what happened. Get me to Emory."

Sue leaned down and kissed Tim. "I will be right behind you. Okay?"

"Just call the doc right now, okay? I will be fine."

The paramedics started pushing the stretcher towards the door. "We have to go, ma'am."

Sue stepped back and let them take him out. "I am right behind you."

A quiet "Okay" came from the stretcher. Sue grabbed Tim a change of clothes and his wallet. The paramedics were getting him in the ambulance as she reached her car in the garage. One of the paramedics came over and told her the route they would be taking and told her to follow along. They would not be traveling with sirens, only flashing lights. He urged her not to do anything dangerous. Sue agreed and they left for the hospital.

As soon as they were on the road, she opened his wallet and started looking for the card. There were two cards in Tim's wallet, Dr. Hampton's and one for a Robert Stewart, Private Eye. She stared at the card and could only imagine what Tim was doing with this card. Had Tim arranged for this man to find him later? She threw the card in her purse; she didn't have the time to deal with that right now. She got Reid's card and dialed the number.

A receptionist answered. "Good morning, Research. How can I help you?"

"This is Sue Billings. I need to speak to Dr. Hampton right away. It's an emergency."

"Mrs. Billings, what's wrong? Dr. Hampton is in surgery right now. Can I help?"

"Tim is paralyzed and on the way to Northside in an ambulance. I am following them. They won't bring him to Emory; I need Dr. Hampton to call the emergency room there right away. We are about 20 minutes away. You have to go get him."

"I will get a message to him for sure, Mrs. Billings. What number can he reach you at?"

Sue gave her the cell phone number and told her to call her as soon as she was in touch with him.

The ambulance pulled into the emergency area and Sue parked. They took Tim into the back and Sue went into the registration area. After showing all the insurance information and signing paperwork, she was finally led to the back. Tim was in a small exam room; the x-ray techs were there to take him for a CAT scan.

Tim was speaking softly, and then saw Sue and called out. "Sue! Did he call yet?"

'No, not yet, he is in surgery right now; they are getting a message to him. He will call, Tim, don't worry."

"Jesus, Sue, I'm scared."

"I know I will get through to Dr. Hampton. Don't worry."

"Don't let them operate on me here. I have to go to Emory. They may mess something up."

The nurse wheeled him out of the room and headed down the hall to X-Ray. Sue walked into the hall looking for a doctor. She went to the nurse's station and asked who the doctor in charge was.

The nurse pointed at a young Doctor standing with a chart. "That's him, Dr. Grant."

As she said his name, he looked over. Sue approached him. "I need to talk to you about my husband."

"Okay, ma'am, who's your husband?"

"Tim Billings. The guy that just came in paralyzed."

"Oh yes, they just took him to X-ray. Don't worry, Mrs. Billings, we will take a look at the CAT scan and figure out what's going on. We can get him in surgery right away if it's a disc problem."

"Dr. Grant, he has a brain tumor. He is scheduled to go into Emory today for surgery. I need you to call Dr. Reid Hampton at Emory and talk with him. You guys cannot operate on him."

"Mrs. Billings, I understand, but if your husband's tumor is pushing on his spinal cord, moving him to Emory could cause permanent damage. I understand your concern, but I am not going to jeopardize your husband's future. If the tumor has moved he needs to be in surgery right away. Do you have this doctor's number at Emory?"

"Yes, right here."

"Okay let me get him on the phone. We are still going to send him down to X-ray so we can see what's going on. I need you to stay calm for me. We work with Emory all the time, don't worry. We will take good care of him."

The doctor nodded at one of the nurses and she asked Sue to follow her. She took her to a small waiting area near the x-ray area and explained he would come through the doors right outside the room. She could see and be with him as soon as he came out. Sue was a nervous wreck, waiting for Tim. She kept staring at her cell phone, but it had not rung. Where was Dr. Hampton? Why hadn't he called?

It was almost an hour before they finally brought him back out. Sue ran up to the stretcher and took Tim's hand. To her surprise, he squeezed it.

Sue smiled. "You can move your hand."

Tim smiled back. "A little, it's slowly getting better. Have they talked to Dr. Hampton?"

"I don't know. I have called twice, but he is still in surgery. They know you are going to Emory; they want to make sure you are not in any danger first."

"I really hope this doesn't mess things up."

"I know. I'm sure he will call soon, don't worry, it will be okay."

Tim smiled and squeezed her hand again. "Thank you! Thank you for being with me."

Sue squeezed back and smiled. They went down the hall and to a room. The doctor came back in and began to show them x-rays of his neck and head. The tumor was larger than what he had seen before and it was pushing against the nerves at the base of his skull. The doctor explained the dangers and the risk of moving to Emory. He had not heard from Dr. Hampton yet, but did not want to wait too long. Tim's symptoms and paralysis were getting better; however, he was in trouble and was at risk of permanent damage.

As they were talking, the nurse came in and told the doctor he had a call waiting. The doctor smiled. "There is your doctor now, I bet."

He stepped out of the room and Sue took Tim's hand again. "Thank God."

Dr. Grant was gone for about twenty minutes and finally came back in. "Okay, Dr. Hampton and I had a long conversation about you and what needs to take place."

Sue spoke up. "Are they coming to get him?"

"No. We are going to do the tumor removal here."

Tim tried to move. "No, I will have her drive me to Emory. I do not give consent for you to operate."

Dr. Grant held up his hands. "Hold on a minute. Dr. Hampton and I agreed the removal of the tumor is not that big a deal. Moving you right now would be very dangerous and neither one of us want to take that risk. We have some fine surgeons here and Dr. Hampton is on the way to assist. He said he would call you shortly and fill you in on the rest of things, not to worry."

"When will I go to Emory?"

"You will go up to the 4th floor to our specialist area first. A neurosurgeon will work with Dr. Hampton to get you fixed up. Once you are stable and you're able to move, then you will go to Emory for the cancer treatment."

The doctor stood up, "I will check in on you as my shift ends. Please don't try and get up, Mr. Billings. Now, good luck, and I hope everything works out okay."

"I am sure it will," Sue said.

The nurse came in and told them where they were headed. She started wheeling Tim out just as Sue's cell phone rang.

Sue began fumbling in her purse for the phone, "Hello!"

"Sue, it's Dr. Hampton. Are you guys doing okay?"

"Yeah, we're just nervous that this has messed things up. Are you on the way here?"

"I am. It hasn't messed anything up so relax. The surgeons at Northside are excellent. Dr. Peavey will be doing the surgery and I will sit in. He is excellent. I already talked with the hospital administrator over there and told him what was going on. He understood and has given us permission to use the hospital for the entire procedure if we need to. So, relax. We will get Tim in good shape and things will proceed as planned. Tim's safety is our concern right now. We sure don't want to cure him of cancer and have him paralyzed."

"No, we sure don't. How long before you are here?"

"About 30 minutes. I will see you guys in your room. We are trying to get a surgical suite now to get you in today. I don't want that tumor doing any damage."

"No, me neither. Thank you, Doctor."

"No problem, Sue. Tell Tim not to worry. He's still my guy. See you soon." The phone went dead.

Sue told Tim and he smiled and closed his eyes. "I'm exhausted," Tim said.

"Me, too!"

Sue sat on the edge of the bed and thought about all that had happened over the past few weeks. From divorce to back in love and from healthy to paralyzed. It had certainly been an interesting few weeks. Sue looked down at Tim and he was staring at her smiling.

Sue smiled. "What?"

"I had forgotten how beautiful you are."

Sue smiled. "You forgot a lot of things Tim."

"I know I did. I won't again!"

Sue laughed. "Yes, you will, but soon, I will teach you all kinds of things."

Tim laughed. "I'll bet you will."

"Yep, I will! You will be the loving kind man you used to be."

"That's fine with me. I've been a jerk for too long."

"Yes, you have. If it wasn't this way, I wouldn't be here."

"I appreciate this, Sue, I really do."

Sue sat there thinking about how much Tim's circumstances had changed his attitude. Why hadn't she been enough? If he had not gotten cancer, nothing would have changed. They would have gotten a divorce, and Tim would have moved on and forgotten her and the kids. She was hurt by Tim's actions, and was still angry, even though things were better between them.

Tim noticed Sue quiet again. "What's wrong?"

"God, Tim, I am still so angry at you."

Tim closed his eyes. "I know. I have said it so many times, Sue, but I am really sorry for who I became. I do hope you give me the chance to make it up to you and the kids once I recover."

"You know, if you hadn't gotten cancer, we would be getting a divorce and you would have walked away. How could you do that to me and the kids? I really want to know, before you go into surgery and forget everything. I want you to tell me why."

"Sue, I have no good reason. I just got lost in the power of my career. The appetite to conquer doesn't stop after awhile. The courtroom wasn't enough anymore. There was no challenge at home, and I know that's wrong. You deserved better than that. Out there, I was a king!"

Sue shook her head. "God, your ego is out of control."

"Hear me out. I'm not talking about in the courtroom. I was good in court, for sure; I'm talking about out in the world. I could go to a bar and tell the people there anything I wanted. I was respected and adored. I was wanted. It became my conquering ground. It became the only place I felt alive. I'm sorry."

"Did I ever not respect you? Did you ever feel unwanted? I thought I was a good wife. Yes, I got wrapped up in the kids, but hell, Tim, you weren't there. Someone had to!"

"You didn't do anything wrong, Sue. You were being everything you needed to be. If I had been more involved and not so in love with myself, it would have been very different. Please don't blame yourself for anything. It was me, all me!"

"How do I know it won't happen again?"

"It won't."

"How do you know? You won't remember today, much less what not to be. What if this is just who you really are? What if this part of you is not memory? Tim, I can't take going through another eight to ten years, just to have you walk away. It will kill me."

"Sue, I won't let it happen. Go get a recorder and I will record a message to myself telling me everything not to do. I don't ever want to hurt you again. This is a chance for me to erase the past and start over. It's a chance for me to be what I was supposed to be for you for the rest of my life. Sue, can you forgive me and erase the past?"

Sue sat on the bed and cried. Tim could not pick up his arm to touch her. He wanted to so badly. He wanted to reach up and pull her close to him, to promise her it would never happen again. But he couldn't. His body had not improved at all in the last hour.

"Sue, please come close to my face. Let me feel your skin against mine. I know you are scared, but it will be different. It will be so much better."

Sue stood turning to Tim. "Shut up!"

Tim blinked hard. "What?"

"I swear I don't want to hear another word, or I will walk out of here and your life at the same time. How dare you think I was not enough! I am enough. I am worth coming home for. I am smart, and beautiful, and I deserve better, both then and now. God, how could I let you back in last night? You are so smooth. Of course you are. That's how you make a living, isn't it?"

"Sue, I . . ."

She cut him off. "Not another word. Is all of that money in my account?"

"Yes, all $800,000."

"Good. You won't remember that and I bet I can hide money too, if I try. I will get you through this, but I don't know about us. I really don't."

She turned and walked out of the room and down the hall. Tim was fighting back the tears as Dr. Hampton walked through the door.

"Wow, Tim, you and Sue fighting? I just saw her walking down the hall and she looked a little upset."

"Doc, I have been a real jerk the last several years. I hope she stays with me after this is done. I know saying that jeopardizes my eligibility, but she is really mad."

"It will be okay, Tim. You will be in rehab for months after surgery and that will give her some time to heal. Hell, she might even miss you."

"I don't know, Doc. She's got some pretty deep scars."

"Maybe, but having the chance to make you into the man you used to be will be good for her. I will talk with her some more. Now, let's talk about you and what caused this little paralyzing problem."

"Little problem! Doc, I can't move anything below my neck. I can feel my fingers some but can't seem to really move them. They did a CAT scan."

"I know; I just looked at the shots of your brain. Isn't science cool?"

"Am I going to be okay? This is freaking me out a lot."

"You'll be fine. The tumor has grown in size this last month to the point that it is now pushing on your spinal cord at the base of your skull. It's a complication, but not a show—stopper. Did anything happen last night out of the ordinary?"

Tim started smiling. "Well, Sue and I had sex. It was fantastic. Nothing happened to my neck though."

"No swinging from the chandelier, or outrageous gymnastics moves? Something pushed it to the point it has swollen."

"Nothing, really. I mean, it was great sex. The best we have had in years!"

"Okay, okay, I just need to know about your neck, nothing else."

Tim blushed. "Oh. Nothing happened that I know of or remember. I just went to sleep right after and woke up like this."

"I see. Let's check a few things."

The doctor began to check reflexes. He scratched at his feet and he didn't move. He checked his hands and did get some movement in the fingers.

The doctor raised an eyebrow at that. "That's a good sign."

Sue entered the room. "Can we do the surgery today?" The doctor spun around to see Sue standing in the doorway.

"Well, hey, Sue. Come on in and let's talk."

Sue said again. "Can you do the surgery today?"

"We can. Being paralyzed makes it a little more complicated but I truly believe the paralysis is temporary. Once we remove the tumor you will be good as new."

Sue sat in the chair next to the bed. "That's good, because if he stays who he is now for much longer I will walk away. I'm just telling you the truth."

Reid looked at Tim. "I think she is serious!"

Tim looked at Sue. "You are good enough, Sue. I was a fool. Please give me a second chance."

Reid took a step back. "Why don't I give you two another minute; I have some preparations to make."

Tim smiled. "Thanks, Doc, I am ready to go as soon as we can."

Dr. Hampton touched Sue on the shoulder. "Hang in there, Sue, it will be okay."

Dr. Hampton left and Sue sat quiet. Tim was afraid to speak. Sue seemed calm for the moment and Tim thought it was best to just be silent. He was so used to reading people and their body language, but not Sue. He was lost and wrong and he knew it. So did Sue. She finally looked up at Tim, helpless, in both body and mind.

Sue shook her head. "What a mess. You have made a mess, and for what? A good time?"

Tim sighed. "Sue, I was stupid, and it took a near-death experience to show me that. This cancer has saved me from myself. Please don't let who I was dictate our future. I will be a brand new man, just for you. I will be whatever you want me to be. Please let me have that chance. Please give me the chance to get to know my kids. Hell, give me the chance to get to know you again."

Dr. Hampton came back through the door with a slight knock. "We're ready. Is everybody okay in here?

Sue sat staring at Tim and then smiled at the doctor. "Take him away, he's all yours."

The nurse came in behind Reid; she unlocked the bed and disconnected the monitor. "Here we go."

Tim looked at Sue. "I love you, Sue. I will see you when it's done."

Sue didn't speak. She watched Tim roll away and then lowered her eyes to the floor. She began to think about all that had happened. The door slowly closed, but she didn't feel alone. She looked back up to see Dr. Hampton standing next to the door.

"Dr. Hampton. You scared me. I thought I was alone."

"Please, Sue, call me Reid. I know this is hard. We talked about Tim and how he was. Remember what you have to gain. He will not be the same when I am done. People are who they are from their life experiences. Tim is the son-of-a-bitch he is because of what his life was. His parents, his career, friends and money made him that way. It could be something that happened to him as a young man or something that happened to him during his career. People are their memories. Tim will be brand new. He will be whatever you make him. He will be all yours. His memories will only be of you, your kids, and your life together—whatever you show him of his past. Don't give up. He was a good man, and he will be again. Don't give up!"

Sue stood up and hugged Reid. "Thank you. I have to catch him and tell him I love him. As mad as I am, if this goes bad, I don't want my last words to be in anger."

"Go!"

She ran out of the room and down the hall. Reid was right behind her. They got to the elevators but Tim was gone. "No, Reid, I have to see him."

Reid hit the "up" button. "You will. Don't worry."

As they came off the elevator onto the sixth floor, Tim was being rolled down the hall. Sue took off running. As she got to his stretcher, she grabbed the frame and stopped the nurse pushing the bed. The nurse reacted by grabbing her arm. "Ma'am!"

Reid was right there and grabbed the nurse by the shoulder. "It's okay, just give them a moment."

Reid and the nurse stood back as Sue came around the end of the bed. Tim began to smile as he saw Sue. She picked up Tim's hand and touched it to her face. "Do you feel that?"

"A little" he said as tears rolled down his face.

Sue wiped the tear away. "Don't cry, Tim. I have always been here and I always will be. I hate what you have done, but I love you! I forgive you, and I know that you will be a good man again."

"I am so glad. I will be, I promise."

"I will be here when you come out. You won't know me, but I will be here."

"I won't forget you. Not ever again. Somehow, I will remember. I love you, Sue."

"I love you, too, Tim. See you on the other side."

The nurse began to push the bed again and Reid took Sue's hand. "He will be a new man. I will get you your Tim back. I promise okay?"

"Okay! You better or I am going to have to kill both of you."

Reid grinned as he went through the surgery door. He waved and the door closed. Sue stood in the hallway all alone. She slid down the wall to the floor, exhausted and nerves shot, uncertain of the future and everything that she was. Today would be the beginning of a new way of life. The tears slowly fell and Sue tried to get it together. Thankfully, the hall was quiet and there was no one to interrupt her thoughts. She sat there for a long while. Finally, she gathered herself and stood up, realizing she had no idea how long he would be in surgery or what she was supposed to do. The hall was still empty and she roamed down to the doorway that Tim had gone through. There was no one there to ask. She turned and started heading for the elevator. The door buzzed and a nurse came out.

"Excuse me, Mrs. Billings."

Sue turned to see the young nurse that had been pushing the bed. "Yes."

"Dr. Reid told me to tell you that they are going to do both surgeries back to back. Dr. Peavey will remove the tumor and Dr. Hampton and his team will treat the cancer."

"Okay. So what should I do?"

"He said to tell you to go home for now. The surgeries will take hours. He said he will call you between surgeries to let you know how things are, and then again when it is all done. Oh, and he said, don't worry, the new Tim will be here soon; whatever that means."

Sue smiled. "Thanks for the update. I was not sure what to do. Thank you."

The nurse turned and went back into the surgery area. Sue looked back down the hall at the emptiness. "All alone now," she spoke out loud. She headed for the elevator and went home.

Tim's last day as a big time attorney was here. He looked up at the faces in the room staring down at him as the anesthesia took effect. Dr. Hampton smiled, "You'll be fine, Tim. You're in good hands."

Tim smiled. "I better be or I am suing all of you!

Tim closed his eyes and thought about Sue. The last memory he wanted was her face, her saying she loved him. The darkness flooded his brain and Tim went under.

Surgery

Chapter 11

The first surgery was a routine procedure as far as tumor removal goes. They went in and found the tumor. After two hours of carefully cutting the tumor away Dr. Peavey felt confident the tumor had been fully removed. Dr. Hampton watched on as Dr. Peavey performed his work. The surgery was a success and they began to bring Tim back around. They needed to see if the paralysis was gone before they went further. As they did, Reid stepped out to call Sue.

Sue was sitting at home, waiting for the kids to get home, especially Annette. She wanted some alone time with her to talk about all that was going on. Things had been a little out of control over the last few days, and she really wanted to get inside Annette's head. She seemed so hostile towards her dad. Sue could see the bus pulling up in front of the house as the phone rang.

"Hello!"

"Sue, it's Reid. How are you?"

"I am fine, Doc. How is Tim?"

"He's good so far. The first surgery went well. We were able to remove the tumor with no problems. It had pushed against his spinal cord, but fortunately, it had not grown around it. So, he is good."

"Have you done both surgeries?"

"No, not yet; we need to bring him back to the surface to see if the paralysis is gone. We want to make sure there are no problems before we proceed. We also have to prep a lot for the next surgery. It will be filmed, since it is the first of its kind, and we have to transport the portion of the donor brain from Emory as well. We will be under way in a few hours if everything is good with Tim."

Annette came through the door and Sue held up a finger signaling her to be quiet. She dropped her book bag at the table and fixed something to drink. Annette watched her mom as she finished the phone call.

"Reid, thank you so much for the call. Please call me when it's done. It doesn't matter what time. I want to know how it turns out."

Reid said he would, and again told Sue not to worry. He had done the surgery on several monkeys and that couldn't be much different than Tim. Sue laughed and said goodbye. Sue put the phone back on the charger and turned to talk to Annette.

"What was that about?" Annette asked.

Sue came over and sat at the table. "Annette, why do you hate your dad?"

Annette looked shocked at the question. "I don't really hate him. I just . . ."

Sue reached out and touched Annette's hand. "Annette, you were practically happy when you found out he had cancer. Help me understand why you feel that way. I know he's been a jerk lately, but is there something else?"

"No. I hate the way he treats you, Mom. He doesn't come home and he cheats on you. Why are you not divorcing him?"

"There are some things in life that can be forgiven. If someone changes, it is okay to forgive. Your Dad is changing."

"No, he hasn't. Mom, you know he hasn't."

"So your wealth of life experience has taught you this at age twelve!"

Annette stood up. "God. Mom, you won't listen to me. You have made up your mind and that's fine. I will be quiet and listen to you cry yourself to sleep, again and again, just like always."

Sue understood the hate now. "Annette, sit down."

Annette rolled her eyes and sat. "Mom, we really don't need to talk about this."

"Really, we do. Yes, your dad has hurt me and yes, I have cried myself to sleep a lot of times, but love is stronger than that. I love your dad and he is changing. He doesn't have a choice."

Annette rolled her eyes again. "No, he won't, Mom. You said it yourself."

"The surgery he is having today will erase his memory. He will not know anything about his past after today."

"He's having surgery today?"

"Yes. He had a brain tumor and that caused him to be paralyzed this morning. We had to rush him to the hospital. They decided to do both surgeries today. When he wakes up, he will have no memory."

"I don't understand. How can you have no memory? He won't remember you, me or Jonathan?"

"No. He won't remember anything. He won't remember being a lawyer, his childhood, or anything he has done to me or you kids."

"So, is that why he started being nice to you? So you would take care of him?"

Sue laughed at the wisdom in this twelve year old child. "He started being nice because he has cancer. That scared him and made him realize just what he had. Sometimes people have to lose what they have to understand how important it is to them. Your dad almost lost his life to cancer. That woke him up. He now realizes what a great family he has. He knows he screwed up."

"And you're willing to just take him back and forgive him for all that?"

"Yes. God says we are to forgive, sweetie. Your dad needs us. He won't remember anything about who he was or what he did. We have to forget it as well. He will only be what we teach him to be when he comes back."

"What do you mean, what we teach him to be?"

"Literally, he will not remember anything about his life at all. The surgery he is having will remove the part of his brain that stores memories. He will come home like a new baby. It will be up to us to teach him everything about who he is."

A smile broke across Annette's face. "So if I tell him he gives me cake before bed every night, he won't know any different?"

Sue grinned and cocked her head sideways. "Alright, Annette, this is not an opportunity for you to get away with stuff. Do you hear me?"

Annette started laughing. "When will he be home? He won't remember anything?"

"Your dad won't be home for about six months. He will stay in rehab where he will re-learn how to eat, how to walk and how to talk again. After that he will come here for us to take care of."

"That's kind of creepy. He won't remember me or anything I have done, when I was born or anything?"

"That's right. The good news is, he won't remember how badly he treated you, either. He won't remember how he hurt you by not coming to school events, or birthday parties, or all the other stuff, either. If you tell him he never missed a single thing, then he will think that's how it is, and he will never miss another one."

Annette started to cry. Sue pulled her close and hugged her. "Baby, your dad does love you. He just got all caught up in the power of his career. It happens. We have been given a gift. We get him back brand-new. We can make him into a great loving man, a loving father. He wants that. That's all he has talked about. He was thankful he got cancer because he gets the opportunity to start over. He wants to be in our lives and forget everything he was. I think we need to help him do that. Will you help him?"

"I want to. I'm afraid, Mom. What if he turns out to be the same?"

"He won't be, Annette, but we have to do a few things to make sure of that."

Annette looked puzzled. "Like what?"

Sue took a deep breath. "We're moving!"

"What? No, Mom, all my friends are here. My whole life is here. I don't want to move. I like living here. Why do we have to move?"

"Baby, we have to get away from your dad's life here. I don't want anybody to come back into his life and remind him of who he was. Do you understand?"

"You're talking about some girl; aren't you?"

Sue looked embarrassed. "That and his drinking buddies. I don't want any ties to his old life. Anything that would remind him of the jerk he was."

"Great now my life gets ruined because of him too. How soon will we move?"

"Annette stop. Your life is not ruined. I have already talked to the realtor and she will be here tomorrow with the For Sale sign. As soon as someone buys the house, maybe sooner, if I find the right place for us."

Annette looked sad at that news. "Can I have my friends over this weekend to just hang out?"

"Sure you can, baby. We aren't moving tomorrow. It will be at least a month, maybe longer. You'll have time for goodbyes, but you can still have them over this weekend."

Back at the hospital, Tim was beginning to come out of the anesthesia. Dr. Hampton and Dr. Peavey stood by waiting for movements of hands or feet. Tim's eyes fluttered and he raised his hand to his face. Both doctors smiled and Reid patted Dr. Peavey on the back. "Good job!"

Dr. Peavey leaned in closer. "Tim, can you hear me?"

Tim blinked hard again. "Yes."

He felt the bandages on his head and looked over at Dr. Hampton. "Did you erase my memory? I still remember everything!"

Reid laughed. "No, Tim. If I had, you wouldn't remember everything. We took the tumor out. Can you move your legs?"

Tim slowly moved his left leg and then his right. He smiled. He picked up his right arm and then his left. "Doc, I think you guys did it."

Dr. Peavey took Tim's hand. "Can you squeeze my hand?"

Tim did but not too hard. "Sorry, Doc, I don't have that much strength right now. I have been a little under the weather."

Dr. Peavey laughed. "That was fine. The fact that you are making a joke is good, too."

Tim looked at Reid. "What's next?"

Dr. Peavey looked at Reid as well. "Yeah, you got to watch me do mine. Mind if I watch you?"

"Not at all! Having you in there would be good. You do good work. Tim, you're in good shape. We are going to put you back under now and continue. I called Sue and told her everything was good. She will be here when you wake up."

"Thanks, Doc. Maybe you could introduce me to her. I look forward to meeting her again."

"Tim, you're going to be just fine. Sue is a good woman and you are lucky to have her. Anything you want me to tell her?"

"Yeah, you tell her she is worth coming back home to. She always has been and I will be home soon."

With that, Tim faded back into sleep. Dr. Hampton scrubbed up and went in to prep the donor brain. This was not his OR at Emory, but it would do. The surgery was really very simple, with the exception of repairing the brain after removal of the cancerous sections of the memory. Reid had done it hundreds of times with animal subjects and was at a 100% recovery rate now, but Tim would be the first human. Not his first brain surgery on humans, but his first for this particular surgery.

As they wheeled Tim back into the OR, the view gallery began to fill. Reid could see all the big shots from Emory had showed. Many of the world's finest oncology doctors had cleared their schedules and flown to Atlanta for this, and the camera was in place. It was time for Dr. Reid Hampton to claim his place in history. Everything he had been working for, for the last six years, was here on the table. This patient would mark the beginning of the cure! Reid was excited and nervous at the same time. So many researchers and scientists had worked countless hours to get here.

Reid was lost in his thoughts when he felt Dr. Peavey touch his arm. "Reid, you ready?"

Reid turned and nodded. "I am!"

"Then let's do this."

Reid began the procedure. He started by talking about what would take place. "Ladies and gentlemen, thank you for your support over the years.

We have found, in brain cancer patients, the production and life line, if you will, is located in the hippocampus part of the temporal lobe. This memory area of the brain produces the cancer cells. We have always treated the symptoms of cancer, but never the source. Today we will be removing the patients left and right hippocampus portion of his brain and replacing it with a clean cancer free donor section. Once the cancer-producing area has been removed, the cancer dies in the body. Only in cases where the cancer has caused damage to organs, or severe tissue damage, do we need to treat further. In this case, the patient had a small tumor that had not grown around any vital areas, so we were able to remove the growth entirely without any damage to his brain. Normally, that would be followed by chemotherapy and other leading treatment possibilities. This procedure will stop the cancer growth and the body's ability to produce the cell structure creating cancer."

The anesthesiologist looked at Reid. "We're ready."

They began to cut into the side of Tim's head, small incisions for the surgery that will be arthroscopic. Technology had come so far. Dr. Hampton slowly maneuvered through Tim's brain making sure not to damage anything else in the process, slowly making cuts and folding back lobes of brain. Three hours in, Reid had secured both sections of the hippocampus. Tim was now free of the cancer.

Reid took a fifteen minute break from surgery to rest his eyes and hands from working the lasers, and viewing the world he was in through a microscope. He was up for the challenge and had done this multiple times. The excitement was still running through his body.

Dr. Peavey came over with a cup of coffee and handed it to Reid. "Reid, you are doing fantastic in there. You are a gifted surgeon as well as a scientist. That gig at Emory goes south, you call me. I will get you on over here in a heartbeat."

Reid laughed. "The gig at Emory is going pretty great, actually. I suspect the next several years will be spent figuring out how many other types of cancer my procedure will cure. It would be fantastic if it cures them all."

He patted Reid on the back. "It sure would. You let me know if there is anything I can do in there, okay? I am right behind you all the way."

"I appreciate it, Steve. I respect your skills as well. You removed the tumor with precision, clean! Great work with my patient; I appreciate you helping pave the way today here at Northside."

"Don't mention it. Once you told me what was happening I wanted to be a part of it. So did Northside. Anything you need, my friend, you just say."

"Thanks. I guess we better get back at it. We have a brain to put back together."

The two men went back into surgery and started back. The anesthesiologist gave the thumbs up and Reid stepped back into place. The team came in with the ice chest containing the donor brain pieces and Reid carefully took out the left side. He prepped the piece and very carefully inserted it into Tim's head. Tim's heart rate began to climb and Reid looked to the anesthesiologist.

"Are we okay?"

He nodded okay and Reid continued. Two hours later, Reid had successfully completed the left side. He took a small break while the team relocated the microscope and laser to the right side; the process was very time-consuming and intense. Reid noticed as he came back in that some of the onlookers and selected members of the press had gone from the viewing area. Reid really didn't care about the publicity as much as the outcome of a cure. This was an event like no other. He was just glad to be a part of it.

At home, Sue was getting anxious about the surgery. It had been hours since Reid's last call. The kids were in bed and she was stuck there with no information. She wanted to go to the hospital and wait for an answer, but couldn't. She resorted to reading and working around the house. Sue ventured into Tim's office and began looking through papers on and around his desk. There was nothing there of any importance. Tim had cleaned out and thrown away everything. She turned on his laptop and waited for it to boot up. As she sat back in his chair, she looked around the room. She had so much to do. Moving without the help of Tim would be brutal. What to throw away and what to keep? How much of Tim's life to erase from existence? She was overwhelmed in the moment of all the change that had to take place.

The laptop dinged and the screen came up. She looked and there in the center was the log on icon with a blank space for a password. She had no idea what it might be. At first she just hit enter to see if there was one. The screen blinked and the password request remained. Sue typed in some of his usual ones. Nothing worked. Sue closed the laptop. That could wait for another day.

Sue heard a sound and Annette was standing in the doorway. "Any news yet?"

Sue stood and walked over to Annette. "No. I wish they would call. The silence is driving me crazy."

"Go down there, then. I am home. I can handle it."

"You are strong like me, aren't you, girly! I know you could handle it, but it won't do me any good. Dr. Hampton will call when they are done."

"Are you okay, Mom? Why are you in here?"

"I'm fine. Just looking at all the stuff we have to get rid of to move. You know your dad won't know anything when he wakes up. I am trying to figure out how much of his life I want to teach him about."

"I say none of it. Let's tell him he was a garbage man and you made all the money. That would be awesome."

Sue laughed. "Annette! Go to bed, you clown."

"I was just trying to make you laugh. It's been a long time, Mom. I miss you laughing."

She hugged Annette even tighter as she began to cry. It had been forever. For the last several years, Sue had felt so alone. Tim was never home and she handled everything. Sue longed for the day when Tim would be there to help her.

Sue kissed Annette on the top of her head. "I love you, Annette. Come on, I will walk with you to bed. It's late and you need to get some sleep."

They walked upstairs and Sue tucked her in and kissed her again on the forehead. Annette smiled and turned off her lamp. "Good night, Mom."

Sue closed the door and went into her room. She turned on the TV and lay in bed. It had been a really long day.

At Northside, Dr. Hampton was wrapping up the second half of the transplant. Everything had gone well so far, and Reid had even let Dr. Peavey work for an hour or so while he took breaks. The surgery was very fatiguing. Brain transplants are more specific than any other. Each section has to be aligned and attached with precision. Reid was one of the leaders in this field.

At 1:00 a.m., the surgery was complete. During the course of the surgery, Tim's heart had stopped twice, but was revived immediately each time. Each time the team reacted quickly and shocked him back into life. Reid stood back for the hour it took the anesthesiologist to slowly pull him back to the surface. They would keep him in a state of coma for the next 48 hours to give his brain a chance to begin healing before he tried to move at all.

Tim's vitals came in strong and he began to breathe on his own. Reid checked eye movement and muscle reaction and all checked out well. The surgery had been a success.

Reid stepped into the hallway with his cell phone and a cup of coffee at 2:20 a.m. He dialed Sue's number and waited for her to answer. One ring, two rings.

Quietly the phone picked up. "Hello."

"Sue, it's Reid."

Sue sat up in bed. "Yes, Reid, thank God, how did it go?"

"It went great, Sue. He is still in a coma now."

"What? Why?"

"It's, okay Sue, we put him there. We need him to stay still for the next few days until his brain starts to heal. Brain surgery is very invasive. It causes a lot of trauma to the brain. We don't want him trying to sit up just yet."

"I see. You scared me, Doc. Can I come see him in the morning?"

"I would wait one more day. He is in extreme ICU for tomorrow, but the next day I can get you in. We just don't want any chance of any infections right now. You understand. I will call you tomorrow and give you updates on his progress. The next 24 hours are the most critical."

"Everything went okay, though? No problems during surgery?"

"Nothing out of the ordinary, he did fine. Soon you will have a brand new Tim. Oh, by the way, he said to tell you that you were worth coming home to. I guess that means something to you, I bet."

"It does, Doc. Thank you for saving him. I hope I can thank you later for saving us."

"I am sure you will, Mrs. Billings. Get some sleep and I will call you tomorrow. Tim will be good as new soon. Good night."

Sue hung up the phone and fell back into bed. Relief flooded her body. She pulled her pillows in tight and closed her eyes. Sleep took over quickly and she dreamed of better days coming.

Recovery

Chapter 12

The next morning Sue got the kids off to school and headed for the hospital. Reid had said not to come, but how could she stay away? She was afraid to call Reid, thinking he may still be sleeping from the late night. She got to the hospital and headed for ICU. She didn't know if there was a separate "extreme ICU" as Reid had put it last night or not. She followed the signs and walked onto the fifth floor ICU. There was a waiting room and a phone on the wall. Everything else was locked off by automatic doors. Sue looked in the waiting area, but it was empty. She stared at the phone, knowing she would not be able to go back and see Tim. She stood there for fifteen minutes, hoping a nurse or doctor would come through so she could ask. No one ever did, so she picked up the phone and it started ringing.

"ICU, how can I help you?"

Sue froze for a second.

"Hello, is anyone there?" the voice continued.

"Yes, I am Sue Billings."

"Yes, Mrs. Billings, how can I help you?"

"My husband is somewhere in the ICU. I wanted an update or to see him if I can."

The nurse hesitated. "He is on the No Visitor list. Apparently, he came in late last night. I'm sorry I can't let you back here now. I suggest you call his doctor for an update. I have his number here I can give you."

"I have it. Thank you."

"I'm sorry, ma'am. I wish I could help."

The phone went dead. Sue hung up, walked into the waiting area, and sat down. She had been so mad at Tim yesterday, but today she truly felt lost without him. The not knowing was killing her far more than she thought it would. She sat in the waiting room for almost an hour, trying to get the courage up to call Reid. Several people had come in and were waiting to go back to see their loved ones. They were clearly families full of love and concern for each other. Sue sat alone, watching the other families, and thinking how she hoped her family could be that way one day.

Sue's cell phone rang. It was Dr. Hampton. "Yes, Reid, how is Tim?"

"He is doing well. I am checking his vitals and incisions now. Everything is looking good. How are you doing?"

"I'm good. I am up here too, in the waiting room."

"In the waiting room? Sue, I told you it would be 48 hours before you could see him. Why did you come?"

"I don't know Reid, I'm lost!"

Reid was silent for a moment. "Where are you?"

"Fifth floor waiting room. I just wanted to know. I don't know why I came."

"Give me a minute and I will come get you. We can talk."

Sue paced the floors as she waited on Reid. The other families made small talk with her and each other. She could not imagine why it was taking so long. The hospital was not that big. Even if he was on another floor, why would it take this long? Sue finally sat back down, taking out her cell phone and checking the signal. Where was he?

Reid walked up to the door but he didn't come in. He motioned for Sue to follow him. They walked to the elevator and got in. Reid had clothes in his hands. Sue was completely confused.

The doors closed and Reid pushed the button for the basement. "Put these on quick."

Sue took the scrubs. "What? Here?"

"Right now. You want to see Tim?"

Sue looked shocked. "Turn around!"

Sue pulled her shirt off and put on the top, then pulled her jeans off and quickly put on the bottoms. Both were about two sizes too big, and she began to laugh.

"Geez, Reid, what do you think, I'm fat?"

Reid turned to look slowly, she was holding the bottoms up and the top was so loose her bra was showing. Reid made a face.

"You look like a slob!" He grabbed the drawstring on the pants and pulled them tight. This bunched up the waist all around Sue.

"Great. Now I look like I am wearing hand-me-downs."

"Sorry, it's all I could grab without getting seen. It will be fine. I can fix this."

Reid turned Sue around and started pulling all the extra fabric to the back of her pants. Just about then, the elevator dinged and stopped. The doors opened and there stood an elderly man. Reid looked at him and the man hesitated. Sue threw her hands over her face.

Reid smiled and hit the "door close" button. "How about leaving this one to us, young man," Reid winked at the old man as the doors closed.

The old man just smiled and waved as the doors closed.

Sue let out a cry, "Oh my God! I can't believe I am doing this."

Reid spun Sue around. "Come on, we don't have much time. What about the top?"

"It's huge!"

"Okay, we need a safety pin or something."

He pulled the top by bunching the material up in the back, making the front look tighter. He twisted the material in the back into a roll. Reid told Sue to hold it and let him take a look. She looked pretty good, considering.

"Okay, now put this on." Reid handed her the white surgical coat and she slipped it on while Reid held the wad of fabric in the back. Reid picked up her clothes and handed her back her purse. Sue took over, holding the wad of fabric at her back.

"Now you look like a doctor. You're here to see the patient, that's all. Got it? Just let me do all the talking. You're a research assistant from Emory."

"Okay."

The doors opened and they were in a basement corridor. "Are these expensive jeans?"

"No. Why?"

Reid threw them in the trash can. "You just came from Emory, that's why. Already looking like a doctor. Do you have your driver's license?"

"Yeah, of course. What are we doing down here? Is he in the basement?"

"No, Security is, and you can't get to where Tim is without a badge. I'm already breaking the rules letting you see him, is lying to security really gonna matter."

"You have got to be kidding me. I can't answer any questions for these guys. I also don't want to jeopardize Tim. Are you sure this is okay Reid?"

"They don't pay that much attention. I will do the talking. Just look like you are out of time and need to hurry. They won't ask you anything. It will be fine."

"I think I might throw up!"

"Can you wait until after we get your badge?" Reid smiled.

They walked down the busy corridor and into Security. The receptionist asked how she could help and Reid asked for a temp badge for Dr. Billings, one of his assistants from Emory. Sue smiled at the lady.

She smiled back. "Can you sign in, Dr. Billings?"

Sue did and the lady told them to wait while she got a badge. Reid said they would and the lady walked away from her desk. Reid reached down and took one of the black paper binders off one stack of papers sitting on the girl's desk. He turned to Sue and reached under her white coat, clipping the wad of fabric Sue was holding with her left hand. She let go and the top stayed in place. Sue smiled, and Reid smiled back.

In a few minutes, the lady came back and asked for Sue's ID. Sue showed it and the lady handed her a badge. "Just return it here when you guys are done." Reid took the badge and handed it to Sue.

"We sure will. Thanks for your help."

Reid turned, took Sue's arm and headed for the door. As Reid held the door for Sue, he looked back at the lady who was picking up the stack of papers now missing its clip. She looked up at Reid and he smiled and walked through the door. As he got into the hall, he laughed and so did Sue.

"I can't believe that was so easy."

Reid held his finger up to his lips. "Well, Dr. Billings, life should not be so hard. Sometimes you just need to know what you're doing first. Now, let's go see our patient."

Sue smiled. "Doctor, lead the way. I need to evaluate your surgical methods on this patient!"

"Right this way, Doctor."

They both laughed and headed for the elevator with Sue adjusting her outfit here and there to look more professional. They went back up to the fifth floor and Reid hit the buzzer. Once again, the nurse came on, asking if she could help.

"Dr. Hampton and my associate, we are here to see my patient, Billings."

Sue looked panicked. "Reid, I spoke to her earlier and told her I wanted to see my husband, Tim Billings. She will know it's me if she looks at the badge."

"Relax, she won't look. Just stay professional in here. No touching Tim. I am taking you to see him. Remember he looks a little scary. His head is shaved and bandaged, so keep your cool. He's fine."

The door buzzed and Reid pulled it open. "Stay cool."

They went in and the nurse looked up. Reid waved and they walked right past her without any problems. They stopped at the outer doors and put on gloves and masks.

Reid looked at Sue one more time. "You ready?"

"I am. Let's do this."

They walked into the ICU and back to an isolation room where Tim was. He was lying there with his head bandaged; a breathing tube in his mouth, IVs in both arms and monitor wiring all over the place. Sue's eyes began to water.

Reid touched her elbow and whispered. "Keep it together now. Remember, he is fine."

Sue smiled. "I know. I will."

Reid pointed at the bandage. "Doctor, we made our incisions here and here. We removed the hippocampus sections of the brain that are responsible for long-term memory in the brain. They also produce the cancer cells in the brain. We used a donor brain to replace these sections."

Sue looked puzzled. "Doctor, explain how you clear the memory of the donor brain so the patient won't wake up with existing memories of the donor?"

Reid smiled. "That's a good question, Doctor! We perform mild shock to the donor brain, which erases all existing nodules storing memories in the brain without damaging the hippocampus. New nodules will form and begin storing new memories."

Sue nodded. "I see. So how long is the recovery time with this type of surgery? How long before the patient can begin rehab?"

"Recovery is about three weeks. During the three weeks prior to rehab we will begin some minor rehab in bed. After that, we can move the patient to our rehab center and begin to reintroduce his family and friends to him. Often it helps patients during that time to be around family as much as possible. It gives the patient hope. Makes them want to get better and work hard to get back home to people that love them."

"I am sure it does. I would think this patient's family would be glad to see him and want to help him learn all about them."

"I am sure they will."

A nurse came in and excused herself while she checked Tim's vitals and all of the equipment. Reid motioned to cover her badge as the nurse was checking his bed pan. Sue crossed her arm covering her badge.

Sue smiled at the nurse. "How are you today?"

"Fine."

She finished her round and headed out of the room. Reid smiled. The two stayed with Tim for another few minutes and then Reid motioned to the door.

"We better head back over to Emory, Doctor. This patient will be in this coma for at least one more day. Then maybe we can move him over to the ICU area where family can visit on a limited basis."

Sue smiled. "That would be good. Let's head out, Doctor."

They walked out waving again at the nurse on the way out. They got to the elevator and went in. When the doors closed, Sue hugged Reid hard. She thanked him repeatedly for taking her to see Tim. She felt so much better being able to see his face, hearing his heart beat on the monitor. Knowing he was now recovering.

They signed out at security and Reid walked Sue to her car. "Sue, it will be a few weeks before Tim is really ready for family time. His memory will not hold anything until the tissue in his brain heals. The nerves and nodules in his memory have to reconnect for the long-term memory to begin storing anything. Do you understand?'

"I do. I just want my husband back. I miss who he was so much and now that I am on this side of getting that I can't wait."

Reid smiled. "I know; you will have him soon. Trying to rush that will frustrate Tim, though. He will see the disappointment in your eyes every time he doesn't remember you. Be careful. Stay positive and upbeat every time you are with him. Eventually, he will begin to remember. It may take a while. Best case is two or three weeks, but it could be longer."

"I understand. It will be hard at first, but I can do it."

"Good. Now, go home and take care of those kids. I will call you when he is awake and let you know how things are."

Sue hugged Reid again. She thanked him for being such a good friend to her. He had become more than just a doctor. She hoped she, Tim, and Reid could be friends forever.

Tim woke up three days after being paralyzed, blinking and trying to understand where he was and who he was.

Reid stood over him, smiling. "Tim, can you hear me?"

Tim focused on Reid. "What?"

"Tim, try and relax. I am Dr. Reid Hampton. We just did surgery on you for a brain tumor and cancer. Everything is fine, but your memory has been affected; erased actually. We are here to help you and make things better. Do you feel okay?"

Tim was trying to understand what had happened to him and he couldn't remember anything. His mind was blank. Anxiety began to flood his mind and Tim felt overwhelmed by the complete feeling of not knowing what to do. He began to reach for the bed rails to sit up. Reid put his hand on Tim's shoulder and asked him to stay lying down for now.

"Sit up," Tim said.

"I know you want to, Tim, but please just go real easy for now. Let me explain a little more to you. We removed the part of your brain that stores and creates long-term memories. We transplanted new in its place. Now, it will take several weeks before you remember things. We are going to put a whiteboard at the end of your bed that will help you when you wake up for the next week. This is the hardest part. The cancer you had is gone and you are much better than you think. In a few weeks, you will be good as new. Try and just relax, I know it might be tough."

"Doc, did I get here? I don't anything know. Is my name?"

Reid smiled. "Your name is Tim Billings. You're married and have two kids. I am sure they will be glad to see you. They will help you remember everything you need to. Your speech and things will get better with time."

Tim sighed. "I don't remember Doc, everything."

"Anything, you don't remember anything."

"Yeah, that."

"It's okay Tim. You will. For the next few weeks, you will continue to forget everything until your brain begins to heal back and the neurons reconnect. In fact, you won't even remember that in a few hours. It's okay. We will help you through it. Do you have any headache or numbness at this point? Can you move your legs for me?"

Tim moved his legs. "No headaches. What is numbness?"

"Tim, that's great. You came in paralyzed, so we are doing very well. Let's check for numbness. That is when you can't feel anything. I am going to touch you around your face and neck. You tell me if you feel it."

Reid took out a pen and began to touch the cap on Tim's forehead. Tim said yes. Then his cheek and so on. At Tim's neck, he didn't respond. Reid touched again, nothing from Tim. Reid continued, finding the numbness at Tim's neck and shoulder area. Tim looked concerned.

"I don't feel that."

"It's okay, Tim. It will come back. We cut into the side of your head and at the back to remove the tumor. We cut through some nerves, but they will grow back with time. Let's go ahead and sit you up a bit, okay. I will raise you up with the bed. Just relax."

Reid began to raise the bed and Tim smiled as he sat up. "That feels."

Reid stopped. "That feels what?"

"What?"

"What do you feel?"

"Good!"

"Oh, you feel good."

"That's what I said."

Reid smiled. "Not really, but it's okay. I am glad that feels good to sit up."

Reid continued to check Tim and help him begin to make sense of his life. Several times during the conversation, Reid went back to why Tim was there. He didn't remember. Reid just laughed each time and explained again. Tim had come through the surgery just fine. In the next few weeks, his brain would heal and he would begin to start remembering.

The next week was very frustrating. Tim's recovery was very slow. Sue went each day but Tim didn't remember anything about her visits. Reid explained this was normal. The transplant had to reconnect itself to all the inner workings of the brain. He kept encouraging her and she kept coming.

Each day she came, he would smile as she came into the room. He knew how to speak but forming sentences was hard. Words were out of place and he was truly a blank page. She would tell him she was his wife and he would ask what that was. Every day, Sue would laugh and explain.

As they talked, she could see him searching his mind for what to say. She would try and help, but the conversations were slow.

After the first week, Tim was moved to a regular room for the first time. Sue came in as they were getting him settled. Tim looked up and saw Sue. "Hi, lady girl!"

Sue laughed. "It's hi, ma'am, or hey lady. Not hi, lady girl. Lady is an older woman, girl is for young women."

Tim looked sad. "Sorry, I memory not right."

Sue sat on the bed. "It's okay, Tim, I am your wife and I love you. I will help you get better."

Tim looked puzzled and Sue expected to explain again what a wife was. "Do I love you?"

The question almost knocked Sue over. She reached and held Tim's hand. "Yes, you do, very much."

Tim smiled. "Is that for me, good?"

"Yes Tim, that's good for you. Love is very good and I have loved you for a long time. I will take care of you."

"Thanks you!"

Sue laughed and patted Tim's hand. "Do you remember me being here yesterday?"

Tim smiled. "You were here yesterday? Was I?"

Sue giggled and scooped up some Jell-O off the tray and started to feed him. "Yes, we were both here. I will be here every day until you get better."

"Yeah, I'm here, why?"

"You had a tumor and cancer, but they made you all better now."

"Are those bad?"

"Yes, they are."

The days went on and on like this. Sue left crying many days. It was so hard to go day after day and Tim not remembering anything from the day before. Reid was in often and he and Sue would talk about hanging in there. Reid told Sue that even though she didn't think it was helping, it was. The primates reacted and began to remember better when the same trainer worked with them every day. Reid explained the brain was very resourceful, and when one part is damaged, the surrounding areas will begin to take on functions to help recover. Sue just wanted to walk in one time and have Tim remember her.

Finally, Tim was transferred to the rehab facility. It was on the north end of Atlanta and Sue began to look for houses north of that part of town to buy. Their house was on the market already, and hopefully there would be a buyer soon. She had already decided to just pay cash for something when she found it, and move. Selling their house could happen faster with it empty. She didn't want any of his friends coming around looking for him, anyway. If she had to explain, they might try and contact him later. Sue had decided after talking to Reid that first day a clean get away was best.

She walked into the rehab facility and told them who she was. They told her Tim was in the common area playing and socializing with other patients. There was everything in this rehab facility, from quadriplegics to severe brain injuries, plenty of people for Tim to sit and talk with for hours.

She walked into a large room full of exercise equipment and floor mats. The walls were very plain but the view through the back windows was of a beautiful lake. Attendants were working with both men and women. Tim turned to look at her. He smiled and waved. Sue's heart jumped as she walked toward Tim.

Tim stood up. "Don't know you?"

"Do you mean, 'Don't I know you?' And, yes, you do know me, Tim. You do know me."

She hugged Tim. "You're from the hospital. I know you there."

Sue laughed. "Yes, you do. I came to see you every day. I am your wife, Tim."

Tim smiled. "That's good for me. You're pretty."

Tim turned to the man in the wheelchair he had been talking to. "She's wife! My wife."

The man smiled. "That's good, she is a beautiful lady. You're very lucky."

Sue took Tim's hand. "Come on, let's sit and talk. Tell me what else you remember."

They sat on one of the couches in a quiet area and began to talk about everything he could remember. He explained there was a doctor he saw all the time. He couldn't remember Reid's name, but he did know he was from Emory. He remembered Sue, but still was not sure what a wife was. Sue laughed at that, thinking what fun it would be showing Tim at some point what sex was.

They talked for an hour until it was time for his therapy session to begin. Tim's hair was growing back now and Sue touched the side of his face when it was time to go. He smiled at her and held her hand on the side of his face.

"I love you, Tim."

Tim sat there not responding. Tears began to rise in Sue's eyes. "What's wrong, Sue?"

She smiled through the tears. "Nothing, getting your memory back may be tougher than I thought."

Tim frowned. "I'm sorry, I memory is bad."

"My memory is bad." Sue said wiping tears away.

"Huh, you have a bad memory, too?'

Sue laughed. "No, you said 'I'm sorry I memory is bad.' It would be: I'm sorry, my memory is bad. It's okay, don't worry. You remembered me, that's huge."

Tim smiled. "Will you come back tomorrow? I don't like you come."

"I hope you like it when I come?"

Tim shook his head. "Yes. That's what I meant. The get words confused."

Sue laughed. "I understand. Yes, I will come back tomorrow. Will you remember me?"

Tim smiled. "Oh yes. You're my wife and you smell . . ."

Tim stood perplexed and Sue looked at him waiting. "Good!"

"Huh?"

"I smell good!"

Tim nodded. "Yes, you smell good."

Sue hugged Tim and kissed him on the cheek. "I love you, Tim, I will see you tomorrow."

"Okay. I will see then."

Tim went with the nurse and Sue stood watching him shuffle away. He was still learning to walk and his speech was in need of some major work. What a funny sight it would be to put him in front of a jury now. Tim waved as they went around the corner and Sue waved back.

She felt fantastic today. He had remembered her. She pulled out her cell phone and called Reid immediately. She got his voicemail and left the message. "He remembered me today, Reid! Call me."

Sue hung up and went looking for houses. She was smiling the entire time. Today had been the first day Tim showed real improvement. Now Sue felt like life would begin to move forward. To get better and better every day.

Later that night Reid called back. "Hey, Sue, so he remembered you today; that's fantastic news!"

"Oh, Reid, it was great. I walked in and he waved at me. He just remembered that I was from the hospital, but it was great."

"That's terrific, Sue. I am very glad for you. It will get better. Just keep going. I will go see him next week. We have to start testing him for cancer now to make sure he is still cancer free. Once we do, it will be official. He will be the first person to have been cured of cancer with no treatment like chemo."

"You'll be busy then, Doc!"

"Gosh, Sue, I already am. I have been speaking all week at different locations. Two more procedures are scheduled for next week. It's really great, what's happening. Tim will be famous."

As the words left his mouth, Sue felt panic rush through her. "Famous." That is not what she needed. She wanted to disappear, not to be famous at all. The last thing she needed was for Tim to be plastered all over the news.

"Reid, I don't want his name used when it hits the news. I don't want his past to find him. I don't want anybody from his past trying to find him."

Reid was quiet. "I understand. I will keep his name out of it as much as I can. Hopefully the media will just pick up the story once it breaks and not focus on Tim. I didn't think about this part of it on the front end when we talked about your situation. Don't worry for now. We will figure it out."

As they spoke Sue was in Tim's office shredding paperwork, erasing his past and everything she could to keep him away from it. It would all be for nothing if his name got plastered all over the news. She pulled open his bottom drawer and saw the bottle of Scotch. She opened it, smelling the bitter butterscotch scent. Sue poured some in her empty coffee mug. Sue sat back and slowly sipped the scotch, feeling its warmth as it went down her throat. She leaned back in the high backed chair, wondering if she would ever escape his life. It didn't seem to matter what she did, trying to erase someone was hard. Maybe she needed to look further away from Atlanta. Maybe up north, or somewhere in California might be better. At least there, no one would make a drive over to drop in and see him, even if he was in the news.

Sue finished shredding the paperwork along with the glass of scotch. She headed to bed and tried to forget the day's troubles.

Tomorrow she would go see Tim again and start looking for houses in other states. She would fight hard to get away from this life. She would fight to get the husband back she had lost so many years ago. Nothing would stop her from having what she wanted this time.

The New Tim

Chapter 13

The next three weeks Sue spent going back and forth to the rehab center, visiting Tim. His speech was improving and his motor skills were almost back to normal. Reid had been in several times, checking his memory and the healing process from the surgeries. Tim's progress was great. He was remembering Sue now, and understanding she was his wife. He had progressed from just remembering her from the hospital, to knowing things about her, things Sue had told him. She had begun to tell Tim about the kids and he was nervous, but wanted to see them.

Sue had decided to buy a house in the North Georgia Mountains and was busy making a new home for all of them. She would tell Tim they had moved there when he got sick but nothing else. The kids were getting adjusted but weren't that happy with the new surroundings yet.

Most days, Sue was home waiting for the kids to get home from school. Most everything of Tim's was gone now. She kept his degree from Georgia but trashed his law degree and everything that had to do with that career. She decided not to tell him about being an attorney. She wanted him to do something less stressful with his new life, whenever that would be; something that didn't require any travel.

The kids were getting adjusted to their new schools; however, up in the mountains of Georgia the schools were very different than in Roswell. A little more "redneck," as Annette was glad to point out whenever they talked about it. The house was beautiful and overlooked the Blue Ridge

Mountains. The bad economy in Georgia had made the house a deal, and Sue had the cash to grab it up when it went into foreclosure the month before she really started looking.

Sue took a position in town with one of the older lawyers, who was looking to retire in a few years. Divorce and lawsuits are not absent in small town USA, either. It was not what she really wanted, but it was a living, and would suffice since she was able to pay cash for the house. She had traded Tim's car in on a nice pickup truck and her BMW in for a Jeep. She had always wanted one, anyway, and now there was no one to say no. Sue kind of liked making the decisions for a change. Tim had always been so in charge of everything. Now it was Sue's turn, and she liked it.

The house was two stories and she set the kids' rooms up in the basement. The house came with a pool table and a nice Jacuzzi on the deck. It had been a rental property for the first five years. The owners never really did anything special with the place, so Sue was enjoying a little yard work now. Upstairs was the master bedroom and another bedroom which Sue had turned into the study. It had a nice big living room area and a good kitchen. She hired one of the local handyman guys to do some work getting the place livable on a full-time basis. The kitchen appliances were upgraded to stainless steel and she added travertine tile and granite to make the kitchen just right. All in all, it was smaller than the house in Atlanta, but it was perfect at the same time. It was secluded, and that's what Sue wanted the most. Not too many reporters would make the hour and a half drive up here to try and interview Tim, she hoped.

Reid, as promised, kept Tim's name out of the spotlight as much as possible. A few reporters interviewed Sue and Tim at the rehab center and the news did make the papers for about a week. It was a headline on the major networks for a while, but then it began to die down and for that, Sue was thankful. The old Tim would have loved the attention and grandstanded for sure, but the new Tim was a little shy and not so sure of himself. Sue loved it.

Reid began to talk to Sue about Tim coming home. "How are things going with you and Tim?"

"It's going great, Reid. Tim is really starting to remember more now and I have begun telling him all about the kids. He wants to see them, so Saturday we are all going down."

"Are the kids ready for that?"

"Jonathan sure is. Annette is still holding back; I think she misses him and wants the new Tim, too."

"I avoid talking about his past anytime I go see him now since he's remembering what you say. What is the official story going to be?" Reid asked.

"Well, I kept his degree from Georgia but I trashed the law degree. I don't think I am going to tell him he was an attorney."

"That's risky, Sue, what will you tell him he's been doing for the last 15 years then?"

"I thought I would make him a project manager for one of the construction companies in Atlanta that is now out of business. Makes it easy to explain why we can't find anyone he worked with, no reference checks. What do you think?"

"I think you're pretty scary! Sounds like a good plan. How's the new house?"

"It's great. The remodel work is done and it's very secluded. The driveway is about 600 feet long with a gate at the end, so, no surprise visitors. I think he will like it. Good place for him to recover; the view is incredible. You will have to bring your wife and come up for dinner sometime. I decorated the study with old contractor gear. I found an old surveyor's site in an antique shop downtown. I think it will help me sell the deal to Tim."

"I am sure it will, and my wife and I would love to come up sometime. Listen, Sue, let's talk about Tim's coming home. When are you going to be ready for that?"

"I can be ready whenever. Is Tim ready for that?"

"Not yet, but real soon. He is remembering things well now. His speech is back to normal and he is walking and doing things pretty well. I think about another week and we will be ready to start phase two of his recovery."

"Phase two? What is that? I never heard you say anything about a phase two before."

"Sorry, rehab term. Phase two is when we introduce the subjects back into their own habitat. Put them in to play with the other monkeys, so to speak. Tim is ready for some other monkeys, I think. I just wanted to give you a heads up so you could prepare yourself and the kids."

"I think we'll be fine, Doc. The kids are ready to have a dad for the first time in years. I think it will be good for Tim and for them. I might enjoy having a husband, too. Although I must say I have been in charge for a while now and I kind of like it."

"Well, I don't think he will be challenging you on that for some time. You have to teach him how to be a project manager first."

"Right, I think I'll just try and get him a job at the grocery store or Home Depot; something with no stress."

"Just don't let him get hit in the head for the next six months. We want everything to grow back completely before he takes a 2x4 to the head!"

"I think for the next year I am just going to teach him to be a dad and a husband. I can't wait to show him all about sex."

"Oh my God, Sue. Take it easy on him for a little while, okay? Too much of that too soon might break something."

"Really?"

"No, not really. He'll be fine. Nothing too crazy for the first few months, the last time you guys did that, as I recall, he ended up paralyzed. So be careful, huh."

"I will; gee, thanks for bringing that back up! I'll tell the kids tonight and we'll tell Tim this weekend that he'll be coming home soon. What day, do you think?"

"Let's say next Friday. That will give us just over a week to wrap up therapy and help Tim transition."

"That sounds great Reid, thanks for everything you've done."

"No problem at all Sue, you do realize, Tim is the first! We have checked his body and his blood work is completely cancer free. The cancer cells in his brain died within one week of his surgery. He is officially the first human to be cured of cancer."

"That's incredible, Reid. You must be so proud of your research and hard work and everyone in your department."

"I am. I have a great team. We will have an official ceremony at Emory in a few months. I would love to have you guys there, if you think it will be okay."

"I bet there will be press there, right?"

"I'm sure of it, Sue. I think if you answer questions and then disappear back to the mountains you will be fine, though. By the time it airs on the news you will be long gone."

"I hope so, Reid. I really don't want any part of his old life back."

"I know, Sue. He is such a different person now. So gentle and such a nice guy, he even hugs me every time I come in there. Was he like that before?"

Sue laughed, "No, I told him he was though, just to see if it would work. He hugs everyone now. It's really funny. I think he will be a great guy now."

"I am sure you guys will be very happy."

"Me too, Reid, thank you so much for saving my husband and my marriage. If we had not met you I would have lost both."

"I hate that it took cancer for Tim to realize what he had at home was worth saving, but I am glad he did. You're a great woman Sue; Tim is very lucky. Listen, I wouldn't be too worried about his past. He will be so out of touch over the next year, it won't matter much even if someone did find you. He won't remember them and he won't be that person they remember, either."

"Thanks. Reid. I am not as much afraid of his friends as I am of him. He had become someone I didn't want to live with anymore. I don't ever want him to become that man again. The money and power made him that way. His friends were just along for the ride, for the get out of jail free card."

"A lot of men let their egos get the best of them. He just let himself be a victim of that, but that's gone now. That person may never be able to come back, even if he wanted to. It was his life circumstances that made him that way, Sue. Those circumstances don't exist anymore. You control the circumstances this time."

"That's true. I think Tim and I will be just fine. We have enough money put aside to live for awhile. I will make enough so he may just stay home and be retired. Fish, and play with the kids. Fortunately, he won't have the pressure of earning a living for us like before."

"It sounds like things are headed in the right direction, Sue. Let's get him home to you so he can begin the wonderful life that awaits him."

"So, we will see you next Friday at the rehab center?"

"Yes, you will. Take care, Sue."

The phone went dead and Sue felt herself getting a little nervous. Tim at home would be the beginning of what would be. Hopefully, she and the kids could pull it off, and Tim would go on to live a great life. She wanted her old Tim back and the kids did, too. Even Annette had indicated that if he was like he used to be, she would be happy.

When the kids came home, Sue sat them both down to talk. Jonathan was anxious to go see him and Annette was still reserved. Sue explained the job details and why she didn't want him to know about being a lawyer. For Jonathan's sake, Sue said it would be too sad for Dad to try and get that life back, and that it would be easier if he thought he was a project manager. Jonathan bought in and Annette knew the real reasons. Sue smiled at Annette and touched her on the hand as they exchanged looks about the truth.

The next day, Sue went to see Tim again. It was Friday, and she would bring the kids on Saturday. He was remembering so much more now and greeted her with a hug and kiss. He still got an occasional word backwards or out of place and still forgot pieces of conversations he and Sue had, even the day before, but all in all, he was doing very well.

He took Sue around the center and began introducing people, explaining to her that it was part of his therapy. Remembering everyone's name was difficult and this exercise helped his brain grow. Sue laughed and told Tim she was very proud of how hard he was working. She asked him if he was scared of coming home. He admitted he was. He was very familiar with the rehab center and everyone there. Home would be all new with things he didn't understand. Sue reached out and took his hand as they walked along the path behind the buildings.

"I will help you with everything. I promise it will be okay."

Tim smiled and squeezed her hand. "I feel stupid, Sue. I don't know things. I don't know your kids."

Sue smiled. "Our kids!"

She took Tim's face in her hands and kissed him. He smiled at that and kissed her back.

He began to blush. "Sue, was I good at . . ." Tim's words fell short.

Sue looked at Tim's eyes. "Sex? You were fantastic and I am sure you will be again. Don't worry, baby; I will show you all about that soon. Where did that question come from?"

Tim smiled big. "I asked one of the guys about it. I didn't want to get alone with you and not remember anything."

"What! What did you ask him? That's embarrassing!"

Tim laughed. "I asked him what to do. I kind of had an idea, but I wasn't sure. I saw it on TV one night. We watch in the main room. This movie was on and they were having sex and I didn't know what it was. Frank and I were talking afterwards. He's the guy in the wheelchair."

"I remember. What did he say about it?"

"He said it was wonderful between a husband and wife. That our bodies were made for each other by God and that it felt wonderful. I think I want to try it soon. It looked like it would be fun in that movie. I don't know who God is, but if he invented it that's cool."

Sue started laughing. "It is wonderful, Tim. So, you don't know who God is? I don't know what to say to that."

"Who is he? What did Frank mean by, God made our bodies? I have a lot to learn again. I'm sorry, my brain is a mess. Will we be okay? I need to work and earn money, too. so I can help pay the bills, right?"

Sue took Tim's hand and started walking again. "No. baby, you took good care of us before you got sick. We have plenty and I have a good job. I think for awhile you are just going to be home and be with your kids and me. Don't worry about us. We will be just fine. I will tell you all about God, too."

"That's good. I think I would like to meet him and shake his hand."

"No, you don't, not for a long time, I hope. You can get to know him, though. There is a book all about him. I will get you your very own copy to read."

Sue and Tim walked around the lake and back up to the main building. Tim asked Sue question after question about their life. What he used to be and how they lived. With each question, she stuck with the story of Tim being a project manager.

"Do they want me to come back? I don't remember anything about the job. What kind of projects did I manage?"

Sue swallowed hard as it was her turn to lie. "You managed big construction jobs, but the economy went down, and the company went out of business because of all the money they lost. There is no job to go back to."

"How long have I been job lost?"

Sue laughed. "Job lost! You mean how long have I been without a job?"

"Yeah, sorry I still mess up words sometimes. How long?"

"Not long. The company went under a few months ago, but we were smart with the money, so we are good for awhile. You did very well over the years, a lot of bonuses, Mr. Billings."

Sue smiled, and Tim did, too. "That's good, huh? I am glad I was good at the job. What do you do?"

"I am an attorney."

"What's that?"

"An attorney represents someone in court."

Tim smiled big. "A lawyer! Joey said lawyers were like rats. I don't know what that means. Can you tell me?"

Sue laughed. "That means that there are a lot of lawyers in the world. There are a lot of rats, too, and rats are gross, disgusting little furry creatures. Lawyers are not always good."

"Are you a good lawyer, wife?"

Sue laughed. "You don't call me wife, baby. Sue, or honey, or baby is good, a pet name. Wife is just what I am. Yes, I am a good lawyer, a very good one."

"Maybe I could be one too, then. You could help me since you're one."

Sue coughed and choked. "God no Tim, that is a terrible idea. Being a lawyer is a lot of work and I don't even really like it that much. You are much better off trying to be a project manager again or something like that. Maybe if you try and do the same thing your brain will already know some things."

Tim smiled. "You're smart, baby. I'm glad you're my wife. I feel safe with you. Not so stupid. Thanks for helping me."

By this time, they were back up at the front of the building and Sue started to say goodbye. Tim had really gotten to a point that he hated when she left. He loved learning about his life from her. She made him feel good about who he was. How loving he had been to her and the kids. Tim was so excited about seeing the kids on Saturday. He wanted her to get back there as soon as she could. She told him again she would head up as soon as both kids were up and done with school work. Tim looked puzzled and asked Sue again what school was and why they had it on Saturday. She laughed and told him it was exactly what they had been doing for weeks now but just for kids. She explained that both kids had projects due and would need to work some on Saturday to finish them.

Tim looked puzzled. "They learn about who they are in school, too?"

Sue laughed. "No, they learn about the world and math and how to talk properly. They still have to become who they are going to be. You can help them do that. You were a great father before."

"I was? I am afraid, Sue. I am afraid I won't be a good dad now. I don't know anything to teach them. How can I make them better if I don't know anything?"

Sue took Tim's face in her hands again. "All you have to do to make them better is be there every day. Love them every day and make sure they hear it every day. If you can do that Tim, you will be a great father; better than most, in fact."

Tim pulled out the picture of the kids he carried with him everywhere since Sue gave it to him. "Well, that should be easy. Look at them. They're beautiful kids."

Sue began to cry. "Yes, they are, Tim. Just make them feel that way and you will be great."

Sue kissed Tim and said goodbye. He always stood at the window and watched her leave before he turned away. As he turned, his friend Frank was there behind him.

"Tim, you sure are lucky to have such a great wife. She comes to see you almost every day."

"I know, she is great, Frank. She is bringing my kids tomorrow. I'm a little scared. Should I be?"

"Come on Tim; let's go get something to eat. You help me with that and I will tell you all about family."

Tim and Frank went to the dining room and got their dinners. They picked a table where they could be alone.

Frank settled in at the table and Tim placed his tray in front of him. "Sue is great, from what I can tell Tim. She comes up here and spends time with you. A lot of wives wouldn't do that."

Tim looked puzzled. "Your wife won't come see you, Frank?"

Frank tilted his head a little. "No, Tim, she left me when I had my accident. She couldn't take the stress of having a paralyzed husband."

"I'm sorry to hear that. Why, Frank? You're a nice guy. Where did she go?"

"She divorced me. I don't know where she is now."

"What does divorce mean?"

Frank smiled. "I hope you never learn what that means, my boy. My point in telling you this is, she left not because I am paralyzed, Tim. She left because I was a terrible husband before the accident. I treated her like she didn't matter and when I needed her she couldn't be there. You make sure you treat your wife good all the time. You make sure you listen to her and take care of her. Women can be complicated, but if you just learn to listen, everything will be alright."

"I know how to listen, Frank, it's talking and remembering that give me trouble."

"Well, that's good, then. You listen to Sue and you will do just fine."

Tim looked sad. "Where will you live when you leave here, Frank? Who will take care of you and help you?"

Frank smiled. "I won't leave here, Tim. I don't have anywhere to go. My wife took everything after I was hurt and moved away. By the time I was out of the hospital, she was gone. This is my home now."

Tim stood up and hugged Frank. "Sue and I will come see you, Frank, all the time. We will be your family now. Okay?"

Frank smiled. "Tim, that would be great, but you will have your hands full getting to know your own family. I'll be fine. I have my own family of people right here. You just make sure you always take care of the people who love you."

"Okay, Frank, I'll do what you say. You have been a good friend to me here. I will come see you. I can take care of my family and add you to it, no problem."

Frank smiled and picked up his glass of tea. "Here's to family!"

Tim sat there not sure what to do. Frank nodded at his glass and then at Tim's. Tim picked it up and Frank clinked the glasses together. "To family!"

Tim smiled, understanding now. "To family!"

The two men sat there, eating dinner and talking about family. Tim decided he wouldn't be anxious about the kids coming. Sue had told him that he was a great father, so the kids would be glad to see him. They would help him remember everything about them. Frank really helped Tim be positive about his new life. Frank was older than Tim, and he had in a short time become a dad to Tim.

Tim went to his room that night and stared at the pictures Sue had brought, one of him and Sue, and the other of the kids. Tim lay in bed, searching his mind, trying so hard to recall any memory at all of them. As hard as he tried, nothing came. Tim closed his eyes, frustrated at the memory loss. He thought about Sue, and how wonderful she was to him. He wanted to be great to her. No matter how he had been before, he wanted to be great now. She deserved it. She was so kind and loving, so giving.

Tim fell asleep, excited about meeting his kids. Life was good and got better and better every day.

Meeting the Kids

Chapter 14

It was 6:00 a.m. Saturday morning, and Sue was already awake. She lay in bed thinking about the kids meeting their dad for the first time since his surgery. Panic ran through her, as she imagined the kids slipping about their dad's past. Tim questioning the lies she had told him about who he was, Annette pulling away when Tim hugged her. So many things could spin everything out of control. Had she really prepared the kids well enough? She tossed and turned in bed until seven and then gave up. She threw back the covers and got up. The house was cold this morning; 50 degrees outside, and it felt the same inside. Sue turned up the heat and made her way to the kitchen for coffee. She was glad spring was just around the corner.

In the kitchen, she began to empty the dishwasher and clean up. She started a load of clothes in the washer and then made some toast. She wanted to read the paper, but the long driveway made that a very chilling proposition on this cold mountain morning. It sure wasn't Roswell, where the paper was on her doorstep each morning. She turned on her laptop and sat at the table to eat. As she did, she heard Annette coming up from downstairs.

"Mom, why are you up so early making noise? My bedroom is right under the kitchen."

Sue frowned at her. "I'm sorry, baby. I forgot about that. I couldn't sleep, worrying about today. So I just got up. Do you want some breakfast since you're up?"

"Can you just be quiet and let me go back to sleep?"

"I can. I'm sorry I woke you up."

"It's okay. Why are you worried?"

Annette came into the kitchen and sat down at the table. "What's the problem with today, Mom?"

"I am just afraid your dad will somehow figure out I have told him a lie about who he was. Then he will question everything I say."

"We won't tell him. We don't want the old dad back. It will be okay, Mom, don't worry."

"Yeah, what if Jonathan slips and asks him why he's not a lawyer any more or something like that? Annette, he is still so young and doesn't know about keeping secrets yet. It's just a lot to risk. I told him he was a great dad and loved you kids very much. He doesn't know about the past."

"So, he won't know about it then."

"Okay. So what are you going to do when he tries to hug you today? That is what's going to happen. He hugs everyone now. He is going to expect that. If you pull away, he will wonder why."

"Okay, I won't pull away. I hated who he was, Mom. From what you've told me he is nothing like that anymore. It will be fine. Don't worry so much. Okay?"

"Easier said than done, I'm afraid. I just don't want to lose him again. I miss my husband, Annette. I want the daddy you used to run to so he would throw you up in the air, over and over and over. I want our family back."

Annette stood up and hugged her mom. "You will have it back, Dad will be home next week and we will be a family again. I'll make sure Jonathan doesn't slip up."

Sue smiled at Annette. "You're pretty grown up; do you know that?"

"Not that grown up, Mom. How about that breakfast? I'm all awake now, thanks to you."

"Why don't you go wake up Jonathan, and let's talk to him, too. We might as well just head to the city and see your dad early. You guys can work on school stuff later."

Annette let a woo who and bounced back downstairs. Sue started breakfast. She stood at the sink and looked out over the mountains, as the sun was breaking over the mountain top. It was going to be a beautiful day, and now she felt better about everything. Maybe it would all be okay. Annette and Jonathan came in and she hugged her son, who was still mostly asleep.

"Why are we up so early, Mom?"

"We are going to see Daddy today. Isn't that exciting?"

"Yeah, can we leave right now?"

"No, but you can have some breakfast with your sister and me. How do you want your eggs this morning, sir?"

"Scrambled, please." Jonathan sat down and put his head on the table.

"What about you, sweetie?"

"Sunny side up for me, please. Can I have some coffee?"

"No! You are way too young to drink coffee. How about orange juice? Make your brother a glass too."

"I am not too young for coffee. I had some at Jen's house before we moved. Nothing happened."

"Oh really? Who gave you coffee at Jen's house?"

"Her dad, we were helping make breakfast and he gave us a cup. It was good. Please can I have some?"

"No! I will have to have a talk with Mr. Wright about serving my child coffee. Jonathan, set the table for me, okay little man?"

"Okay!" Jonathan dragged himself up and crept towards the drawer to get the silverware.

Sue made a nice breakfast and the three of them sat down to eat. The house was peaceful and the view out the sliding glass doors was spectacular. The house sat at the crest of one of the taller mountain tops, so when the morning fog cleared, you could see for miles. Sue smiled thinking about how much Tim would like the view. It would be a great place for him to recover and learn all about life again.

Jonathan interrupted Sue's thoughts. "Mom, when is Dad coming home?"

"Well, we need to talk about that. You know we are going to see him today, right?"

"Yeah."

"Well, he is coming home next week. Do you remember what I told you about telling Daddy about his past?"

"Yeah, but why do we have to lie? You said I should never lie to you or daddy. I don't want to lie about who he was."

Sue's stomach turned as she looked at Jonathan. "I know, baby, and that is the truth, but we don't want to hurt daddy. He has been through a lot and he was a really good lawyer. It's easier to tell him he worked for a construction company that went out of business than to tell him he had to give up his career. You don't want to make him sad, do you?"

"No, but . . ."

Sue touched Jonathan's hand. "It's okay this one time to lie. Daddy needs all the help he can get to get better. If he asks you anything about what he used to do, just tell him you don't know. He won't push you about that, anyway. You teach him how to throw a baseball and wrestle. Okay?"

"Okay. I might even beat him wrestling if he doesn't remember anything."

"Oh, that might not be good. You need to take it easy, because Daddy had brain surgery. You don't want to hit him in the head!"

"Okay. Can I have some more eggs?"

Sue laughed. "You bet. Annette, how about you? Want some more eggs?"

"No, I want some more sleep. How long before we leave?"

"We can go as soon as you guys are ready. It takes about an hour to get there and visitation starts at 9:00."

"Let's just go then. I'll throw some clothes on."

Annette got up and started to walk away. "Annette, put your dishes in the dishwasher. What's wrong with you?"

"I'm tired. It's 7:30 in the morning."

"I don't care what time it is. You don't leave dishes on the table.

"Can I teach Dad that he always wants to do the dishes? That would be awesome."

"Get your stuff put away and go get ready. If not, I will teach him that he should spank first and then find out what's wrong."

"I would call DFACs on you."

"Really, want the number? Here, I have it in my cell phone. You can use mine. Tell them to come get you right away."

"Ha ha, you're real funny."

"You, too. Now go get ready. Besides, if DFACs took you today they would bring you back tomorrow and understand why we spanked you so much." Sue started laughing.

Annette finished her dishes and headed downstairs. Sue made Jonathan some more eggs and sat down beside him. As best she could, she tried to explain to her son that his dad had changed and their lives had changed because of it. The move to the mountains, not telling him about his past, all those things would help Dad move on with his new life and that was what was most important. Being part of Jonathan's life and Annette's was more important than what he used to be. Jonathan seemed to understand, but inside Sue was still nervous that he would slip up, being so young. Sue would have to distance Jonathan from Tim for a while until things settled down.

Jonathan finished eating and Sue took his plate. "Did you get enough?"

"Yeah, that was good, Mom. Do you want me to go get ready?"

"I do. It's cold out, so wear jeans and your white sweater. We are leaving in about thirty minutes, okay, so don't start playing. Get dressed and come upstairs and watch cartoons."

Sue stood at the kitchen sink staring out the window again at the beautiful mountains. The sun was up now and she could see the fog drifting across the range. So much had changed in the last few months. Tim, herself, their marriage, everything had changed. Everything was so fragile. Keeping Tim's life from him may be a mistake Sue thought. If he finds out it could ruin everything she had worked towards. Sue wondered if it would be better to tell him the truth and just teach him to be better. It really wasn't too late. She had trashed all of his things but she could just confess that she was scared and maybe he wouldn't want to try and reconnect with that old life. Sue was wrenching the dish towel so hard it began to hurt her hands. She noticed her white knuckles and let go of the towel. Sighing loudly, she put the last plate in the dishwasher and headed for her room.

She didn't know what to do anymore. All of this weight on her shoulders was wearing her out.

Sue got ready and came out to find Annette and Jonathan watching TV. "You guys ready to go?"

Annette turned the TV off and they headed for the car. Once they got on the road, Jonathan fell back asleep and Sue looked over at Annette. She had her iPod turned up and was staring out the window.

Sue tapped her on the leg. "Can I ask you something?"

Annette looked over and pulled an ear bud out of one ear. "What?"
"Can I ask you something about Dad?"

"Yeah, what?"

"Do you think I am making a mistake telling your dad he was a project manager instead of a lawyer?"

"I don't know. I sure don't want the old Dad back; do you?"

"No, I don't. I am so afraid something will slip out from one of us, or we will run into someone that knows him and he will find out. He would doubt everything I say then. Everything I have said. It would be very bad."

"He won't find out, Mom. There is nothing around him now that would make him question the past. Don't worry so much. We won't slip up. We don't talk to you guys about work stuff anyway. I don't even know what you do at work. I think it will be okay."

Sue patted Annette on the arm and she put the ear piece back in her ear. Annette turned and smiled at Sue and she did feel better about it. Annette was so much more grown up at twelve than she had been at that age. Another thirty minutes went by and they were pulling into the rehab center. Sue reached back and shook Jonathan to wake him up.

"Okay, guys, we are here. Are you ready for this?"

Jonathan, in his best "Rocky" voice, said, "Let's do it!"

Sue laughed. "How about you, Annette; you ready to go give your Dad a big hug and tell him you love him?"

Annette rolled her eyes. "Yeah, I'm ready."

"Alright, remember he doesn't remember anything about you guys, or me, or where we lived, except what I have told him, which is not that much. So, just be patient and show him that you love him. He needs to know we are ready for him to come home and be with us. He needs us to get better."

They parked and walked to the front entrance. They were earlier than she had told Tim, but Sue could see him standing in the common area when she came through the door. Tim turned and saw her. He looked surprised and scared to death all at the same time. He started walking towards them as Sue signed in at the front desk. Jonathan broke out in a run towards his dad. As they got close, Tim fell to his knees and Jonathan hugged him hard. Tim began to cry as he picked Jonathan up and walked towards Sue and Annette. Sue looked at Annette who was also crying and she began to lose it herself. As Tim got to them, Annette stepped forward and hugged her dad. The tears were rolling down Sue's face now and Tim leaned into her, telling her he loved her very much. Sue threw her arms around all of them and they stood there forever it seemed just hugging.

Tim whispered in Sue's ear. "Thank you for loving me. Thank you for helping me."

Sue pulled away, feeling like Tim knew the past already. "Why would you say that?"

Tim set Jonathan down and let go of Annette. "Because I think a lot of people would not be as good as you have been to me, if they had to deal with everything like you have. You are a good person and I think I am very lucky."

Tim smiled at Annette and Jonathan. "Are you guys hungry? They have good food here. I am very glad you're here. Your mom has told me so much about both of you. I wish I could remember. You will have to tell me all about yourselves. I want to know everything so I can be the best dad ever."

Annette hugged her dad again. "I will. I want you to be the best dad ever!"

Sue started crying even harder and turned and walked out the front doors back into the parking lot. Tim looked confused.

Annette spoke up. "She was really nervous about today. She'll be okay."

Tim smiled and touched Annette's face. "You are so smart, just like your mom said. I better go see about her. You guys come with me and I will introduce you to Frank. He is a really good friend of mine and he can show you around while I talk to Mommy, okay?"

Tim took them into the common area and introduced them to Frank. Frank was glad to show them around for a bit while Tim went after Sue. When he found her, she was standing by the entrance, trying to pull it together so she could come back inside.

Tim walked up quietly. "Sue, are you okay?"

"No, Tim, I'm not!"

Tim stood there not sure what to do. "Sue, I don't know what to do to help you. I'm sorry, I just don't know how to handle this right. I don't know what to say."

Sue turned and looked at Tim. "Tim, you weren't such a good dad before. You were never home. You were always working. I'm sorry I didn't tell you the truth, but I wanted you to be a great father this time, so I told you that you were. When I saw you loving the kids and so glad to see them, I just lost it. I haven't seen you act that way in a long time."

Tim reached out and pulled Sue close, wrapping both arms around her tight. "Sue, I don't know who I was before, but this is who I am now. I love you and those wonderful kids very much. I have thought about everything you have told me over and over. If I was something less than that, I don't want to know. I want to be who you have told me I was, not who I really was, if that was bad. Don't ever tell me any of it. I want to be good to you and them forever."

Sue hugged Tim so tight he almost couldn't breathe. "I love you, Tim. I love who you are. I don't ever want you to be like you were, ever again."

Tim drew a breath. "You're making me not breathe!"

Sue laughed and loosened her grip. "Sorry, don't die on me now."

Tim smiled and wiped tears off Sue's face. "I won't. I won't ever be a bad father to those kids again. I won't ever be a bad husband to you. Whoever I was before is gone, and I must have been pretty bad for you to be so scared."

Sue thought about her reaction to everything and how it was her, and not the kids, jeopardizing what she had told Tim.

"It's okay. You weren't that bad. You just worked a lot on the jobs. It kept you away from home and you were always tired, so you didn't have time for them like you will now. Everything will be great now. This cancer and stuff is the best thing that ever happened to us."

Tim smiled. "Well, I wish I could have not gone through all this, but I understand what you mean. Come on, let's go get the kids. I left them with Frank and there is no telling what he is doing with them by now."

Sue smiled and wiped more tears from her eyes. "Okay. He wouldn't do anything bad, would he?"

Tim laughed. "No, he is a great guy. In fact, I want to stay friends with him once I leave here. He has no family at all Sue. His wife left him when he got hurt. She is not good like you. I feel bad for him. Can we do that?"

"Of course we can, baby. We can do anything you want."

"I want to come home. Dr. Hampton just says soon. I'm ready, Sue, I want to come home now."

"Let's go find the kids and we can talk about that."

Tim began to hurry inside. "Did Dr. Hampton say I could come home now? Sue, tell me."

"Ask your kids. They can tell you."

Tim ran inside now searching for the kids. He went into the cafeteria and there was no sign of them. Tim thought about the TV room and grabbed Sue's hand as he ran by her.

"Tim, slow down, you might hurt yourself."

"Come on, Sue, I know where they are; the TV room. Let's go, I need to know."

Sue was laughing as they ran through the common area, Tim dragging her along like a kid in trouble. Once they got to the room, Tim couldn't wait any longer.

"Guys! When can I come home?"

Annette and Jonathan looked at Sue for approval. Sue nodded that it was okay to tell.

Jonathan spoke first. "Next Friday. They said you were ready."

Tim grabbed up Jonathan and began to chant. "I'm going home. I'm going home."

As he did, Sue noticed that Frank hung his head. She knew he was sad that it was not him going home. Sue walked over to Frank and put her hand on his shoulder. He reached up and patted her hand, understanding that Sue cared.

Frank looked up and smiled. "It's okay, Sue; I got over being left behind a long time ago."

When Frank said that, Tim stopped chanting and put Jonathan down, who was still in chant mode.

"Frank, I'm sorry I was celebrating right in front of you. That's not nice of me is it?"

"Tim, it's okay. I know families come and go here. I'm happy for you. You're a very lucky guy. No need to be sad for me. Celebrate, dance and shout out loud. I would get up and dance too, but my legs just won't listen to my brain saying get up."

Sue hugged Frank. "Thank you for being a friend to Tim. He has told me of several of your conversations. Some embarrassing for me, by the way."

Frank laughed. "It's okay. He needed some guy time. I was glad to help. You guys will have a great life. Sue, you are a real good person to stick with Tim and take care of him. I wish I had been so lucky."

"I know; Tim told me a little bit of your story. I'm sorry, Frank. Tim wants to keep coming to see you and I agree. I think that would be fun. You could even come up to the mountains sometime with us. It's beautiful there, I'm sure you'd like it."

"That's very nice of you, but it's hard for me to go anywhere in this chair. Mountain houses don't have ramps or elevators. I appreciate the thought, though."

Sue studied Frank for a second. "Why do you assume no one would care enough to make the effort for you Frank? What have you done in your life that makes you feel that you're not worth it?"

Tim stopped playing with the kids and turned to face Sue and Frank. "Sue, that's kind of a harsh question."

"It is, but I want him to know we aren't that kind of people, Tim."

Frank smiled at Tim. "Tim, it's okay. Sue asks real questions and I like that. Sue, my experience is that people say things like that but they really don't mean it. It's all superficial. The reality of my situation is tough to handle outside of a facility like this. Even restaurants that are supposed to be handicap-ready aren't. It's tough being like this. It's also okay. This is my burden to bear. I know you enough Sue to know you mean what you say. I would love to go to the mountains sometime. That would be nice."

"Well, okay then, once we get Tim all settled and things level out we will make arrangements."

Frank nodded and smiled. "Okay. Now, Tim, show your kids around this place."

Frank guided his wheelchair out the door and into the common area. Sue came over and kissed Tim. She took his hand and they headed towards the back to go walk around the lake. Sue took Annette's hand and Tim took Jonathan's. Tim was very happy. He could only guess that this was probably the happiest moment of his life. It certainly was, from what he could remember.

They walked around and talked about his coming home next Friday. He still didn't understand why he couldn't go home now. He felt good. His speech was back to normal and he was functioning on his own. Sue tried to explain that Dr. Hampton thought he needed one more week, but he didn't want to hear it.

"I want to call him myself. I don't need another week away from you guys."

"Baby, they have the whole thing planned so you will be the best you can be when you come home."

"I'm fine now. I just need to start learning about you guys now. I need to be home being a dad, helping you."

Annette let go of Sue's hand and took her dad's. "Daddy, don't fight with them. We're not going anywhere. You have the rest of your life to be with us. If they want you to stay, it must be for a good reason."

Tim looked at Annette as tears began to form in his eyes. He stood there speechless looking to Sue and then back at his wonderful daughter holding his hand. Letting go of Annette's hand, Tim bent down and picked Annette up. He held her in his arms hugging her, telling her he loved her very much.

Sue began to cry again, seeing the transformation in Annette. This once angry young girl was loving her dad beyond what Sue ever thought she would. Annette had shown a side that just blew Sue away. Jonathan stood there watching, not quite understanding all the emotion, so Sue reached out and picked him up as well. Jonathan smiled and kissed his mom, putting his arms around her neck as they continued to walk down the path. Tim never set Annette down as they walked. She went from his front to riding on his back as they walked. Annette and Sue traded looks several times, and Sue smiled huge at Annette. Annette could feel her Mom's approval every time.

For Annette, she truly felt like she had gained her dad back after all this time. She was happy for her and for her mom. They both had gotten what they wanted.

As the day ended, they returned to the main building. Tim had always hated when Sue's visits ended, but this time was the worst. He had gained his whole family back this day. He was so happy. His kids were more than he could ever imagine. He just wanted to get in the car and leave with them.

Annette hugged her dad again. "Daddy, I love you and I am so glad to have you back."

Tim got down on one knee to be eye to eye with her. "Me, too, sweetheart. I can't wait to be home with you guys all the time. I will talk to that doctor on Monday."

Annette stepped back, putting one hand on her hip and pointing at Tim, "Young man, don't make me ground you to your room. You do what the doctor says and don't be bad."

Tim started laughing and hugged her again. "Okay. Who taught you to be so tough? Did your mom teach you to be like that?"

Annette laughed. "No, you did!"

"Wow. I guess I was a tough guy before. I guess that's what being a good project manager teaches you, huh."

Sue coughed. "Yeah, it does. Okay, guys, we have a long way back. Let's head out."

Jonathan came over to hug his dad. "I love you, man!"

Tim busted out laughing and grabbed up Jonathan. He took Sue's hand and they started for the parking lot. Tim helped them into the car and blew kisses as they pulled out. He was standing in the parking space, when suddenly Sue put on the brakes and got out.

Sue ran back to Tim, throwing her arms around his neck. "I love you, Tim Billings, for everything you are becoming."

Tim squeezed hard. "I love you, Sue Billings, for everything you already are."

Sue ran back to the car and drove away. Tim stood there with tears rolling down his face until they were gone.

The Last Week of Rehab

Chapter 15

Monday morning, Reid was at the rehab center with a team of doctors. Tim met them at the door, ready to do battle. Reid began to talk about tests and procedures, and Tim interrupted with talks about going home right away.

"Good morning, Tim; glad to see you so ready to go."

"Doc, I am ready to go home. I want to leave today. I don't need to be here any longer. I can come to your office for these tests. Wouldn't that be easier, anyway?"

Reid studied Tim for a second. "Tim, I'm glad you want to go home. That's a good sign; but it's better if you stay here and let us wrap things up this week. You are going home on Friday. Did Sue tell you that this weekend?"

"Yeah, Doc, she did, but I miss being around my kids. I need to go home now."

Reid took Tim by the arm and led him into a small conference room to talk. Reid sat down and asked Tim to join him. "Tim, I know you are anxious to be with your family. It is completely understandable, but I need you to listen to me and try to understand."

"No, Doc, I need you to listen to me! I want to go home."

Reid leaned closer to Tim and put his hand on Tim's shoulder. "Tim, we have to take biopsies of your brain this week to make sure the cancer is completely gone. Do you know what that means?"

Tim looked puzzled. "No!"

"That means we are going to make a small incision and go in with a needle all the way to the center of your brain and take a small sample."

Tim's face contorted. "I think that would hurt me a lot. Why do you need to do that?"

Reid smiled and let go of Tim's shoulder, sitting back. "We have to do it to make sure there is no cancer. We will put you to sleep and then keep you sedated afterwards. It's better if we do that here. It's only a few more days. Just hang in here with me and maybe by Thursday we can get you home. How does that sound?"

Tim frowned. "Fine, I guess. I want to go home, Reid. I want to be with my family."

"I know you do, Tim. That's really good. A lot of patients that suffer severe memory losses are afraid to leave the familiar surroundings of rehab. It's good you want to be home. I know Sue will be glad when you are. I promise we will make everything as quick as possible this week. Are you ready to get started?"

"No. I don't want you taking a piece of my brain out. Can't you just draw some blood or something? Now I'm afraid for sure."

Reid smiled. "We are going to draw some blood and do some more X-rays as well. A lot of stuff this week, Tim, but it will go by fast. We will give you some good drugs for the bad parts. You won't remember much of that."

"Great, now I am taking drugs to forget. Alright, so what's on the list for today?"

"Well, today we are doing a lot of talking with a group of doctors. We will do some physical and motor skills tests in the gym and draw some more blood. They will ask you a bunch of questions and study the effects of brain transplants. You're a little famous. Everyone in my world wants to see the guinea pig."

"What's a guinea pig?"

Reid laughed. "That means we tried something new out on you and it worked. Shall we go?"

The two went back out and joined the other doctors. First, they went to the gym and began some of the physical testing, hand-eye coordination, as well as strength. After lunch, they began to test Tim's IQ levels. By the end of the day, Tim was exhausted. Everyone had left except Reid, who stayed to eat dinner with Tim.

"Well, how did I do? Did I pass?"

Reid laughed as they sat down at the table. "It's not really a pass or fail deal. You did just fine, though."

"Did you guys do any of these tests before the surgery?"

"Well, we would have, but you developed some complications that sort of rushed things along. Things don't always go as planned in this business."

"What sort of complications?"

Reid smiled. "Honestly, you had sex with Sue and you woke up paralyzed. We kind of skipped all the preliminary stuff we had planned and took you straight into surgery. Has Sue not told you about any of that?"

"No. I got paralyzed from having sex? Holy cow, Doc, what kind of sex causes that? I'll make sure I don't do that again."

Reid started laughing. "Sex doesn't cause that Tim, you're good to do what you want. Your problem was the tumor you had was already pushing on your spinal cord and that last night was the straw that broke the camel's back. We got you all fixed up, though. Good as new!"

"I'm glad we met, Reid. Sue has told me that what you did saved my life. I want to thank you for that."

"Tim, what we did to you will save millions of lives. When the FDA approves this procedure, we will begin to perform it on all brain-related cancer patients. It may even be a cure for all cancer. That's the next step in the process, to see what else works now that we know it worked on you. How does it feel to be the first?"

"I don't know, Doc. I just met my kids yesterday. I don't know how it feels to be a human, much less to be the first of some kind. A month ago, Doc, I learned how to go to the bathroom and what toilet paper was for."

Reid shook his head. "Oh, man, not at dinner, please."

Tim started laughing. "Come on, Doc. With some of the stuff that goes on in here, that's nothing. You should hang around here at night. There is less staff and some of these patients need around the clock care. It's gross. I am ready to be home."

Reid nodded. "I know you are. We'll try and rush things along this week. If you can take it, we will try to do multiple tests in one day instead of spacing them out. I will make the calls tonight and see what I can do. Is Sue coming tonight?"

"No, the kids had something at school and I told her I was testing today, so she will come tomorrow, if that's okay. She gave me a cell phone. I have her number programmed so I won't forget it. Numbers are still tough for me. I guess that's strange since I was a project manager and dealt with numbers all the time. I need to work on that."

Reid looked up from his plate. "That's right. Sue told you about your career before? What do you think about that?"

"What do I think about what? I don't remember it at all. I guess the company I worked for went under, anyway, so not much chance of going back to that. Sue said the construction industry was really slow, anyway. Maybe I will be something different this time. Maybe I can be a doctor. What do you think about that? I could work at Emory with you."

"Tim, I think that's a fine idea. You go through school and get your degrees and I will make sure you have a spot in the research department. That would be a great success story."

"Yeah, that would be cool, the first patient to get this procedure eventually performing the procedure on someone else. That sounds really cool."

"Yes, it does. So tell me about the kids. How did that go?"

"I was a mess, Doc. I was so excited and nervous about seeing them, but when they got here, all that went away. They both ran in and gave me a big hug and told me they loved me. It was the greatest day of my life, Doc. You should have been here."

"I would have liked that, I really would have. So both kids came in and gave you a hug. That's really great. Most kids are a little afraid when they see a parent in this kind of atmosphere. Sue must really be a great mom."

"She is, Doc; she has been amazing. She told me I wasn't always such a great dad, though. That bothered me a lot. Did you know that about me?"

"Well, Sue and I had several talks while you were out of it. She told me some. It doesn't matter now Tim. You aren't that person anymore. Just like the job thing. It doesn't matter who you were before. You can be anything you want to be now. You can be the greatest dad in the world to those kids and the best husband in the world to Sue."

Tim smiled at Reid. "You know, you're right, Doc. I can be anything I want to be now."

Frank rolled up to the table just about then. "Mind if I join you guys?"

Tim turned and smiled at his friend. "Sure, Frank. This is my Doctor, Dr. Hampton. Dr. Hampton this is Frank. He has been a great friend to me here." Leaning towards Reid, "He told me about sex, too, Doc."

Reid started laughing as he shook Frank's hand. "Well, good to meet you Frank. I hope you told Tim to take it easy for awhile."

"I did, Dr. Hampton."

"Please, just call me Reid. I am a research doctor. We're not so formal."

"Very good, Reid, you can call me Frank because I'm not formal at all. In fact I just shit my pants twenty minutes ago, nothing formal about that at all."

Reid laughed and the three of them ate dinner and talked about life around the rehab center. Tim felt good, like he had friends and he belonged. Dinner was soon over and Reid said his goodbyes. Tim knew tomorrow would be a scary day for him. Drilling into his brain with a needle didn't sound fun at all. That night he called Sue.

Sue answered on the first ring. "Hey, Tim, how did it go today?"

"Fine, Sue. I missed seeing you today."

"I know, baby, me too. I have gotten used to seeing you every day and I like it."

Tim was quiet for a minute. "Didn't you see me every day before?"

Sue froze, getting caught off guard by the question. "Well, yeah, almost every day. You traveled some with the old job, too. I meant I was just getting used to seeing you everyday now since the surgery."

"Me too. I don't know if tomorrow will be good or not."

"Why? I want to come there tomorrow and see you. What are they doing tomorrow?"

"They are putting a needle into my head to take brain samples. Reid said they would put me to sleep and then keep me subbed for the day."

Sue laughed. "You mean sedated?"

Tim laughed too. "Oh yeah, sorry I still get confused on some words. I may not remember you coming tomorrow."

"Do you know how many days I came to see you that you don't remember?"

"No. Was it a lot?"

"A lot! I will be there tomorrow no matter what. I don't care if you are out of it or not. I need to see my husband."

"I love you, Sue. You are everything to me."

Sue was silent on the other end of the phone. She was remembering their days of college when Tim had said that so many times to her. The night he proposed, he had said the same thing as he got down on one knee in the middle of the restaurant and gave her the ring. With those few words, she knew she had the old Tim back, finally.

Tim listened to the silence. "Sue, are you there?"

Quietly, "Yes, I am, Tim. I will always be here."

"What happened? You were silent for a long time. Did I say something wrong?"

"Tim, I haven't heard you say that in a very long time. It is so good to have you back."

Tim's eyes filled with tears. "I won't ever go anywhere again, Sue. I want to be home with you so bad, you and the kids. I can't wait to be there. Reid said maybe Thursday. Won't that be great?"

"Yes, it will. I am ready for you to be home. So are the kids."

"Tell Annette I only fought a little bit today. I was a good boy."

Sue laughed. "I will, but you will have to deal with her on your own. You broke the rules, now it's hell to pay."

Tim smiled. "I hope she doesn't ground me. I have a lot to see when I get out of here."

Sue and Tim talked into the night about the kids and coming home. Tim told Sue all about dinner and that Dr. Hampton had stayed. Tim told Sue how afraid he was about tomorrow. Any procedure that messed with his brain worried him; it made him wonder if he may lose memories again. Sue assured him everything would be fine. Sue asked Tim what time things would start and end so she could plan her day. She wanted to be there when he was finished. Tim told her that Reid had said things would begin around 9, and he would be back in his room by 6 that night.

"Gosh, Tim, that is a lot of time. Are they taking you back to Emory?"

"No, they are doing everything here. Reid said it was better that way so I was not traveling right after the procedure. I wanted to come home and just go there for everything, but he said no."

"Well, I will be there when you're done. I already have a babysitter for the night, so I will be there for sure."

Tim paused. "Sue, I will understand if you don't come tomorrow. I'll be out of it, anyway. It's okay if you stay home, I understand."

Sue frowned. "Do you not want me to come?"

"No! Yes! I mean, I do want you to come, but I will understand, is what I am trying to say."

"You need to go to bed, you confused man. I'll be there tomorrow. I don't care what you are trying to say."

Tim smiled. "Okay, I'm glad; I want you to be here. I'm going to bed now. I can't wait to see you again, baby. I can't wait to be with you in bed."

"Tim Billings! Are you getting fresh with me?"

Tim paused. "Huh?"

Sue laughed. "Are you saying you want to have sex with me?"

Tim blushed. "Well, no, but yes! I do want to have sex with you, but I meant I just can't wait to be next to you when I sleep. I want to know you are near me all the time."

Sue rolled over in bed cupping the phone close to her face. "I love you, Tim. I am so happy now."

Sue and Tim hung up and Tim turned off his light and closed his eyes. Sleep was quick to follow. That night for the first time, he dreamed of Sue. She was far away and Tim was running through sand to catch her. No matter how hard he tried, the sand would slow his run to a crawl. Tim yelled for Sue to stop but no matter how hard he yelled she couldn't hear him. Occasionally, Sue would turn to Tim and wave for him to catch up, but Tim could not. Eventually, Sue was out of sight and Tim fell to exhaustion in the sand. He began to roll down the hill, falling head over heels, gaining speed as he went down the hill. Each time he got face-up, he would look for Sue, but she was nowhere to be seen. Tim hit the bottom of the sand hill with a hard smack, waking up to find himself landing on the floor of his room, slamming into the floor with all the force with which he had been falling in the sand.

Tim gathered himself together, trying to figure out what that was he had just experienced. In a panic about losing Sue, he grabbed the cell phone and called her, not paying any attention to the time at all.

Sue looked at the clock to see 4:30 a.m. "Hello!'

"Sue! Thank God it's you."

"Tim?"

"Yes, it's me. Have I ever been to a place with lots of sand?"

"What? Tim, it's 4:30 in the morning. I don't know. No, why?"

"I don't know. I was asleep, but I was in a place with tons of sand mountains and I was chasing you but I couldn't . . ."

"Tim."

"I couldn't get to you."

"Tim, it was a dream and it sounds like you were in a desert."

"What is that?"

"A desert or a dream?"

"Both?"

Sue smiled to herself, realizing he had not had a dream yet, or at least one that he remembered. "Tim, it's okay. It's your imagination. Your mind is playing a trick on you. It's hard to explain. Can I try and explain tomorrow?"

Tim, now feeling bad for waking her, said, "I think it is tomorrow. I'm sorry I panicked. I didn't know what to do, so I called you. I fell out of bed and it woke me up."

Sue, very sleepily, "It's okay, Tim. Go back to bed. I will be there tomorrow."

The phone went dead as Tim said, "I love you, Sue."

Tim got back into bed, lying there staring at the ceiling for awhile. He had no idea what to think of the dream. He had never experienced anything like that. It terrified him to not be able to catch Sue. To lose sight of her in all that sand. To fall down the hill, all hope being lost. Tim lay there, afraid now to close his eyes, afraid of another dream and where he might land next time.

As the moments went past, Tim's eyes got heavier and heavier until finally he fell asleep again. This time, no dreams came, and he slept until the attendant came in to wake him. Tim sat up and began to tell her of the dream. She shook her head and told him that everything would be fine. This troubled Tim, that she felt she needed to comfort him after such a dream. Did dreams mean something, or were they just the mind's playground at night?

Tim got dressed and went for breakfast. As he made it to the cafeteria, Reid met him, explaining he couldn't have food this morning before the procedure. Tim couldn't understand, and became even more frustrated than he already was. Reid explained that the anesthesia would make him sick to his stomach, but Tim was barely listening as Reid spoke.

Reid stopped Tim. "Tim, what's wrong this morning?"

Tim met Reid's eyes with his. "I dreamed last night. It was terrible."

Reid began to laugh. "Tim, that is fantastic. We don't see dream behavior for months after a procedure like this. That is great news. Your brain is healing much quicker than we hoped. What did you dream?"

"I was in a desert chasing Sue. No matter how hard I tried, I couldn't catch her. I kept calling out for her, but she couldn't hear me. I ended up falling down a huge hill of sand. When I got to the bottom I woke up from hitting the floor of my room."

Reid's eyes got big. "Did you hit your head? Are you okay?"

"Yeah, I'm fine; but why would I have such a dream? Are all dreams bad like that? I feel terrible today. I called Sue at 4:30 in the morning in a panic because I didn't know if it was real or not. Doc, I don't want to have another dream."

Reid put his arm around Tim's shoulder. "Tim, it's okay. Dreams come from thoughts we have, fears or insecurities. The mind takes those inside thoughts and creates a reality in our dreams. Some can be very accurate and some can be completely random and make no sense whatsoever. Your dream is most likely because you feel inadequate with Sue. You are depending on her to teach you. You are chasing her and it is hard, like walking in sand. The dream makes sense, but it's not real, Tim. Sue would stop and help you. She would wait for you . . ."

Sue spoke behind them as Reid said the words. "I would wait for you where?"

Tim spun around, rushing to Sue. Hugging her tightly, he asked, "Sue, why are you here?"

"I couldn't sleep after your call. I tossed and turned and finally just got up. As soon as I got the kids off to school, I headed this way. Hopefully, the next time you have a bad dream, I will be in the bed next to you."

"It is so good to see you Sue. I was chasing you through the sand and you couldn't hear me at all. It was terrible."

"I know. Bad dreams are never good. I could hear the fear in your voice, so I wanted to see you this morning before the procedure."

Reid stepped in to hug Sue. "Sue, it's great to see you again. How are you?"

Sue smiled. "Reid, I'm great, anxious to get my husband back. Would you hurry up?"

"I'm trying my best. Tim, remind me sometime to tell you what your wife made me do at the hospital. She can be a little crazy when she wants something. You better prepare yourself. She will not take no for an answer."

Tim looked at Sue. "What is he talking about?"

Sue glared at Reid. "I have no idea. Don't believe everything you hear, Tim. People lie and I need to teach you about not believing everything you hear."

Tim hugged Sue again and turned to Reid. "Okay, I'm ready to get on with this."

Reid smiled back at the two of them. "Well, me too, but Sue, I'm sorry you can't go in with us."

Sue began to smile big. "You mean Dr. Billings; don't you, Doctor?"

Reid laughed and Tim looked confused. "Ha, ha. No, Sue, this time you can't go in."

Tim spoke. "What are you guys talking about?"

Reid grinned at Sue. "Say goodbye, Mrs. Billings."

Sue turned to Tim and hugged him hard. "I'll tell you the whole story later. I'll be here when you wake up. Don't worry; you'll be fine."

Sue kissed Tim and said goodbye. Reid pulled Tim by the arm into the procedure room and closed the door. Sue looked around at the common area and saw Frank. Frank waved, and Sue went over to say hello.

"Sue, we are going to have to stop meeting like this. Tim will be jealous."

Sue laughed and hugged Frank. "I know, right! How are you, Frank?"

Frank smiled. "As good as a paralyzed guy can be on a Tuesday morning. I will have to say, starting the day off with a hug from a beautiful lady makes it better than most. How about you? What brings you here so early? Is Tim okay?"

"He's fine. Just having a brain biopsy this morning and he had his first bad dream last night. He panicked and called me at 4:30 this morning. Frank, he really didn't know what to do. I felt so bad for him. I just had to come down and see him before he went in."

Reid came out to talk to Sue, interrupting the two of them. "Hey, Sue—excuse me Frank—I am glad you haven't left yet. I wanted to give you the rundown for the next couple of days."

Sue smiled at Frank and focused on Reid. "That would be great, Reid. Tim said he thought he might be able to come home on Thursday."

"I think so. Today is the last of the big tests. He will be out of it for most of the day, so if you don't want to stay, I don't think it will matter."

"I don't mind, Doc. I think Tim likes it when I am here. Frank will keep me company, she responded, looking back at Frank, and smiling.

Frank smiled. "My lucky day!"

Reid laughed. "Well, suit yourself. Tim will be out around four, but we will keep him sedated so he is not too active tonight. This procedure is pretty tough."

"So, why can't he just come home tomorrow then?"

"The other doctors here want to wrap up therapy and they kind of give a little party at dinner for the ones who are graduating. It's nice. You are welcome to come as well. Then, Thursday morning, we will discharge him and he is all yours."

"Okay, if that's how it has to be. I still don't see why he can't just leave after dinner."

"Go with Frank. Frank, would you take her out of here? Please!"

Frank smiled. "Sue, you are some kind of woman! I've got to say it again, Tim is so lucky to have you."

Sue blushed. "Thanks, Frank, but I'm just doing what I have to. Tim is a good man."

Frank looked puzzled. "Are you trying to convince me or you?"

Sue quickly looked into Frank's eyes with surprise at the question. "What do you mean?"

A Twist of Faith

Chapter 16

Frank motioned for Sue to follow him. They went outside and down to the walkway to the lake. There, by the water, it was quiet and there was a swing for Sue to sit in. Frank motioned to sit and Sue did so, reluctantly.

"Frank, did Tim say something I need to know about?"

"No, not at all, Sue. I thought maybe we should talk, and it's so nice down here. Don't you think so?"

Sue stared hard at Frank. "B.S., Frank. What's on your mind? What did you mean up there by the 'who am I trying to convince' statement? I don't like games, Frank."

Frank smiled at Sue. "Did Tim tell you what I used to do, or how I got in this chair?"

"No, he didn't. What did you used to do, Frank? What happened to you?"

"A year ago, I was a detective for the Atlanta PD. I was a hot shot cop! I made detective way before I should have and was all about the job."

Sue's stomach started to knot. "Did you get shot?"

"Nope. My partner and I were eating lunch one day at one of the sidewalk cafés downtown. I looked up and saw a guy we had been watching for a while. We never could quite get this guy. He always seemed to beat the rap, or be gone before the bad stuff happened. He was slick. When I looked up and saw him, he was walking with a known drug dealer."

"Wow, that's pretty lucky that you were right there. So what happened?"

"I hit my partner and pointed at the pair of them. He confirmed the drug dealer was on our wanted list and we might be able to get the other guy on a drug possession charge or something."

Sue was into the story now and had relaxed. Frank seemed glad someone was listening, and they had most of the day to kill. It was a pretty day and the lake was beautiful.

"So then what happened?"

Frank smiled at her enthusiasm. "We took to the chase! The two guys split up almost immediately. My partner took the drug dealer and I took the other guy. We were running down through the streets in heavy traffic. I was yelling 'Stop, police!' and he didn't care."

"Did you get hit by a car?"

Frank smiled. "Don't get ahead of the story, now. We ran into this parking deck. This guy was fast. I was doing my best, but he was getting away. I called in for backup and was hoping someone would show up before I threw up my lunch."

"Oh, that's bad, Frank. Come on, did you get the guy?"

"Well, he ran out of the parking deck and across a street into the loading dock of the building across the way. As I crossed the street in a full run, a little black 350Z hit me, doing about thirty."

Sue flinched. "Oh my God, Frank, that's terrible."

"Sue, I never even saw the guy. I went flying through the air. My momentum shot me almost to the entrance of the loading dock that the guy ran into. The last thing I remember when I hit the ground was seeing the suspect standing on the loading dock thirty feet away, laughing and pointing at me."

Sue was upset at the story. "Frank, that is unimaginable. I am sure the pain must have been unbearable."

"It was bad. I crushed two discs in my back, severing my spinal cord. Luckily, I passed out for awhile and couldn't feel a thing. My leg was broken and I was skinned up from head to toe."

"Did they catch the guy?"

"They did. My partner had lost his guy and saw me run into the parking deck. He doubled back and was coming down the street as we ran across. He cornered the guy in the loading dock and took him down."

"Oh that's good Frank. I hope they got something on him that would stick."

"Well, here is where the story turns. I woke up as my partner got back to me with the guy. Two uniform cops in cars arrived and were blocking the street by then. I was lying on the sidewalk, dying, while they read this guy his rights next to me. One officer was trying to help me, while my partner was making sure the arrest went right this time. The thing I remember the most about that day was lying there in the street, leg and back broken, thinking I was going to die."

"God, Frank, that must have been terrible. I can't imagine. I think I would have shot the guy if I could have gotten to my gun."

"Easy there, Dirty Harry! This ain't the wild wild west, you know."

Sue laughed. "I know, but being a lawyer myself, I could never represent that kind of person like . . ." Sue stopped her sentence.

"Like what, Sue?"

"Ah, like some lawyers do."

"Let me finish the story. So I am lying there. The ambulance was on the way and this jerk is looking at me the whole time he is being arrested. My partner got through reading him his rights, and do you know what he did?"

"No what? Took off running again?"

"No, he looked right at me and said, 'You ain't got nothing on me, cop. My lawyer will have me out of this in no time!'"

Sue stared at Frank, her stomach churning a little bit more. "So what happened next?"

"Well, I spent the next four months getting surgery and going through physical therapy. Got myself a nice new set of wheels to live in for the rest of my life, and saw the end of my career come and go."

"That's it? What happened to the guy? Is he in jail now? Please tell me after all of that, you got the guy?"

"His trial came up about six months later. I was a key witness to what happened that day, so they waited until I could be there. The guy sat there on that stand and told that jury he was jogging. He said he never heard me say 'Stop, police' because the traffic was so loud and he had his music in his ears at the time."

"What? Surely they could get around that defense. What happened?"

"His lawyer set up a sound system in the courtroom and played a recording of street sounds in downtown Atlanta during average traffic time. More like five o'clock on Friday. It worked like a champ. He stood in the back of the courtroom and yelled 'Stop, police.' The jury couldn't hear crap."

"Frank, that's crap. What did the prosecutor do?"

"Nothing, we didn't really have a case after that. It was his word against mine and his lawyer was good at his job. Ruthless."

"What are you trying to say, Frank; you don't like me because I am a lawyer?" I do family law, not criminal law."

"No, Sue, I like you just fine. You want to know who his lawyer was?"

Sue's heart sank. "No. Frank, I need to go."

Sue stood turning her back to Frank. "It was Tim, Sue. I'll never forget it. I've been to court a thousand times with a thousand different defense attorneys. I can't tell you one of their names, but that day I watched Tim Billings, attorney at law, get the guy that put me in a wheelchair for the rest of my life off the hook. Now that's a day I will never forget."

Sue began to cry. "I'm sorry, Frank. I have to go."

Frank started after her. "Sue, wait. That's not the end and I am not going to tell Tim."

Sue stopped and turned back to look at Frank. "You're not?"

"No, Sue, I'm not. Please come back and let me finish."

Sue came back down the path and sat on the bench. Frank pulled back around in front of her, closer this time than before.

"So finish. I'm all ears."

Frank smiled at Sue. "As that thug piece of shit walked out of court, he laughed at me. Sue he looked right at me and laughed. I was so angry. Tim walked out behind him and never blinked an eye. Didn't smile, didn't look at me, nothing. He was ruthless. He was victorious. Did you ever go to court with your husband and watch him?"

"No. Not my place."

"Well, you should have. He's the best, or was."

Sue held up her hands. "Frank, stop. You know who Tim is. You know I told him he was a project manager, yet you say you are not going to tell him. You clearly hate Tim for what he did. What are you waiting on? What do you want for me."

"I don't hate Tim, Sue. Besides, the Tim that is in that building right now is not the same Tim I saw in court, a completely different guy. With his head shaved when he first came in, I didn't even recognize him. He and I started talking at night and I had no idea he was Tim Billings. I just knew him as Tim. Once he started remembering things, he started introducing himself to everyone, over and over. Honestly, the first time he came over and said, Hi I'm Tim Billings, who are you? I about crapped myself."

"What did you say to him?"

"I said, the lawyer?"

Sue closed her eyes. "Oh God!"

"It's okay, Sue. He doesn't remember that. It was early on. After that, I just decided to get to know the guy. He obviously was not the same guy. No memory whatsoever. He didn't even hardly know his own name."

"I hope he doesn't remember that. God, please, no."

"Help me out here, Sue. Why not tell him the truth? It's not like he is going to be an attorney again anytime soon. What does it matter?"

"Frank, you don't know the old Tim. You don't know what I have been through."

"Oh yeah, I do. A cold, calculating asshole. I met him Sue. I saw what kind of man he was. Why hide it?"

"Frank, our life was a mess before the cancer. We were getting a divorce. Tim cheated on me several times and had no relationship with the kids at all. He was a jerk. He didn't care about me or the kids at all. It was awful."

"So you decided to wipe his life clean. Sweet revenge for you. Let me guess, I bet you had a house in Buckhead or Alpharetta, didn't you?"

"Roswell. Beautiful place! With his memory being wiped clean, I felt like it was my chance to start over. Get the old Tim I fell in love with back. I moved us. Got rid of our cars, his clothes, everything. I erased his life, but it wasn't revenge Frank; it was survival."

"So what will you do when someone like me shows up and says, Tim, good to see you, are you still a lawyer? What will you do, Sue?"

"I don't know Frank. I moved us to the mountains to try and avoid that. If enough time passes, people will forget him, don't you think?"

"Some will. Some, like me, won't. It's a gamble, Sue, a big one. You may need to get out of the state to get far enough away from it to survive."

"So what kept you from telling him all this time?"

"A lot of things, but I will tell you the main thing, and it's the most important. Tim! That's why I am not telling. Tim is different now. I really like him."

Sue looked confused. "I don't get it."

"He didn't know anything at first. Once I figured out who he was, I was just curious as to who he was now. Pretty soon you came into the picture, and I was impressed by your dedication. I guess the detective in me wanted to find out why. How could a jerk like Tim Billings have a wife so dedicated?"

"Frank, stop. I was just doing what any wife would do."

"No, Sue, not every wife. When I got hurt, my wife came to the hospital one time. I never saw her again. Five months later, I got divorce papers in the mail with a one paragraph note, saying, I can't take it any longer. I'm never coming back. Not everyone hangs in there, Sue."

"Frank, I'm so sorry. I didn't really know. Tim told me you didn't have anyone and that he wanted us to be your family. I didn't know."

"That's why I won't tell him, Sue, that right there. Whoever Tim was before, he's not that way now. Tim was willing to take me in as family, no questions asked. He called us brothers. That's not the Tim Billings I saw in court that day, and I bet that's not the Tim Billings you lived with, either. That Tim, I believe, would step over you if you were bleeding in the street and never look down."

"Frank, don't say that. Tim just let the money and power get the best of him. He was a good man and I believe he is again. He just got lost."

"Sue, he is a good man now because of you. The old Tim is dead. He died of cancer and from the sins of his past. God has literally renewed him. He is reborn; a new man full of love and kindness, and compassion for others. He vows he will come visit me and take me back up to the mountains as often as he can and I believe him. When he told me he was a project manager, I had to know more. I had to find out why someone would erase his life like that. The detective in me stayed silent, just to know the rest. The answer is you."

"Frank, life was hard before all of this. Tim was hard to live with. When the cancer came, I really wasn't sure what to do. I told him to have one of his girlfriends take care of him, at first."

Frank grinned. "You did? Wow."

"I know, but we were at the point we were hardly even talking."

"So, why lie to him? Really, would it have mattered?"

Sue stood. "Can we go down the path and talk?"

Frank started to roll down the path. "Lead the way! You have to keep talking though. The suspense is killing me."

"Okay! Okay! When the cancer came, his doctor told me about him losing his memory. I told him I didn't think I could do it. After several conversations, he convinced me it would be a new beginning for me and Tim. At that point I decided to move, erase his friends, his life, everything. I wanted him to be disconnected from everything in his past. I don't ever want the old Tim back, Frank, ever!"

"I understand, Sue. That's a lot of change. What if someone like me walks up a year from now?"

"I'm very afraid of the people who knew him. I have thought a lot about telling him lies, but it's too late now. If I tell him, it will only make him question everything."

"Yeah, but finding out a year from now will make it even worse."

"Frank, I can't do it. If I have to move us to California, I will."

"How realistic is that, Sue? You have a family and friends here, a career yourself. Are you sure that's the right decision?"

"I know, Frank. If I can just seclude him for a year or so, I think we will be fine. People will forget him."

"Sue, did you know you can Google him and it will come up with multiple hits? He has been in the news several times, including my case. You are taking a serious risk and betting everything on it!"

Sue sat on the next bench along the path, holding her hands over her face. "Frank, what am I supposed to do?"

Frank laughed. "I have no idea!"

Sue looked up at Frank. "Frank! What kind of friend are you?"

Frank wheeled the chair in front of Sue, taking her hands with his and squeezing tight. "Sue, stick to what you have started. Keep Tim away from everything. Fortunately, it will be months before he even tries to re-enter the working world. Hopefully, by the time he comes back, enough time will have passed that no one will remember. I would change his appearance as much as you can. Tell him to grow his hair longer, grow a beard, anything to make him look far from what he used to."

"God, Frank, I really screwed up?"

"Oh, hell, it's not that bad Sue, but I think I would have stuck to the truth about his career. It was smart, though, to get out of the city, away from all his friends. I am sure it will be fine. Just stay below the radar. Fugitives get caught all the time because they get a ticket or do something that gets them noticed. Just keep Tim simple for a year or more. Tell him you want him to just be a stay-at-home dad for now. No computers at the house. No cell phone that has internet. Keep him stupid. Do you know what I mean?"

Sue was beginning to smile. "I do. I can do that. Where we live is out in the middle of nowhere. I can keep it simple for months. Probably a year even."

"I would keep from making too many new friends as well. People get bored and nosy. You don't want new neighbors Googling you or Tim for the heck of it. Stay very low-key. Stay very to yourselves. Cook at home. Get movie channels on cable instead of going to the movies. All that will keep you out of the spotlight."

"That's another problem."

"What's another problem?"

Sue pulled her hands away from Frank and stood. She looked out onto the rippling water of the pond and at the ducks swimming looking for food under the surface. "The spotlight. Tim's the first patient to be cured of cancer. They will be asking for interviews and stuff. I just know it."

"What do you mean, cured of cancer? I thought he just had a tumor and was operated on."

"No. They actually found out what causes brain cancer and maybe even more, maybe all cancer. Tim was the first patient ever to receive the treatment. He did have the tumor removed, but he also was cured of cancer."

Frank shook his head. "You're screwed!"

"I know. I'm so confused."

"Tell him the truth, Sue. If you start living a lie it will only be worse later."

"Frank, I threw away everything from his past, even his law degree. He would be furious with me."

"Who cares? It's better than him finding out everything he thought he knew was a lie. I say tell him, the sooner the better."

It was almost lunch time so the two of them headed back. Frank had been telling Sue how good their lasagna was and she had told him she would have to cook hers for him. He could pick which one was better. As the two headed back, they continued to talk about how to tell Tim. Sue still was not convinced it was the right thing to do. Frank agreed to stay quiet, no matter what the decision. He had grown to care about both of them now, and would support Sue either way.

As Frank and Sue sat at lunch, Sue asked Frank about his wife. "Why did she leave?"

"It's not worth telling, Sue. I was never home. Just like Tim, I let my career ruin everything."

"Do you think she would come back now, if she knew you were better?"

"I didn't lose my memory, like Tim, and neither did she. There is way too much damage there to recover from."

"I'm sorry, Frank. I will call her if you want me to. I think you're a great guy."

Frank smiled. "Thanks. Unfortunately, we were beyond repair before the accident. She couldn't take it any longer. For the first six months after my injury, I hated everyone. She would have been in a no-win situation trying to live with me. She is better off. Hopefully she found a nice insurance salesman who is home every day at the same time and worships the ground she walks on. She deserves a quiet life after what I put her through. Being a cop's wife isn't easy."

"I am sure you are not the same guy anymore, either. Maybe you should call her?"

"I don't think so. Thanks for the vote of confidence. I'll be fine. Besides, I have you guys now. I'll just hang out at your house for the holidays."

Sue smiled. "I think that's a great plan! I know he would like that."

"Sue, I hope everything turns out for you and Tim. You deserve a good life, too. Whether you tell him or not, I hope it works out. He needs you, just like I needed my wife when I was hurt. He is lucky to have such a dedicated woman by his side."

Sue blushed. "Come on, Frank, you are embarrassing me. I just had different circumstances that made my decision easier. If Tim would have kept his memory I don't know if I could have made it through."

"Don't kid yourself, you have strength inside you that most don't. You would have made it either way."

Sue looked at Frank and shook her head. "Do you want to know the real truth about why I stuck around?"

Frank's smile faded to a serious look. "Sure, I love a juicy drama."

"He paid me to, Frank. Eight hundred grand. What do you think of me now?"

Frank sat there silent trying to get his head around what she had just said. "He paid you? That is classic! An 800 hundred grand payment and he doesn't even remember it. Now that is sweet revenge for bad behavior."

Sue shook her head back and forth, lost in the thought of things in the past. "I was divorcing him. The doctor told him if he was not in a supportive family unit, he couldn't be in the program. Tim was desperate and offered me money. I took it. Not such a great person after all, am I?"

"BS! I've seen you here with Tim. It's not about the money. You love him so much and I can see it in your eyes. My business was reading people and I am good at it. You would have done it with or without the money."

"You know what Frank? You're wrong. At that time I was done. He had hurt me so much that I couldn't take it anymore. I hated him, but I knew if I divorced him he would have made sure I didn't have a dime. I took the money to survive. I took the money for my kids."

Frank was silent and slowly looked at Sue. "So what changed your mind?"

"Just like you, Frank; it was Tim! Before he went into surgery, I saw him fall apart. I saw the man I once loved reaching for the surface. I saw the father in him with my kids. For the first time in many years, I saw him care again. Once the surgery was done, I saw the young boy in Tim. A shy, scared, insecure Tim that I had never seen before, ever. I fell in love with him even more than I did when we met the first time. Now, he is already the man I want to spend the rest of my life with, and he doesn't even really know who he is."

"He's who you've told him to be, Sue. He won't ever be who he was again. Even if you told him, he wouldn't be that man again. He can't; he doesn't know how."

Sue grabbed Frank's hand. "What if it's just part of his DNA, Frank? What if he regains his confidence and becomes just a new version of who he was? I couldn't take it."

Frank patted her hand with his free hand. "He won't. You are in control now. Teach him to be gentle and loving. You said it yourself; it was the money and power that made him that way. Hide the eight hundred grand from him and live simple. He'll never know any other way."

Sue pulled her hand away and covered her face. "I am scared of that more than anything."

Reid came back out and let them both know everything was completed. Tim would be fine and would be moved back to his room for the rest of the night. He had been given heavy medication to keep him sedated through the night. Sue wanted to see him, but it would still be a while before she could. Frank had his own therapy to go to, so Sue was now alone.

She roamed around the center, waiting for Tim. Finally, they brought him out and took him to his room. Sue followed them in and watched as they got him into bed. He was still completely out of it and didn't even know Sue was there. Everyone left, and Reid gave Sue a hug on the way out. Sue looked at Tim, so peaceful in the bed. She still could remember a much nastier Tim. Thinking back to what Frank had said about not being home for his wife, Sue could relate. She wondered what made her different. What made her stand by this man who had lied and cheated on her for years?

Sue was now sitting by Tim's bed, watching him sleep. She reached up and took his hand. He didn't move, and there was no life in his grip. She began to think about everything she had done. The lies she had told him to protect him from himself. Was it the right thing, or should she tell Tim now, like Frank had said? She didn't know.

In the quiet stillness of the room, Sue stood by Tim and began to pray over him. "God, help me to be this man's protector, to help him become whoever he can be now. God, please let him remain a good man and father. Help us to be all that we were. I love him God, and want the best for him. Help me stay strong. God, be with Frank as well. Give him hope for the future. Let him know he is not alone. We will be his family."

She felt Tim's hand tighten on hers as she said Amen. She opened her eyes to see Tim looking at her and smiling.

In a quiet voice, Tim spoke. "Who are you talking to?"

Sue leaned in close and kissed him. "God!"

Tim smiled and faded back away. The grip loosened and Tim's eyes were closed again. She decided to let him rest after that; it was time to go home for the day. He was fine and would be home soon. She had a lot to think about and decide. She leaned over again and kissed him. The corners of his mouth turned up in a grin as she did. A faint, whispered, almost non-existent, "I love you" came out.

Sue smiled and put her lips close to Tim's ear. "I love you, too, Tim, so very much."

Sue left that afternoon with her mind going a million miles an hour. Was Frank right or was she? The truth had always been the easier way to go and she knew it, but this time the choice was hard. If she changed the story now, it would still take him by surprise and may make him question everything she said. She didn't want to take any steps back. Since he found out he had cancer, they had taken huge steps forward in their life together.

By the time she was home, she decided to sleep on it and decide later. A few days wouldn't make any difference.

The kids were already home and watching TV when she came through the door.

Jonathan bounced into the kitchen. "Is Dad with you?"

Sue smiled. "No little man, not today. He will be home on Thursday. Are you ready for him to be here all the time?"

Jonathan hopped up on the counter. "Yep! How about you, Mommy?"

"I am. It will be nice to have our family all in one place again."

Annette walked into the kitchen. "Are you sure you're ready, Mom?"

Sue turned and stared at Annette. "What do you mean by that?"

Annette started laughing. "I think you like being in charge around here."

Sue looked strangely at Annette. "Get out of here, kid. I don't have to be in control of everything. Having Dad home will be nice. I miss him."

Jonathan was now playing with the sink sprayer. "What's for dinner?"

Annette exclaimed. "You miss the new dad!"

"Enough!"

Sue gave Annette the "shut up" look she deserved. Annette turned and walked out of the kitchen. Sue told Jonathan to stop playing in the sink and to go wash up for dinner. She stared out the window, as she often did when she needed to think. So much in life had changed. Tim would be home soon and life would move on. She laughed to herself, wondering who she was trying to convince now.

Coming Home

Chapter 17

Thursday morning finally came. Sue had been at the graduation dinner the night before, and Tim had been given official releases from all the doctors. He would now be listed in every medical journal as the first patient to ever be cured of cancer with no radiation treatments, and no expectations of recurrence.

Sue and Tim gathered all of his belongings from his room and loaded them in the car. Reid was there, and Tim went around the center saying goodbye to all his new friends. Tim covered everyone but Frank, who was at the front, talking to Sue.

Finally, Tim made it to the front. "Frank, I am going to start getting jealous of you hanging out with my wife so much!"

Frank laughed. "Well, I would say I will fight you for her but I think you have an advantage, your reach is longer than mine."

Tim laughed. "I thought it was because you were in that chair."

Frank looked around. "What chair?"

Everyone laughed. Sue went over and hugged Frank. "Frank, we will come back next week. Fourth of July will be here soon and I think it would be nice if you came up for a few days."

Tim smiled. "See, Frank, I told you we would make you family. We're brothers now."

"I believe you, Tim. You take care of yourself, okay?"

Tim walked over and hugged Frank. "Thanks for being my friend. You made life here bearable. I never felt alone. Thank you for that Frank."

Tears formed in Frank's eyes. "Tim, it was my pleasure getting to know both you and your lovely wife. I hope you guys have a wonderful new life together. You listen to her Tim. She's a smart lady and she loves you very much. I will see you soon."

With that, Frank rolled away. Tim signed the paperwork at the front desk and they were done. Reid followed them out to the car.

Reid shook Tim's hand. "Tim, you pulled through with flying colors. The whole thing is a huge success. How do you feel about that?"

Tim smiled. "Good, I guess. I'm still working on those 'how to feel' emotions."

"It will all come with time. A year from now you will feel like this never happened. Frank was right, though, you've got a great woman beside you. Listen to her and she will get you through it."

Tim put his arm around Sue. "I will. I will be a good husband and dad. I don't know how to be anything else. I guess I will learn to cook first so I can be a help at home, right Sue?"

Sue laughed. "Boy, that will be fun. Teaching you to cook will be hilarious. We can do it, though. I sure would like the help."

Reid hugged Sue and Tim hugged Reid. "Thanks for saving my life, Doc. I sure am glad we met, even if I don't remember it."

"You were a man on a mission and I'm glad you were. Your timing was perfect. Another day and I would have picked someone else. God was looking out for you."

Tim's face got serious. "Who is this God person everyone keeps talking about?"

Sue and Reid looked at each other and laughed. "We have a lot to learn about, Doc. The next year should be fun; ain't that right Tim?"

"I just can't wait to get home and try some of the things I have been told about!"

Sue blushed. "Oh, lord! Reid, we will see you soon. I am getting in the car."

Tim laughed as Sue got in the car. "It will be okay if we have sex, right? Baby do you want me to drive?"

Reid threw up his hands. "No! You do not need to drive and yes it will be just fine if you have sex my friend. Don't do anything crazy though, okay!" Reid slapped Tim on the shoulder.

"Okay Doc, I won't. Can I ask her to when we get home?

"Sure you can; she's your wife."

"I'm scared of that side of things, Reid. I don't know what is okay and what's not."

Reid laughed. "Tim, everything is okay as long as it's your wife. If it doesn't hurt, it's okay! Now go have fun."

"When do we need to come see you again?"

"Well, the reception at Emory will be in about a month. Other than that, I won't see you for another six months. We will need to do some blood work then, and that's it. You will be all done."

"Wow, Doc, it's hard to believe. Thanks again for everything."

Reid stopped with a thought. "Tim, let me tell you something just in case you didn't understand my comment a minute ago. Sue is the only person it's okay to have sex with; no one else."

Tim smiled. "Why would I want to, Doc? She's my wife."

Reid started to laugh again. "That's right. I was just making sure you knew the deal."

"Doc, I lost my memory but I'm not stupid."

"That's good, I just wanted to make sure you knew. I think a lot of Sue. She has been great to you. You couldn't have found a better woman. Take good care of her and treat her well."

"I will, Doc. I know she is special. I don't know how I was before, but I will be good to her from now on."

"That's good, Tim, very good. I'll see you soon."

Tim got in the car, and Sue looked puzzled. "What was that about?"

"Just guy talk!"

Sue smiled. "Guy talk about what?"

Tim smiled big. "Sex!"

"Oh really. What did the young Dr. Hampton have to say about that?"

"He said we could do whatever didn't hurt, whatever that means."

Sue laughed. "Oh my God, Tim! Do you talk to everyone about sex?"

"Not everyone, just Frank and Doc. I'm sorry; I want to be with you. I have for a while now. Frank said that was being turned on. You turn me on!"

"Well, that's good. That's how it's supposed to be; but only me."

"That's weird—Reid said the same thing, almost. Was I turned on by someone else before? Seems like both of you are quick to tell me that."

Sue looked shocked at the question. She stuttered, "No, not at all; we both just want to make sure you understand how things work. Being turned on by someone else can destroy a marriage. I don't ever want that to happen to us. Do you?"

Tim took Sue's hand and kissed it. "No way, baby. I know I have a good thing. You're the best. I see that. I'm not stupid."

"I know you're not, and when we get home we will see what we can do about you being turned on!"

Tim smiled big. "Let's get home, then."

Sue and Tim headed home. As they went, she questioned him on how he felt. He was happy about going home, but anxious at the same time. He wanted to be able to feel normal and have a sense of belonging.

"What scares you the most?"

"I think, not knowing what to do."

"Why do you think you need to do anything? We are in good shape at home. We have money, thanks to you, and we have a nice home. All you have to do is enjoy being there."

Tim smiled and squeezed Sue's hand. "I'm sure I will. I'm just nervous about saying something stupid or not doing something I should. The rehab center was easy to feel like I belonged, but there are so many things out here that I don't know. Things I don't remember, that are simple. I had to be taught how to go to the bathroom again. I can't imagine what else I don't know."

"Let's just take things one day at a time. I have taken the week off so I can be home with you. I will help you. Anything you don't know, just ask. We will all help you."

"Don't I need to be working somewhere to earn money or something? On TV, all I saw was how bad the economy is and everybody is broke. I want to help."

Sue smiled. "You already did before you ever got sick. You were very smart with the money. We own our house with no mortgage at all. Our bills are minimal. We can easily make it on my income and what we have in the bank. If you want to stay home for a year without working, we will be fine."

"How often can we have sex?"

"Tim! You are terrible. Is that all you can think about? You're like a teenage boy."

"I'm sorry. I don't remember when we met or how we were all these years, all I know is whenever I am around you I get excited. My thing grows."

Sue burst out laughing. She pulled the car over in a deserted area off the highway. Tim questioned what she was doing. Sue just smiled. Once she got stopped, she put the car in park and climbed into the back seat. Tim sat staring at her.

"Get back here!"

Tim climbed into the back seat with Sue. He sat staring at her, not knowing what she was intending. Sue laughed again and began to kiss Tim. Tim kissed her back. Sue pulled his shirt over his head and began to kiss him down his neck and across his chest. Tim froze in excitement and fear. She took his hand, placing it on her chest.

Looking into Tim's eyes, "I'm yours! You can do anything you want. You can touch me anywhere you want. I'm all yours."

Tim pulled Sue's shirt off and then her bra. As he kissed her down her neck and across her breast, she pulled him on top of her down in the seat. She took her time with him, guiding him as they made love. Tim's excitement was like she had never seen. He had become a virgin all over again and she was glad that she was his first. God had given her a brand new Tim and she would get to be in every first that he experienced from now on. Sue laughed, thinking how they had made love for the first time in a car when they were in college. That time had ended with a policeman's tap at the window. She was praying that this time would not end the same way. As he climaxed, he screamed with excitement. She wrapped her arms around him and pulled him close. Kissing his sweat covered forehead and lips, she felt young again. She felt like the relationship had gotten a brand new start.

Tim kissed Sue back while trying to catch his breath. "That was fantastic!"

Sue laughed. "Yes, it was. Wait until I get you home in a bed!"

"I am sure that will be fantastic. I love you, Sue!"

Sue kissed Tim again. "I love you, too. Now, do you feel better?"

"I feel fantastic. Can we do this again sometime? It was exciting getting in the back seat like this."

"Sure we can, but when we were younger and doing this, we got caught. That was not so fun."

Tim contorted his face. "Oh no, caught by who? What happened?"

"We were out one night and things got heated and you pulled into an abandoned neighborhood. We started fooling around, and just as we were going at it, a cop knocked on the window. He scared the crap out of me. He made you get out, holding nothing but your shirt over your front and you had to tell him just what you were doing. It's funny now, but back then I thought we were going to jail."

"What did I say?"

"You started telling him we were just making out, but he told you to stop lying; he saw us doing it. It was a mess. You were as red as a stop sign. Eventually, he let us go, but not before he checked our ID's to make sure we were both of age. He told us never to come back. It was great."

Tim laughed. "So car sex is a regular thing for us, huh?"

Sue laughed. "No, but it's exciting, so it can be. We can see if we can get caught again. See how well you talk your way out of it this time."

With that, Tim looked outside. "You're right; we better get out of here. I at least could say I didn't know it was wrong. I would be telling the truth."

They both laughed as they got dressed and got back on the road. Tim was now leaning over towards Sue, holding her hand and touching the back of her head. She kept smiling at him, glad to have her husband back. They talked about life at home and how things would be. He told her more of his fears and she talked about how she would help. Tim was smiling constantly as they spoke.

Sue could still see some worry in Tim's eyes. "Tim, what else is bothering you about home?"

"I feel like it will take forever for me to learn everything again. Even as I look around, I don't know what these places are, what you would buy there. Where I would go for clothes or milk? I just don't remember."

"You have clothes, and I will take you with me to get milk. I am not sure I want you driving anywhere for awhile."

Tim laughed. "Afraid I will get lost and not come back?"

Sue didn't laugh at that. "No, afraid you will run a light or not yield because you don't remember the laws. I don't want you to get hurt on the road after going through all of this."

"I see your point. You're pretty smart, aren't you, baby?"

Sue smiled. "I try to be."

"You are. I may have lost my memory, but I didn't lose my common sense. When I picked you, I was pretty smart, too."

Sue laughed. "Yes, you were; handsome and smart."

They pulled into the driveway and then into the garage. Tim sat there, not moving. Sue started to get out, and noticed he had not moved. She looked in through the windshield and then got back in the driver's seat.

"Honey, are you going to get out?"

"Yeah, I'm just taking it slow."

She sat back in the car looking at him. "This is your home. No one will make fun of you or judge you. We all love you here, and it will be fine. Now, come on so I can show you around before the kids get home."

Tim smiled at Sue and got out. She took his hand and led him inside. As they came in, he stopped and stared out the back windows at the view of the mountains. She stood beside him, and marveled at the view herself.

"Beautiful, isn't it?"

"Yes. What do you call it?"

Sue started to laugh, but caught herself. "Mountains. Those are the Blue Ridge Mountains."

As they looked out across the mountain ridge, the sun was high and the mountains were full of all kinds of colors from the winter. Many of the pines were tall and green while the hardwoods were still brown and bare. The clouds were low for the day, and the top of the mountain ridge almost touched them. Tim didn't speak a word, and Sue looked from the mountains to Tim.

Smiling, she put her arm around his back and squeezed him tight. "Welcome home, baby."

"Wow. They are beautiful. Did we build this house? The company I worked for, I mean."

"No. I bought it after you got sick. The other house we had was just too much. I wanted a peaceful place for you to recover and for our family to be together. This place was perfect."

"I agree, and I don't even remember the other place. I love it, baby. Show me the rest. Show me our bedroom!"

"The kids will be home in just a little while, young man. You will have to wait until they are asleep."

"Oh, man!"

She led him around the inside and then the outside, giving him the grand tour. She called out everything she thought of as they went. The garden hose, wheelbarrow and rake. Finally, they were back inside and in the kitchen.

Tim looked around. "This is my new job, huh? Stay at home dad. What can I fix you, Mrs. Billings?"

Sue smiled. "Okay, let's start with something simple, like a grilled cheese sandwich—one of the kids' favorites. Make them that and they will love you forever."

"Okay. That sounds like a good plan. You teach me something simple every day, and that will help me learn where and what everything is. Teamwork!"

Sue laughed. "That's right. We are a team, a good one."

"Then later you can teach me more about sex, right?"

She laughed and smiled. "What am I going to do with you? Yes, I will show you all about it. Today was fast. Tonight will be slow!"

Tim smiled. "I like the sound of that. Okay, what's a grilled cheese sandwich?"

Sue smiled and showed Tim the stove and pots and pans. She went through the fridge, pointing out things, calling them by name. She made sure he knew about the heat on the stove, and what Teflon coating meant. They both laughed and kissed as the afternoon went on. As the kids arrived home from school, they were both waiting at the front door. Jonathan came running in and hugged his dad like he had not seen him in forever. Tim was so glad they were home. Annette was a little slower, but hugged her dad and told him she was glad to have him back home.

Tim looked at Sue as he had both kids wrapped in his arms. "Thank you," Tim whispered. Sue waved it off and went into the kitchen.

"Who wants grilled cheese?" Sue yelled out.

Both kids said, "I do," and dumped their book bags off at the door. Sue smiled at Tim.

"Coming up," Tim said as he walked into the kitchen.

Annette looked at her mom. "Are you sure that's a good idea?"

Tim cleared his throat. "What do you mean? I can cook a grilled cheese just like Mom. I got this!"

Jonathan yelled out, "Go, Dad!"

Tim reached over and tossed Jonathan's hair. "Thanks, buddy."

Tim leaned over to Annette's ear. "Mom taught me earlier; don't worry." He winked at her as he picked up the pan.

Annette laughed, "Two please, kind sir!"

"You got it, kid. Anything for you?" looking at Jonathan.

Jonathan spoke up, "Two for me too, please."

"You got it. And for the lady?"

"No, I am good until dinner."

Tim turned and looked at the kids now sitting at the bar stools next to the counter. "She's still afraid of my cooking. She'll come around."

Annette laughed, looking at her mom. Sue held up her hands in defense. "I am going to change my clothes and clean up before dinner. Don't you guys eat too much. I am making spaghetti tonight. Sorry, your dad is making spaghetti tonight!"

The bedroom door closed and Tim looked at the kids. "No idea on that one. She'll teach me, though. How was school today?"

Tim sat and talked about school and him coming home. He answered questions about the cancer and being healed and anything else the kids wanted to know.

Sue came to the door at one point and opened it just enough to see the kids and Tim. They were laughing and talking like never before. They finally had the father back they had wanted, and she was so happy. She could feel the tears rolling down her cheeks as she watched Tim talking and laughing. He made gestures with his hands, and noises, and the kids laughed out loud. Somewhere along the way, he had found a sense of humor, and Sue couldn't have been happier. She closed the door and let them enjoy the time together. For the first time in a long time, Sue felt like she was at home.

As she ran a bath, she lit some candles around the room. She thought she would relax for a while and let Tim just be a dad.

While she enjoyed the bath, Tim caught up on all that was happening in each of their lives. He asked if they were mad about moving and starting a new school. Both kids said they understood and wanted to help. Annette told Tim she missed her friends, but she had already made some new ones and they were pretty cool. Jonathan had already been exploring all through the hills and couldn't wait to take him. Tim looked forward to the adventure and told Jonathan that, on Saturday, when he didn't have school, they would take off for the hills.

Sue could hear the laughter from time to time as she soaked. She was very happy things would slow down now and they could become a family again.

Life at Home

Chapter 18

A week after Tim came home, things were falling into place. Tim was becoming quite the house dad. Sue would help get the kids up and going in the morning before she left for work, but Tim would cook everyone breakfast and keep the house clean. He thought he would try to go back to work around the end of the year, so he began some classes online to help. Sue was a little afraid of him being online, but Tim wanted to learn and she didn't want to say no. He had become fascinated with home repair shows and had even started a few projects around the house.

Sue would get home and he would help her make dinner. They sat at the table as a family now to eat, something they hardly ever did before. He was becoming a good cook as the months went by.

The family truly had become what Sue wanted all along. The kids and Tim were doing great and he knew everything about their lives. Sue and Tim both went to school functions together, and if there was an event, Tim made a point to be seated in the front row.

Spring came and now the mountains were alive. All of the summer festivals had started up and the kids made friends all over the place. Sue and Tim would go to town and shop or eat, depending on where the kids were and who they were spending the night with. They had grown to love the little mountain town and it felt like they had always lived there.

All of Sue's fears were gone. The celebration at Emory had come and gone with very little excitement. The reporters had interviewed Tim briefly and it did make the papers, but the news was the cure for cancer and not Tim. Sue was glad of that, and they had retreated back to the mountains with no problems.

They made regular trips back to see Frank and he had come to the house for Memorial Day and the 4th. He was family, and the kids looked forward to his visits. Tim built a ramp that could be temporarily added to the front stoop, allowing Frank's wheelchair to come right in. Frank never brought up the past, as promised. Sue appreciated Frank's trust in her. He really had become a friend to both of them.

Life was good!

One Saturday, Sue and Tim were in town shopping, while the kids were with their friends. They had been in the square, and were headed to one of their favorite spots for lunch. The place had a great burger. Tim was standing on the sidewalk as Sue put some of the shopping bags in the Jeep.

As she did, a man and his wife approached Tim. "Tim, is that you?"

Instant fear ran through her. She knew just about everyone that Tim knew in their lives, but she had no idea who this was. Tim looked lost as he answered.

"Yeah, I'm Tim."

The man was older and stuck out his hand to shake with Tim. "It's Pete. You don't remember me, do you?"

Sue took Pete's hand. "From the old neighborhood, right?"

Pete looked surprised. Turning to Sue, "Yeah, that's right."

"Tim doesn't remember any of our old neighbors because of the cancer. How have you been?"

Pete paused, looking between Sue and Tim. "Just fine. Do you guys live up here now?"

Tim spoke first, "Yeah, what about you? You say you know me from the old neighborhood?"

Pete smiled, still trying to get a grip on Sue's demeanor. "No, we live in Roswell still."

Sue stepped between Pete and Tim. "Well, you know how things change in life. We enjoy a much simpler life now. No city hustle and bustle for us. We just stay quiet up here in the hills. What brings you guys up here?"

Pete stepped back slightly, feeling the tension from Sue. "We have a place up here. We come up often."

Tim spoke up again. "You know I was cured of cancer, the first person ever. Maybe you saw it in the paper. I don't know if Sue or I told you I had cancer. Sue never really mentioned any of our neighbors before. You say we were friends? I lost my memory during surgery. Sorry I don't remember you."

Sue glared at Pete as Tim spoke. She needed this conversation to end. The only friends Tim had around the house were drinking buddies at Scully's. She didn't want Tim to start drinking again or missing the old bar scene.

Pete picked up the stare from Sue. "It's okay, Tim. I just saw you and wanted to say hello. We won't keep you guys. Glad to see you are doing well, Tim."

Tim looked puzzled. "Oh, okay. Glad to see you again—Pete, did you say? Tell everyone we said hello, okay?"

Pete nodded. "Sure will, Tim. You take care now."

Sue grabbed Tim's arm. "Baby, can you go get us a table. I want Pete to give our old next door neighbors a message for me. I will be right in. You know how they get crowded on Saturdays."

Tim hesitated and then turned to walk inside. "Okay, babe. Bye, Pete. Good to see you."

Sue waited for Tim to go inside. "Pete, the only place he could know you from is Scully's. I'm sorry, but I don't want him to reconnect to any part of his old life. I am sorry to be rude, but we moved up here to get away from that whole life. If you don't mind, please don't ever try and make contact with Tim again."

Pete's wife was tugging on his arm now and taking steps back, looking at Sue like she was a crazy woman.

Pete held his ground. "It's Sue, right?"

"Right. Can you do that for me, Pete? Just forget Tim. I'm sure the friendship was all superficial, anyway."

Pete smiled at Sue. "You are as tough as Tim said you were. I think maybe even tougher."

Sue softened her stance. "Tim said that about me?"

"He did just before the surgery. He told the guys how much he loved you and wanted to make things work. He said you would probably move and he would not be back. I knew Tim pretty well; it wasn't superficial. I understand what you are trying to do."

The anger Sue was holding began to fade. "I . . ." She couldn't find the right words.

Pete reached up and touched Sue's arm. "It's okay. Take care of him, Sue. I hope you guys have a wonderful life. Don't worry if we see you again, though. The secret is safe with us."

Sue looked at Pete's wife. "Sorry, I didn't mean to scare you."

Pete let go of Sue's arm. "It's okay. No problem, take care, Sue."

With that, Pete and his wife walked away. Tim came back out the door. "Our table is ready."

Sue turned to face Tim. "Oh good, let's eat!"

Tim looked down the sidewalk at Pete and his wife leaving. "Did they want to eat with us? I got us a table for four in case they did. They seemed nice."

As they sat down, Tim questioned Sue. "You didn't want me to talk to them, did you?"

Sue looked surprised at Tim's question. "Why do you think that? I just wanted Pete to tell our old next door neighbor something for me."

"Sue, I lost my memory, not my ability to see. If you needed to get them a message I am sure you would have just called. You have shielded me from my past all along. I've let it go because I figured maybe I was not such a nice guy. You already told me I was never around for the kids. Let me guess: I was never around for you, either."

Sue became distraught. "Tim, I can't do this here!"

Tim reached out and took Sue's hand. "Do what? Just tell me, Sue. I'm not going anywhere."

The waitress came to the table. "Hi folks, what can I get you to drink?"

Sue stood up. "Nothing. I have to go!"

The waitress looked confused as Sue walked away. Looking back at Tim, she asked, "Is she okay?"

"Yeah. Sorry about this. I guess we'll eat later."

She stepped back. "Okay, did I do something, sir?"

Tim touched her on the shoulder as he stood up to go after Sue. "No, not at all."

Tim hurried to catch Sue. She had made it through the front door and out to the sidewalk. The tears were flowing now and she was walking faster to put distance between her and Tim. Tim came out the door and looked for Sue. She had stepped around the end of the building and leaned against the brick, sliding down the wall and sitting on the ground. She wiped the tears from her face, both mad at herself for not just telling Tim in the beginning, and mad at Tim for being who he used to be. The Tim she had now was all she ever wanted. Why couldn't he have been like this all along?

Tim started left out the door, but the buildings were continuous and there was no sign of Sue. He turned around and began to jog towards the end of the buildings to the right. Maybe she had turned the corner.

For the next few seconds, Sue thought she should just tell him everything. Why put off what would eventually come out? Why wait until he finds out on his own, or he runs into someone who knows him again? She was tired of living in fear of this day. She wanted him to choose her and the kids, knowing everything, and be the man he was going to be. She wiped the tears again from her face as Tim ran around the corner, passing by her, not even noticing her sitting low against the building.

"Tim!" Sue yelled out.

Tim stopped and turned back to Sue. He came over to her and knelt down in front of her, wiping more tears away from her face.

Tim smiled while he held Sue's face. "Tell me who I really was. I need to know."

Sue started shaking her head. "No, you don't. That man died at Northside Hospital and you need to let him stay there."

Tim wiped more tears. "Sue, how can I ever be the husband and father you want me to be, if you don't let me apologize for whatever it was I did to you? You know I have been reading that Bible you gave me. God said confess your sins and ask forgiveness."

Sue was now crying uncontrollably. "I need for you to let me do that, Sue. I need to know who I was, no matter how bad, so I can ask forgiveness from you and God. I'm not going anywhere."

Sue just stared at the ground as she began to talk. "I hated you so much, Tim!"

Tim sat down in front of Sue. "Why?"

"Can we go home and do this? Please!"

"No. It comes out right now, right here!"

Sue swallowed hard and looked back at the ground. "I don't know how to do this, Tim. It's too much. Can we please just go home?"

As Sue started to try and stand up, Tim pulled her back down. "No, Sue, we are doing this right here. I don't care who hears or sees. You need this more than me. You have been living a lie and it is killing you inside. Now let's have it. Start by telling me about my job."

Sue laughed through the tears. "Well, you sure weren't a project manager!"

Tim smiled. "I didn't think so; I don't have any tools. So, what was I?"

"I didn't think about that. I'm not as good of a liar as you were."

Tim frowned. "That doesn't sound good!"

Sue was shaking her head now. "It's not. You were a lawyer just like me. The difference is, you were way better at it than I am; you were bigger than life and you went to work for a big firm right out of law school."

"Was I arrogant about that with you?"

"Not at first. You were making good money, so we decided I would pursue a pro-bono career and let you go after the money. That way I could stay home with the kids."

"That sounds good. So what happened?"

"Tim, I really don't want to do this here. Can we just go to the car?"

"No, we need to keep talking. I don't want this between us anymore."

"Okay, fine; but you are not going to like it, and if I do this and you leave again, I will kill you. Do you hear me?"

"Leave again?"

Sue sat there looking at Tim. "Tim, you became very successful. You made partner at the firm; you had money, power and women!"

Tim's face began to fill with sadness as Sue spoke.

"You took on clients in Colorado just to be away from home. You were gone all the time. You had no idea who your kids were. Before the cancer, you hadn't been to a school function in five years. You would work, or whatever, or be with whoever, until six or seven and then usually go to Scully's to drink with Pete back there and your pals."

"Sue, I'm so sorry."

"Oh, I'm not done, it gets worse. Most nights, you would get home at ten or eleven and not even speak to me when you came to bed. We hadn't had sex in over a year before you got sick! Hell, Tim, sometimes you just didn't come home. With all the power and money, you became someone I didn't even know anymore. It was awful. I lied to you about who you were because I didn't want you to ever be that person again."

Tim stared at Sue. "I'm . . . it must have been awful."

"It was, Tim. It was more than awful, it was unbearable. We were getting a divorce when you found out about the cancer. I didn't want to help you. You found out about the Emory deal, and they wouldn't let you into the program unless your wife was with you. Tim, you paid me to get you through it! You had to pay me! How screwed up is that?"

Sue cried harder as she spoke. "I can't handle this, Tim. These past months have been hard on me. Hell, this whole year. I went from hating you to loving you again, and I just don't know if I can take you leaving again!"

Tim wrapped Sue's legs with his arms. "Look at me, Sue. I'm not going anywhere. I love you and I love our life. I am so sorry you have gone through all that you have with me. I would never do that to you now. I can't even imagine it."

"If it wasn't for Dr. Hampton, I wouldn't even be here. He did more than just save your life Tim; he saved us."

Tim leaned in to Sue and kissed her. "I love you, Sue. I am never leaving you. I want to be with you and the kids for the rest of my life. I can't imagine what I was thinking. I must have been crazy. I'm so sorry I put you through all of that. I'm so sorry that I was such a jerk you felt like you couldn't tell me who I was."

Sue put her arms around Tim's neck. "I was so afraid, Tim, afraid that if you got connected to any part of your old life you would find your way back there. When you went into the hospital, I erased you from everything you knew. From everyone that knew you. I sold the house, took our kids out of the school system they loved and away from all their friends. I quit my job and started over. I bet everything on this, Tim."

Tim pulled away and took Sue's face in his hands again. "It will be okay, Sue. I don't want any of that life back. You are everything to me! I couldn't be a lawyer again now if I wanted to, anyway. I don't remember anything about it. Just like being a project manager. I don't know what to do, other than be here for you and the kids."

Sue smiled and kissed Tim again. "That's more than enough, Tim. It's so nice having you home. I can't even begin to tell you how different and how much better our life is now. To see you just sitting and talking with the kids makes me cry every time. Just to see you smile at me when I get home is incredible. To hear you say I love you makes me melt inside. Tim, you were so cold and mean before."

Tim kissed Sue. "I love you, Sue. I am so sorry for who I was, for what I had become. I won't ever be that person again, I promise. I have a wonderful life now. I love where we live. I love knowing all about my kids and who their friends are. I love being with you. Walking in the square today, shopping and just being with you, holding your hand. I even like doing the handy work around the house. Maybe I will just do that, to earn some money and keep busy. I love this life, Sue. I don't want any of the jerk back in me, ever!"

Sue hugged Tim hard again and kissed him. "God, please take me home so we can make love right now!"

Tim smiled and picked Sue up off the ground. "You got it, baby!"

They hurried towards the car. Tim held Sue's hand tight in his as they walked. She wiped tears off her face and tried to pull herself together. Tim opened the passenger side door and Sue got in.

As he sat in the driver's seat, Sue looked at Tim. "What are you doing?"

Tim laughed. "Can you teach me to drive again? I kind of feel funny always having you drive."

Sue laughed. "Yeah, I can. Just take it easy and go slow. I must look a mess. I am so tired of crying over you, boy."

"I don't want you to ever cry over me again, unless they are tears of joy from laughing."

Sue took Tim's hand as they pulled away. "That sounds good to me. A life of laughter beats a life of tears any time."

They were on their way home when the full impact of what Sue had done set in. Tim shook his head. "So, this whole time the kids were in on this lie about my life?"

Sue looked at Tim. "I'm sorry about that. They didn't want the old you back, either."

"How did you get them to handle that? Jonathan is so young. Weren't you terrified he would let it slip?"

"Every day! Every time you would get alone with him, I was so afraid he would say something that made you question the past. I hated every minute of it."

"It must have been terrible for them to keep such a secret. How could I have ever not wanted to be around them? They are such great kids. You have done such a good job raising them."

Sue began to cry again. "Stop talking like that. I can't cry anymore today. I'm exhausted."

Tim reached over and wiped a tear away from Sue's cheek. "I love you and I will find a way to make this all up to you for every day you suffered. You will never be treated that way ever again by me. I promise. Besides I don't even know how. I only know how to love you baby and I like it that way."

Sue smiled. "Now that the truth is out, you need to apologize to Annette. It is amazing how she changed to make this all work. She hated you, Tim. She wanted me to divorce you as much as I wanted to divorce you back then."

Tim had started to cry now as well. "She never showed it!"

Sue reached over and wiped a tear away and pulled herself closer to Tim. "It was hard for her, I know. The first visit at the rehab center when she hugged you was too much. That's why I lost it and went outside."

More tears from Tim. "Why did she hate me so much?"

"Tim, little girls need to know their father loves them. That's where all women learn how to love. We learn from our fathers, the first man in our lives to show us love. Annette didn't have that and she was angry."

"How could I have been like that? I never showed her any love?"

"Not for years. You were gone. You would stay in Colorado for at least a week every month and the rest of the time, if you were home, you were in your office or on the phone. We didn't exist to you."

Tim shook his head. "I can't believe you agreed to stay with me. You are truly an amazing woman. I have got to be the luckiest man on the planet. It sure sounds like I don't deserve it."

"You were a good man when I married you. You just let the job and your ego get out of control. Reid convinced me by saying I would have the rare opportunity of teaching you to be whoever I wanted you to be. I chose to teach you to be loving and kind."

Tim gave her a strange look. "How much did I pay you?"

Sue started laughing. "I'm not telling. That was an arrangement between the old Tim and me. You're not even on that account. If you don't act right this time, big boy, you're screwed!"

Tim laughed. "I ain't scared. Besides, I'm not going anywhere. I love my life, and my wife, and my kids! . . . Was it a lot?"

Sue laughed again. "It was enough for us to pay cash for a house and live for some time without worrying about money."

"From the sounds of me before, I don't think I want to know much more about the old Tim Billings. He sounds like a real jerk, and baby, please don't ever stop teaching me to be what you want me to be."

"He was a jerk, but he died and you came along, a wonderful, caring, loving, beautiful man. I would do it all again to have what we have now."

Tim took Sue's hand and kissed it. "I would die again to have what I have now."

Sue smiled as they pulled into the driveway. "The kids will be home in about an hour, so I suggest you get in the house and get naked."

Tim parked and Sue grabbed the packages out of the back seat. They got out of the Jeep and ran for the house. As soon as they got through the door, Tim pinned Sue against the wall and began kissing her. She kicked off her shoes and started pulling at his belt. They stumbled a few more steps in the living room as he pulled her shirt over her head and dropped it to the floor.

As Sue's shirt hit the floor they heard, "Mom, oh gross!"

Annette stood in the living room as Sue grabbed her shirt and ran for the bedroom. Tim began to laugh as Sue ran away.

Annette still had her hands over her eyes. "Why are ya'll doing that in here? Go to your room."

Tim was still laughing. "You can take your hands off your face. Mom is in our room and very embarrassed, I am sure."

Annette moved one hand slightly and looked. "We need to talk about some rules! You may not know, but none of that in front of the kids."

Tim laughed hard as he came into the living room and sat next to Annette. "Sit. Let's you and I have a little talk."

"Eww, go wash your hands. There is no telling where they have been."

"Seriously, sit down; I want to talk to you about something."

Annette looked a little afraid. "What?"

"Come on, it's nothing bad. Just something about us I want to get straight."

Sue came out of the room and saw Tim and Annette sitting. Tim held up a hand signaling Sue to give them some time. Sue nodded and went back into the bedroom and turned on the TV.

Annette sat, cautiously, staring at her dad. "What do you need to get straight?"

"Mom told me."

Annette looked confused. "Mom told you what?"

"It's okay. Mom told me I was a lawyer before, not a project manager. She also told me I was a jerk and I didn't care about you guys at all."

Annette stood, angry. "Why would she tell you that? Now you're gonna leave. Why would she do that to me?"

Tim stood and grabbed her. "Whoa. I'm not going anywhere. It's okay, baby. Daddy is never leaving you, ever."

Annette started crying and hugged her dad tight. "Please don't change. Please don't."

Tim stroked Annette's hair as tears rolled down his face. "I won't, baby, I promise. I will never be that man again. I will never leave you guys. I have years to make up for that I lost being someone else. Can you forgive me?"

Tim bent down so that he looked up at Annette, tears now covering his face. "Please forgive me."

Annette hugged her dad again. "I do. I do. Don't cry, Daddy. I love you."

Sue made her way out of the room and watched as the exchange took place. She joined the two of them kneeling on the floor next to Tim. Annette wrapped one arm around Sue and the three of them just stayed there for a long while.

Tim wiped his face on his sleeve, kissed Annette on the cheek, and then kissed Sue. "I love you guys so much. I don't want to ever do anything to hurt you again."

Sue kissed Tim on the cheek. "You won't. You're not even close to the same man as you were. Is he, sweetie?"

Annette smiled and kissed him on the other cheek. "Not even close!"

Tim pulled both of them in tight again and squeezed hard.

As they embraced, the front door opened and Jonathan came in. He stood there, trying to figure out what the heck was going on. Slowly the three of them broke out into a laugh. Jonathan just stood there.

Tim spoke first. "Come here, buddy, and get some of this love!"

Jonathan took off in a run, slamming into the three of them and knocking them over. Tim held on and all four of them went to the floor in a massive hug! Laughter rang out through the house, and the pile quickly turned into a tickle fest, with Tim leading and soon being overcome by Sue and the kids. Tim was now on the bottom with the three of them tickling wherever they could.

Tim was happier than he could ever imagine he had been. He had nearly died from cancer but instead he had been saved from himself. He had a wonderful wife and family that he loved and was loved by. It just couldn't be better.

The rest of the day they hung around the house and played and talked. Tim told Jonathan he knew about being a lawyer and not such a nice guy. He thanked Jonathan for helping mommy get daddy through by not telling. He talked about lying, and how it was still not good, but he understood why mom wanted him to just this one time. Jonathan just smiled and hugged his dad, asking if they could wrestle now. Tim laughed with a loud, "Yes!" as he picked Jonathan up over his head and slammed him down on the couch.

As they cleaned up that night in the kitchen, everyone helped do their part. Tim and Sue were swapping looks and little quick touches, indicating the behavior that was stopped earlier that day would continue soon in their bedroom.

Annette caught one of the looks followed by a touch. "Gross! Rules, people! Rules!"

Sue and Tim both started laughing. Jonathan was clueless. Annette turned and went into the living room.

Sue laughed. "Come back. We will behave!"

Annette looked at her. "God, you guys went from not ever touching to sex maniacs! Get a room!"

Jonathan put his hand over his mouth. "Sex! She said sex!"

Everyone laughed!

Tim turned to look at Annette. "Why were you home early today, by the way?"

Annette turned red with embarrassment. "I got a ride from someone."

Tim looked at Sue and then back at Annette. They both said, "Who?"

Annette flopped down on the couch and turned on the TV. "Just a friend!"

Tim stood. "Whoa! Like a guy friend drove you, or what?"

Annette didn't turn to look at them. "No, a friend's mom."

Sue started walking to the living room. "Guy friend or girlfriend?"

Tim raised his voice slightly. "Annette, turn the TV off and answer your mother."

Annette turned the TV off, still not looking at her parents. "A guy friend. It's no big deal."

Sue walked around to where she could see Annette's face. "It is a big deal when you leave school with someone and you don't ask one of us, young lady. It better never happen again. Do you like this boy?"

Annette turned red again and put a pillow over her face to hide the embarrassment. "I won't do it again. Do we have to talk about this?"

Sue looked at Tim and grinned. "What's his name?"

A muffled "Hunter" came from behind the pillow. Tim walked over and pulled the pillow off Annette's face. Annette replaced the pillow with her hands.

Sue sat down beside her, pulling her hands away. "Why are you so embarrassed? Is he your boyfriend?"

Annette was dying. "No! He's just a friend in my science class. He's my lab partner, that's all."

Tim sat beside Annette, grinning ear to ear. "Annette's got a boyfriend!" he sang.

Annette began to smile and Sue started tickling her again. Jonathan came running into the living room, singing the same thing as his dad. Annette was now the center of the tickle fest this time, as the four of them tumbled from the couch to floor. Annette yelling, "Stop" the entire time.

The living room was full of laughter, and the heaviness of the day seemed to drift away. What Sue had dreaded from the day of the surgery was now behind them. She knew there may be more questions from Tim, but the truth was out, and it was not anywhere near as bad as she thought it would be. Tim had grown so much as a person and as a husband and father. This life was so much better than anything they had before. He was everything Sue could hope for in a man now. She was glad he didn't want the past in his life. He had chosen her and the kids this time, and that made her very happy.

Annette was the last to head off to bed as Tim wiped the counters down in the kitchen. Sue poured a glass of tea at the island as Tim turned to face her. Twisting the towel in his hand making the perfect weapon!

Sue saw what was coming, and put both hands up in self-defense. Tim quietly moved closer to take the shot. Sue broke into a run, leaving the tea pitcher and glass sitting on the counter. Tim began to chase after her, focusing on the spot he wanted to strike, both his hands rigid in the towel ready to strike at the first opportunity. Sue screamed as she ran towards the bedroom. As Sue ran through the bedroom door, the towel popped the doorknob!

Sue yelled out. "Ha! You missed me!"

Tim, now laughing, pulled the towel back again, ready for another strike. Sue grabbed the towel and pulled him to the bed on top of her. Tim let the towel go and began to kiss Sue passionately. Sue rolled Tim over and kissed him hard as she got up. Tim looked sad at this, but Sue took a few steps and closed the bedroom door.

Tim smiled but that soon faded as Sue bent down next to the bed and quickly picked up the dish towel, popping Tim on the leg. Tim now yelped and grabbed for Sue. The two of them rolled off the end of the bed onto the floor. Tim's smile melted Sue and her resistance turned quickly into desire.

The dish towel fell between them and was pushed out of the way along with their clothes. They made love passionately on the floor, then the bed, ending up in the bathtub in each other's arms.

Sue's head rested on Tim's chest as the warm water and bubbles covered their bodies. Tim stroked the back of Sue's head, amazed at how lucky he was. He had been lucky enough to win this wonderful woman so many years ago, only to be stupid enough to lose her because of his career. She had fought for him and he would never let her down again. He understood her lying about who he was to protect their life now. He was, however, a little curious; but had decided earlier in the day to just let it be. His life was wonderful now and he didn't want anything to change that, certainly not his past.

Sue looked at Tim smiling. "What's up? What are you smiling about?"

Tim squeezed Sue tight. "Just thinking about how wonderful my life is with you. I love you so very much."

Sue laid her head back on Tim's chest squeezing him tightly. "I love you very much, too."

A Visit from a Stranger

Chapter 19

O ver the next few months, things really began to come together. Sue and Tim were better than they had ever been, even better than when they had first met. They had regular date nights and family nights as well. Tim had not brought up the old career since he found out about it. Sue had told him some more about who he was, but it was so bad that eventually Tim just quit asking.

Tim and Annette had several more conversations about a father's love and he had apologized to her every day for a week. Annette finally told him to stop; she was over it. Tim hugged her tight and told her it was dropped forever. Jonathan continued to be the boy he was, loving the fact that his dad was so available to wrestle and explore with him. They had been fishing and hiking all over the mountains together.

Sue had given Tim a few driving lessons and he was getting the hang of it. His license had expired and they planned to get that taken care of, eventually. He would make the run to the school to pick up the kids now and then, but otherwise didn't drive much. It kept getting put off.

Tim was still mostly at home, working on several projects around the house. He had gotten quite good at working with wood. He built a small workshop in the back yard, not half bad for a beginner. Several of the neighbors had him fix things around their houses and he made good money here and there. Most of the cabins in the area were rentals and Tim quickly got to be known as a cheap, but reliable fix-it guy. He was enjoying staying busy but still being near the house. He would see the kids off and then go work for a few hours. He had become pretty efficient at Googling any problem he couldn't figure out.

Tim and Sue made a trip to see Frank after all the truth came out, and Frank thoroughly enjoyed busting Tim's chops about getting the perp off after he put Frank in the chair for life. Tim felt bad every time the old Tim was discussed.

Frank looked at the two of them. "Are you guys doing good?"

Tim smiled. "Frank, sex is fantastic, buddy. You didn't do it near enough justice!"

Frank laughed. "Well, I wanted it to be a surprise for you, nothing like being a virgin twice in one lifetime!"

Sue got embarrassed. "I think I am going to leave you two alone for awhile. Think I will walk around the lake."

Sue got up and headed out the back, leaving Frank and Tim sitting there watching her go. Tim sat smiling as she left. Frank looked at Tim and laughed.

"She's got a nice butt, huh?"

Tim turned quickly back to Frank. "Hey, pal, watch it!"

Frank laughed. "Whatcha gonna do, beat up a guy in a wheelchair? Besides, look around dude. Not much to look at here."

"Hey, don't get any ideas about my wife, pal. She's all mine."

Frank laughed. "I know she is. It's just fun to mess with you. So how did the conversation really go when she told you she had lied all this time?"

"Frank, it was bad. She started telling me what a jerk I was, and it was bad. I don't think I know anywhere near all of the truth about me. I hate it. I guess you know firsthand how bad I was, huh?"

"Yeah, I watched you work your magic with that jury, and boy you had them from the beginning. You were good. Any desire to try and be a lawyer again?"

Tim shook his head. "I don't think so. It's weird knowing you were the best at something, but having absolutely no memory of it."

"I'm sure. It would be hard. It's hard enough knowing I was a good cop and not being able to do it anymore. I would hate to be physically able but have no knowledge of it. I feel you; must be tough."

"Frank, have you ever thought about contacting your ex and trying again?"

"No way, she left me lying in a hospital, dude. I don't ever want to see her again. I'm just glad we didn't have kids. I think that probably helped Sue make the decision to stay with you. To take the risk, you know?"

"Maybe she loved me, man. Through all that crap I did, she loved me anyway. That's a strong woman right there."

"Yeah, you're a lucky man. 'Cause she has a great butt!"

Frank laughed as he rolled away from Tim. Tim swung at Frank's arm, trying to give him a charlie horse for the comment. Tim caught the back of his chair within a few steps and messed Frank's hair up as he drove away. "Ah, man!" is all he could hear as Frank grabbed his head.

Tim laughed. "Say something else, and next time you're at the house I will have Sue put laxatives in your food. See how you like having the runs in that chair, dude!"

Frank stopped and looked at Tim. "Don't make me call some of my cop friends up in the mountains and cause you all kinds of trouble. Them redneck boys will mess you up, son."

Tim laughed. "Okay! Okay! Lay off the butt comments!"

Frank smiled. "Hey, I can't help it if God put me permanently at butt level. I just see what's in front of me. That's all, one butt at a time."

Tim sobered. "Hey, I'm really sorry I got the guy off that got you hurt. He sounds like a real scumbag. Sue told me the story on the way here."

"Hey, it is what it is! I'll be okay. Meeting you guys has given me some new hope anyway. I actually have been looking into some jobs online and might just move up near you guys. Maybe I will buy a small house, get you to renovate it for me so it will fit a wheelchair, and I just might get a life and venture into the working world again. I think I could handle it."

"Frank, that would be awesome. If you find a place near us, we could help out. You know I would be glad to do that. So would Sue."

"I believe you, Tim. I never thought you would continue to come see me like you have, but you did. You're a good friend Tim, you and Sue both."

Tim laughed. "You get out of here and you just might meet a girl, too. Does that thing work still?"

Frank swung at Tim now. "Get out of here, asshole. Go get your wife before I take her from you."

The two of them went out to the back; they could see Sue walking back up the path towards them.

Frank asked. "Have you gotten her to take you by the old house yet? Any interest in seeing it?"

"No. I need to let that past be past, you know?"

"Yeah, that's probably best, nothing but trouble with those old friends. Of course, if you can find my friend that put me in this chair I might like to pay him a little visit. I bet I can put him in a chair for the rest of his life, too."

"Nope! Not helping you out on that one, Frank. I don't want to come see my brother through bars."

Frank smiled as Sue walked up. "How was the walk?"

Sue smiled. "Good. What are you two up to? Still talking about sex?"

Tim smiled and kissed Sue. "Nothing, just asking for forgiveness for the old Tim again. I seem to do that every time he gets brought up."

"I was just telling Tim here how walking is good for your butt muscles." Frank began to laugh.

"Babe, let's get away from this pervert. I would hate to hit a man in a wheelchair."

Frank smiled. "I told you before, don't let this chair fool you. A lot of fight still in this old man."

Sue leaned over and hugged Frank. "Behave, both of you. Frank, it was good to see you as always. We'll come back soon."

Tim spoke up. "He may be moving up our way. He said he has been looking into jobs he can do online and might move up near us. Wants me to renovate a house for him. What do you think about that?"

"Frank, that's a great idea. When are you thinking about doing it?"

Frank frowned at Tim. "Can't you keep quiet about anything? I see Sue is the secret-keeper. I don't know. I have been interviewing, and if something comes up, we'll see. I think I am ready to get out of here. You guys have inspired me to live again."

Tim shook Frank's hand and they headed home.

The next few weeks were quiet. The kids were back in school now and Tim was working on several projects. Sue was working regular hours, and the house was quiet.

The weekend came where they celebrated Tim's one year anniversary from being cancer-free. Reid and his wife came up for dinner, and Frank did as well. It was hard to believe it had been a year. They all sat at dinner listening to Reid tell how many more cases had successfully been completed now, and how they were having good results in the lab attacking other types of cancer as well.

Frank kept pushing Reid to get into spinal cord injuries so he could find a cure for that, too. Reid laughed and said he would think about it, because soon there might not be a need for cancer research. Frank liked that, and told Reid he was willing to be the first, just like his buddy Tim. It was like Thanksgiving again, and Tim was surrounded by everyone he called his family.

Reid did a quick exam of Tim towards the end of the night and drew some blood to run at the lab the next day. He wanted to do a quick check to make sure things were good.

Tim was a little reluctant because things were going so well in his life. No reason to invite bad news. Reid laughed at the statement and reassured him that he was sure there would be none.

Tim sat impatient at the house all day waiting for Reid's call. Sue had called Tim four times to find out if he had called. Tim assured her he would call immediately as soon as he heard from Reid.

At two, Tim's cell phone rang. Tim snatched the phone open. "Hello, Reid! Is everything okay?"

"Yeah, Tim, I'm sorry it took so long. We can't do the testing in house for this. We have to send it to the lab for verification, FDA rules and stuff."

Tim sat down relieved. "So, no cancer, for sure?"

"No cancer, Tim. You're in good shape. All your levels look great. Cholesterol is a little high, so watch those fried foods; other than that you are good to go."

"Thanks, Doc, you had me freaking out all day. I got to go and call Sue. Talk to you soon."

Tim hung and called Sue. "Everything is fine!"

"Thank God. Why did it take so long?"

"It was the lab. They had to send it off to be compliant with the FDA rules. Anyway, I am just fine."

Sue sighed. "I'm glad."

"When are you going to be home?"

Sue sighed again. "I don't know. I am stuck with this lawsuit crap that goes to trial tomorrow. I wish you were still a lawyer right now. I would get your help."

"Sorry, baby. I couldn't help you at all. Don't remember a thing. I do understand working hard, though. Do what you have to, and I will keep dinner warm."

"Okay, baby. I won't be too long. Maybe by seven, okay?"

Tim said, "I love you!"

Sue replied. "I love you, too. See you soon."

As Tim hung up, there was a knock at the door. Tim was puzzled, wondering who it could be. No one ever came to their door in the middle of the day. Tim went over and looked outside. It was a man with a large envelope in his hands. Tim thought, Something for Sue, I'm sure.

He opened the door. "Hey there, how can I help you?"

The man smiled. "Good afternoon, Mr. Billings."

Tim looked surprised. "Do I know you?"

"I am Robert Stewart. I'm the private detective you hired a year ago to deliver this package to you, sir. You told me then that you may not remember me."

"I did? Well, come in."

"No need to. You paid me in full last year. Here's your package. Good luck, and I appreciate the business. Call me any time."

Tim shook the man's hand and closed the door. The envelope said across the front, "For Tim—open alone." Tim looked at his watch: 2:15. It would be an hour before the kids were home from school and Sue would be late. He went into their bedroom and opened the package, dumping what was inside on the bed. The stack of papers was clipped together. Tim flipped the stack over to see the front. In bold letters it said, YOUR LIFE BEFORE!

Tim left it lying there and went into the kitchen. He poured a glass of tea and sat at the table. The mountains were beautiful as he looked out the windows all across the back of the house. Tim sipped his tea, wondering whether reading what was in the package would change things. He knew his past at this point; how much more could there be?

Tim walked back into the bedroom and sat down next to the papers. He stared at them, almost scared to touch the stack. "What is your problem?" he said to himself. With that, Tim picked up the papers and took the clip off. He took the top page off and began to read about his career, where he worked and who his important clients were. He read about Shelly, his assistant, and the firm. Who his friends were, and who to be careful with. As Tim read, he could not believe he had written it. It was angry and direct. It was nothing like who he was. Tim put the papers back down and walked back into the living room.

He pulled out his cell phone as he walked out onto the back deck. He called Frank.

Frank picked up right away. "Hey, Tim, what's up?"

Tim was silent. "Tim, are you there?"

"Yeah, Frank, I'm here."

Frank knew something was wrong. "Tim, what's wrong? Is everyone okay with Sue?"

Tim shook his head. "Frank, I got something today that I had a private detective hold for me from a year ago."

"What is it?"

"It's a write-up about me, my life before. On the envelope it said, 'Open away from Sue.'"

"Tim, I am telling you as your friend, throw it away. There is nothing but pain in there for you."

"I know that, Frank, but part of me really wants to know. I know Sue held back some stuff about me. Maybe even stuff she didn't know about is in there. Wouldn't you want to just know?"

"Tim, that part of your life is dead. You said it yourself, you want this life. What could you possibly gain by looking at that stuff? Throw it away now, before Sue gets home."

"Did you know I was a partner in that law firm downtown? I was making almost half a million a year in salary alone."

"Yeah, I know. I also know you were a world-class jerk. I also know you were about to get a divorce and you didn't even know your kids. Come on Tim; think about what you're doing here."

"Frank, part of me agrees with you completely, but the other part wants to know. Not so I can do anything about it, but just to know. I can't ask Sue that stuff. It tears her apart to even talk about it."

"Dude, I'm telling you, don't. Listen, if you have to, then do it with Sue. Tell her what happened and you guys go through it together."

"I don't know about that, Frank. What if there is stuff in there she didn't know, like women? She told me I cheated, but I don't know who or how many times. She may not, either."

"What good will come from this?"

"I gotta go. Thanks for listening."

"Do the right thing, Tim. You have a great life, my friend; don't screw it up."

Tim hung up the phone. From the porch, he could see Jonathan's coat on the floor next to the couch. Hanging on the back of one of the kitchen chairs was Sue's sweater, the one she wore when they walked. On the counter was Annette's iPod that Tim had taken from her last night so she would study. As he looked at all these things, he could see his life. His family was all around him, and he knew them. He knew everyone but himself.

Tim stood from leaning against the rail. He took a deep breath of the cool mountain air and headed for the bedroom. It was his life and he wanted to know. Good or bad, he wanted to know, and he didn't want to hurt Sue with it any more.

He got to the bed and began to spread the pages out. The first pages were his work life. He had read some of that already. The next group was his friends. He had some good ones. CEOs of a bunch of companies in Atlanta and Colorado, several politicians, and a list of clients that Tim was sure were mostly criminals.

The next few pages were his friends at Scully's and a few other bars he hung out at instead of going home. Among these pages, he found Pete's name. He realized then how much Sue was trying to protect him from this life. He saw that his favorite drink was scotch. Also something Sue had told him he never did.

Then Tim came to the pages that listed girlfriends. He read about Tracy and Jenny and several others around town. As he did, Tim felt sick knowing what he had put Sue through. He was angry with himself. Tim wadded up the papers at this point and walked into the kitchen. He threw the stack into the trash. The papers scattered across the floor as he did. Tim cursed as he watched his old life float to the floor. He stood there disgusted with what he had learned. Finally, bending down to pick everything up, he threw each piece in the trash, with anger and regret. All he could hear were Frank's words, "There's nothing but pain there."

Tim cleaned up the mess and walked out the front door. He was disgusted with who he was before the cancer and disgusted that he was so weak that he fell to temptation. Tim got in his truck to go for a drive. He needed to clear his head before everyone came home. He couldn't let this affect his new life. He wouldn't. He would protect Sue like she had protected him against Pete that day in the square. Tim thought about Pete. How random it was to see him up here, of all places. How terrified Sue must have been that day. What a mess, he thought.

Tim found himself driving down 75 towards Atlanta, and didn't realize how far he had gone until he saw a sign that said, 'Atlanta 15 miles.' He looked at his watch; it was four o'clock. The kids were home already. He hadn't been home before when he was working, and Annette could handle Jonathan for a while. Tim thought about the address where they had lived. He was curious about what the house looked like, the neighborhood. He was even a little curious about Scully's. What had made that place so great to him that he spent night after night there? Would it hurt anything to just ride by?

Tim had gotten over to get off the highway to turn around, but at the last moment decided to go on and see for himself. Hell, at this point it was only twenty more minutes. He would be back before Sue got home, and then he would know.

Tim punched the address into his GPS and in just a minute, it said, 17 miles to your destination. With that, Tim went back into his thoughts of past and present, feeling the breeze of fall through the truck window. In the distance, Tim could see the Atlanta skyline and he wondered how it was to live there. How he must have had the city under control as a big time lawyer.

He turned onto Roswell Road; he was within a few miles of the house now. As he took in all the sights and buildings along the way, he could see it was a nice area. It was obvious that money lived here.

As he drove along, looking for his turn, he noticed something on the right, off the road a little and with a few trees around the front. On the street, the brick sign in neon said, "Scully's."

Tim hit the brakes and pulled in the parking lot.

A Mistake

Chapter 20

Tim pulled into a spot right by the front door. The lot was crowded for 4:30, and he sat debating whether he should go in or not. He knew he didn't want to start drinking again, even though he didn't remember it. In the last year, he had seen enough TV and movies to know it could wreck a home, but he was still curious; if he went in, would anyone know him?

Tim looked at his watch again: 4:45. "Just enough time to ride by the old house and get back home."

Tim shook his head and reached for the key to start the truck again. A knock came on his window, scaring him half to death and out of his trance of thought.

George stood beside the truck. "Tim, is that you? It's George!"

Tim smiled. "Yeah it's me."

Tim got out and George hugged him. "Good to see you, man. Pete said he saw you and Sue in the mountains, but we never thought we would see you down here again. Is Sue with you?"

Tim was not sure what to do. "No and I think I need to go. I just wanted to see . . ."

"Oh, Tim, you have to come in. Charlie and Pete are inside. I know they would like to say hello, just one drink for old time's sake."

"I don't know, George, I'm not sure that's a good idea. Sue would not like any of this."

"Boy, you sure are different. Come in and at least say hello."

Tim sighed. "Alright, but just for a minute and then I have to go."

George slapped Tim on the back. "That-a-boy, the gang will be so excited to see you."

The two walked in and Billy looked up from behind the bar. "Holy crap! Mr. B, how the hell are ya?"

Tim looked at George. "The bartender knows me, too?"

George laughed. "Everybody knows us here, my boy. This is our place, almost every night."

"You guys should stay home with your wives more. It's not good to be away so much."

George rolled away from Tim, laughing. "Wow!"

"What? It's the truth. This place nearly cost me a divorce and the best woman on the planet. I have to go."

Tim turned and started walking back to the door. George ran to catch him holding his arm, "Wait, Tim."

"No. I have to leave now. I shouldn't be here."

George walked with Tim into the parking lot until he reached his truck. "Tim, wait. I agree with you, and told you that very thing the night I watched you hit on three girls at the bar. It's not this place that almost cost you a divorce; it was you. You almost cost yourself a divorce."

Tim stood there by his truck embarrassed by who he was. "I'm sorry I did that. I read a little about myself today and I really don't like who I was. I was a jerk and a cheater. I shouldn't be here, George. I shouldn't have come to Atlanta at all."

"Tim that was a different life for you, cancer has made you wake up. I can certainly tell the difference. The guys are good guys and they were friends of yours. If you have to go, I understand, but at least come in and say hello."

Tim sighed again. "All right, but just for a minute, I need to get back home."

George slapped Tim again. "Good man. The guys will not believe it when they see you."

Tim and George went back in and Billy spoke again. "Mr. B, how the heck have you been? It's good to see you."

Tim looked at George lost. "His name is Billy."

"Thanks. Hey, Billy, how are you?"

"I'm good Mr. B. I'll bring the usual."

Tim didn't even catch what Billy said as the guys erupted when they saw Tim. Pete, Charlie and the others rushed over to greet him. Tim was overwhelmed by the handshakes and hugs. It was a lot of love for grown men. Everyone wanted to know all about everything since he left. Pete stayed back a little, keeping his distance at first.

Tim finally locked eyes with Pete. "So, now you're afraid to talk to me?"

Pete chuckled. "No, just not sure what you're doing here. Sue was pretty adamant about you having nothing to do with us ever again. Are things okay?"

Tim walked over and shook Pete's hand. "They are, Pete. That day we saw you actually was a good day. Sue told me a lot about my past that day. Sorry I didn't know who you were."

Pete laughed again. "You still don't!"

Tim laughed. "You're right about that. I don't know who any of you are, but I feel like I just found a bunch of old friends."

Charlie joined them. "You did, son. How the heck are you? Do you remember anything? How did you end up here? Pete told us you guys live in the mountains now."

Billy walked up and handed Tim a scotch on the rocks. "Here ya go. This one's on me Mr. B. Welcome back."

Tim looked at the drink. "No, I . . ." and then Billy was gone.

Charlie yelled out, "A toast to our long lost friend, Tim."

Everyone cheered and took a drink. Charlie looked at Tim. "Aren't you drinking with us?"

Tim looked down at the drink and remembered his own letter, saying how he loved a good scotch. He slowly pulled the glass up to his lips and sipped. He didn't remember the taste, but it was good. He took another deeper draw from the glass and the guys cheered. Tim decided one drink would be harmless and then he would go.

He began to explain how he had lost all memory. His life wiped clean. He talked about getting to know Sue and how strong she had been. He had finished the drink and sat it on the table as he spoke. Charlie had motioned to Billy to bring another round. Tim didn't realize what was going on until the new drink showed up in front of him. By that time, Tim was looser and the thought of another drink was not so hard to justify. The scotch was good, and he felt good among his old friends.

Tim talked for an hour about the kids, Sue, and how great life was. As he sat there talking, he didn't notice the pretty woman walking up behind him.

Jenny tapped Tim on the shoulder. "Well, if it isn't the disappearing attorney!"

Tim looked at the guys and turned to look at Jenny. "I'm sorry, ma'am. Do you know me?"

The woman threw her drink in Tim's face. "Do I know you? You slept with me and I spent the weekend with you, and two days later, you disappeared. No returned calls. No emails, no nothing. Now you act like you don't know me."

Tim was at a loss for words. The guys had scattered when the drink flew. They each stepped away, telling Tim they would give him a minute.

Tim stood wiping his face. "Look, I'm sorry. About a year ago, I had cancer and the surgery wiped my memory clean. I don't remember anything or anyone."

Jenny pointed at the guys now ten feet away. "Whatever, Tim, you sure are hanging with your buddies like nothing ever happened. What was I to you, just an easy lay?"

Tim took her arm and asked if they could talk on the balcony. Jenny snatched her arm away from Tim. "Here is just fine."

Tim pointed to the chair. "Please, take a seat. I'm not lying. I don't remember anything that happened in my life before last year. I'm sorry if I didn't call you or whatever."

Jenny crossed her arms. "So, where have you been?"

"Well, for six months I was in rehab learning how to walk, talk and eat again. I finally began to retain memories and then they let me go home." Tim's words fell quiet.

"Home to your wife?"

"Yes. I'm sorry if I didn't tell you. I am married and I didn't mean to treat you bad. I was a different person then and I am not proud of that."

Jenny laughed under her breath. "That's just great. What a slut I am. Thanks, Tim. Where is your wife now, or are you just getting back into the same old routine?"

"No, I'm not. She and I worked it out, and because I didn't remember anything, we just started over. We're very happy now and I am very faithful. I am sorry about before. You seem like a very nice girl, not a slut. I was getting a divorce just before the surgery."

Jenny stood. "Well, isn't that just great for you, Tim. You sweep a girl off her feet and then disappear back into your wife's arms."

"I'm really sorry, Miss."

Jenny laughed. "You seriously don't even know my name, do you?"

Tim shook his head. "No. I don't remember you at all."

"Well, it's probably better that way. You can buy me another drink though since mine got spilled. I think I will get drunk tonight and try and forget a few things myself! My name is Jenny by the way."

Tim shook his head. "Jenny!"

Jenny looked at Tim like he was crazy. "Yeah, did that spark some kind of lost memory in there, Tim?"

"No, I just read about you today." Tim felt the mistake as he said the words.

"You read about me. What are you talking about? What did you have some kind of journal or something before? Please don't tell me you wrote about our weekend in some freakin' journal that your wife has read."

"No, not at all. I wrote some things down and had it put away. I found it today and you were in there. I . . ."

"Just stop talking, Tim. Buy me a drink and leave me alone. Don't you ever talk to me again!"

Tim motioned at Billy to take care of her drink. Billy nodded and got to work. Jenny walked towards the bar and never looked back. Tim turned to the guys who were still wiping drink off their clothes.

George started to laugh. "Wow, boy, your past is coming back hard, ain't it?"

"Man. I felt bad for her. I really don't remember any of that. I hate who I was back then guys. I'm sorry."

Charlie took Tim by the shoulder. "It's okay, Tim. You were lost and now you've found yourself. It's good! Good for you."

Tim looked for his cell phone to see what time it was. He realized that when George startled him in the truck earlier, he had left his phone on the seat. Panic went through him as he looked outside and it was dark.

"Crap! What time is it?"

Pete replied. "It's almost seven."

"Oh God, I'm in trouble. Guys, I have to go. I have to get home. I am going to have a huge amount of explaining to do."

George grabbed Tim's arm. "Hey, are you okay to drive? I'm guessing it's been a while since you drank."

Tim stopped. "Yeah, I'm fine. I just have to go. It was good to see all of you. Maybe Sue and I will come back sometime. I really don't like going anywhere without her."

Pete smiled. "Tim, take care and tell Sue I said hello. Hopefully, the next time I see you, we can talk a little."

"That sounds good. Guys, I have to go. Take care."

Tim ran out of the bar and got in his truck. He reached for his keys as he saw the message light blinking on the phone. He felt the pain of trouble and knew most likely Sue had called worried about where he was. What the heck would he tell her?

He started the truck and began to back up. Tim stopped as he hit the curb several car lengths behind his truck. He sat there for a moment, realizing he was a little bit drunk. He had only had two drinks, but his system wasn't used to alcohol anymore and it let those two double scotches go straight to his head. His phone rang again. It was Sue. Dear God, what would he say? He hit "ignore," put the truck in drive, and pulled out of the parking lot, headed for the expressway.

As he went up Roswell Road, he could feel he was drifting a little. He was in trouble here, and it was more than just being gone and not answering the phone. Tim was almost to the interstate when the blue lights came on behind him.

He swore as panic ran through his body. He began to slow down as he heard the siren. Tim turned into the next parking lot, hitting the curb as he did so. He put the truck in park and hit the steering wheel hard.

The officer was standing at his window now, and Tim, still wet from the drink that had been thrown on him, rolled it down.

"Can I see your license and insurance card?" The officer leaned into the window and sniffed Tim.

Looking at the license, "Mr. Billings, have you been drinking tonight?"

Tim sighed. "Not much, but I know I smell like it. I got a drink thrown in my face by this woman."

"I see. How about you step out of the truck?"

Tim looked at the cop in desperation. "I am begging you, please, just let me go home. I haven't had that much to drink. I'm fine. I promise."

"Sir, I'm gonna ask you one more time to step out of the truck. Shut it off and hand me the keys." The officer took a step back from the door.

Tim shut the truck off and stepped out. "I really am fine."

Tim handed the officer the keys and the officer told him to follow him to the back of the truck. The blue strobe lights on top of the police car hurt his eyes as they walked. Tim looked away to see the strobe effect of the lights bouncing of all the buildings around them. The officer explained to Tim that he wanted him to stand on one foot with his arms stretched out to his sides, and, with his eyes closed, to touch his nose with just the tip of his finger.

Tim laughed. "You have got to be kidding me!"

At that, the officer began to read Tim his rights. He cuffed Tim and escorted him to the back seat of his car. On the front seat of the truck, Tim's phone began to vibrate again with Sue calling. The phone fell off the seat and onto the floor.

Tim sat in the back of the police car, as he watched the tow truck pick up and haul away his truck. As it did, Tim's cell phone slid up under the front seat. Tim was so angry with himself for stopping at Scully's at all. What had he been thinking? Now Sue was probably wondering where he was, and worried, as well. Tim felt stupid and ashamed.

The officer came around and opened the back door. "So, do you want to tell me yet how much you had to drink?"

"I just had two, but I guess that's more than I should have."

"Yes, sir, it is. I watched you back all over the curb leaving the bar. I followed you down Roswell and saw you weave across the yellow line twice. Did you know you are driving on an expired license as well, Mr. Billings?"

Tim looked at the officer and banged his head on the seat in front of him. "Great!"

"I am charging you with DUI and driving without a valid license." The door to the police car shut, and off to jail Tim went.

Back at home, Sue was pacing through the house. Annette and Jonathan had no idea where their dad had gone.

Sue slammed her cell phone down on the counter after trying to reach Tim again. "You guys didn't call him when you got home?"

Annette shrugged her shoulders. "No. He works now. Sometimes he's not here right when we get home."

Sue was worried at this point. "Have you guys eaten anything?"

"No."

Sue sighed. "This is killing me, not knowing where he is. What if he got hurt and it messed his brain up or something?"

Jonathan hugged his mom. "I'm sure he's okay, Mom. Maybe his cell phone just died and he is on the way home."

Sue hugged Jonathan back. "I hope so, baby. Let me go get changed and I will fix something to eat."

Sue walked to the bedroom and started getting undressed. On the bed, she noticed a piece of paper lying just under the edge of the bed. Sue walked over as she pulled on a t-shirt. She reached down and slid the paper out to read it, the words were written in Tim's handwriting.

YOUR LIFE BEFORE!

Sue fell to the bed, putting her hands over her face. "No!" She muttered under her hands, "No."

Sue came back into the kitchen and began to fix dinner. She opened a can of beans, sliding the empty can on the counter. She took out some pork chops from the fridge and turned on the oven. Leaning back against the counter, she was in a fog thinking about where he could be.

Annette walked into the kitchen. "Mom, are you okay?"

Sue looked at Annette. "I don't know."

Annette hugged her mom. "He will be okay. I'm sure there is a good reason for him being gone. He's probably helping someone or working."

A tear rolled down Sue's cheek. She was still staring off into space. "I'm not so sure!"

Sue laid the page on the counter for Annette to see. Annette picked it up. Sue took the empty can off the counter to throw it away. When she did, she saw all the rest of the papers. All of the crumpled pages were in the trash can. She started pulling them out one by one, faster and faster as she saw the headings across the tops of the pages. Work, friends, women and money!

Finding all of this confused her more about where Tim was. If he threw all of this away, he clearly was not acting on what he had seen. Some of the pages were still paper clipped, as if they had not been read. Annette was trying to see. Sue realized, and stepped between the trash and Annette.

"Ah, Mom, let me see, too."

Sue got everything and held it close to her chest. "No, baby, you don't need to know anything more than you already do. You and your dad are great together now, and I don't want anything to stop that. This stuff is between him and me. I just can't figure out where he is if he threw all this away. Nothing is making sense right now."

Sue pointed at the stove. "Make dinner for me, okay? Let me go look through this to see if I can figure out where he went."

Annette turned in a huff. "Fine, I'm not a kid anymore. I'm 14; I can handle it!"

Sue kissed Annette on the head. "You are still my kid and I love you. Now cook like an adult. You're thirteen and half by the way so chill out."

Sue went into the bedroom and spread the papers out section by section. She looked at Work, then Friends. She picked up Women and put it back down. She picked up Money and was amazed.

Tim had six different off-shore accounts, each with somewhere between $350,000.00 to $585,000.00 at the most. Sue quickly did the math, and all total it was near two and half million, plus the eight hundred thousand he gave her. Sue sat on the bed, trying to figure out how this man she had been married to for 16 years now had managed to hide over three million dollars without her ever knowing it. That thought brought Sue to the papers labeled Women.

Sue's stomach turned at that. "The same way you manage to have three pages of girlfriends!"

She looked at the pages. There was info on Tracy in Colorado. Sue knew about her. Jenny, here in Atlanta, apparently one of the current girls at the time he went into surgery, and four others that were scattered between the states. She suddenly dropped the pages to the floor as if they were diseased. She shivered, thinking how dirty Tim was. How secretive and manipulating he was. Sue sat trying to understand why he would have stayed with her all those years. Why not just get the divorce and go on with life as a single guy?

Then Sue looked at the pages again. The work pages were apart and had been read; so had the pages on his friends. However, the women and money pages were not. They were both still paper clipped together in the trash can. So where was Tim? He didn't take the money and run! It didn't look like he took the girlfriends, either, so it had to be friends.

Sue looked at the friend pages. She found Pete, but no phone number. She saw others listed under Scully's.

"Scully's!" Sue knew that was where he was and she was going to kill him when she got there. He went to town and went to Scully's. Sue got dressed. She could be there in an hour and she would drag this man out by his ear. She had not come through all of this to have him become a drunk again. She could feel the anger as she threw on jeans and a sweater. Sue charged out of the room into the kitchen.

"Guys, I have to go get your dad."

Jonathan jumped up. "Where is he? Is he okay? Can I come?"

Sue looked at Annette. "He's fine. He went to see some old friends. I am just going to see them, too. Annette is in charge, young man. No, you can't come this time. I will be home in a little bit. Get your baths and go to bed by ten."

Sue kissed Jonathan on top of the head. "Love you."

"I love you, too. Tell Daddy he scared me."

"I will."

Sue walked over to Annette standing at the stove. Annette whispered, "Women?"

Sue shook her head no. "The old bar. He didn't even look at the pages that talked about girlfriends."

Annette frowned, "Girlfriends!"

Sue grimaced, "Just one."

"Mom, you said *girlfriends*. That's more than one."

Sue saddened. "More than one, but that's not where he is. He is at the old bar with his friends. I'm going to get him. I'm not having him start drinking now. We have all been through too much and I love him too much for that."

Sue started to turn when Annette grabbed her arm. Sue turned back to face Annette. "Tell him I love him, Mom. Tell him I want him home, too."

Tears instantly filled Sue's eyes. "So do I, baby, so do I."

Sue hugged Annette and headed for the garage.

Finding Tim

Chapter 21

S ue flew down 75. She knew where Scully's was, and she would drag
Tim out of there, drunk or not. As she drove, she couldn't help but
get angrier. It didn't matter what the motive was; he shouldn't have
gone without her. If he had asked, she would have gone. He knew the truth
now; there was nothing to hide. This was the old Tim resurfacing. Sue was
amazed that even with no memory, Tim still had the ability to disappear
on her. Why wasn't he answering the phone? Was he just ashamed because
he was caught, or something worse? Was there a woman?

Sue pushed the Jeep to over 80 mph now. Roswell was fifteen minutes
away. She was both angry and scared.

She pulled into Scully's, but didn't see the truck. Sue parked and headed
inside. The place was dark inside. It had been 16 years since Sue had been
in a place like this, and she felt like a fish out of water.

Sue went to the bar. Billy came over. "How you doin'? What can I get you
tonight?"

"I'm looking for my husband."

Billy turned away. "Not sure I can help you there, ma'am."

Sue laughed. "I haven't even told you his name yet. God, you men are all
alike, protecting each other. My husband's name is Tim Billings; have you
seen him tonight?"

Billy turned and looked at Sue. "Who's asking?"

"His wife! I'll take that as a Yes. Can you tell me where he is? Did he leave with anyone?"

"I really don't know where he went, ma'am. He was here earlier, but he left alone. I don't know where he was going. Ask the guys in the back. They're playing cards. Ask George, or Charlie."

Sue headed for the back room. She remembered Pete, but had never met the other men. The room was dark except where the lights were centered over each table. There were three tables in the room, but only one had a game going. The men sat around it with cigars in hand, all holding their cards close. She spotted Pete sitting at the table, and he spotted her. Pete reached over and hit George's arm, and pointed.

Pete stood. "Sue, how are you?"

"Cut the crap, Pete. Where is Tim?"

"He left a few hours ago. Is he not home? He left here going home, I swear. He was talking about how he made a mistake coming here and he had to get home. He lost track of time, something about his cell phone being in the truck."

Sue looked at the others. "Anybody else got anything? Did he say he was going home right then, or did he say he was going somewhere else and then home? I've been trying to reach his cell all night."

George spoke up. "He did say his phone was in the truck. He wasn't going to come in but I saw him and talked him into it; sorry about that. We didn't mean anything by it. I just wanted him to say hi to the guys. Sue, he loves you very much."

Sue looked at George. "Did I say he didn't?"

George stuttered. "I—I meant he didn't come here to find anybody or do anything. I think he was just curious about us. That's all."

Sue's face was blank. "Did he drink while he was here?"

George's eyes fell to the table. "Yeah, a couple, that's all, but he wasn't drunk or anything."

"You know, guys, I have spent the last year telling Tim he was a good man. A family man—and that's who he is. If he ever comes back here, please just tell him to go home. Don't drink with him or anything. Just send him home."

With that, Sue turned to leave. Pete got up and started after her. "Sue, wait."

Sue turned. "What? I need to go check the police departments and hospitals to see if my husband has shown up at either. This is just what I needed, thanks to you. Now what do you want?"

Pete smiled. "We are not the problem, Sue. He showed up here and the bartender bought him a drink. He only stayed for a little while, just to tell us about the cancer and you and how happy he is."

"What did he say about me?"

"How much he loves you and loves the kids. Sue, he is 100% yours. He did have a few drinks, but not because he wanted them; they just got bought for him. I promise all he talked about was you. He is a different man, not because you taught him to be, but because he wants to be, Sue."

Sue stood there, not sure what to say. "Thanks, I guess; but that doesn't help me right now. He has been missing for more than two hours, and I still can't get him on his cell. That means he is either in a hospital unconscious, or in jail or worse."

Pete nodded. "Okay, the boys and I will help you. What do you want us to do?"

"I am going to take the more likely of the two first, and call the police. If you guys want to start checking the hospitals around here, that would be great. Here is my cell number. Call me if anything turns up."

Sue gave Pete the number and started for the door. As she went back into the front room, a very drunk woman grabbed her arm.

Sue turned, glaring at the woman. "What's your problem?"

Slurring her words, the woman asked, "So you're his wife?"

Sue turned to face the woman. "Whose wife?"

"Tim's!"

"Yes, I am. Who are you?"

"I'm the girl that told him to fuck off tonight and threw my drink in his face. He missed out on a good thing with me. I'm definitely better than you. You tell him that when you see him."

The anger in Sue rushed to the surface. She balled up a fist and decked the woman. Jenny hit the ground flat on her back. Blood began to trickle from her nose. Her drink and purse flew all over the floor.

Sue leaned over her. "He's mine, whore! You tell him that if you ever see him again."

Sue turned and walked out of the bar, still angry with adrenalin pumping— God, that felt good, she thought, as she fired up the Jeep.

Sue pulled out her phone and dialed Information. "City and state, please?"

"Roswell, Georgia, Police Department."

The operator came on and gave the non-emergency number and offered to dial it for free. "Yes, please."

The next sound was ringing and then the answering, "Roswell Police Department, how can I help you?"

Sue paused at the officer's question, afraid to ask. "Can I help you?"

"Yes, do you have a Tim Billings in custody?"

"Who is calling, please?"

"I am his wife."

"Hold."

The phone went to music and she waited. She began to laugh at the song playing, "The Devil Went Down To Georgia." A few minutes passed. "Yep, he's here."

"What's the charge?"

"DUI and driving on an expired license. Want directions?"

"What's the address?"

The officer gave her the address and instructions on getting there. It was five minutes away and Sue headed that way.

She called Pete who answered on the first ring. "Sue, any news?"

"He's in jail Pete. DUI."

"Oh God, Sue, I'm sorry. This is our fault. He told us he hadn't had a drink in a year, but I didn't think two drinks would do anything."

"Well, Pete, having his old girlfriend throw one in his face probably didn't help. I am sure he reeked of alcohol when they pulled him over."

Pete was quiet. "How did you know about that?"

"She decided to confront me as I walked out; bad decision on her part. I think I broke her nose!"

Pete started to laugh. "Holy cow, you're one tough woman."

"Yeah, well, stay away from my husband or I might punch you next. We had a great life up until tonight."

"I can respect that, Sue. I will, I promise if he ever shows up around here again I will send him home right then. Listen, Sue, me and the boys know some folks over at the police station, you want us to make some calls?"

"Not right now. I will call you if I need you."

"Please do, we want to help. We really do care about Tim, Sue. We didn't mean to cause you any trouble."

"Thanks." Sue hung up.

Pete heard the line go dead and Billy came around the corner. "You cats missed it! Tim's wife knocked the piss out of this girl, broke her nose and everything. Man, that woman can hit!"

Pete started laughing. "I feel bad for Tim when she gets a hold of him. He may end up with a broken nose, too."

Billy started laughing.

Sue got to the police station and went to the front desk. It was small and not that many people were in there. The officer asked her if he could help.

"I'm Sue Billings, you have my husband here."

The officer pulled up Tim in the computer. "Yes ma'am, DUI and driving on an expired license. You here to post bond?"

"Yes! What was his blood alcohol level?"

The officer paused and went back to the screen. He hit a few buttons. Hit a few more. Looked at Sue, and then back at the computer.

"What's the problem? I am sure you checked it at the time of his arrest."

"Yes ma'am, I'm sure we did, but it's not in the computer."

Sue thought for a second. "Officer, let me reintroduce myself. I am Attorney at Law, Sue Billings. Can you go get a supervisor for me?"

The officer hit a few more buttons. "Yes ma'am, just let me find this in the system first."

"It's either there or it's not, officer. Now, go get your Sergeant or Captain or whoever is in charge here."

The officer looked up at Sue. "Now!" Sue barked.

The officer stood up. "Yes ma'am. Have a seat."

She looked where the man pointed and saw several very dingy looking chairs in a row against the outside wall of the lobby. The tile floor was worn in a pattern from the front door to the front desk, where every person had walked for the last however many years since the place was built. Sue paced as she waited. Sue thought if they can't produce a verifiable statement, that either blood work was done, or at least a breathalyzer test was administered, she would have him out of here in no time. She paced back and forth. Finally, the sergeant came to the desk and sat down. Sue started to speak, but the man held up a finger at her to be quiet.

Sue squinted and stood her ground. The man hit a few keys and looked at the other officer and then back at the screen. Sue watched as the man searched. He looked up at Sue and then back to the screen.

Sue had had enough. "It's not there! Either go get my husband, or administer the test now. Otherwise, this is a false arrest and I will sue this police department from now until Christmas time."

The Sergeant motioned for Sue to come around the desk. He led her to a small conference room just inside the doors. "Have a seat."

He left the room. About ten minutes later, he came back with the file on Tim, including the officer's notes. He sat down at the table. He opened the file and began to read. Sue sat patient. He finally looked up.

Sue grinned. "It's not there; is it?"

"The arresting officer observed the suspect hit a curb and then weave in traffic down Roswell Road. At the time of arrest, the subject refused to take a field sobriety test. In our book that is admitting guilt."

Sue smiled. "Who cares about your book? We are talking about my client's rights. Was a test given once he was here at the station?"

The Sergeant put his hand on his forehead and looked back at the file. "Not that I can see."

"Okay, then go give him a breathalyzer test now and if he is not over the legal limit I will expect you to release him immediately."

The officer eyed Sue. "Wait here!"

The sergeant left, leaving Sue staring around the room. She looked at each wall and at the ceiling. The grey paint with a blue line and the very large Roswell Police Department logo on one wall was a little intimidating, Sue thought. In the corner, she noticed a video camera aimed at the table. She wondered if the sergeant was going to administer the test, or if he was just making her wait to be mean. She sat for thirty minutes. She picked up her cell phone and called the house.

Annette answered. "Mom!"

"Hey, baby."

"Is dad okay?"

"He is. We will be home in a little while."

"Where did you find him, in a bar?"

"No, he's in jail."

"What? Why?"

"He drank some and got pulled over. I am working on it. You guys get ready for bed and I will see you soon, okay. If I am not home by ten, I want you to get in bed."

"Mom, it's almost ten now. How long will you be?"

"I don't know. Just lock up and I will be home soon."

"Will Dad? Are you guys fighting?"

"No, I haven't even talked to him yet. He's okay. I wish he had not come here and I am really not happy about the DUI, but it's okay. He really didn't do anything wrong. Go to bed and we will be home soon."

"All right. Tell Dad he's an idiot, but I love him. Jonathan said to tell you he loves you, too."

"I love you both; now off to bed."

Sue hung up and looked at her watch. Forty-five minutes now. The door opened and the sergeant came back in.

"Well?"

He cleared his throat. "He's below the legal limit, but that doesn't mean he wasn't over the limit at the time of the stop. He refused the field test."

Sue held up her hand. "Sergeant, you know in a court of law that won't stand up for crap. If he refused the test, you guys should have immediately done blood work or at least a breathalyzer when he came to the station.

Go get my husband or I am going to sue this department for false arrest, harassment and anything else I can think of. A lawsuit is free for me; is it free for you?"

The Sergeant sat there for a few minutes, just looking at Sue. "Let me see a card that says you're an attorney."

Sue opened her purse and pulled out two sliding them across the table. "There's two; one for you and one for your captain, whom I will be seeing first thing in the morning to tell him what a bunch of screw-ups his men are."

The sergeant picked up the card reading the title. He looked back at Sue. "Screw it! I don't have time for this crap. Come on, I will go get him."

Sue smiled. "Now, that's smart thinking. One more thing."

The sergeant looked at her. "Don't push your luck, sweetheart!"

Sue held up a defensive hand. "I would like to go talk to him while he is still in the cell. Can I do that?"

"No!"

Sue grinned, pulling a pen from her purse. "What was your captain's name again?"

Sergeant Donavan shook his head. "Lady, you are something else. Sit down and let me move him to a small holding cell. He's in the drunk tank with twenty other idiots! Just give me a minute."

Sue smiled. "Thank you, I will send a note to the captain telling him what a helpful night shift he has here. Could you not tell my husband it's me that's here? Just tell him his lawyer is here."

The Sergeant smiled. "Have a seat. I got a feeling you might be worse than the DUI he would have gotten."

Sue smiled and the officer left the room.

In the back, the sergeant came to the holding cell. "Billings, come with me."

Tim stepped to the door. "What now? More breathalyzing?"

"Just come with me. Your pain-in-the-butt lawyer is here."

"Lawyer? Who called a lawyer for me?"

"Just come on."

Tim followed the officer out and into a smaller cell. He shut the cell door and walked off."

Tim stood there. "Hey, aren't I supposed to be going with you if my lawyer is here?"

The sergeant kept walking. He went up front and got Sue. "Follow me."

They walked back into the cell area. Sue came around the corner and Tim was sitting on the bench in the cell.

Tim stood, "Sue, thank God."

Sue walked up to the cell and looked back at the sergeant. "Can I have a moment?"

He stepped away. "I'll be over here; call me if you need me."

Tim stepped up to the bars. "I really screwed up, Sue. I'm so sorry."

"You can say that again."

Tim stuck his hand through the bar to touch Sue. "I can explain."

Sue stepped back out of his reach. "Okay, why don't you do that? You've got time."

Sue laughed. "Get it! Time! You're doing time. That's hilarious, see me laughing."

Tim stayed silent and Sue straightened back up with a serious look. "Explain!"

"I got a package today from a private detective that I apparently hired a year ago."

"Yep, I know all about it."

Tim looked confused. "You do?"

"The trash, Tim, you threw it in the trash."

"Oh, I'm sorry. I was angry and just threw the whole thing away. I should have burned it!"

"We can do that when we get home. What were you angry about?"

"Some of the stuff in there. I'm so sorry I put you through all of that. How did you stay with me through that? The Sue I know wouldn't."

"I wouldn't now. I won't if this is what I have to look forward to."

"You don't. I wasn't down here to drink or anything else. I was just curious."

"Curious about what, Tim? Why didn't you just ask me? What made you come here?"

"I started reading about work and then friends. I know you don't want to talk about that stuff and I understand."

"Tim, you still haven't answered my question. Why did you come here?"

"I was angry."

"Angry at what? Me?"

"God, no Sue, I was angry at myself. The work stuff and friends was fine, but when I got to the section on women, I was furious with myself. How could I have been that kind of person? How could I do that to you and the kids? Annette must know, too; God, she is way too smart not to. How could I have been that person? How could I have been a person that would write that shit down to be delivered a year later?"

Sue's stare went to the floor. "I've asked myself that a million times."

"I got so disgusted with myself that I threw the whole package in the trash and left. I wanted all of that out of my head before you got home. I started driving and before I knew it I saw a sign that said 15 miles to Atlanta."

"Why didn't you just turn around then, Tim? Why?"

"I don't know. I was curious about the old house and curious about Scully's."

"You couldn't just let it go, let it be part of the past?"

"I just wanted to see it. Nothing bad about that, but I made a mistake. I pulled into Scully's and sat in the truck. I was about to leave, and George, one of my old friends, came up to the window. He scared the crap out of me. I didn't know who he was. I got out, figuring he knew me, and we started to talk. I told him I was leaving, that I shouldn't even be there."

"Why didn't you?"

"He wanted me to at least come in and say hi to the guys. I felt like it would be rude not to at that point."

"So what got the drinking started? I thought you were never going to drink again."

"I walked in the door and the bartender bought me a drink for old time's sake. The guys started toasting me, and I drank it. I don't know why."

"And the girl that threw her drink on you? Want to tell me about that?"

Tim looked up at Sue. "How do you know about that? Nothing happened, but—the guys, they must have told you."

"No, I met her on the way out. She decided to confront me; that was her mistake!"

"How did she know who you were?"

"When I came in, I asked the bartender if you had been there. He asked who I was and I said, 'Your wife.' I guess she was sitting at the bar."

Tim shook his head in anger. "She approached me, too, and I had no idea who she was. She was angry when I told her I didn't know her and that I was married. She threw her drink all over me."

"Yeah, well, she told me to tell you that you missed out on a good thing with her and I broke her nose!"

Tim started laughing. "You did?"

"Yeah, I think she got the message. So what happened then? How did you end up in here?"

"The guys bought another round, and by then I guess I was a little tipsy. Not drinking in a year, I don't know. I drank the second drink while I told the guys all about you and the kids and what I've been doing since I left. It was harmless, really; but I lost track of time. My cell phone was in the truck, and I . . . I just screwed up, Sue. One of the guys said it was seven o'clock, and I panicked."

"Why? Why didn't you just call me right then? I would have come and gotten you if I needed to."

"I know, but I was ashamed. I never meant to be gone that long. I wanted to clear my head and get back home before you did, and forget all about the past. When I realized it was seven, I freaked. I ran out of that place and jumped in the truck. I saw I had several missed calls from you and the house, again, just another screw up. I backed out and ran all over a curb. Apparently, the cop was sitting nearby and saw me. He followed me out onto Roswell Road, and in my hurry, I crossed the yellow line, too. The blue lights came on and the rest is history."

"Hmm. So now you're in jail. You've been gone for six hours and didn't answer me when I called. You know I can leave you in here, right?"

Tim laid his head against the bars. "Yeah, I do."

"Good thing for you, you have a good lawyer."

Tim looked up at Sue. "Do I have you?"

"Tim, you didn't do anything wrong. You just did it without me. You disappeared and you didn't call. I was scared to death. You can't do that to me anymore."

"I don't want to ever do this again. I'm sorry I came down here. I shouldn't have. You probably want to punch me in the face, too."

Sue laughed. "Maybe. You should have just asked me, and I would have come with you. I understand curiosity about who you were. I don't ever want you to be that person again, but I understand."

"Can we go home? Will you post bail for me?"

Sue turned to the sergeant who had laughed at half of what was being said between them. "Let him out!"

The sergeant walked over and opened the door. "Come on and I will get you your personal effects."

(clearing)

Tim stepped towards Sue to hug her. Sue punched him in the stomach, and Tim doubled over, coughing and gagging. The sergeant spun around, looking at Sue.

Tim held up a hand. "It's okay."

Sue smiled at the sergeant. "Now I feel better!"

Sue walked past the officer. "I'll be out front. Sergeant, I want his truck brought here, too. I'm not going to any impound lot. Thank you!"

The sergeant helped Tim stand up straight. "I think you might be better off staying in jail, brother!"

Tim stood up. "I love that woman!"

The sergeant patted Tim on the back. "Well, good for you. Make sure you get that license renewed right away. You don't want any more trouble with the law."

Tim nodded. "Will do, sir, sorry about the trouble."

Home Forever!

Chapter 22

They both pulled into the driveway just before midnight. Tim got out and walked around to Sue's door. She was gathering the paperwork together from the package Tim had thrown away. Tim saw what she had and shook his head.

Sue got out holding the papers. "Why do you still have that stuff?"

Sue looked at Tim. "Did you want me to leave it at home so Annette could read through it?"

Tim face contorted with stupidity. "No! I think she knows enough bad stuff about my past already. Good thinking."

Sue looked at Tim standing there. "At least one of us was thinking tonight. Don't ever put me through what you did tonight again."

Tim took Sue into his arms. "I won't. I love you too much to lose you to something stupid like that. I just found you! I can't lose you now."

Sue pushed away from Tim. "Did you look at the whole package or did you stop at your girlfriends?"

"Ouch! I stopped at the girlfriends. I was so disgusted that I didn't want to read anymore."

"So you didn't look at the section labeled 'Money' did you?"

"No. What was in it?"

Sue stopped and turned to look at Tim. "So you have no idea what kind of money you had hidden away, do you."

Tim smiled. "Is it a lot?"

Sue's face got serious. "It's enough for you to live any way you want."

She handed Tim the stack of papers and turned to walk into the house. "I am starting a fire inside. You can take those papers and go live your life alone, or you can come inside, burn the whole thing and be with your family. It's up to you. Either way, you decide right now, right here!"

Sue turned and walked in the house, closing the door behind her. Tim looked down at the paperwork in his hands and noticed the girlfriend section was on top. He wadded the papers into a ball and walked inside. Sue was standing at the fireplace with a lighter in her hand. Tim took it from her, bent down and dropped the ball of papers on top of the logs. He lit the paper and closed the screen. He stood up, dropping the lighter to the floor. With that, he took Sue's face into his hands and kissed her hard. She raised her hands to Tim's back and pulled him tight.

As the papers went up in flames, Sue looked at the fireplace. "You didn't want to take the section about money out first?"

"Nope, I don't want any part of that life, if it comes between us. I chose you and the kids."

Sue grinned. That's what I wanted, Tim. That's all I ever wanted was to be first in your life."

Tim smiled. "You are, and you have been for as long as I can remember."

Sue laughed and looked back at the fireplace. "It was a lot of money."

Tim looked too. "Do we need it or are we okay. Maybe I could get it real quick."

Sue laughed more, and pulled the white page from her back pocket. "You mean this one?"

Tim stepped back from Sue. "I can't believe you kept that. This whole thing with the papers was just a test, wasn't it?"

Sue held the page over by the fire. "I can toss it in if you want me to."

Tim took Sue in his arms, not even looking at the page. "Well, if it's enough for you to retire, then we could be together all the time. I think that would be great, don't you?"

Sue smiled and kissed Tim. "I do. I just needed to know you were willing to walk away from the old you, knowing what the possibilities were first. I needed you to choose me."

Tim kissed her back. "I will always choose you first, baby. Always!"

The End

Epilogue

T im and Sue were hardly ever apart after that day. Tim never went back to the city. He started playing in the stock market and found that he was pretty good at it. He turned that 3.2 million into almost 6 million over the next few years. They are both retired now, and still live in the house in the Georgia Mountains. Tim's past was never discussed after that night in jail. The old Tim had died with cancer, and they were both glad.

Frank moved to the mountains that spring and Tim helped make his house completely wheelchair-friendly. Frank met a local girl that summer, and they were married the next winter. Sue and Tim were their maid of honor and best man at the wedding. Frank had called Dr. Hampton several times to find out who at Emory was working on research for spinal cord injuries. Frank now has an appointment with the head of spinal injury research.

Dr. Reid Hampton eventually left Emory to work for the National Cancer Institute. He now leads the country in cancer research and cures. His procedure didn't stop cancer from forming, but in six different types of cancer, removing the hippocampus portion of the brain cured the patients with no recurrence. Tim was recognized two more times over the next few years, and is still in the record books as the first person to ever be cured of cancer. Reid is now looking for a cure altogether so that cancer can be gotten rid of forever. The new cancer research building at Emory is named Reid Hampton Hall.

Sue and Tim did see Pete and his wife a few more times in town, but the friendship never happened. Pete's wife didn't like Sue from their first encounter. Tim didn't want to reconnect with any of the old group after his night in jail, anyway. Too many bad memories there for Sue. Tim never took another drink!

Jenny had two nose surgeries after she met Sue in the bar that night. After the second one, she swore she would never date a married man again. She got married the next year. Her husband is having an affair with Fay, Jenny's best friend! Jenny is clueless.

Annette grew up with loving parents that supported her through every adventure she ever took. She eventually became an attorney, just like mom and dad. Her dad is still her hero and she talks to him almost every day.

Jonathan wrestled and played football in high school and then at the University of Alabama. He went pro with the football but now is thinking about becoming a professional wrestler for the WWF! He never stopped wanting to wrestling with his dad as he grew up. Annette is his attorney and reviews all his contracts. His stage name is "The Redneck Inferno!"

Tim did send off to get a copy of his law degree, but never pursued the career again. He still cooks dinner for Sue three nights a week, and his life remains dedicated to his wife and kids. He never missed a school function or a phone call from Sue after that night. He was always where he said he was, and Sue never wondered about him again. Tim was faithful to Sue for the rest of his life.

Printed in the United States
by Baker & Taylor Publisher Services